Ash lowered his head and kissed Brenna again...

This time it was achingly slow and thorough, his mouth whispering over her eyelids, her cheek, the corner of her mouth until, with a guttural moan, Brenna laced her fingers around his head, clinging to him as her lips found his.

Ash's hands were in her hair, though he couldn't remember how they got there. He pressed Brenna against the closed door, his body imprinting itself on hers as he took the kiss deeper still, his mouth restlessly seeking what he really wanted.

The quick, jittery charge to their systems had them practically crawling inside each other's skin. And still it wasn't enough...

"This story is action packed and fast moving...A good solid story with fantastic characters and an interesting story line."
—NightOwlReviews.com

Quinn

"Ryan takes readers to Big Sky country in a big way with her vivid visual dialogue as she gives us a touching love story with a mystery subplot. The characters, some good and one evil, will stay with you long after the book is closed."
—*RT Book Reviews*

"*Quinn* is a satisfying read. R. C. Ryan is an accomplished and experienced storyteller. And if you enjoy contemporary cowboys in a similar vein to Linda Lael Miller, you'll enjoy this."
—GoodReads.com

"Engaging...Ryan paints a picturesque image of the rugged landscape and the boisterous, loving, close-knit Conway family."
—*Publishers Weekly*

Montana Glory

"These not-to-be-missed books are guaranteed to warm your heart!"
—FreshFiction.com

"Wonderful romantic suspense tale starring a courageous heroine who is a lioness protecting her cub and a reluctant knight in shining armor...a terrific taut thriller."
—GenreGoRoundReviews.blogspot.com

Montana Destiny

"5 stars! Watching this wild rebel and independent woman attempt to coexist was so much fun...The author, R. C. Ryan, delivers an ongoing, tantalizing mystery suspense with heartwarming romance. Sinfully yummy!"

—HuntressReviews.com

"Ryan's amazing genius at creating characters with heartfelt emotions, wit, and passion is awe-inspiring. I can't wait until *Montana Glory* comes out...so that I can revisit the McCord family!"

—TheRomanceReadersConnection.com

Montana Legacy

A *Cosmopolitan* "Red Hot Read"

"A captivating start to a new series."
—BookPage

"Heart-melting sensuality...this engaging story skillfully refreshes a classic trilogy pattern and sets the stage for the stories to come."
—*Library Journal*

"A fresh, entertaining tale that will keep you wanting to read more."

—RomRevToday.com

THE MAVERICK
OF COPPER CREEK

ALSO BY R. C. RYAN

THE MAVERICK OF
COPPER CREEK

R. C. RYAN

FOREVER

NEW YORK   BOSTON

Copyright © 2014 by Ruth Ryan Langan
Excerpt from *The Rebel of Copper Creek* Copyright © 2015 by Ruth Ryan Langan

Forever
Hachette Book Group
237 Park Avenue
New York, NY 10017

www.HachetteBookGroup.com

Printed in the United States of America

First Edition: September 2014
10 9 8 7 6 5 4 3 2 1

OPM

Forever is an imprint of Grand Central Publishing.
The Forever name and logo are trademarks of Hachette Book Group, Inc.

The Hachette Speakers Bureau provides a wide range of authors for speaking events. To find out more, go to www.hachettespeakersbureau.com or call (866) 376-6591.

The publisher is not responsible for websites (or their content) that are not owned by the publisher.

ATTENTION CORPORATIONS AND ORGANIZATIONS:

Most Hachette Book Group books are available at quantity discounts with bulk purchase for educational, business, or sales promotional use. For information, please call or write:

Special Markets Department, Hachette Book Group
237 Park Avenue, New York, NY 10017
Telephone: 1-800-222-6747 Fax: 1-800-477-5925

To my family.
You lift me up.
You make me proud.

And to Tom, always and forever.

THE MAVERICK
OF COPPER CREEK

PROLOGUE

MacKenzie Ranch
Copper Creek, Montana—2005

Nineteen year old Ash MacKenzie was so cold he could no longer feel his hands or feet. His clothes were frozen to his skin. He was soaked through from the spring blizzard that had sent him and the team of wranglers into the hills, hoping to save the herd trapped there. It was calving season, and every rancher knew that newborns dropped during such a storm had a diminished chance of surviving.

Brady Storm, foreman of the MacKenzie Ranch, dropped an arm around Ash's shoulders as they made their way to the truck for the drive home.

"Your old man is going to be proud of you, Ash. Half the wranglers gave up from exhaustion or cold halfway through the night and had to head to their bunks. I don't know how you're still standing."

"Believe me, Brady," the young man said between chattering teeth, "I thought about giving up hours ago. But I've watched Pop push his way through a lot of pain and misery over the years, and I just didn't want to let him down."

"No doubt about it." Brady shook his head in admiration. "You're Bear MacKenzie's kid. Nobody but a MacKenzie could take that sort of beating and still be standing."

High praise indeed. People in this part of Montana referred to Bear MacKenzie's ranch as part of the Scottish Highlands, and Bear himself as a Highland lord, tough enough to command an army of warriors.

"What about you, Brady? You're still here."

The foreman grinned. "That's different. Your old man pays me a lot of money to do this job. But you..." He shook his head again. "All I'm saying is, you've got what it takes."

Ash beamed at such rare praise. Now if only his stern father would say the same. He'd tried everything he knew to get his father to notice and appreciate his efforts. By the time he was eight or nine, Ash had learned to tumble out of bed an hour before Bear got up in the morning, just to get a head start on his chores. He often stayed hours later than the wranglers, working in the barn, just to make his father proud. He took on the jobs none of the others wanted to deal with, in order to get his father's attention. So far, all he'd received for his efforts was a litany of complaints about the things that still needed to be done.

He cranked up the heat in the truck and closed his eyes, exhausted beyond belief, but before he could fall asleep, they rounded a curve and caught sight of black smoke billowing in the dawn sky.

"What the...?" Brady swore and floored the gas pedal. As they came to a screeching halt at the ranch, they leaped out of the truck to find one of the horse barns burned to the ground. Bear, Ash's mom, Willow, and his younger brother, Whit, were standing in the frigid dawn, staring dazedly at the smoke and rubble. In a corral, frightened horses circled and whinnied, spooked by the oppressive smoke and flames.

On the porch, Maddock MacKenzie, Bear's father, sat in the wheelchair he'd been confined to for the past few years, since a ranch accident had left his legs paralyzed. Nearby stood the few remaining wranglers who had stayed behind in the bunkhouse overnight.

Seeing his oldest son, Bear turned on Ash with a snarl of fury. "Where the hell have you been all night?"

"You know where I've been." Startled by his father's anger, Ash's response was harsher than usual. "Up in the hills with the herd. When Brady spotted those storm clouds, we hightailed it up there to make sure any newborn calves weren't caught in the blizzard."

"And you left me without enough manpower to put out that fire."

"How was I supposed to know the shed was going to burn, Pop? I—"

"Look at your mother's hands. All charred and blistered because she had to lead dozens of horses through the fire to safety."

"Are you all right, Mom?" Ash grabbed his mother's hands. "I'm sorry—"

Bear shoved him backward with such force Ash stumbled and fell. "You leave me here with a woman and a little kid—"

"Little?" Ash picked himself up, eyes hot with fury. "Damn it, Pop, Whit's fourteen—"

"Don't you mouth off to me, boy." Bear closed his hand into a fist which he stuck in his son's face.

Brady stepped between them. "Bear, neither of us knew about the fire. We were too far away to spot any smoke. But you'd have been proud of Ash last night. He saved dozens of calves from freezing to death. Half the wranglers couldn't take any more of that blinding blizzard, and had to retreat to the cabin. But Ash never stopped. He was still working this morning, even though he's frozen clear through his clothes and boots. Look at him. He's half dead with fatigue. You should be glad your son saved those calves."

"I should be glad that I've got a dozen calves, while my barn burned? Is that what you're saying, Brady?"

"I'm saying that Ash—"

"I can speak for myself." Ash stepped around the foreman and stood toe to toe with his father, the famous MacKenzie temper in full fury. "All my life I've done everything I could to please you, Pop. But no matter what I did, you always picked it apart, looking for the flaws. I've worked harder than any wrangler on this spread. But you know what? I'm sick and tired of trying, and then getting put down by you. I'm sick and tired of butting heads with you, Pop. I'll never be good enough for you. I'll never live up to the mighty Highland warrior Bear MacKenzie. Well, guess what? I'm through trying. I've had enough."

He turned away and stalked toward the ranch house.

Behind him, Bear MacKenzie shouted, "Don't you walk away from me, boy. I'm not through yet."

"Maybe you're not. But I'm through with you. Through with trying to please you." Ash climbed the steps of the porch.

His grandfather caught him by the wet, frozen sleeve. "Your pa doesn't mean any of this, laddie. He picks at you because you're the oldest, and he wants the best for you and your brother."

"The best for me? If this is his best, Mad, I need to get as far away from him as I can before I become just like him."

"You're already like him, lad." Maddock, who had always been called Mad by his family and friends, clung to the young man's sleeve. The hint of Scottish burr always present in his speech thickened with emotion. "He just wants his lads to be able to handle every facet of ranching. If you're going to take over this spread one day, you need to know how to do it all."

"It'll never be enough to please the powerful Bear MacKenzie. I'm done, Mad. Finished. I'm leaving."

"Just like that? Where will you go, lad?"

"I don't know. I guess I'll just have to figure it out along the way. What I know is this." Ash snatched his arm free and plucked a parka from a hook just inside the back door. Tugging it on, he turned and headed for his battered pickup truck. Over his shoulder he shouted, "I'm done, Pop. You can find somebody else to be your whipping boy."

"Ash." Willow's voice was filled with anguish. "Please don't do this."

At his mother's plea, he paused and caught her hands in his. "I can't stay. Don't ask me to. I love you, and Pop, and Whit, and Mad, and this ranch." His voice lowered with passion. "I love it all so much. But it's like you always say about too many grizzly bears in the same cave. If two of them are grown males, that's one too many. We both know it's way past time for me to make my own way, and figure out my own life."

"What about me?" Standing beside his mother and older brother, Whit's lips quivered. To cover his unmanly tears, his voice was rough with fury. "What am I supposed to do without you?"

"I don't know, Whit." Ash clamped a hand on his younger brother's shoulder, but the boy shook it off and stepped back out of reach.

"And Brenna?" Willow asked in nearly a whisper.

At the mention of Brenna Crane, Ash flinched as though he'd been whipped. The pain, at the thought of hurting the girl he loved more than his own life, was almost more than he could bear. "Tell her..." With a look of sorrow he realized there were no words. What could he ask his mother to say to a girl who'd lived a life of hardship from the time she'd been born, and refused to give up the hope that things would be better?

Wasn't that one of the reasons he loved her so? Despite all that she'd been through, she had a heart and soul filled to overflowing with goodness. She was sunshine on a bleak day. Laughter that chased away tears. She lifted him up when his edgy relationship with his father got him down.

Most of all, Brenna had learned to trust him. To depend on him, even though she'd been let down so many times in her young life. He knew that she would see his leaving as a betrayal of that trust. But, he reasoned, if he truly loved her, he had no right to ask her to share his uncertain future. She'd already been through so much turmoil, he had no right to burden her with more. Brenna had a better chance here, among people who knew and loved her, than she'd have with him on his journey into uncertainty. Hell, he didn't even know how he'd survive the next day, let alone a lifetime. What kind of man asked a woman to share that kind of misery? Brenna deserved only the best, and right now, he felt like the lowest man on the face of the earth. By cutting all ties swiftly, cleanly, he'd be doing her a favor and freeing her to find someone good, someone deserving of the tender love she was capable of sharing.

Someone good. Someone deserving of her.

Someone else?

It was too painful to contemplate. Since he'd first met Brenna, he'd pictured her in his life forever. He couldn't imagine her with anyone else.

He would contact her, he promised himself. When he could prove to himself and to the world that he was worthy of her. When he had proven to himself that he could provide a way of life that she deserved.

Absorbing a sense of loss that had him sucking in a breath, Ash climbed into his truck, and with his family watching, stunned and silent, he drove away with nothing but the clothes on his back and less than a hundred dollars in his pocket.

He broke a lot of hearts that frigid March day, including his own.

CHAPTER ONE

Hawk's Wing, Wyoming
Present Day

'Morning, Ash." The fresh-faced banker looked like a high school junior, with wire-rimmed glasses and short-cropped hair. He offered a handshake before indicating the chair across from his desk.

"Jason." Ash shook the young banker's hand and sat, setting his wide-brimmed hat on the chair beside him.

Ash MacKenzie had thought about dressing up for this meeting but decided against it, settling instead for a quick shower and shave. He'd been up before dawn and had already completed a couple of hours of ranch chores. Right now he just wanted to get this nasty business behind him before returning home to face the rest of the day in one round after another of back-breaking work. Work that would all be in vain if he couldn't persuade the bank to increase his loan so he could pay off his debtors, who were snapping at his heels.

"What can I do for you this morning, Ash?"

"I'm here to talk about extending my loan."

The banker's eyes narrowed slightly. "Extending the length of the payback?"

Ash gave a quick shake of his head. "I'd like to borrow more money and have it added to the back end of my original loan."

"You already owe fifty thousand. Why would you want more?"

Ash dug out the documents and passed them across the desk. "My taxes are due, and I just put a new roof on the barn. There was a leak in the irrigation system, flooding the south pasture, and the company that installed it for the prior owner refused to admit that they were at fault. The lowest bid I could get for the repair came to more than thirty thousand."

The young banker blew out a breath. "Wow, Ash. Looks like you got yourself a whole ton of troubles."

Ash had learned at his father's knee to never show fear. His tone was rock-steady. "I can handle them, Jason. I just need a quick infusion of cash, and a little time, and I'll be operating on all cylinders again."

The young banker looked him in the eye. "I'm not authorized to handle something like this. I'll have to take it upstairs."

Ash nodded, knowing that upstairs meant asking permission from Jason's father, Jason Collier III. The Collier family owned the only bank in this tiny town, and they treated every dollar like their own.

"I'd be happy to go with you and present my case."

"That's not the way it's done." Jason pushed back from his desk and walked to the door. "I might be a while."

"Take your time." Ash leaned back and stretched out

his long legs, crossing his feet at the ankles, watching the young man's retreating back. Though he looked relaxed, it was only a façade. Inside, his muscles tensed as he thought about the importance of this request.

Since he'd left his family ranch all those years ago, his workload had doubled. But at least now, he was working to please nobody but himself. Though he missed his family with an ache around the heart that would never heal, he didn't miss his father's constantly finding fault with everything he attempted to do.

Mad might have believed that Bear just wanted the best for his sons, but to Ash's way of thinking, it simply meant that he would never be able to please his implacable, rock-headed father, no matter how hard he worked. Now, at least, he was no longer busting his hide for someone else. If he chose to spend his life working like a dog, he had the satisfaction of doing it for himself.

Oh, he'd had years of working on other men's ranches, while he saved every dollar and plotted and planned for his own future. But he had a good piece of land now, and a working ranch, and though his life was lonely without the comfort of family and friends, he was not only surviving but thriving.

He frowned. Not really thriving. More like just barely getting by. But at least he was doing it on his own terms. He just needed one more break, and he could be free of the dark memories of the past.

Ash's musings were interrupted with the return of the young banker.

He made his way to his desk without looking at Ash. "I'm sorry. The bank just can't take the risk of giving you any more money."

Ash fought to keep his tone level. "I've made every payment on time. I never missed a single one. Besides, if I default, the bank holds my mortgage. The way I see it, you won't be risking a thing."

"We're not in the business of owning ranch land." Jason glanced at the documents before passing them back to Ash. "And from the looks of all this debt, you stand a very good chance of losing yours."

"I'd stand a better chance of holding on if you'd extend my loan."

The young man stood. "Sorry. I tried."

"Mind if I talk to your father?"

"It was my father who said emphatically no." Jason held the door, indicating an end to their meeting. "Unless you agree to ask your father to cosign the loan."

And there it was, out in the open.

"You know how I feel about that."

Jason nodded. "I know. I told my father you've already said you'd never ask your father to cosign."

Without a word Ash left the bank and stalked to his truck. Once inside he turned off the radio and drove the entire distance in silence.

His father.

That was what it all came down to. Even here in Wyoming, it seemed, everyone knew Bear MacKenzie was good for the money. Hell, he could probably hand over a million dollars without even going to the bank. Petty cash for Bear MacKenzie. Chump change, he'd call it.

Ash swore. He'd rather lose the ranch and everything he'd worked for than ask his father for one red cent. It would be an admission of defeat. An admission that these past years had all been a mistake, and now he was ready to crawl home and become the good, docile son his father wanted.

His father. There was no pleasing Bear MacKenzie. Hadn't he spent half his life trying? That part of his life was over.

Come hell or high water he'd make it on his own, or move on and start over yet again, with nothing but the clothes on his back.

MacKenzie Ranch

Bear MacKenzie stood on the banks of Copper Creek, his all-terrain-vehicle idling nearby. For the third time he glanced at the threatening storm clouds and swore loudly before walking over and turning off the ignition. The sudden silence was a shock to the system until his ears caught the lowing of cattle, the buzz of insects, the chorus of birdsong. At any other time he would have taken a moment to enjoy the serenity of his land. For as far as the eye could see, this was all his. His little slice of the Scottish Highlands, where his ancestors had ruled. His heaven on earth.

But for now, he was simply annoyed at this waste of his precious time.

He kicked at a stone, sending it spiraling into the creek. While he studied the ripples on the surface, he felt a sudden prickling sensation at the base of his skull, like cold fingers on his spine. Or eyes watching him.

Before he could turn, the sound of a gunshot broke the stillness. Liquid fire seared his veins. His legs failed him and he dropped to the ground. Blood formed a dark, sticky pool around him.

While cattle and birds and insects continued their songs, the life of one man was slowly seeping away.

Willow MacKenzie stopped her pacing when she spotted headlights through the rain-spattered window.

"Finally. Bear had better have a good excuse for being this late for supper." She patted her father-in-law's arm as she hurried past his wheelchair and through the mudroom to throw open the back door of the ranch house.

Instead of her husband, the man striding up the porch steps was Chief Ira Pettigrew, the tall, muscled head of the Copper Creek police force. A force that consisted of three men.

Ira's great-grandfather, Ingram Pettigrew, had been a legendary hunter and trapper in Montana, and he had been a bridge between the Blackfoot tribe of Native Americans and the homesteaders who'd settled the wilderness. Keeping the peace had become a way of life for the men who followed, including Ira's father, Inness, and now, Ira. The father of four, Ira had worked for the state police as a trained marksman before accepting the position of police chief in his hometown. Ira knew every square mile of land in his jurisdiction, and he zealously guarded the people who lived there.

Willow managed a smile, despite the tiny shiver of apprehension that threaded along her spine. "Ira. What brings you out here on a night like this?"

Instead of replying, he whipped his hat from his head and took a moment to hang it on a hook by the door, watching it drip a stream of water on the floor, before laying a hand on hers. "I've got some news, Willow."

He shut the door and led her past the rows of cowboy

hats, parkas, and sturdy boots, and into the kitchen. With a nod toward Maddock MacKenzie, he indicated the high-backed kitchen chair beside Mad's wheelchair. "Sit down, please, Willow."

She was about to protest, until she caught a glimpse of the tight, angry look on the police chief's face. Woodenly she sat, stiff-backed, suddenly afraid.

The door was shoved open, and Whit MacKenzie and Brady Storm blew in, shaking rain from their wide-brimmed hats and hanging them on hooks before prying off their mud-caked boots and jackets.

When they spotted the police chief, both men paused.

"Hey, Ira." Whit stepped into the kitchen ahead of Brady.

"Where're you coming from so late?" Ira words were not so much a question as a sharp demand.

Whit frowned at the impertinence of it. "Checking the herd like always."

"And you, Brady?"

The foreman nodded toward Whit. "With him."

"Which pasture?"

Catching the note of tension in the chief's voice, Whit bristled slightly. "North pasture, Ira. What's this about?"

"It's about my reason for this visit." Chief Pettigrew turned his full attention on Willow.

At fifty-one she was still the tall, graceful model she'd been at Montana State, when she'd turned the head of every boy and man on campus, until Bear MacKenzie, ten years her senior and already a seasoned rancher, had claimed her for his own. From the moment he'd set eyes on her, Bear had been head-over-heels smitten, and determined to make her his wife. And who could blame him?

Thirty years later she was reed-slender, with a dancer's legs and muscles toned from years of ranch work. With that mane of fine blonde hair and green eyes, even in faded denims and a soiled cotton shirt, and without a lick of makeup, she was still the prettiest woman in town.

"I'm sorry to tell you this, Willow, but Bear's been shot."

"Shot. My God." She was up and darting past him when his hand whipped out, stopping her in midstride.

"Hold on, Willow."

"No. I have to go to him. Where is he, Ira? Did you send for an ambulance?"

"No need." He put his hands on her shoulders and very firmly pressed her back down to the chair. "Willow, honey, you have to listen to me now. There's no easy way to tell you this. Bear's dead."

Time stopped. The utter silence in the room was shattering. No one spoke. No one even seemed to be breathing.

The four faces looking at the police chief revealed a range of intense emotions. Shock. Fury. Denial. And in Maddock MacKenzie's eyes, a grief over the loss of his only son that was too deep for tears.

Except for Willow's hiss of breath, nobody spoke. Nobody moved. They seemed frozen in disbelief.

"How?" This from Bear's son, Whit.

"A bullet to the back."

"Where?" Brady Storm's hand clenched and unclenched, itching to lash out in retaliation.

"On the banks of Copper Creek. North ridge."

"How long ago?" Maddock demanded.

"Couple of hours at least." Ira didn't bother to go into

detail about the temperature of the body, or the tests that would be run in the medical examiner's lab in Great Falls, or the amount of days or weeks that would be needed to determine the exact time of death. Copper Creek was too far away from the facilities afforded by big cities. Ira and his three deputies had learned to take care of their own needs. When they couldn't, they knew how to wait. And wait. Small-town crimes in the middle of cattle country were low priority for big-city authorities.

"You said he was shot in the back." Willow's voice nearly broke. She swallowed and tried again. "Do you think Bear would have known the one who shot him if he'd been able to face him?"

"I won't know anything until all the tests are concluded. My guess is that the shooter was a good distance away when the shot was fired. Probably relied on a long-range sight."

Willow's lips quivered and she pressed a hand to her mouth. "So this could have been done by anybody? An enemy? Even a friend?"

"Or someone who calls himself a friend." Mad MacKenzie hadn't just earned his nickname because it was an abbreviation of Maddock. In the blink of an eye, he morphed from grieving father to avenging angel.

Pounding his fist on the arm of his wheelchair in fury and frustration, he looked from Whit to Brady. "We'll find the son of a bitch who did this, lads. And when we do..."

"You'll do the right thing and let me handle it, Mad." Ira's voice was pure ice. "If any of you learn anything at all, you're to call me immediately. Got that?"

He fixed his glare on Maddock, and the old man returned his look without a word.

Whit gave a barely perceptible nod of his head. "I hear you, Ira."

Finally the chief turned to Brady, who mouthed the word *yes* grudgingly.

Satisfied, Ira turned his attention to the widow, closing a hand over hers. "Willow, I'm sorry that I can't allow you to take possession of Bear's body until the authorities have concluded their tests. I hope you understand."

She blinked twice, the only sign that she was listening. She'd gone somewhere in her mind, locked in her pain and grief.

"Good. Good." Fresh out of words, Ira started toward the door. Then, thinking better about it, he paused and turned. "I can't tell you how sorry I am. You've lost a good husband, son, father, and friend. And the town of Copper Creek has lost a born leader. Bear will be mourned by a lot of people."

He plucked his hat from a hook by the back door and let himself out.

In the kitchen, the only sound was the ticking of the clock on the wall.

The headline in the *Copper Creek Gazette* read:

BEAR MACKENZIE KILLED BY A SINGLE BULLET IN THE BACK

GUNMAN STILL AT LARGE

The news spread like a range fire through the tiny town of Copper Creek, Montana.

The headline and news article were read and discussed

in every diner and saloon and ranch, where cowboys and their women speculated on the shooter and the motive for the killing.

And though everyone in the small town claimed to know everyone else, there was the nagging little thought that one of them just might be the vicious gunman who'd ended Bear MacKenzie's fabled life.

Willow's mount was lathered by the time horse and rider topped a ridge and the house and barns came into view. The chestnut gelding had been running full-out across the meadows ever since its rider had left the stables and given him his head. Now, sensing food and shelter, the horse's gait increased until they were fairly flying down the hill.

At the doorway to the barn Willow slid from the saddle and led her mount toward a stall. Snagging a towel from the rail, she removed the saddle and bridle and began wiping him down. After filling the trough with feed, she picked up a pitchfork and began forking dung, even though the stalls had been thoroughly cleaned earlier in the day.

She worked until her arms ached. When she could do no more, she hung the pitchfork on a hook along the wall and dropped down onto a bale of hay. Burying her face in her hands, she began sobbing. Great wrenching sobs were torn from her heart and soul.

"Hey now." Brady Storm stepped out of a back room and crossed to her.

Without another word he wrapped his arms around her and gathered her close, allowing her to cry until there were no tears left.

When at last she lifted her head, he handed her a hand-kerchief. She blew her nose and wiped her eyes before saying, "Thanks. Sorry." She ducked her head, avoiding his eyes. "I got your shirt all wet."

"It's okay, Willow."

When she continued staring at her feet he caught her chin and lifted her face until she met his steady look.

Her voice was choked. "I thought I was alone. Don't tell Mad or Whit. I never want them to see me like this."

"It's nothing to be ashamed of. You've got a right to grieve. We're all grieving."

"I know." She stepped back. "But I need…" Her lips trembled and she fretted that she might break down again. "I need to be strong while we sort things out."

He kept his hand on her arm to steady her. "You're the strongest woman I know, Willow."

"I'm not feeling strong right now. I feel…" She looked up at him, and tears shimmered on her lashes. "I feel broken, Brady." She turned away and hugged her arms about herself, as though trying to hold things together by the sheer strength of her will.

The foreman placed a hand on her shoulder in a gesture of tenderness, before quickly withdrawing it and lowering his hand to his side. His voice was gruff. "You stay strong, Willow. What's happened has you down on your knees. I know what it feels like to be that low, when your whole world ends. But each day, you'll find a little more of your strength. And one day, when this is behind you, you'll realize that no matter what life throws at you, nobody and nothing is going to break you."

She turned and pinned him with a look so desolate, it tore at his heart. "What if all my strength really came from Bear? What if I never find any of my own? How do you know it will get better, Brady?"

His words were laced with pain. "Because I've been where you are now. And know this—I'll be here for you whenever you need to lean on someone until your own strength returns."

He turned on his heel and strode from the barn in that loose, purposeful way he had.

Watching him, Willow thought about what he'd just said. It was the most he'd ever revealed about himself.

Though Brady had been in Bear's employ since she first had come here as a bride, she knew little more about him now than she had in the beginning. Whenever she'd asked, Bear had insisted that Brady's past was nobody's business. When pressed, Bear had told her that he would trust his life, and the lives of his family, to Brady Storm, and that should be good enough for all of them. He'd explained that he'd found that one-in-a-million cowboy who he believed would put their interests above his own. When she'd asked how he knew, Bear had said only that Brady'd been through more of life's trials than most men, and he had come out the other side stronger than steel forged in fire.

And now she had to face a fire of her own. She had her doubts that she would morph into a woman of steel. For now, she would settle for the courage to face one more day.

She took in a deep breath, squared her shoulders, and wiped her eyes before making her way to the house.

CHAPTER TWO

W illow. I'm so sorry for your loss." Mason McMillan, long-time lawyer for the MacKenzie family, paused in the doorway to give the woman an awkward hug while juggling his briefcase in one hand and his wide-brimmed hat in the other.

"Thank you, Mason." She took his dripping hat and draped it on a hook before looking past him to the tall, handsome man standing behind him.

"Oh, sorry." He turned. "Willow, this is my son, Lance. I've been easing him into my law practice, and now I'm comfortable leaving all my clients in his capable hands."

"Lance. If you're half as good as your father, I know you'll make him proud." She shook his hand before leading both men into the kitchen.

"The roads are practically washed out by all this rain." Mason stepped around her and set down the briefcase on the kitchen table before offering his handshake first to

Brady Storm, then to Maddock, and then to Whit, murmuring words of sympathy as he did. His son smoothly followed suit.

"Thanks, Mason. Lance." Mad pointed to the kitchen counter. "Would you prefer coffee or something stronger?"

Lance smiled his gratitude. "After a hundred miles in this weather, I wouldn't mind a splash of your fine Irish whiskey in my coffee." He turned to Mason. "You could probably use some, too, Dad. And all of you."

Mad turned to his daughter-in-law, his grandson, and the ranch foreman. "Care to join us?"

Willow glanced at her son, then at their foreman, and when both nodded, she did the same.

"Done." Mad wheeled his chair across the room and filled six cups with steaming coffee, then added the bottle of whiskey to the tray that fit perfectly over the arms of his chair.

Seeing it, Lance remarked, "My father told me you invent things, Mad. That tray one of your inventions?"

"Yeah." Mad looked pleased that the younger lawyer had noticed. "I'm always looking for things that can make my life a bit easier."

Minutes later, as they gathered around the big oak table, Mason lifted his cup in a salute. "Here's to Bear."

The others followed suit and sipped while he shook his head. "Sorry. I still can't believe he's gone." He looked around the table, seeing the lingering shock in all their eyes. "I know I'm preaching to the choir, but of all the people in this world, Bear MacKenzie seemed the least likely to ever die before me."

Taking a deep breath, he opened his briefcase and removed a sheaf of papers. "Willow, you asked me to try to locate Ash, to alert him of his father's death."

She looked up hopefully. "You found him?"

"It took some digging, but Lance located him on a ranch in Wyoming."

Whit's head came up. "Are you telling me that all the time we've needed help here, my brother's been working for someone else?"

Lance shook his head. "He works for himself. It's Ash's ranch. It was small when he bought it, but he acquired the land on either side until it's grown into quite a spread."

While his son spoke, Mason handed Willow a document, which she scanned quickly before handing it over to Maddock.

The old man looked it over. "So much land. The lad took quite a gamble buying that much."

Mason nodded. "Seems to me gambling runs in the family."

That had Maddock smiling. "Yeah. But a gambler's got to be prepared to lose as often as he wins."

"That could be in Ash's not-too-distant future." Mason pointed to the upper portion of the document before turning to his son to let him explain.

Lance said matter-of-factly, "If Ash can't come up with enough to pay some heavy-duty debts, he could lose everything, including the original ranch. Right now, with family holdings being auctioned off every week, I wouldn't put my money on Ash beating the odds."

Willow interrupted. "Has he been notified about his father's death?"

Lance shook his head. "I have an associate driving out

there now. Dad didn't think it was something you'd want him to hear over the phone."

"No." She turned to the old lawyer. "Thank you for thinking of that, Mason."

He patted her shoulder.

She folded her hands atop the table. "Do you have a phone number for Ash?"

Lance spoke for his father. "There's no landline. I figure he has only a cell. But I'll have that information for you by tomorrow evening."

"Thank you. I need to hear his voice. To know that he'll be here for his family."

She started to shove away from the table, but Mason and Lance exchanged a look before Mason stopped her. "There's something else."

At the tone of his voice she sat back down and arched a brow. "This sounds like bad news, Mason."

The older lawyer cleared his throat. "Do you remember a woman named Melinda Warren?"

"Sorry. No." Willow shook her head. "Should I?"

"She was a teacher in Copper Creek until she left town about thirty years ago."

Willow shrugged. "Then she wouldn't have taught either Ash or Whit. What's this about, Mason?"

The lawyer frowned and tapped a pen on the stack of papers in front of him. "Maybe you'd prefer the privacy of Bear's office, where we could talk alone."

Willow sat up straighter. "Now you've got me worried, Mason. Why don't you just say whatever it is you have to say and get it over with?"

He took in a breath. "After leaving Copper Creek, Melinda Warren settled in Billings and taught school there for the past twenty-nine years. When she was recently diagnosed with a terminal illness, and learned that she had only a short time to live, she wanted to set the record straight for the sake of her only son and heir. Bear got a letter documenting the birth of a boy, Griff Warren, to Melinda Warren, formerly of Copper Creek, Montana, and listing Bear as the biological father. He was stunned and brought the documents to me to have all the facts verified. From time to time," he added softly, "I employ some very discreet investigators."

Willow's eyes were wide and unblinking.

Across the table, Whit and Maddock had gone as still as statues, while the foreman kept his gaze fixed on Willow's pale face.

"That would have been the time you broke your engagement to Bear and flew to New York about that modeling job, Willow." Mason's tone lowered. "At least that's the way Bear remembered it. He said he was like a wounded grizzly, and the pretty young teacher was willing to give aid and comfort. A month or so later you were back in Montana, and back in Bear's life. He swore to me that he never saw the teacher again, and when she left town, he didn't have a clue that she was having a baby. His baby. Apparently she told nobody, not even her son, about the affair. She never married. But when she learned that she was dying, she wanted her son to have a chance at a real family."

Whit's eyes blazed. "Are you saying you want to bring that bastard here, Mason?"

"I'm saying that when the results of a DNA test proved her claim once and for all, your father asked me to contact this Griff Warren, to arrange an introduction, and to list him in his will as his son and legal heir. Bear thought it was the right thing to do. The letter went out weeks ago."

"Weeks ago." Whit leaned forward. "Could it be that you've just found Pop's killer?"

Mason shook his head. "That thought occurred to me, too. He certainly had a motive. But I learned that Griff is currently serving with the Marine Corps in Afghanistan." He spread his hands, palms upward. "I'm sorry to be the messenger of such painful news, especially at a time like this. But Willow, it was Bear's intention to invite this stranger here when he returned to the States and give him the opportunity to be part of the family."

Willow's voice sounded suddenly weary. "What of the mother?"

"Dead."

She hissed in a breath. "And now this stranger...Griff Warren...will have to be told that his father is dead, too. Does he know yet?"

"The Red Cross has notified him. When he responds...if he chooses to respond...I'll let you know, of course." Mason turned to Whit. "But there's a good chance he'll want nothing to do with any of you."

As the silence stretched out, Lance removed several documents from his briefcase. "I've brought copies of Bear's amended will. He added the latest changes as soon as he learned about this...surprise." He studied the stricken look on the pretty widow's face. "You should know that Bear was as shocked as you at the news. But once he processed it, he was determined to do the right thing for this...son he never knew."

Whit was on his feet. "Are you saying my father put this bastard in his will?"

"Whit..." Willow reached for her son's hand, but he snatched it away.

"Tell me." Whit's eyes blazed with fury. "Did he leave any part of this ranch to a stranger?"

Lance glanced at his father before the older man nodded. "He did, Whit. He told me that he knew how painful this would be for everyone, but he figured Griff Warren was the innocent victim in all this. He said a fatherless kid probably paid a dear price for the mistakes of his parents in the past. Bear didn't want to make things worse by denying him a future."

"So he just cut up the family ranch to include this stranger?"

"The ranch was Bear's to do with as he pleased." Without looking at Whit, Lance passed the documents to Willow. "I'll leave these amendments for you to read. If you have any questions, you know where to reach me."

The older lawyer snapped shut his briefcase and stood before offering his hand to Maddock. "Again, I wish you didn't have to endure this pain, Mad."

"Thanks, Mason."

The lawyer shook Whit's hand without a word before drawing Willow close for a firm hug.

"You call me anytime, with anything you need to know. You hear?" He patted her shoulder. She nodded, as he added, "We'll let ourselves out."

Behind him, his son followed with handshakes all around, then the two men headed for the door. In the back room they retrieved their hats before stepping into the rain-drenched night.

In the kitchen, the four figures remained at the table,

lost in thought, until Willow snatched up the documents and got to her feet.

Before she could leave, Maddock reached for her hand.

"I remember that time, when you broke the engagement and flew to New York."

Willow held her silence, while pain and anger warred in her eyes.

"You were gone for over a month."

"Six weeks." Her words were stiff.

"To Bear, it seemed like a lifetime."

"Really?" Her voice nearly broke. " It's nice to know he managed to find some...comfort."

Maddock held her hand firmly when she tried to pull away. "Men grieve differently than women, lassie. As I recall, you went on a modeling assignment to some sun-drenched island and had yourself a fine time. "

"Where I worked from sunup to sundown. And when it was over, I realized it wasn't the life I wanted. I came home. Back to Bear, who acted like a man who'd been on a starvation diet and I was a feast."

"You were, lass. He may have taken comfort with someone else, but you need to know this. Bear never loved anyone but you. And from the day you married him, he never even looked at another woman."

"How would you know, Mad? Were you with him day and night?"

"I'm his father. I know. My son was a one-woman man. In Bear's eyes, in his heart, the sun rose and set on you, lassie. Don't you ever forget that."

She did pull free then, and strode quickly out of the room.

The three men sat in the kitchen, listening to the sound of her footsteps on the stairs. Minutes later they heard the slamming of her bedroom door.

And then there was only the sound of the rain streaming down the windowpanes like tears.

Morning dawned clear and bright.

Willow sat slumped on the edge of the king-sized bed, her mind in turmoil. It was all too much to take in. Bear dead. Shot in the back by a cowardly killer. He was never coming back. Never going to fill the room with that booming laugh, or rattle off every rich, ripe curse in a voice that could freeze a man's blood when he'd been crossed.

Since the moment she'd heard Ira Pettigrew say those words, she'd been unable to make sense of them. How was it possible that Bear had been murdered?

Willow unconsciously clenched her fists. She couldn't even imagine anyone, friend or foe, daring to threaten Bear MacKenzie, let alone any man following through with such a threat.

You just didn't kill a man like Bear MacKenzie.

But someone did.

And now, to learn that the man she'd loved and trusted more than anyone in this world had betrayed her, was almost more than she could take in. Oh, it might be true that he hadn't cheated while they were married. But that didn't alter the fact that he'd fathered a son with another woman. A son who might or might not decide to satisfy his curiosity about the man who'd been absent from his life, and come here to further complicate things.

It had been such a source of pride to her that she'd

been the great, the only, love of Bear MacKenzie's life. To learn now, while grieving his sudden, shocking death, that there had been another woman, the mother of his firstborn son, was almost too painful to bear.

Too agitated to sit, she got up, walked to the window, and stared at the tranquil morning scene spread out below. For as far as the eye could see there were hills dotted with herds of cattle. Their gentle lowing drifted through the closed windowpane. A truck was moving along the ribbon of road that led from the highway to their ranch. A tractor rolled out from behind the barn. Up on the north hill Whit was on an all-terrain vehicle, trailed by several horsemen, heading up to high country.

It all was so deceptively peaceful. But she knew that everyone on this ranch was reeling. For that matter, everyone in the town of Copper Creek, whose life had been touched by her husband, had to be experiencing this sick feeling in the pit of their stomachs.

Everyone except the shooter.

"Why, Bear?" The words were torn from her lips and the tears welled up again, spilling down her cheeks.

It had been like this ever since she'd heard the news. This sudden, wrenching grief that had her throat raw, her heart breaking over and over, until she thought she'd go mad from the pain.

"I can't do this." She paced the length of her room and back, letting the tears fall. "I don't even know where to begin without you here. Whit thinks he can step into your shoes, Bear, but he's wrong. He's not ready yet. And Maddock may be wise enough, and tough enough, but his body won't let him do what he once did."

She slumped back onto the edge of the bed and buried

her face in her hands. Bear was dead. Though she hadn't yet been allowed to see his body, Ira Pettigrew had said so.

Her hands suddenly clenched. She couldn't do this. Couldn't run this ranch alone. And certainly couldn't handle the arrival of a stranger claiming to be her husband's son. She had an almost overpowering desire to run and hide. She would rather be anywhere than here, dealing with the mountain of misery that had been dumped on her.

She stared at her clenched fists and slowly opened them. She'd had a good life with Bear.

Bear MacKenzie was the strongest, smartest man she'd ever met. He was her husband, her mentor, her protector. Her best friend.

He'd literally ridden into her young life like an avenging angel. Her father had been a teacher and part-time rancher. Her mother had raised chickens and cooked a fine chicken dinner once a month as a fund-raiser for the Copper Creek Church. They had been standing with their daughter beside their broken-down van when the most handsome cowboy Willow had ever seen rode up on his horse and offered to help. He'd fiddled under the hood and got their van started, then followed along all the way to town to make certain they arrived safely. Then he'd stayed to enjoy her mother's cooking and had flirted shamelessly with tall, slender Willow Martin, a sun-bronzed, blonde college junior home for the summer. By the time she returned for her senior year, she was wildly in love with her cowboy and sorely tempted to abandon her plans to go to New York and become a model. And though she gave modeling a try after graduation, she simply couldn't stop missing the man who had stolen her heart.

After that singular modeling·assignment, she had returned to Bear's arms. Once married, Willow had embraced ranching with an all-consuming passion.

She blinked, struggling to put aside her gut-wrenching musings of the past and think of something positive to hold on to this day.

She had a father-in-law and sons who would no doubt do whatever they could to ease the road that lay ahead. She had a strong, loyal foreman. And in truth, whatever doubts plagued her, she would have to find her way through the layers of grief, anger, fear, confusion, and utter despair, and uncover her strengths.

She would deal with all of this because she had no choice. The hand had been dealt. Now, like it or not, all she could do was play the cards.

The voices in the kitchen were muted.

Brady was saying, "I've already given orders to the wranglers. Since we don't know who shot Bear, or why, I want someone looking out for Willow at all times. Wherever she goes, one of us goes with her."

Mad nodded his agreement. "You're a step ahead of me, laddie."

Whit's eyes narrowed. "You think the shooter will come after Mom?"

The foreman shrugged one powerful shoulder. "Right now I don't know what to think. But until we know the who and why of this mess, we need to take precautions."

"I agree." Mad clenched a fist on the arm of his wheelchair. "If there's a grudge against Bear, what better way to pay it back than to kill the woman he loved, too?"

"But why? What would be the point of killing Mom now? With Pop gone, it's too late to hurt him."

"For all we know, the whole family could be targeted." Brady stared into Whit's stormy eyes.

Mad nodded his agreement. "Just to be safe, whenever you're off the ranch, I think you should travel with one of the wranglers, lad."

"You want me to have a babysitter?"

Mad placed a hand on his grandson's arm. "Think of it as the buddy system. Whenever you went swimming in Copper Creek as a lad, I always told you to take along Ash or one of the wranglers, just in case."

"I was six, Mad. I'm not a kid anymore."

"It's just a precaution." Brady lowered his voice, hoping Willow didn't choose that moment to come downstairs and catch them conspiring. "But especially where your mother is concerned, I don't want her alone until this matter is resolved."

When Whit gave a slight nod of his head, both men breathed a sigh of relief.

It was just another minor bump in a week that had seen one major crisis after another.

They were all bracing for whatever might happen next.

CHAPTER THREE

Ash trudged across the field separating his land from his nearest neighbor's. He could have driven his truck, but he figured the walk over and back would help him do some heavy thinking.

Old Fred Covington had been making noises about wanting Ash's ranch ever since he'd learned that Ash's bid at the county auction had been higher than his. It had been an uphill battle, but Ash had finally managed to break through the old man's icy wall until they were now, if not friendly, at least neighborly.

It hadn't been easy for Ash to request this meeting with Fred Covington and openly admit to his financial problems with the bank.

"Ash." Fred stuck out his hand.

"Fred. Thanks for agreeing to see me."

The old man glanced up at the layers of clouds rolling

in from the north. "Afraid I can't give you much time. Got to see to my herd. What's this about?"

As briefly as possible Ash told him about his meeting with the banker, and the disastrous outcome.

His words were met with narrowed eyes and a tightening of the lips, a sure indication that the stern-faced neighbor was about to gloat and offer him a lowball figure to take the land and buildings off his hands.

In truth, Ash was prepared to accept whatever offer was made. He'd run out of options.

The old man spat a wad of tobacco. "I could have told you what you'd get from the Colliers. Father and son are both more concerned about squeezing every drop of blood they can from the hardworking ranchers around here than they are with lending a hand when it's needed." Fred pursed his lips, considering. "How much do you need to get that irrigation system repaired?"

Ash shrugged, trying his best to hold onto his dignity. "They're asking thirty grand."

"Thirty." Fred shoved back his hat to scratch his head. "Then I figure they'll probably take ten up front, and ask for the rest in payments."

"Yes, sir. That's what I'm figuring, too."

"And your taxes?"

"I thought I'd be able to cover them, but everything started piling up."

"Yeah. That's a rancher's reality." The old man stared off into space before turning to meet Ash's eyes. "All right. Come on up to the house. I'll write a check for the irrigation company and the bank." He started away.

Ash was choking on the lump in his throat. "You..." He swallowed and tried again. "You'll have yourself some fine land for the price of taxes and an irrigation system."

Fred stopped dead in his tracks and turned. "Is that what you think? That I'm hoping to take over your place?"

"Aren't you?"

Fred Covington gave him a long, assessing look. "Since you took over this place, I've been talking with some other ranchers in the area. They tell me you were one of their best workers, and you've been saving every dollar you earned to buy this ranch. That right?"

"Yes, sir."

"I figured you'd just asked your daddy to buy you a place of your own, but I've heard you haven't taken one red cent from your pa." When Ash held his silence he said, "This land was built by men like my granddaddy. I like a man who lives by a cowboy's rugged code of independence. That's why I'm offering you a loan so you can hold on to what you've earned by the sweat of your brow."

As his words sank in, Ash's eyes rounded. "I don't know when I'll be able to pay you back."

Fred's lips curved. "I figure you're good for the money. And if you don't pay me back, son, I know where you live."

Ash swallowed. Had this dour old man actually made a joke?

He followed Fred to the house and stood awkwardly in the kitchen. Minutes later Fred returned, holding out a check.

The old man was smiling. "I wish I could be a fly on the wall at the bank tomorrow when the Colliers, father and son, see this. The stingy bastards."

Ash's smile came slowly, before it bloomed on his lips, in his eyes. He accepted the check and shook Fred Covington's work-worn hand. "I'll never forget this, Fred. I...I was prepared to let it all go and start again."

"That's what I like about you, son. You remind me of myself at your age." His voice lowered. "I started over a number of times before it all began working for me. But once it did, I never took it for granted. I appreciated everything I had. And still do, truth be told."

Ash studied the old man with new respect. "How many times did you have to start over before you got it right?"

"Half a dozen, at least. But I tell you what, son. If it weren't for the love of my good woman, I'd still be trying to figure things out." He looked at Ash with those dark, piercing eyes. "You listen to me. If you find yourself a good woman, you make damned sure you never let her get away."

"I'll remember. Thanks, Fred."

Clutching the check, Ash shook the old man's hand again before turning toward his ranch in the distance.

As he made his way across the fields, his smile grew.

Thanks to the kindness of a neighbor he barely knew, he'd saved his ranch for at least a while longer.

He hadn't admitted to Fred that he'd already betrayed the trust of the only good woman he'd ever known. Finding another like Brenna Crane wasn't likely. And meeting any woman would have to take a back seat to ranch chores, at least for the foreseeable future. He intended to pay Fred back every penny before the year was up. If he had to work longer hours and tighten his belt even more, so be it. He intended to do whatever it took to make sure that Fred Covington never regretted putting his trust in him.   •

That was Ash's last thought before he spied the shiny black car bearing a Montana license plate parked in front of his ranch house.

The man stepping out, dressed in a dark suit and tie and looking like the grim reaper, was no rancher. And the fact that he was from out of state meant that he wasn't from the bank, either.

Whoever he was, and whatever brought him way out here, Ash figured he hadn't come all this way bearing good news.

Ash stepped up onto his front porch and eyed the man.

"Ash MacKenzie?"

"Yeah."

"Phil Bradley. I've been sent by Mason McMillan."

"My father's lawyer? You a private investigator?"

The man nodded. "Could we go inside?"

Ash made no move to open the door. "So my family resorted to hiring an investigator to find me. Now that you have, you can get off my property and hightail it back to Montana with the news that you were successful. I'm sure that'll earn you a fat bonus."

As he opened the front door and stepped inside, the man's hand shot out, preventing Ash from closing it in his face.

Ash gave a sigh of disgust. "Okay. Why don't you say what you came here to say and let me get back to work."

"I'm sorry to tell you that your father is dead. He was..."

Ash never heard the rest. His hand lowered to his

side and he stumbled inside like a drunk before dropping down heavily on a kitchen chair.

Phil Bradley followed him inside and watched as Ash struggled to clear his mind.

"My father...When? How?"

"Two days ago. Shot in the back by an unknown killer."

"Murdered?" Ash couldn't seem to wrap his mind around such stunning news.

"I had to do a lot of digging to find you. Your family didn't want you to hear this by phone."

"My family." Ash closed his eyes on the pain. His mother, his brother, dealing with this for two days while he was wasting his time worrying about a piece of land.

"What should I tell them?"

"Tell them...? My family?" Ash's head came up and he struggled to focus.

He would phone Fred Covington and make whatever arrangements he could on the spur of the moment. Nothing else mattered now except being with his family. "Tell them I'll be there as soon as possible."

Bradley nodded. "Your mother requested a phone number where she could reach you."

Too stunned to speak, Ash held up his phone, displaying the number. The investigator punched the numbers into his own cell phone before letting himself out.

Ash lowered his face to his hands.

His father dead. Murdered. It was too much to process.

It couldn't be true. It couldn't. Bear MacKenzie was too tough, too ornery, to die.

Grief welled up, choking him. There was a terrible band around his heart, making it impossible to take a breath.

He roared up from his chair and stormed across the room, pounding a fist into the wall. Even the pain that shot up his arm wasn't enough to overcome the terrible, black grief that had him by the throat, squeezing all the air from his lungs.

He'd worked so hard. Denied himself so much, just to be able to go home one day and prove to his father that he could make it all on his own. It had been the thought of seeing his father's respect that had driven him like a man possessed.

And now, he could never stand before Bear MacKenzie and say the one thing he'd wanted to say more than anything in this world.

"Oh, Pop." Anger and anguish and guilt rolled through him in a storm of emotions that dropped him to his knees. "Why did I let the MacKenzie curse take me this far? Why did we always resort to our fists? Why couldn't one of us have said we were sorry?"

He got to his feet and began to pace. *This is my fault. My fault. My fault. I deserted everyone I love because of this damnable temper. And though I've spent years blaming you, Pop, I'm the one who made the choice to go so far away from all the people I love.*

The people I love.

Despite all the bitter battles of will, the shouting, the cursing, the angry words spoken in a haze of fury, he had loved his father. And knew in his heart that his father—though critical of everything he'd done, and ready to stand toe to toe with his oldest son every step of his journey to manhood—had loved him, too.

What had Mad always said? Bear just wanted his sons to be tough enough to survive this harsh land and the almost superhuman demands made on anyone who chose ranching for a lifetime.

"Oh Pop. What a waste. What a terrible waste of years " With an arm across his eyes, Ash sank down on the ancient sofa that had been left by the ranch's former owner.

Overcome with a blinding, bitter grief, he wept scalding tears over his loss.

Kabul, Afghanistan

"Hey, Griff. Got a cigarette?" Jimmy Gable had just celebrated his twenty-first birthday the previous week. When he'd entered the Corps at eighteen, he'd been a pudgy kid fresh out of school. Now, despite his babyish face, muscle replaced the fat, and there was a toughness in his demeanor that came from facing death in the hills of Afghanistan. He considered thirty-year-old Griff Warren his closest friend despite the difference in their ages and backgrounds. The two had bonded over long nights spent under the heavy cloak of darkness punctuated by bursts of enemy fire.

"Here." Griff tossed aside the last of his cold coffee and handed over the pack after taking a cigarette for himself.

"Thanks. I thought you quit." With a grin, Jimmy struck a light to his own, and then to Griff's.

"I did. For about an hour."

The two men stretched out their legs and inhaled deeply.

"You still thinking of doing another tour?" Jimmy blew out a stream of smoke.

"Yeah." Griff did the same, watching the smoke dissipate into the night air. "Nothing else to do with my life now."

"Tough about your mother."

When Griff said nothing, Jimmy figured that the pain of loss was still too fresh. Griff's plans for a grand reunion when he was discharged had all somehow gone up in smoke.

"Maybe I'll stay in with you and do another tour."

At Jimmy's words, Griff looked at his young friend and shook his head. "There's no future here for you."

"And there is for you?"

Griff shrugged. "It's different for me. I've got no future back home, either. I've got nobody. But you've got that big family just waiting to smother you with love."

"Yeah. *Smother* being the operative word." Jimmy gave a dry laugh. "With two older brothers and three sisters, I've been smothered from the day I was born. When I joined the Marines, I became plain old Jimmy Gable. Here, I'm not Artie's little brother, or Audrey's cute brother. Or John Gable's kid."

"You should be proud to be someone's kid."

At the rough tone of voice, Jimmy fell silent, embarrassed at that slip of the tongue. Though Griff kept his personal life pretty much to himself, he'd once said that he grew up without a father, or any family except his mother. To Jimmy, that sounded like heaven. But seeing the look in Griff's eyes, he knew his friend considered it more like hell.

Over these past months Jimmy had begun to look up to Griff Warren as the epitome of a man and a Marine. Griff was strong, silent, and absolutely fearless. His muscled body was rock solid, his mind razor sharp. During their rare breaks away from combat, Jimmy had seen the way women looked at his friend. And no wonder. Even with that hint of danger in those dark eyes that warned everyone to keep their distance, Griff Warren was handsome in a rugged, dangerous sort of way. To Jimmy's way of thinking, though, any woman who dared to take on Griff would have to be prepared to take on the devil himself. It wasn't just the scar that ran from below his ear to his chest, a souvenir from a crazed enemy soldier. There was something dark and wounded that showed itself in those brief moments when Griff let down his guard. Something that spoke of a pain too deep for words. And maybe an anger that simmered and boiled deep inside. Jimmy just hoped he never caused that anger to boil over. It wouldn't be pretty.

When the mail was distributed, Jimmy clutched half a dozen envelopes, taking his time opening each one and chuckling as he read the long, newsy letters from his family.

He was surprised to see Griff holding an envelope. "Hey. Look at you. You got some mail."

"Yeah." Griff studied the letterhead on the legal-size envelope before slitting it open.

He read through the official letter once, then read it again before carefully folding it and placing it back in the envelope.

He stood and tucked it into his breast pocket before saying casually, "I guess I'll be taking that discharge after all."

As he started away, Jimmy called, "You win the lottery?"

Griff paused and looked back. His eyes were dark and

fathomless. Whatever he was feeling, it had been carefully banked.

"Something like that."

Copper Creek, Montana

When Whit MacKenzie volunteered to babysit the herd on the western ridge for the night, nobody gave it much thought. Whit was known by his family and by the wranglers of the MacKenzie Ranch as a loner. He was a cowboy through and through. Whit ate, slept, and dreamed about ways to make his father's ranch bigger and more successful than any other in Montana. And because of his father's constant criticism, he'd learned early in life to put as much distance as possible between himself and the man to whom he would never measure up.

The odd thing was, even though Whit had inherited the same hair-trigger temper that plagued all the MacKenzies, he'd also been blessed with a zany sense of humor. In fact, his friends often referred to him as "Whit the wit" in the MacKenzie family.

Whit often spent weeks, even months, up in the hills, without ever feeling the need for companionship. The wranglers knew him to be tough, independent, and a free spirit. He carried a stash of books in his saddlebags, and would often curl up on a cot in the bunkhouse and read while the wranglers were passing the nights playing poker. They loved having Whit along, because they all knew that he would willingly take on the late-night hours keeping watch over the herd so that he could be alone with his thoughts.

This night, as he and his horse patrolled the perimeter

of the camp, he could hear the faint bursts of laughter or swearing from the bunkhouse.

His thoughts turned to all the crazy events of the past week. His father dead. Murdered. It didn't seem real. He had the feeling that he'd ride back home in a few days and find his father seated at the table, talking and laughing with his mother and Mad, and explaining that it had all been a misunderstanding.

Then there was the fact that Ash had been contacted, and had sent word that he would be home as soon as he could make arrangements for someone to tend his ranch and herds in Wyoming. Though Whit still resented the fact that his big brother had abandoned him all those years ago, he couldn't deny that he was eager to see him again. His heart beat faster just thinking about their reunion.

And then there was the bastard. Whit liked thinking about the stranger that way. A bastard. A sneaky thief in the night, hoping to cash in on the accident of his birth.

Mason McMillan had already received word that Griff Warren was planning on paying a call on the family as soon as his discharge from the Corps was finalized.

Well, Whit had news for Griff Warren. He was free to visit and pay his respects, but after that, he'd better be prepared to head back to wherever he came from.

Whit's hand fisted the reins.

Griff Warren would learn soon enough that there was no room on the MacKenzie Ranch for someone pretending to be one of them.

CHAPTER FOUR

As his truck ate up the miles, Ash MacKenzie took note of the changes in the landscape around the town of Copper Creek since he'd left. More of the once-desolate land had been claimed by small ranches. Cattle and horses shared pastures. Trucks and campers were parked beside freshly painted barns.

The town itself hadn't changed much, he thought as he rolled along Main Street. Green's Grocery looked the same, as did Reels, the small movie theater that showed movies so old they were currently playing on TV. Most folks weren't lured by the movie, but rather for the nostalgia of an old-time theater. As for the younger set, it still afforded a chance to make out in the dark. Wylie's Saloon looked just as honky-tonk as ever, and the row of little shops and stores looked the same, except for the names. It was a dusty little town, with a main street that led to a jail, a courthouse, a medical clinic, and the Copper Creek

Church, with its tall spire gleaming in the late morning sunlight. There were people out walking, talking, shopping, and crossing the street, waving to neighbors.

There was nothing about Copper Creek to set it apart from every other tired little town in the West.

Yet, he'd missed it. All of it. With an ache that caught him by surprise.

If anyone had told him nine years ago that he would miss all this, he'd have called them crazy. But there it was. Despite the sad reason for his return, he was glad to be here, back where it had all begun.

Of course, it helped that he was returning without feeling like too much of a failure. He'd sold off enough of his herd, plus some equipment, to Fred Covington to pay Fred back for the taxes and the repair of the irrigation system. Fred had agreed to care for the rest of his livestock until he returned.

He would deal with the next crisis tomorrow.

Today, he would deal with the biggest loss of his life.

Out of the corner of his eye he caught the blurred image of a fuzzy yellow puppy darting into the street. He had to stand on his brakes to avoid hitting the poor thing.

He was out of his truck in a flash and grabbing the wriggling little animal before it could get hit by the truck traveling in the opposite direction.

"Hey, little guy." Kneeling, Ash was rewarded by a face-licking before a female swooped down on them and dropped to her knees in the middle of the street.

She was close to tears. "Oh, Sammy. I was sure you'd been killed."

At the sound of that familiar voice, Ash sucked in a breath. It wasn't possible, and yet...

He turned and caught sight of her face. A face he'd carried in his heart all these years.

"Brenna." The word came out in a whoosh of air.

Her eyes rounded. "Ash?"

For a moment both were rendered speechless.

Brenna swallowed, before saying in a rush, "I shouldn't be surprised that you're home. I heard about your father." She lay a hand on his in a gesture of tenderness that was so typical of the girl he'd known in his youth. "I'm so sorry, Ash. It must have been a horrible shock for you."

"Yeah. Thank you." He was surprised he could get a word out. His throat had turned to dust, and he was so startled that all he could do was stare. With her hand on his there was a quick rush of heat, and then a slow trickle of ice along his spine.

Brenna Crane had always had that effect on him. She only needed to look at him with those big blue eyes, and display those dimples in a dazzling smile, and his brain turned to mush.

She'd always been a cute, pert tomboy in braces and threadbare denims. Now she was movie-star gorgeous, her long blonde hair straight and shiny, her jeans molding long, long legs, and no braces on those white, even teeth. There was the faintest scent of spring flowers that had him wanting to lean closer and breathe her in.

He felt an even stronger need to just drag her close and kiss her. There had been a time when it all would have been so easy. But that was in the past. And now, thanks to the years of silence and avoidance that stretched between them, all he could do was stare in awkward silence. To cover his reaction he handed over the wiggling puppy, and his hand brushed the underside of her breast. If this had been in the past, she would have teased him about doing that deliberately. In the past, he'd have grinned like a fool and said she knew him too well. But now, all that had once been easy and familiar between them was strained and awkward.

He pulled back has hand as though burned and stood watching as she cuddled the little guy.

The sight of it had his insides tangling as memories of her hands gliding over him had his throat going dry as dust. When the puppy began happily licking her face, he had to close his hand into a fist at his side to keep from reaching out to her.

He managed a smile. "I can't believe you're the first one I've seen since returning..."

A truck seemed to come out of nowhere, barreling around the corner and heading straight for them. Ash reacted instinctively, grabbing Brenna in a bear hug and drawing her to one side. The truck narrowly missed them, so close they could feel the rush of air as it rocketed by them.

"Damned fool." For a moment Ash remained protectively on top of her, stunned by what had just transpired. And even more stunned by the press of her body beneath his.

When the vehicle roared off, he looked down into her face, seeing her eyes wide with shock. Her mouth was mere inches from his, her breath whispering over his cheek, and he wanted, more than anything, to taste her. To cover her lips with his and kiss her until they were both breathless.

"Ash." At the sound of his name, he blinked and struggled up before helping Brenna to her feet. She was still holding the wriggling pup, while Ash, reluctant to break this tenuous connection, continued holding tightly to her as if to lend support.

"Well, that will teach us to hold a reunion in the middle of the street." Her voice was soft and a little too breathy.

"Still, he had to see us here. He didn't even bother to stop and make sure we were all right."

Brenna looked down at his hand, still holding tightly to her.

He was forced to release his hold on her. That was when he caught the glint of sunlight reflecting off the diamond on the ring finger of her left hand.

His mind went numb. For the longest time, his heart forgot to beat.

On the long drive here he'd tried to prepare himself for any number of changes. He'd even tried to picture Brenna married and with children. But the truth was, it had been an impossible image. The closer he'd come to town, the more he'd begun to allow himself to hope that she would be the same Brenna he'd left all those years ago. Sweet and generous and somehow willing to forgive him and even wait for him.

Though he'd tried to prepare himself for the worst, now that he saw that ring winking in the sunlight, mocking him, he couldn't speak. Could barely breathe. He felt his jaw clench until his teeth ached.

Seeing the direction of his gaze she flushed. "I guess you wouldn't have heard. I'm . . . getting married."

"Married. Well. Con . . . gratulations." The word stuck in his throat. "Who's the lucky guy?"

She nodded toward the man in suit and tie just exiting

Green's Grocery with a bottle of water tipped up to his mouth.

Ash absorbed a wave of absolute fury. He hated this stranger on sight.

Adjusting his sunglasses, the man smiled at Brenna and strolled into the street. "You hitching a ride with strangers now, Bren?"

"Sammy got loose and ran before I could stop him. I'm grateful he wasn't run over. In fact, we were all nearly run over by some crazy driver who didn't even slow down. It was a close call."

"I thought I heard the screech of tires. I guess that's what happens when you stand in the middle of the street," the man said drily.

"Chris, this is Ash MacKenzie. Ash, my fiancé, Chris Revel."

"Revel." Ash studied the man through narrowed eyes.

"MacKenzie. Of course. I heard about your father. I guess everyone in Montana has, by now." He offered a handshake. "I'm really sorry."

"Thanks." Noting the suit and tie, Ash couldn't help saying, "I guess it's a safe bet that you're not a local rancher."

"I work for the government. My temporary assignment has stretched out into a six-month stint." He shot an admiring look at Brenna. "And for that I'm grateful."

Ash fought to ignore the jealousy that pulsed through him. It was an emotion alien to him. But though he knew he had no right to envy this stranger, he couldn't deny what he was feeling. It was raw and deep and completely irrational, and it had him by the throat as if it were a monster.

"What is it you do for the government?"

"Collect data for the Farm Bureau."

It was on the tip of Ash's tongue to call him a paper pusher, or something equally denigrating, until he managed to push aside his irrational anger and return to civility.

Hearing the honking of a horn, he looked over. "Unless we get out of the street, we may not get a second chance." He turned to Brenna. "It was great seeing you."

"You too, Ash."

As Ash climbed into his truck, Chris Revel put a proprietary arm around Brenna's shoulders and guided her back to the sidewalk.

Ash put the truck in gear and watched in his sideview mirror as the man bent to press a kiss to Brenna's cheek before taking the puppy from her arms. Once the leash was attached, the couple continued walking with the puppy following at their feet.

They were looking into each other's eyes and smiling.

Ash felt a knife enter his heart.

And then they were out of sight.

He leaned an arm out the window, trying to focus on the reason for his return to town. But it was impossible to concentrate on anything except Brenna Crane.

His first love. His only love, if truth be told. Even though he'd left her without a word of good-bye, he'd never stopped thinking about her. And somehow, he'd always entertained the idea of coming back to find her still in love with him, and still waiting.

Another dream shattered. With his record, he thought, he ought to be good at dealing with broken dreams by now. But this one hurt so much more than the others. Hurt enough to have him mentally cursing the pain, and cursing himself for his stupidity.

He knew one thing. He'd heard from a friend passing through Wyoming years ago that Brenna had been deeply wounded when he'd left town without so much as a word to her. For a girl like Brenna, it had to have been the final straw in a life that had been one shattering disappointment after another. But though he'd wanted to write her, or call, he'd convinced himself that he had no right. Not while he'd been struggling to figure out his own future. What kind of man would ask a woman as special as Brenna to wait or, worse, to join him in what appeared to be a succession of odd jobs and no roots?

Guilt had been Ash's constant companion all these years. He was still plagued by guilt.

And now, it seemed, he needn't have worried. Brenna had finally moved on with her life.

Ash reminded himself that after the way he'd treated her, she had every right to carve out a bright future for herself. And he had no right to get in the way. Whatever feelings he had for her would have to be buried as deeply, as completely, as the feelings he had for his father.

In these past years, the loss of everyone who mattered had left him feeling adrift. The loneliness had been a physical ache around his heart that had never healed. But he'd learned that it was possible to live with a permanently broken heart.

For now, he would concentrate on repairing the rift he'd caused in his family, and easing his mother through the pain of her loss. He'd been the cause of so much pain, not only for Willow, but also for Whit, the kid brother who had been his constant shadow.

He hoped they'd be able to find their way back to what they'd once had, before all the anger and harsh words had broken them completely.

And then he would figure out what he was going to do with his life going forward, now that all the old dreams were gone forever.

Chris Revel led Brenna inside the temporary cubicle he rented behind the medical clinic before turning to her. "Coffee?" The single word was abrupt.

She managed a smile. "I thought we were going to lunch."

He turned his back on her. "That's what I'd planned, but I got a call from Helena. I've got to get them a mountain of data before their monthly meeting tomorrow."

"How long will it take to finish your work?"

He filled two cups from the coffeemaker on a corner cabinet and handed one to her. "Hours, if I get to it right away. Half the night, if I don't get my hide in gear. I'm afraid I'll have to cancel our dinner plans, too. I hope you haven't already shopped for those steaks."

She sighed, struggling for patience, since his own seemed to be on a short leash. "That's all right. They'll keep. I guess working for the government is just like running a ranch. You dance to the whims of the bureaucrats while ranchers dance to the whims of Mother Nature."

"Yeah. But frankly, I'll take steady employment and a monthly paycheck over the whims of nature any day. Like I told you, I grew up on a hardscrabble ranch in Oklahoma. The day I left for the university, I vowed to never shovel manure again. Unlike," he added with a note of sarcasm, "the cowboy we just left back there in the street."

Ignoring his coffee, he opened a cabinet and began collecting folders and setting them on his desk. His movements matched his terse words. After an extended silence, he turned to her, leaned back, and crossed his arms over his chest. "So that was Ash MacKenzie."

At her arched brow he shoved his hands in his pockets. "Small-town people like to gossip."

"I should have guessed." Brenna sighed with resignation. "What would you like to know?"

"Just one thing." His steely gaze pinned her. "Are you over him?"

"Chris, he's been gone for almost ten years."

His eyes narrowed. "That's not an answer."

When she held her silence, he crossed the room before holding open the door, a sure signal that his patience had snapped and their time together was up.

Brenna set aside her untouched coffee and caught hold of Sammy's leash.

As she brushed past him, Chris bent to kiss her good-bye. Against her mouth he muttered, "Maybe getting no answer really is an answer."

"Chris, I—"

He cut her off with a quick, hard kiss. "I'll see you in a day or two."

When his door closed, she walked to her battered truck and yanked open the driver's-side door. Sammy leaped inside and stuck his head out the passenger side window.

She climbed in and started toward home. But her thoughts weren't on her destination, or on the man she had just left in his office.

All she could think of was Ash MacKenzie.

After the shocking way he'd left her, she'd had way too much time to think about him, and wondering what her life would have been like if he'd stayed.

Did he have regrets for the way he'd betrayed her trust? Did he miss her the way she missed him, with an ache that never ended? Why had he never tried to contact her?

She'd always hoped that they would one day cross paths again. In her fantasies, she'd be wearing something stylish and chic, her hair and makeup perfect, her manner poised and aloof. It shamed her to admit that she'd secretly hoped that Ash would be old or paunchy or at least apologetic about the way he'd left.

He'd been none of those things. He'd been the same rugged cowboy he'd always been, only older, more muscled, and, if possible, even sexier.

He'd taken the news of her engagement in stride. And though she hadn't spotted a wedding band on his finger, that didn't mean he hadn't found someone to share his life. After all, she'd moved on. It was sensible to assume that he'd done the same.

But moving on wasn't the same as letting go. Though she'd tried desperately to get over him, all those old feelings came rushing back the minute they came face-to-face in the street.

And seeing him again, being held in those arms for a brief moment, had shattered her beyond belief.

"Ash." Willow fell into her son's arms and hugged him fiercely before stepping back to study the rugged, craggy face of her firstborn son more closely.

"How are you holding up, Mom?"

"I'm okay. Lost without your father. My heart broken beyond belief. But I'll survive. Oh." She hugged him again, as if to assure herself that he was really here. "I'm so glad to see you, Ash."

When he released her, he leaned down to the wheelchair to hug his grandfather. "Mad. You're looking great."

"I wish I felt great." The old man returned the hug stiffly, before patting his grandson's shoulder to soften the welcome. "These are hard times, Ash."

"Yes, sir. They are." Ash straightened and turned to Whit, who had stood to one side watching the reunion. "Hey, Whit. You okay?"

"Yeah. I'm fine." Whit stuck out his hand, sending a signal to his brother that he had no intention of being hugged.

The two shook hands solemnly.

Ash looked him in the eye, and realized his younger brother was now as tall as he. "You're not that fifteen-year-old kid anymore."

"You got that right." Whit's eyes narrowed on his brother. "How long you planning on hanging around?"

"I don't know. I came without any agenda except to bury Pop."

Seeing Brady Storm just striding up the porch steps, Ash turned to the back door to greet the ranch foreman.

"Hey, Brady."

"Ash. I figured that was your truck when I spotted the Wyoming plates."

The two men shook hands, then seemed to think better of it and gave each other a quick, fierce, bone-jarring bear hug before stepping apart and slapping each other's shoulders. From the warmth of their laughter to the light

dancing in their eyes, it was plain that the affection between them was as strong as ever.

"You got older, Ash."

Ash grinned. "You didn't."

"I guess that's what comes of having salt-and-pepper
hair back in my thirties and forties. I looked old before I
got there," the foreman said with a laugh.

Ash turned to wink at his mother. "And you didn't age
a year. How is that possible?"

Willow laughed and tossed her head. "I can see that
you're determined to be on your best behavior."

"Maybe I'm hoping that will earn me a big slice of
your chocolate cake."

Willow turned to her father-in-law. "I guess he doesn't
know yet."

"Know what?" Ash said.

"I'm chief cook and bottle washer around here now.
I got sick and tired of sitting around watching everyone
else working while I was feeling sorry for myself."

"You're the ranch cook? What does Myrna do?"

"I've been demoted to laundry and household chores
and being your grandfather's legs." The old woman was
grumbling as she waddled into the kitchen wearing an
enormous apron that spanned her ample middle. Her gray
hair had been pulled into a tight bun, from which damp
tendrils had worked free to curl around her pudgy cheeks.
Her blue eyes twinkled with a look of childish mischief.

"Hey, Myrna." Ash gave her a hug and lifted her off
her feet, swinging her around as he always had.

That had her smile returning as she settled on her feet
and touched a hand to his cheek. "Ash, honey, if you don't
look even more handsome than you did when you left."

"Now that's the kind of appreciation I was looking for," Ash said with a laugh.

"Appreciation was never the strong suit of the MacKenzie family." Whit shot a glance at his older brother before adding, "At least while Pop was top gun around here, we all got shot down equally."

Maddock slapped a hand down hard on the arm of his wheelchair. "You'll not speak ill of the dead."

Whit flushed. "Sorry, Mad."

"You'd better be." The old man turned his wheelchair toward the stove. "Lunch will be ready in a little while. I'm making..."

At the sound of wheels on gravel, Maddock looked out the window. The others did the same and watched as a tall, muscled man stepped out of a dusty truck and started up the steps.

Willow wiped her suddenly damp hands down the front of her denim shirt. "That must be...Griff."

At Ash's lifted brow, Whit said in an aside, "Long story short, Pop learned just before his death that he'd had a son with some slutty school teacher before he and Mom got married."

"Whit!" Willow rounded on her son. "You mind that tongue."

"What the hell...?" Ash's jaw dropped.

Before he could ask more, there was a knock on the door.

Willow hurried over to greet their guest.

Pasting a smile to her lips she pulled open the door.

And found herself staring at a face that was the exact image of her dead husband's.

CHAPTER FIVE

Griff?" When she managed to find her voice, Willow
continued her wide-eyed stare.

Ash did the same. He couldn't help himself. The same
dark eyes. The same strong jaw. The same firm mouth.
There was no denying this stranger's heritage. He'd been
cast from the same mold as Bear MacKenzie. Except for
the difference in ages, and a knotted scar that ran from his
ear to disappear below the collar of his shirt, they could
have been twins.

"Yes." The voice was low and deep. Bear's voice. The
same growl. The same inflection. "Are you Willow?"

She nodded, and Ash realized that she was afraid to
trust herself to speak, for fear she would burst into tears.

"I have a letter of introduction from Mason McMillan." He held out the document, but instead of reaching
for it, Willow continued staring at him for long moments.

Finally gathering herself, she stepped aside. "I'm

sorry, Griff. I know about Mason's letter. He copied it to me. Please come in."

"Thank you." He looked beyond her to the others. Their gazes were fixed on him as if they were seeing a ghost.

When nobody stepped forward, he cleared his throat. "My name is Griff Warren." He turned to Ash. "You are?"

"Where are my manners...?" Willow began, but Ash was already speaking.

"Ash MacKenzie. I'm the oldest..." Realizing the error of what he was about to say, his voice trailed off as the two shook hands. This stranger would have been born before Ash was even conceived.

Ash indicated the man in the wheelchair. "This is my grandfather, Maddock. Everybody calls him Mad."

"Mad." Griff stuck out his hand and the old man shook it, all the while staring at him with a look of stunned surprise. To make conversation, Griff added, "I hope that nickname doesn't describe your attitude."

"Most days it does." Mad's tone was solemn enough, but the corners of his mouth were curling in the merest hint of a smile.

"Griff, this is my younger brother, Whit."

Griff offered his hand, and Whit glowered as he shook it, unable to hide his feelings about this man's presence in his family.

"Our ranch foreman, Brady Storm."

"Brady."

"Welcome to MacKenzie Ranch."

"Thank you."

An awkward silence fell over the group when they realized that Brady Storm, the only one of them who was not blood-related, had been the first to offer a word of welcome.

"I'm Myrna Hill. I've been with the family for nearly thirty years. Until recently"—she shot a knowing look at Mad—"I was chief cook and bottle washer around here. Now I guess I'm just the bottle washer."

Her remark broke some of the tension as the others laughed aloud.

"Now *I'm* the cook," Maddock said with a wry smile.

"I'm sorry, Griff." Struggling to pull herself together, Willow kept her hands tightly gripped at her waist. "I'm afraid I'm feeling a bit overwhelmed."

"You're not the only one. I didn't know about you—" he nodded to include all of them "—*any* of you, until I got the letter from your lawyer."

"Yes, well . . . that was a shock for all of us," she admitted. "But seeing you . . ." She swallowed and tried again. "You see, you're the image of Bear."

"I wouldn't know. I've never seen him." The words were as challenging as the look in his eyes.

"Let me show you his portrait. It hangs in his office." Willow opened the door that led down a hallway.

As she walked along beside Griff, the others followed, more out of curiosity than out of welcome.

Bear's office was a purely masculine room, with a stone fireplace that dominated one wall. A bank of windows offered a view of the rolling hills beyond, which were dotted with cattle. A massive desk stood to one side, faced by several upholstered swivel chairs.

Griff's attention was arrested by the portrait hanging above the fireplace mantel.

He couldn't have been more stunned if he'd been

shocked by a cattle prod. It was like looking in a mirror. The man staring back at him had the same dark, curly hair, the same shape of brow and stern, dark eyes. He even had the identical cleft in that strong, jutting jaw.

While Griff studied the man in the portrait, the others were riveted by the man who could only be Bear's son.

Mad's gruff voice broke the silence. "I think we could all use some coffee."

As they turned away, Ash stepped up beside his mother, who was struggling to think of something, anything, to say to this stranger.

"On the way back to the kitchen, why don't we show you the great room?" Ash led the way into a room filled with light from the floor-to-ceiling windows that offered an unbroken view of the hills in the distance. Another massive stone fireplace took up one entire wall.

Griff paused to study the portrait that hung above this mantel.

Ash followed the direction of his gaze, and the irony of the situation once again rendered him silent.

In the portrait, Bear MacKenzie had his arm around his younger son, Whit, while Willow stood proudly with her hand on Ash's shoulder.

A happy moment, captured for all time, of a united family.

It couldn't be made any clearer that Griff Warren was the absent one. The outsider. The illegitimate son of a man no longer here to claim him as his own.

"Something smells great." Because the others had become so subdued, the ranch foreman made an effort to keep things light as they entered the kitchen.

"Split pea soup with ham," Maddock announced. "It's been simmering since dawn. Sit." He indicated the round wooden farmhouse table and high-backed wooden chairs that were the centerpiece of the kitchen.

The table had been set with baskets of rolls and pitchers of foaming milk, as well glasses of water and a carafe of coffee.

Maddock balanced a wide tray across his chair and proceeded to fill bowls with steaming soup.

"What's this?" Ash asked, pointing to the tray.

"An invention of mine," his grandfather said with a trace of pride. "I figure, since I'm stuck in this thing"—he indicated the hated wheelchair—"I'd invent ways to make it more useful."

"Pretty clever, Mad."

At Ash's compliment, Myrna shot him a look. "Oh, yeah. Clever all right. Every time I look for something I've been using for years, I find it's been cut down or cut up to make something 'clever.' And then I have to go to town and replace all the things I'm missing. Like my favorite serving tray."

That had Mad grinning. And even Myrna's words held no sting. She nudged the old man's elbow as she waddled about, distributing platters containing chunks of ham as well as boiled potatoes, carrots, and cabbage in the middle of the table, where everyone could serve themselves.

At a wink from Mad, Ash stifled a grin. The friendly competition between Mad and Myrna had begun when the older man had moved in, and would no doubt continue until the day they were carried out. But, though Myrna's words were strident, there was really no anger behind them. Nobody listening to her was inclined to believe she had anything but affection for the old man she'd spent a lifetime complaining about. It was evident in the way the two playfully contradicted one another, only to break into laughter whenever one or the other managed a really clever barb.

When the others had staked their claim on their seats around the table, Griff held Willow's chair before taking the chair beside her. "Do you usually eat this much for lunch?"

Hearing him, Ash chuckled. "By noon, most ranchers have done more work than most businessmen would do in a week. There's something about hard, physical work that makes a body hungry."

"And lean and mean," Mad said with a grin. "You won't see too many overweight ranchers. We're too busy working off every calorie before it can turn into fat."

Griff nodded. "It's that way in combat, too."

Brady passed him the basket of rolls. "I'd guess being a target for enemy fire would burn off a whole lot of calories."

"Yeah." Griff helped himself to a roll and held out the basket to Willow. "I didn't see any overweight Marines where I was stationed." He glanced across the table at Ash. "So you've been up since dawn working?"

Ash shook his head. "By dawn I was already on the road heading here."

Griff raised a brow. "You don't live here?"

"I have a spread in Wyoming."

"Have or had?" Maddock's head came up sharply. "Mason's son Lance figured you were about to lose it for back taxes."

"I managed to sell off enough cattle to pay the taxes,

and I made a deal with my neighbor to do a land exchange for repair of my irrigation system. So, for now at least, I still own it."

The old man's face relaxed into a smile. "Good for you."

Willow sat back and regarded her older son. "If you decide to settle here, there's more than enough land for you."

"This was Pop's. Now it's yours, Mom."

"It's ours, Ash. Your father wanted it to belong to all of us." She glanced at Griff. "Once Bear learned about your existence, he added you to his will, too. He wanted this ranch to belong to the MacKenzie family for generations to come."

"That's a nice dream." Whit's tone of anger, as well as his words, had everyone looking at him. "But we couldn't even live together before Griff came along. What makes you think things are going to be any different now?"

"Because everything's changed." Maddock slammed a hand down hard on the arm of his wheelchair. "Because we've lost my only son, and your father, and we suddenly see how quickly things can change. And if we don't learn how to work together now, we won't deserve a third chance."

A pall of frosty silence settled over the table.

It was Myrna who broke the ice. "While the rest of you are choking on those loving sentiments, I'm starving. Please pass me the ham."

Griff fought back a grin before passing platter after platter to Willow, who passed them to Brady, who passed them to Whit, who held them while Myrna helped herself to a heaping portion of ham, potatoes, carrots, and cabbage from each.

The rest of them followed suit, and soon they were too busy eating to argue.

Willow seized the opportunity to tell them her news. "I heard from Chief Pettigrew..."

Whit's fork clattered on his plate. "They found the bastard who shot Pop?"

Willow felt Griff bristle beside her and realized, too late, that Whit's choice of words had just added another layer of insult to a fatherless man who had probably suffered a lifetime of them. She fixed Whit with a look that every son recognized. "You will not use that word in my home again. Is that clear?"

Whit's gaze slid over Griff as the realization dawned. "Yeah. Sorry. I didn't mean..." He changed the subject. "Did they identify the killer?"

"No. But Ira wanted me to know that they've completed their autopsy, which proved what they already knew. Bear was shot by a single bullet from a long-range hunting rifle. They've identified the weapon as a Remington bolt-action."

"Great. That makes every rancher in the state of Montana a suspect," Maddock muttered around a mouthful of ham.

"Exactly." Willow sipped coffee. "I was hoping they would at least find some exotic bullet and weapon, or something in the area that would reveal more." She sighed. "He used a long-range sight, so Bear didn't have a chance. He never would have suspected that he was being stalked by a killer."

"Enemies?" Griff asked.

"Enough." Ash's lips thinned. "Pop had a hair-trigger temper. Anything could set him off, and once he lost it, he usually went into a full-blown rant."

"But they were only words." Maddock was quick to defend his only son. "And once the tirade was over, Bear's anger was gone as quickly as it started. He was always able to forgive and forget."

"Apparently his killer didn't have the same capacity for forgiving or forgetting." Brady clenched a hand at his side.

Ash looked at the foreman. "You think the shooter was somebody who's been holding a grudge?"

"When somebody stalks his victim and waits to kill him, what would you call it if not a grudge?"

Ash nodded thoughtfully.

Willow glanced around the table. "Ira requested a list of possible suspects and reasons why we might suspect them of wanting to harm Bear. He specifically mentioned the recent spate of cattle rustling, as well as the names of people who owe Bear large sums of money. I've given him every name I can think of, but I'm sure I've overlooked any number of people. So I'd like each of you to make your own list and add it to mine."

"Cattle rustling?" Griff grinned. "As in those old Westerns on TV?"

"This is high-tech rustling," Whit was quick to explain. "They roll up in the night with a caravan of cattle-hauling trucks, and by the time a rancher learns that he's lost hundreds of head of cattle overnight, the thieves have crossed several state lines, covered the brands with new ones, and have already sold the animals to a slaughterhouse."

Griff shook his head in wonder. "I guess that might be worth a man's life."

"You'd be surprised what a man's life could be worth."

Mad slapped the arm of his wheelchair in disgust. "Some ranchers have died just because they threatened to report a poacher of wolves."

"Wolves?" That had Griff's attention.

Whit told him, "Even though they're protected by the government, some ranchers are willing to pay a bounty to keep the predators from their herds. Especially during spring calving."

"Ira even asked if there could be any old friends who might be jealous of Bear's success." Willow set aside her fork and pressed a hand to her stomach.

Maddock, seeing the look of pain on his daughter-in-law's face, was quick to say, "I think we've speculated enough about this for now. Why don't we all make our lists and let the police chief do his job?" He turned to Willow. "When will they release Bear's...the body?"

"Ira told me to contact Mitch Weatherby to arrange a pickup tomorrow at the county morgue. Which means I can plan a funeral service as soon as I talk to Reverend Hamilton at Copper Creek Church. Depending on his schedule, we ought to be able to have something by the weekend. I thought I'd call the pastor today and see if I can arrange the service for this weekend. That way, more of the ranchers will be able to attend."

"Yeah. They'll be in town anyway and can drop by church just before they pick up their feed and grain order, stock up on groceries, and lift a couple at Wylie's," Maddock muttered. "In Bear's honor."

While the others flinched, Willow glanced at Ash and then Griff. "Do either of you have to leave sooner?"

Ash shook his head. "My neighbor agreed to tend what's left of my herd while I'm gone. I'm not on any kind of timetable."

"Griff?" Willow turned to him.

"The Marines sent me home with a pocket full of money, and I'd just as soon spend it in Copper Creek as anywhere. Let me know the date and time of the service, and I'll be there." He thought a moment. "That is, if there's a place in town where I can stay until then."

"You're welcome to stay here, Griff."

He shot a glance at Whit. "I don't want to intrude on your grief."

"You're not intruding." Willow put a hand on his arm. "I know this is awkward for all of us, but you're family now. When Bear and I built this house, we'd designed it so that we could watch our children and grandchildren grow up here without feeling crowded. We have more than enough room for you."

"And half your Marine buddies," Mad added with a laugh.

Griff grinned at the old man's joke before saying to Willow, "You're sure?"

"Positive. Ash, you can have your old rooms back. And you can show Griff the east wing."

To Griff she added, "You can have as much privacy as you want, and when you're in the mood for company, some of us are always around."

"Especially here in the kitchen," Maddock said with a chuckle. "You can almost always find me here."

"Inventing something that will cost a fortune to make and then won't work anyway," Myrna growled.

Ignoring her, Mad continued as though she hadn't said

a word. "And when the rest of the family gets hungry enough, this is where they congregate."

"If I'm going to stay here, I expect to do my share of the work."

"Oh, you can count on that." Brady gave him a knowing smile. "Ranch chores are never really done. By the time we get to the end of the list, it's time to start over."

"Especially mucking stalls," Whit added. "Pop always said it was good for building muscles."

"As well as character, as I recall," Ash said with a quick glance at his grandfather.

"Bear learned that from me. I raised him to believe that mucking stalls was one of the constants that a rancher can never walk away from. So, since you can't beat it, you may as well learn to use it for some good."

"You'd know how good manure is, wouldn't you, Mad?" At Whit's remark, the others burst into gales of laughter.

Griff shrugged. "Okay. What am I missing?"

"I guess we could say that Mad was the butt of Pop's joke. He loved to tell us about the time Pop and Mad got into a real knock-down, drag-out fistfight, and Mad shoved Pop off the hayloft. By the time Mad had climbed down the ladder, Pop was spitting flames and wound up shoving his own father into a mound of fresh manure he'd just shoveled from the stalls. Gram wouldn't even allow Mad to come in and shower until he hosed himself off in the barn," Ash said.

Griff was laughing and shaking his head at the image. "I don't blame her. I wouldn't have let you in either, Mad."

The older man wiped tears of laughter from his eyes.

"What Ash didn't tell you is that it was below zero that day, and by the time I'd hosed myself off and walked back to the house, my clothes were stiff as a board, and so was my hair. I looked like a damned scarecrow."

Around the table, the others joined in the laughter.

Willow took in a deep breath, surprised at how much the sound of laughter lifted her spirits.

"Your rooms are in there." Ash led the way up the stairs and along a hallway until he and Griff paused in front of closed double doors. "If you need anything, just let Myrna know. Mad may claim to be in charge of the cooking, but Myrna runs the entire household."

"Thanks." Griff opened the doors and set aside his bags. "I'll keep that in mind."

Ash continued along the hallway until he came to a second set of double doors. Inside, he dropped his bags and stared around with interest. This had been his room when he was growing up. Even though he'd been gone for almost a decade, little had changed. The bedroom had a huge walk-in closet and a king-sized bed. A desk and chair had been custom-built along one wall. Along another was a wood-burning fireplace. Atop a low, flat dresser something new had been added since he'd left home: a flat-screen TV.

He was deep in thought as he set up his laptop on the desk before crossing the room to the wall of windows.

Here was another thing he'd missed. This view. This land.

His legacy.

He'd been willing to leave it all behind in his eagerness to escape the constant battle of wills with his father. But now, seeing it all again, he felt an overwhelming sense of what he'd missed. Not just the land, the shared work, the comfort of his family. What he'd missed more than he ever realized was the presence of his father.

He tried to remember those times before the anger. Before the constant butting of two heads that refused to soften.

He'd loved his father. Had grown up wanting to be like him. And yet, each time Bear MacKenzie had started one of his tirades, something inside Ash's heart had closed a bit more, until one day, it slammed shut, and there was no solution except to go. To make his own way, and hope that one day he and his father would make things right between them.

Though he'd never given it too much thought, he'd always assumed that they would find a way to heal the wounds.

That day would never come now. And he knew, with absolute certainty, that he would have to live with that gnawing regret for all his life. No chance to say he was sorry. No chance to mend the terrible, gaping wounds that had left his family bloody and bowed. His family.

Though his mother and Brady seemed to have barely aged, the change in Whit was shocking. Ash had left behind a kid brother and had returned to find a man in Whit's place. An angry man. And who could blame him? He must have felt completely abandoned by the big brother he'd shadowed for all his life. Ash could only imagine how much of his father's temper had transferred to Whit, since there'd been no one else around to deflect all that anger.

Ash hoped he could be around long enough to establish some kind of relationship with the now-grown Whit. But such things took years, and he'd already wasted nearly a decade.

And what of Griff Warren? Ash had been prepared to deny any sort of relationship with the stranger claiming to be his father's son, until he'd seen his face. There would be no way any of them could deny Griff's claim. It was there on his face, in his eyes, the shapes of his nose and mouth. And even in the deep timbre of his voice. He was a younger, stronger Bear MacKenzie. And that fact had Ash wanting to resent him. But he couldn't. Not if he wanted to mend his relationship with his mother. She'd made it perfectly clear that she would not permit any disrespect while Griff was here.

Maybe, Ash thought, once they'd buried Pop and he and Griff returned to their lives elsewhere, he'd have time to sort through all that had happened and make some sense of it.

Ash wiped an arm across his eyes and turned away, feeling an overpowering weariness. This was all more than he could take in.

He kicked off his boots and, without bothering to turn down the bed linens, stretched out on the comforter.

He was asleep as soon as he closed his eyes.

CHAPTER SIX

Ash awoke, confused and befuddled, from a deep, soundless sleep. It took several moments before he realized where he was. His bed. His room at his family's ranch.

He sat up and looked around, allowing all the old, familiar sights and sounds to wash over him. Cattle lowing in the distance. From the kitchen, the clatter of pots and pans, and the wonderful aroma of pot roast in the oven. The *flop, flop* of Myrna's slippers on the stairs and the distinct sting of disinfectant in the air, left behind from her cleaning.

Had it really been nearly ten years? So much of the life he'd left behind remained as fresh, as familiar, as though he'd been gone no more than a day. And yet, it had all changed. His mother a widow. His brother a man. A half brother who hadn't even existed in his mind yesterday. And Pop dead.

That realization sent a series of shock waves through his system, leaving him sucking in a quick breath.

A glance at his watch told him he'd been asleep for over an hour. After his long journey, that much-needed sleep had him feeling ready to tackle the rest of the day, and to see what other surprises life had in store for him.

Pulling on his boots, he headed downstairs to join the others.

Mad looked up from the stove. "Caught a little lie-me-down, did you?"

"Yeah." Ash nodded toward the back door. "Where's Whit?"

"In the barn with Griff. I hope they haven't come to blows. Whit's mouth tends to get ahead of his brain at times."

"Yeah. It's the family curse. Guess I'll join them. I can be the referee."

As he started toward the mudroom, Mad's words stopped him. "You've been gone a long time, laddie-boy."

Ash paused and turned to look at his grandfather. "If you've got something to say..."

Mad held up a hand. "I'm not looking to pick a fight. I just want you to know I'm glad you came back, even though it took you longer than I'd expected."

Some of the strain left Ash's eyes.

"And I know your ma's glad to have you home, too. She said so, just before she left with Brady to check on the herd in the south meadow."

At the mention of his mother, Ash smiled. "She looks good, Mad. How's she holding up?"

The old man shrugged. "You know your ma. She may be hurting inside, but she won't let us see her fall apart. She's a strong woman, Ash."

"Yeah. And how about you, Mad? How're you doing?"

His grandfather looked down at his hated chair. "I never thought anything could be harder than this. But losing my son..." His words faltered. "This time the Lord's given me a mountain."

Ash yearned to go to his grandfather and hold him, but he knew the old man was close to breaking down. One sign of sympathy, and he'd probably fall apart. That was something neither of them could bear. So he stood his ground and said simply, "You'll climb it, Mad."

"You sure, laddie?"

Ash nodded. "That's what a MacKenzie does. You told me that yourself the time I got bucked off that spotted stallion and broke both my arms."

"Cracked a couple of ribs, too, as I recall, and bled buckets of blood on your way to the town clinic." Mad blinked away the tears that threatened and managed a weak smile. "You scared the hell out of me. But you never even cried. You were always one tough kid."

"We're both tough, Mad. That's what you and Pop taught me. If you want to be a MacKenzie, you have to take whatever life throws at you."

As Ash turned and walked out the back door, Maddock watched in thoughtful silence.

His grandson was all man now. There was no trace of the quick-tempered youth who'd driven off in a trail of dust, leaving them all wondering how he'd survive.

He'd not only survived, he'd thrived. He'd grown up.

And hopefully he was a better man than those who'd gone before him.

Mad found himself wishing Bear could see his son now.

Hell, maybe he could.

With all his might, Mad hoped and prayed Bear could see all of his sons.

What a high price they'd all paid for that trademark MacKenzie temper.

". . . prefer working in the high country."

At the sound of Whit's voice, Ash paused in the doorway of the big barn.

Whit and Griff were busy mucking stalls, forking filthy straw and dung into the honey wagon and carrying on a running, if guarded, conversation. It was clear that Whit was struggling to be civil, though the fire of resentment was still burning in his eyes. And why not? Except for that scar, the man facing him was a mirror image of their father.

That fact alone would be enough to swallow, but knowing that Bear hadn't had time to share his newly discovered knowledge of Griff with his family before his untimely death made it all the more awkward. It was so unfair, especially to their mother.

"Do you prefer it to other ranch chores?" Griff asked.

Whit worked the pitchfork into a corner of the stall. "I guess there isn't any one chore I prefer over the other. But I like the solitude in the hills. I like being with the herds and feeling like I don't have to make small talk with people."

Griff leaned on his pitchfork. "Sorry. If you'd rather work in silence, we don't have to talk."

"No. I didn't mean now." Whit dumped a load of dung and returned to the stall. "Well, maybe I did. I don't know what to say to you." His mouth twisted into a frown. "Cows don't care if I praise them or curse them."

"If you feel like cursing me, go ahead."

When Whit held his silence, Griff moved closer to touch a hand to his sleeve. "Look, Whit. We're both new at this. I was raised as an only child, by a mother who refused to answer any of my questions about my father. Every time I tried to engage her in a conversation about him, she shut me down. After a while, I gave up asking. And I was resigned to never knowing a thing. Then, out of the blue, a letter arrived from a lawyer telling me I'd been acknowledged by a man I didn't even know." He paused for a moment before saying, "So if you think having a new half brother sucks, think about this. I've now acquired two half brothers, a stepmother, and a grandfather, and all of them strangers. On top of that, the man I'd always dreamed of meeting is dead, robbing me of the chance to ever meet him, to judge for myself whether or not he was a jerk or a good guy. Oh, and one more thing—his killer is still at large, and for all we know, he wants to slaughter the entire family."

Whit stared at him for long minutes before giving an unexpected grin. "I guess your situation trumps mine. So for now, let's just call a truce and figure things out."

"Fair enough." Griff returned to his work. "So you enjoy your solitude. Is that your nature, or just something that's happened since your dad died?"

Whit shrugged. "My nature, I guess. But after Ash left, the urge got stronger. I started volunteering to be with the wranglers up in the hills. It was easier than working alongside Ma in the barns, because she was always sad. And working with Pop was impossible, because of his temper. At first, after Ash left, there was no talking to Pop."

Ash absorbed a quick jolt to his system. He'd known, of course, that a kid brother would suffer the loss of a brother he looked up to. But he hadn't really thought about just how deeply Whit had been affected. It sounded as though Whit had felt completely abandoned.

Ash's feelings of guilt grew.

"Pop always..."

Seeing Ash's figure in the doorway of the barn, Whit let his words trail off before calling, "You finally awake, sleepyhead?"

"Yeah." Ash crossed the space between them and picked up a pitchfork. "I was hoping you two would have this done by the time I joined you."

"We figured as much." Whit shared a knowing look with Griff. "We decided to go slow so we wouldn't deny you your chance to share the load."

"Thanks." Relieved that Whit could make a joke of it, Ash stepped into another stall and started cleaning.

After what he'd just heard, his heart went out to both Whit and Griff. But at least they were still speaking.

As for his own feelings, he'd need plenty of time to sort through them. Right now, he was feeling as unsettled as he'd felt when he'd first left home and realized he had no place where he belonged. After all these years, could he really belong here again? Would it ever really feel like home?

He decided to ask a few questions of his own. "How long were you in Afghanistan, Griff?"

"This was my third tour."

"Third?" Ash looked over. "You got a death wish?"

Griff paused to wipe his arm across his damp forehead. "In the Corps we go where we're sent without question."

"Three tours in Afghanistan." Ash shook his head in wonder. "Were you scared?"

"Too many times to count."

"Why'd you join the Marines?" Ash closed the stall and moved to the next.

"I thought of myself as a tough guy. And I guess, if I'm going to be honest, I wanted to break away from my mother and prove to myself that I could make it on my own."

Whit gave a dry laugh. "Sounds like someone else I know." He stared knowingly at his older brother.

Ash nodded. "Yeah. I guess everybody has something to prove." He turned to Griff. "How did your mother take the news?"

"Like a wounded bear. She knew I was restless, and she figured I was getting ready to leave for good. But the first time she saw me in my uniform, she was able to put aside her fear and tell me how proud she was."

"You're lucky." Ash frowned. "Not everybody gets to hear a parent say that before they . . ."

To cover the awkwardness, Whit jumped in. "Where'd you get that scar, Griff? In battle?"

The Marine automatically touched a hand to the scar that ran from below his ear to the other side of his throat. "An insurgent up in the hills. Took down the guard while the rest of us were catching some sleep. He nearly slit my throat before I was even awake."

Whit's eyes went wide. "How'd you survive?"

"My training kicked in and I managed to wrestle the knife from his hands and take him down. After that, I woke up in surgery, and they told me another inch and I'd have bled to death. I guess it wasn't my time to die."

The three fell silent as they bent to their work.

It was Ash who finally broke the awkward silence. "Why don't we all head to town after supper and have a beer at Wylie's?"

"Not a good idea," Whit said quickly.

"What's Wylie's?" Griff asked.

Ash was quick to explain. "The town's watering hole."

"Sounds good to me." Griff tossed another load of dung into the wagon.

"Me, too." Ash followed suit.

"I don't know." Whit shot a quick glance at Griff's face. "There's bound to be gossip."

"You think that's something new to me? Hey, I'm the guy who grew up without a father, remember?"

"Suit yourself." Whit's nod of agreement came slowly. "Just for the record, they won't just be talking about you. I'm sure the favorite topic of the entire town is Pop's death. When you live in a town as small as Copper Creek, folks thrive on gossip. And when a rancher dies, you're bound to hear the good, the bad, and the ugly."

"Thanks for the warning." Griff set aside his pitchfork.

"One more thing." Whit's smile was quick and dangerous. "I'd better warn you both. If you two hear a lot of females moaning and sighing when we walk by, don't let it go to your heads. They'll be mooning over me. It's just the effect I have on women. Especially in Wylie's."

Griff turned to Ash, who was staring at his brother with a look of complete surprise.

After sharing a laugh with the other two, Ash took a moment to study his younger brother with renewed interest.

"What's wrong?" Whit asked.

Ash lifted a brow and shot him a knowing grin. "I guess that just proves again that my little brother is all grown up."

"As all the women at Wylie's will testify to. And don't you forget it, bro."

Whit gripped the handles of the huge wagon and lifted it with ease, rolling it toward the doorway of the barn. Ash took note of the muscles bulging beneath the rough plaid shirt. No doubt about it. His little brother had become a man while he was away chasing his own dreams.

As he continued his work Ash came to a sudden decision. He'd missed way too many of the important things in life because of an impulsive reaction. An impulse that could have been channeled in a much more positive way if he'd only taken time to think things through.

No matter what hurdles he faced from his fiery family in the future, he would face them head-on. And communicate.

No more running.

If he returned to his ranch in Wyoming, it would be because it was his choice, and not because he was running away.

Ash pushed away from the big oak table and carried his dishes to the sink. "Great supper, Mad. You've really mastered the art of cooking." He winked at Myrna. "Sure you didn't have a little help from you-know-who?"

Maddock practically growled his displeasure at any

suggestion of help. "You-know-who never cooked the beef long enough to be fork tender. And she certainly never added cream cheese to the mashed potatoes."

"Is that what made them so good?" Willow glanced at their housekeeper. "Did you teach Mad that trick?"

Again the old man growled. "I don't need any females teaching me tricks. Don't you know all the really good cooks are men?"

"And pigs fly," Myrna muttered as she deposited her own dishes in the sink. "Good night. I'm going to my room and watch TV."

"Why don't you start your own series, Myrna?" Mad called to her retreating back. "*The Glamorous House-keepers of Copper Creek.*"

"In my day I could have given all those women a run for their money." Her voice trailed off as she closed the door to her suite of rooms.

While the others laughed, Ash turned to his grandfather. "Speaking of TV, have you been watching those cooking shows?"

Mad flushed. "What if I have? I learned more in a month than I would've in a year reading Myrna's yellowed old dog-eared cookbooks. I think they were written when Lincoln was a boy."

"Careful. You let Myrna hear you say that, you may find yourself fending off her rolling pin."

"I'm not worried about that old hen." As an afterthought Mad added, "I made coffee and brownies."

"None for me." Whit set aside his fork. "Against my better judgment, I'm taking Ash and Griff to town for a couple of beers at Wylie's."

The foreman glanced at him across the table. "A couple of beers? Maybe I'd better go along as your designated driver."

"You're just looking for an excuse to jawbone with all the other ranchers," Whit said with a grin. "But come on along, Brady. You're welcome to join us."

"And do the driving." Griff turned to Willow. "How about you joining us, too?"

She was so surprised and pleased by the invitation, she was momentarily speechless. Then, collecting her thoughts, she shook her head. "It's very thoughtful of you, Griff. But no thanks. The last time Bear and I went to Wylie's, Bear nearly came to blows with Luther Culkin over some remark Luther made."

Ash's eyes grew stormy. "Some things never change. But I guarantee that Luther wouldn't dare make a remark when you're surrounded by all of us."

Willow touched a hand to her heart. "I'm grateful for the invitation, but not tonight. Maybe another time."

"Okay." Ash turned to his grandfather. "How about you, Mad? Ready for a beer at Wylie's?"

"Not tonight. Like your ma, I'm not ready to face all the ranchers and wranglers in town yet. The funeral will be soon enough. But maybe next time."

The four men said their good-byes and paused in the mudroom to collect their denim jackets and wide-brimmed hats before heading out the back door.

Minutes later the sound of the truck's engine broke the stillness.

At the table, Willow and Maddock sipped their coffee and shared a smile.

"Funny." Willow nibbled a brownie before pushing it aside. "I thought I'd resent Griff. I wanted to."

Across the table, Mad held his silence.

She sighed. "He represents a part of Bear's life that I didn't share. His mother…" She shrugged. "It doesn't matter now. His mother is gone. So is Bear. And every time I look at Griff, all I see is Bear, and I can't bring myself to resent him. None of this is his fault."

Mad reached across the table and covered her hand with his. "It's not your fault, either. It just is what it is."

She nodded. "Still, his presence in Copper Creek will have tongues wagging."

"No doubt about it. But there's a toughness in that young man's eyes that tells me he's lived through a lifetime of gossip. Tonight will be nothing new for him."

"But tonight he'll be in Bear's hometown. And everyone who sees Griff Warren will be looking at the ghost of Bear MacKenzie."

Mad nodded thoughtfully. Willow sat back, her mood suddenly pensive. "I'll be honest, Mad. When Mason gave us the news about Griff, I was shocked and saddened. But the deepest pain came not from the knowledge that Bear had a son with another woman, but from the fact that he hadn't shared that fact with me when he learned the truth."

Mad was relieved that she could finally speak of it. "I think he would have shared it with you, once Mason assured him that he'd located the lad."

She shook her head. "How can you be so sure?"

"Because Bear had already directed Mason to add the lad's name to the will. That's not something he could keep secret from his own wife. He would have had to explain his reasons to you sooner or later. And I'm thinking that Bear wasn't a man to put off something as important as that. It was only a matter of time before he'd have told you everything. But first, he wanted to have all his ducks in a row."

She reached across the table once more and squeezed her father-in-law's hand. "Thanks, Mad."

"For what?"

"For giving me something to hold on to. It's all been too much to wrap my mind around."

The old man nodded. "That is has. Too much pain. Too many questions about who and what and why."

Willow stared off into the distance. "I keep thinking that if only I'd ridden out to Copper Creek with Bear, this might not have happened."

"Don't you even think that way, lass." Mad's tone grew rough with passion. "Whoever did this didn't have a care about taking a man's life. If he'd had to add one more to the list, who's to say he would have given it a single thought?"

Willow fought back tears. "But I'd have been there with Bear while he lay dying. And maybe, just maybe I would have had time to call for help, and Bear would still be alive."

"Or you'd both be dead. Don't play this game with yourself, lass."

"But what if—?"

"I'll not go there." Maddock slapped his palm hard on the arm of his wheelchair and turned away from the table. Over his shoulder his burr thickened with passion. "Nor will you. Bear is gone, Willow. And if we're to honor his life, we move ahead and make this ranch and this family a living testimony to all that he believed."

Though he heard her crying softly, he didn't turn back to her.

He waited until he heard her footsteps leaving the room.

Alone in the kitchen, the old man buried his face in his hands and wept bitter tears.

CHAPTER SEVEN

Here we are." Brady Storm pulled up in front of the row of buildings, before driving around to the back to park.

Wylie's Saloon looked like every other dingy bar in every small town. It sat on Main Street. An old wooden building that hadn't seen a coat of paint in twenty years or more. A scarred heavy door that creaked and groaned every time it opened or closed. Inside, the smell of stale beer and greasy burgers hung like a cloud over a long wooden bar that bore the scratches of a thousand beer mugs. Tables and chairs were scattered around the room, with booths along the side and back walls. A small dance floor opened up the middle of the room, where two cowboys and their girlfriends danced to Tim McGraw singing about living like you were dying.

The room was crowded with ranchers and wranglers, cowboys and drifters.

"Got what he deserved," Luther Culkin was saying.

"My only question is how he managed to avoid being killed sooner." Luther, tall, muscled, considered himself the toughest cowboy in a town full of tough cowboys. He wore his dark hair in a ponytail, not because of any need for fashion, but because he was too cheap to pay a barber. He'd rather spend his money on booze. The more he drank, the more he hungered for a good fight. "If I were to make up a list of men wanting Bear MacKenzie dead, I'd be here till midnight."

"Who do they think killed Bear?" one of the cowboys asked.

Behind the bar, Wylie shrugged. "If Chief Pettigrew is to be believed, every man, woman, and child around these parts is a suspect."

Over their beers and whiskeys, looks were exchanged.

And though everyone in the saloon knew everyone else, there was the nagging little thought that one of them just might be the vicious gunman who'd ended Bear MacKenzie's fabled life. As soon as Whit and Ash stepped inside, the loud voices, the laughter died. For the space of several seconds, nobody made a sound as all eyes were fixed on the two men who had not only lost their father, but had lost him in the first murder most of this town could ever recall.

As the two MacKenzie brothers moved toward the bar, a few of the wranglers found their voices.

"Hey, Whit. I'm sorry about your pa."

"Thanks, Marty."

"Ash." A cowboy stood and stuck out his hand. "Figured you'd come home for the funeral. Sorry about your loss."

Wylie looked up from the bar, where he'd been pouring drinks. "Whit. Ash. We all heard the awful news. Sorry..." His gaze was arrested by Griff and his words faded. He did a double take before regaining his voice. "Who's this with you?"

Ash had given some thought to how he'd handle the introductions to Griff. Wylie had just given him the perfect opening.

In a clear voice he said, "I'd like you all to meet Griff Warren."

Nonie Claxton was staring at Griff as she sidled up beside Ash. "Since the bar's nearly full, how about a booth?" She lowered her voice. "I've got a big one in the back. Away from the noise."

Ash shot her a grateful smile. "Sounds fine, Nonie."

"I think I'll stay here at the bar." Whit slapped the back of a young cowboy and leaned in to give Wylie his order.

"Me, too." Brady paused to speak to a couple of local ranchers.

"Suit yourself." Ash motioned for Griff to follow him and Nonie.

The waitress leaned close to touch a hand to Ash's cheek. "I'm so glad you're back, honey. You've been missed."

"By you, Nonie?" He placed an arm around her shoulders.

"Of course. But there were...others, too." She nodded toward a table, and Ash caught sight of Brenna and her fiancé talking in low tones.

As he and Griff threaded their way through the crowd toward the back booth, he was forced to pass directly by Brenna's table.

He braced himself as he paused and forced a big smile. "Hey, Bren. Chris."

Brenna's cheeks were flushed, a sure sign that she was feeling conflicted. "Hi, Ash."

Chris frowned, making no attempt at friendliness. "MacKenzie."

"Good seeing you, Bren." Ash turned to include the man with her. "Good seeing you both."

As he moved on he could hear Chris saying, "...why I hate small towns. Everywhere we go, we'll be running into him."

So. Apparently Chris had heard about the history he and Brenna shared. For some strange reason that had Ash grinning as he took a seat in the booth.

From here he had a perfect view of Brenna and her guy.

Another reason why he loved being back in a small town.

His attention was suddenly drawn to the bar, and one voice in particular. "Griff Warren?" Luther Culken downed his beer in one long, noisy swallow before turning to share a grin with the cowboy beside him at the bar. "He sure looks like someone we all knew." He winked at Brady, standing behind the others at the bar. "I thought for a minute or two I was seeing Bear."

Ash watched as the foreman fixed Luther with a challenging look that would have frozen most men's blood. But Luther was apparently too drunk to care.

To break the tension, Wylie shouted, "The house is buying a drink for everyone."

Nonie Claxton loaded her tray and started parceling out drinks to every table.

When everyone was served, Wylie shouted, "Lift your glasses to Bear MacKenzie."

A roar went up from the crowd. "To Bear."

At the bar, Whit and Brady joined the others in the toast before tilting their bottles and drinking.

Luther nudged the cowboy beside him as a signal that he was about to have some fun at the expense of the MacKenzie family. "So, this Griff fellow? He a long-lost relative, Whit?"

"That's none of your business, Luther." Whit walked to a seat at the far end of the bar, while Brady remained standing with a cluster of wranglers from a nearby ranch.

"Maybe I'm making it my business." Seeing that he'd pushed Whit's hot button, Luther's voice lifted a notch so he could be heard above the din. "I figured I was seeing your daddy's twin or—" he looked around, to make certain he had everyone's attention before adding "—or maybe his long lost kid."

"Shut up, Luther. Or—"

Luther cut him off. "Or what?" Whit's scowl was exactly the reaction he'd been hoping for. "You calling me a liar?"

"I said shut up."

"Uh-huh." Now Luther could barely contain his excitement. "Know what I think, boys?" He looked around, enjoying the sizzle of anticipation he could feel rippling through the crowd. "I think when nobody was looking, old Bear was making whoopee behind the barn."

At the rumble of laughter Whit was out of his seat and had his hands at Luther's throat before anyone could react.

"I told you to shut your filthy mouth."

Ash and Griff, hearing the commotion, were on their feet and crossing the room just as Luther clawed at the strong hands around his throat and managed to break free. Sucking in air he slid off his bar stool and threw a punch that landed directly in Whit's face.

Blood spurted from Whit's nose, though he took no notice through the haze of fury that had him returning the punch with one of his own.

The cowboy seated beside Luther tossed a mug of beer in Whit's face, momentarily blinding him.

That had Brady locking an arm around the cowboy's throat before he could pick up another drink to toss.

Against his ear Brady swore. "This is between Luther and Whit. You keep it a fair fight, or you'll answer to me."

Luther took that moment to bring his knee into Whit's groin. "See how you like that, tough guy."

As Whit crumpled to the floor, Luther stood over him with a sneer. "Maybe you'd better ask the bastard to come over and fight your battles for you."

Griff fisted a hand, ready to jump in, but Ash held him back. "Let's let my little brother fight his own battle, as long as it's fair."

While they watched, Whit caught Luther by the ankle and dragged him down.

When Luther fell, two of his buddies leaped into the fray.

Ash nodded at Griff. "Now it's not fair. But we'll even those odds."

Ash threw his first punch, and it was all Griff and Brady needed to join him.

Fists were flying, and bodies dropping so quickly, it looked like half the town of Copper Creek had suddenly joined the free-for-all.

Above the din Griff shouted, "Anybody wants to take on the bastard, here I am. And in case any of you are still wondering, I am Bear MacKenzie's son. And damned proud of it."

Somebody threw a full bottle of beer at Griff's head. He managed to duck, and it landed on the floor, sending shards of glass and foaming beer everywhere.

A table was overturned, and a chair went flying through the air.

Cowboys were hauling their women safely outside before joining the fight. Except for Brenna and Nonie, there weren't any females left in the place.

Chris Revel caught Brenna's hand and started leading her toward the door, hoping they could escape the brawl as quickly as possible.

They were nearly at the door when Brenna spotted Luther, bleeding from his head, picking up an empty bottle. He broke it on the edge of the bar and, with the lethal weapon in his hand, started across the room toward Ash, who was busy fighting off two of Luther's drunken buddies.

"Ash!" Brenna was desperate to be heard above the roar.

As she started forward, Chris caught her roughly by the arm. "Don't be stupid. We have to get out of here."

"Oh, don't you see? Ash can't hear me." She shook off the offending hand and dashed across the room just as Luther raised his arm.

"Ash. Behind you!"

At Brenna's warning, Ash turned and landed a fist in Luther's throat.

The bottle fell to the floor while Luther dropped to his knees, struggling for breath.

"Thanks, Bren..."

Out of the corner of his eye Ash saw a cowboy tossing a chair. Wrapping his arms around Brenna, Ash dragged her to the floor and fell on top of her, hoping to absorb the brunt of the blow.

The chair grazed his shoulder before slamming into the wall beside them.

For several moments they lay in a tangle of arms and legs, heartbeats thundering, their breaths shuddering.

Ash lifted his head just enough to brush his lips over her ear. "Seems to me we were in this same position earlier today." Despite the pain that shot up his arm from the flying chair, he managed a quick, sexy grin. "I think we've got to quit meeting like this."

"How can you make a joke when you were nearly knocked unconscious?" Brenna's words were whispered against Ash's cheek.

At the mere brush of her lips on his flesh he felt a sudden, shocking arousal. Instead of rolling aside, though, he remained where he was. His arms came around her, pinning her even more firmly against him. "Are you sure I'm conscious? I used to dream about having you here in my arms like this. Am I dreaming, Brenna?"

She'd gone very still and watchful.

"I have to find out." He allowed his mouth to nuzzle her jaw. "Umm. So soft. Just the way I remember your skin. I guess you're real and this isn't a dream."

"Ash…"

He continued nuzzling her jaw before moving his mouth closer to hers. "Why didn't you run when you had the chance?"

She remained completely still for a moment longer. Then with a sigh she turned her face just enough that their lips were brushing. "I saw what Luther intended to do, and I had to warn you."

"My sweet little avenging angel." His hands roamed her back as he absorbed the most amazing rush of sexual energy.

Before he could return the kiss Chris was beside them, his voice thick with anger and concern.

"What in hell do you think you're doing, MacKenzie? Brenna. Are you hurt? Here. Let me help you up."

Ash rolled aside and managed to touch a hand to her face. "You okay?"

Heart pounding, all she could do was nod.

Chris stepped over Ash and caught Brenna's hands, helping her to her feet. "That jagged beer bottle could have carved up your face. What were you thinking? I told you to stay away." He swore loudly, viciously. "If you don't have any concern for your own safety, then at least give a thought to the guy who's about to marry you. The last thing I need on my employment record is an arrest for a stupid bar brawl with a bunch of drunken cowboys. Come on." With his arm firmly around her shoulders, he led her away.

Ash continued sitting on the floor, watching through his one good eye as Whit battled Luther's buddy, who suddenly pulled a hunting knife from his waist. Griff, seeing what the cowboy intended, gave a martial-arts kick that had the cowboy's body dropping face-first to the floor with such force, he lay moaning, unable to move.

Whit wiped blood from his mouth before saying, "That was some move. You learn that in Afghanistan?"

"Long before I went there." Griff shook his head. "A bar in my hometown."

"It was a good move." Whit dropped an arm around Griff's shoulders. "I'll have to remember that for next time."

"You planning on doing a lot of bar fighting?"

"You never know. Sometimes it just helps to let off some steam."

The two of them ambled over to where Ash was sitting on the floor. Whit offered his brother a hand, and got him to his feet.

"Going to have quite a shiner, bro."

"And you've got a fat lip."

"It'll heal."

They turned to Griff, who was limping slightly.

Ash nodded toward Griff's leg. "Somebody use a boot on you?"

Griff grinned. "I did it to myself. That last kick. Out of shape, I guess."

"You were in shape when it counted." Whit offered his handshake. "You fight like a pro, bro."

Griff laughed out loud. "Thanks. I consider that the highest of compliments."

"Fighting like a pro?"

"No. Being called bro. That's a first in my lifetime."

The three were grinning as they approached Wylie, who was looking over the destruction to his saloon.

Ash reached into his pocket. "Sorry about the mess, Wylie. I've got—" he counted bills "—sixty dollars."

"I've got forty," Whit said.

"I've got ninety-eight." Griff deposited his money on the bar. "I hope that will cover the damage, Wylie."

Brady Storm ambled up and dropped another fifty on top of their pile of money. "For the drinks you didn't get to sell tonight."

Wylie nodded. "That ought to more than cover everything here. But I doubt it'll cover Luther's visit to Doc Mullin's clinic."

"Serves him right," Whit said with a snarl. "Next time I see him, he'd better keep that big mouth shut, or he'll need another visit to the doc."

Brady started for the door. "Come on, boys. It's time I drove you home."

The three of them followed.

As they settled into the ranch truck for the long drive back, the three kept up a rambling conversation about the punches they'd thrown, the cowboys who were considered stand-up guys for fighting alongside them, and those who had sided with Luther.

When they'd talked themselves out, Brady was grinning.

"What's so funny?" Whit demanded.

"The three of you. If I didn't know that you and Ash had been apart for the past nine years, and that neither of you had met Griff until this morning, I'd think you'd been loyal brothers for a lifetime."

The three men fell silent, each lost in thought.

It occurred to Ash that Brady was right. He and Whit and Griff had forged a bond tonight. A bond that might not be the same as having spent the last years together under one roof, but a bond nevertheless.

Then, as Brady fiddled with the radio, and Patsy Cline sang about being crazy, his thoughts drifted to Brenna. The press of her body beneath his. The dazed look in her eyes when she'd realized how recklessly she'd behaved.

To save his hide.

The thought had him grinning through his pain like a lovesick fool.

She might have already agreed to marry someone else, but she still had some feelings for him.

Old feelings, as he well knew, could run deep and true.

Mad rolled himself into the kitchen and poured three fingers of Scotch. Sometimes, when the pain in his old bones woke him from a sound sleep, his only relief was a stiff drink.

He sat in front of the wall of windows and stared out at the starlit sky. Maybe he should have gone to town with the lads. Hell, he'd wanted to. But he hated leaving Willow alone here. It was too soon. He needed to be here for her, just in case. Besides, he reminded himself, it was a chore for the lads to take him anywhere these days. The lifting, hauling, more lifting weren't only an effort on them but a constant humiliation for him, as well. How he hated being cared for by others. For a man who'd prided himself on his physical prowess, these paralyzed limbs were a painful reminder of how quickly life could change.

He heard the low rumble of a truck's engine, and the crunch of tires on gravel, and glanced at the clock. The lads were home earlier than he'd expected.

He turned as the door opened. Seeing Ash, his hand holding the tumbler halted halfway to his mouth. Then he spotted Whit, Griff, and Brady, and a half grin tugged at the corners of his lips.

"Should I ask to see the other lads? I hope they look worse than the lot of you."

Ash shot him a grin. "Much worse, Mad. You would've had a grand time watching from the sidelines."

"From the looks of you, I think I'd have had to step in to save your hides."

Whit chuckled. "No need. Brenna Crane did that for you."

"Brenna?" Willow's voice from the hallway had them looking over. As she stepped into the kitchen, tying the sash of her robe, she studied their battered faces. Except for raising a brow, she made no comment.

"Sweet Brenna decided to warn Ash about Luther Culkin, who was sneaking up from behind with a broken bottle. And for her effort, she nearly got clobbered by a flying chair."

Ash rubbed his tender shoulder. "It missed her and hit me, instead."

"Sounds like a barrel of laughs." Willow turned to Brady, her eyes stormy. "I thought you were going along to see to their safety."

He merely smiled, though even that small movement had his jaw protesting. That cowboy from the Lazy J packed a punch. "I said I'd go along to drive them home. You know that once a MacKenzie feels insulted, there's no stopping the fireworks."

"Which of you was insulted this time?" Willow demanded.

Whit glanced at Griff. "Luther called him a bastard, and then had a few things to say about Pop. You wouldn't expect me to allow that to go unchallenged, would you?"

Mad caught Willow's eye and winked, defusing the charged atmosphere in the room. "I'd say you lads handled it exactly the way your father would have. I hope you reimbursed Wylie for any damage."

"We did. And even covered any beer sales he may have lost during the brawl."

"And Brenna?" Willow asked. "Did you see that she got home safely?"

"Her fiancé hustled her out of there so fast, we didn't have time to thank her," Whit said with a grin. "And from the look on his face, he wasn't happy to see his future bride lying on the floor under my big brother."

Willow turned to Ash, who merely shrugged. "Don't worry, Mom. There wasn't time for any . . . hanky-panky. I was just shielding her from debris."

Mad took a moment for a long, satisfying drink of his Scotch. "Not that hanky-panky would ever enter your pure mind, laddie."

"She's engaged to another guy, Mad." Ash's tone was angrier than he'd intended.

"And that's got your temper up, has it, laddie?" Mad's eyes danced with humor. "As far as I know they haven't said 'I do' yet."

Willow put her hands on her hips and speared her father-in-law with a look. "I think we've all had enough fun and excitement for one night. It looks as though all Bear's sons will be sporting bruises at his funeral." She turned on her heel. "Good night."

"'Night," they called.

When she was gone, they said their good nights to Mad and made their way to the stairs.

In the kitchen, Brady twirled his hat around and around in his hands until they were out of earshot.

The old man looked up expectantly. "Was it a good fight?"

Brady nodded. "You'd have been proud of them, Mad. Whit took on Luther for the things he suggested about Bear and Griff's mother. When it got ugly, both Ash and Griff jumped in. I held back until I could see they needed a hand. But they were all capable of holding their own against a room full of angry cowboys."

Mad's eyes danced with unconcealed joy. "I wish I'd been there."

Brady touched a hand to his tender jaw. "I know I'll pay hell tomorrow. But for now, I have to say it was a satisfying end to the evening. And Mad, in case you haven't noticed, you've got yourself a houseful of good men."

After Brady let himself out, Mad sat alone, nursing his drink and thinking about the son he was about to bury.

Odd, he thought. Life was strange. He'd lost a son and gained a grandson. And from the looks of the other two, they were beginning to accept Griff as one of the family.

Nothing like a good knock-down, drag-out fight to bring out the best and worst in a man.

He drained his tumbler in one long swallow and rolled his wheelchair toward the suite of rooms that had been built for him on the main floor. Sleep, he knew, would be a long time coming. But at least everyone was home now. All his chicks home to roost.

All but one, who would never walk through that door again.

That knowledge was a blow to his heart, swift and terrible.

CHAPTER EIGHT

Every pew in the Copper Creek Church was filled to overflowing. The MacKenzie family was the closest thing to royalty in this part of Montana, and ranchers and their families had come from a hundred miles in every direction to bury their king.

Brenna sat next to Chris near the rear of the church and watched along with everyone else as the casket of Bear MacKenzie, flanked by Brady Storm and five wranglers, moved in solemn procession along the center aisle.

The stern image that Bear MacKenzie showed the world dissolved in Brenna's mind, replaced by the kind, considerate man few had come to know as personally as she had. After Ash's abrupt departure from Copper Creek and from their lives for all these years, she and Bear discovered that they shared a bond not shared by many. They both missed him and grieved deeply, and they had actually consoled each other. It wasn't something she was comfortable sharing with Chris—or, for that matter, with anyone.

Directly behind was Willow, walking between her sons, Whit and Ash, with Maddock's wheelchair being pushed by Griff Warren.

Once Ash came into view, Brenna couldn't look away. The sight of those broad shoulders, that thick, dark hair that curled slightly over the collar of his starched white shirt, had her riveted.

He glanced around, as though searching the crowd for someone. When his eyes met hers, he gave a brief nod of his head before moving on.

It was enough to have her shivering yet again, as she'd been for days now.

It had been bad enough when they'd met in the street on the day of his return. But the incident at Wylie's was so deeply imprinted on her mind, she couldn't shake it. The strength in those hands as they'd clutched her and taken her down in the blink of an eye, saving her from that chair tossed like a missile. The press of that hard, muscled body on hers as he'd shielded her from harm. The touch of his work-roughened hand moving along her spine, causing a rush of heat to spiral through her in a torrent of raging fire. Added to that was the wonderful feel of his calloused hand on her cheek, as gentle as a snowflake, when he'd looked down at her with such tenderness, such concern. And the deep timbre of his voice asking if she was truly all right.

And, of course, that almost-kiss. The moment his mouth brushed hers, she'd wanted him to crush her against him and take the kiss deeply, until they were both lost in it.

It shamed her to realize that even now, seated in a church, about to witness the burial of a man held in esteem by an entire town, she couldn't stop thinking about Ash and the way she'd felt in his arms.

Chris had been furious at her involvement in the brawl. And still was. He'd gone on and on about the sort of crazy woman who would place herself in jeopardy when fists and even chairs were being thrown.

She knew she'd done a dangerous, foolish thing. But in truth, she would do it again.

Chris was an outsider. Maybe that was why he didn't understand the sort of loyalty she felt for someone she'd once loved.

Once loved.

At least that was what she tried to tell herself. Ash MacKenzie had left her without a word of good-bye. There hadn't been a single letter in all the years he'd been gone, proof of how little she'd really meant to him. She'd been cut to the depths of her soul by his callous behavior.

She felt a sense of pride that despite his ill treatment of her, she hadn't died of a broken heart. Instead, she'd learned to live without Ash. Had made a good life for herself, despite all the obstacles in her way. It was natural to want to step in and help when he was threatened. It didn't mean that she was willing to set herself up to be hurt again.

Or was there more going on than she was willing to admit?

She'd been having this argument with herself ever since Ash had returned to Copper Creek.

Had she been living a lie? She'd convinced herself that she was over Ash, but now, seeing him again, she was

suffering terrible guilt. He'd used her badly. Had left her
without a word, and though there must have been plenty
of opportunities to contact her, he'd never even tried. What
kind of fool would set herself up for even more abuse?
Hadn't there been enough in her life? And yet, seeing Ash
again, and allowing that scene in Wylie's to play through
her mind again and again, she wondered about her very
sanity.

As the eulogy was given, and the music soared, Brenna
saw Ash whisper something to his mother. Saw Willow
nod and wipe a tear with a lace handkerchief. Saw Ash's
strong arm around his mother's shoulder. And deep inside, something twisted in Brenna's midsection.

Chris idly caught her hand in his and looked over with
a smile, and her feelings of guilt deepened.

She'd accepted a marriage proposal from a good man.
And why not? She was twenty-six years old, and she
had every right to find happiness where she could. But
right now, right this minute, she was riddled with doubt.
Though she'd convinced herself that she'd completely
stopped loving that quick-tempered, hard-headed boy
who had stolen her heart when she was just eight years
old and he was ten, she wasn't so sure anymore. How else
to explain why, from the moment he'd returned to Copper Creek, he'd completely taken over her mind? If she
wasn't very careful, and very vigilant, she could very easily give him control over her heart and soul, as well.

The Copper Creek Cemetery stood on a windswept hill behind the church. It was a pretty place, with a wrought-iron
fence and weathered monuments dating all the way back to
the 1800s. Here and there ponderosa pine trees spread their

branches, casting shadows on crosses and marble angels. An occasional granite bench offered rest for those who came to visit and leave flowers on the graves of loved ones. Every Memorial Day—which the folks in Copper Creek still called Decoration Day—the town showed up to mark the graves with flags and wreaths, and the high school's lead trumpeter would play taps.

A small canopy had been erected at the gravesite to shield the family from the elements. But the weeklong rain had fled, leaving only a soft spring breeze and warm sunshine.

After the graveside ceremony was concluded, the townspeople left to conduct business, and the ranchers and wranglers returned to their never-ending chores.

As the MacKenzie family made their way down the hill, Ash spotted Brenna and Chris walking toward them. In Brenna's hands was a large box.

Willow paused to embrace her. "Brenna. How nice of you to come."

"I'm so sorry for your loss." Brenna greeted the others and introduced them to Chris before holding out the box to Willow. "I thought you might like to have this."

Willow opened the box to reveal a sculpture of Bear waving his hat in the air while astride a bucking horse. "Oh, my." She studied it carefully, noting the triumphant look in his eyes, the charming smile parting his lips.

She handed it to Maddock, who turned it this way and that in the sunlight in order to see all the finely sculpted details.

"Brenna, you've captured Bear so completely, it's uncanny." Willow smiled at the young woman. "When did you do this?"

"I photographed him last summer at the rodeo, and when I showed it to him, he asked me to make a sculpture of it as a birthday gift to you. I showed it to him last month, when it was nearly completed, and he was delighted."

"So am I. Oh, Brenna." At a loss for words, Willow gathered her close and pressed her lips to the young woman's temple. "How can I possibly thank you? It had to take so much of your valuable time to make. Will you let me pay you for it?"

"Knowing you like it is all the payment I want."

"Like it?" Willow's voice rang with passion. "I absolutely love it. And to think that Bear had commissioned it as my birthday gift means the world to me."

Brenna's smile deepened. "I'm so glad now that I brought it."

Chris added, "I told her not to bother you with it today. I said it was too soon, and might cause you pain.

"Pain?" Willow turned to study the sculpture, which Mad was still holding. "Just looking at it makes me smile."

Willow put an arm around the young woman's shoulders. "We're going to the Boxcar Inn for lunch. Please join us."

Chris shot a look at Brenna and was already shaking his head in refusal. It was obvious that they'd made plans of their own.

Brenna considered refusing. It was on the tip of her tongue to make her apology and leave with Chris, but one look at Ash, standing to one side, staring at her so intently, his sorrow a palpable thing, had her saying rashly, "We'd love to. Thank you."

Their little party walked through the town until they

came to the diner, which had been made from a train's boxcar, complete with faded red paint and a Santa Fe logo on the side.

Inside it looked much like a train's dining car, with booths along each side of the main aisle, and small windows above each booth.

The food was simple fare, featuring burgers, fried chicken, and homemade soup. Even the pies were baked fresh by the owners, Will and Nell Campbell. Will had retired after thirty years with the railroad, and he boasted to everyone who would listen that instead of leaving the railroad, he'd brought it home with him.

After they had all given their orders, Brenna sat back and studied the MacKenzie family.

Willow looked as model-stylish as ever in a trim black suit, her hair straight and loose the way Bear always liked it. Maddock and his grandsons were dressed in dark suits and ties. Brady Storm wore a dark Western suit and string tie, his boots polished to a high shine. Myrna was dressed in a dark, shapeless dress with a pretty pearl brooch pinned to the lapel.

When Brenna spotted it she smiled. "What a pretty pin, Myrna."

The old woman touched a hand to it. "Bear's gift to me on my birthday last year. It's my favorite. I thought I'd wear it in his honor. You know, I think Bear enjoyed everyone else's birthdays more than his own."

Willow ducked her head, but not before they could see the tears that sprang to her eyes.

"So, Chris." Maddock looked at the young man beside Brenna. "You've decided to settle here in Copper Creek?"

"I won't be settling anywhere for quite a while. This

is just a temporary stop." Chris accepted a glass of water from Nell Campbell.

Mad winked at the young man. "I see. You hoping to run the Farm Bureau one day?"

"Why not? Why settle for less than the top job?"

Maddock chuckled. "Why indeed?"

To change the subject, Brenna turned to Whit, hoping to keep the conversation light and impersonal. "I just found a book out in the barn I absolutely know you haven't read. And since you like to have several in your saddlebags when you're up in high country, I thought I'd save it for you."

"Thanks, Bren. I appreciate that. I'll stop by your place some day this week and pick it up." Almost as an after-thought he asked, "What's it about?"

"As if you care," she smiled and they shared an easy laugh. "So far you've read my how-to manuals on sculpting, my biography on Abraham Lincoln, and even those dog-eared copies of my favorite historical romances."

Ash and Griff were staring at Whit with matching looks of surprise.

"Romances?" Ash said under his breath.

"You ought to give them a try, bro." Whit winked at Brenna. "When you're up in hill country with nothing but a herd of ornery cattle, they can be pretty entertaining."

"So is a round of poker with the wranglers," Maddock said with a frown.

"I can do that anytime, Mad." Whit couldn't help grinning at the look on his grandfather's face. "But I sure am learning what women in your day really wanted."

"*My* day?" The old man glowered. "You think I'm ancient?"

"Okay. Maybe not in your day. But in the days of Queen Elizabeth, those females were some red-hot chicks."

They were still laughing when their meals were served.

As their party made its way from the diner, Brenna and Chris paused to say their good-byes.

Brenna embraced Willow. "Thank you for including us. It means a lot to me."

"And your sculpture of Bear means the world to me. I'll treasure it always."

Brenna could feel Ash's gaze boring into her as she bid goodbye to the others.

She extended her hand. "Goodbye, Ash." With a teasing glint of humor she couldn't help adding, "Nice-looking shiner."

His own smile was quick and disarming. "You should have seen the other guy. If Luther's is anything like mine, in the last couple of days it's gone from black and blue to purple and even green. We started calling it my neon eye."

That had everyone laughing except Chris, who said drily, "I'm just glad it was you sporting that shiner and not Brenna."

Willow couldn't help saying, "Ash told me you were at Wylie's during their brawl."

"Not just there." Whit's voice rang with pride. "When Luther threatened Ash with a broken bottle, Brenna blew into the scene like Wonder Woman."

"And saved my hide," Ash added.

"I knew you couldn't see what Luther was planning."

She turned away, feeling embarrassed at this turn in the conversation. "I'm just glad it all turned out without anything more serious than a black eye." She smiled at Willow, and then at Maddock. "Good-bye. And again, I'm so very sorry for your loss."

As she and Chris walked away, and the others made ready to climb into the trucks for the drive back, Mad turned his wheelchair to watch Brenna and Chris. As he did, he caught sight of his grandson's grim face.

When Ash realized Mad was studying him, he leaned close and lifted his grandfather up into the passenger seat of the truck.

Before he could turn away Mad caught his hand. "Some things are harder to let go of than others. But be careful about rekindling an old flame, laddie. They can burn too hot and bright before they burn themselves out. Remember that you've already trampled on that lass's heart once."

Stung by the truth of his grandfather's statement, Ash kept his thoughts to himself. But on the ride back to the ranch, he couldn't help mulling Mad's words. He'd blown his chances with Brenna. She had a right to a bright, shiny new life. If he were a gentleman he would step aside and not make waves.

He frowned.

He'd never made any claims about being a gentleman. Not now. Not ever.

CHAPTER NINE

Whit bounded into the kitchen and helped himself to a mug of steaming coffee. "Do I smell flapjacks?"

"That you do, laddie." Mad turned from the stove. "With blueberries and warm syrup."

"Did somebody say blueberries?" Ash blew in from finishing chores in the barn and discarded his hat and denim jacket in the mudroom before washing his hands and stepping into the kitchen.

Behind him, Griff did the same.

Willow was seated at the table, wearing the same faded denims she'd worn for her dawn chores. Sipping orange juice, she looked up with a smile. "Feel that breeze every time the door opens. Look at that sunshine. I think spring is here to stay, and the rain is gone."

"At least for today." Brady unrolled his sleeves, the mixture of dark and light strands of his hair glistening from a quick wash at the mudroom sink, and poured a fresh cup of coffee.

Myrna set a platter of crisp bacon on the table, along with a platter of scrambled eggs. Minutes later she returned with an even bigger platter of pancakes.

Willow turned to Griff as he took the seat beside her. "How is your room?"

"Very comfortable. Thanks for making me feel so welcome. But I think it's time I..."

They all looked up at a knock on the door. Myrna opened it to reveal Mason McMillan standing on the porch, his ever-present briefcase in hand. Behind him stood his son, Lance.

"I hope I'm in time for breakfast," Mason called as he walked into the kitchen.

"Just in time." Mad pointed with his serving fork. "Sit. Eat. And then you can deal with business."

Mason studied the young man seated beside Willow. "Sorry we didn't get a chance to meet yesterday at the church. You certainly have no need of an introduction. You could only be Griff Warren."

"I am. And you are...?"

"I'm sorry, Griff," Willow handled the introduction smoothly. "This is my lawyer, Mason McMillan, and his son, Lance."

The three shook hands before Mason set aside his briefcase and took a place at the table, with his son beside him.

While the platters were passed, and plates filled, Mason spoke of the funeral. "I thought it was a beautiful service. I couldn't help thinking that Bear would enjoy seeing so many of the townspeople there."

Willow nodded. "You know you and Lance could have stayed here last night, Mason. We have plenty of room."

"You needed your privacy. And the rooms at the Becket place were really comfortable. Kate and Kevin have put a lot of thought and expense into their new bed-and-breakfast concept at their ranch. I just hope it's worth it. After all, there aren't a lot of visitors to Copper Creek."

"Except at rodeo time." Mad speared a flapjack. "I guess they're hoping the town can come up with other ways to draw in visitors."

"Good luck to that." Lance smiled. "I stopped by Wylie's and heard there was an...incident a few nights ago." He took note of the lingering shadow around Ash's eye, and the slight swelling of Whit's upper lip. "But Wylie assured me everything had been put back in good repair in time for the crush of visitors. In fact, he was able to install a better speaker for the jukebox. So I guess he holds no hard feelings."

"I'm sure the occasional brawl is an accepted cost of owning a saloon," Mad said drily.

When nobody ventured any further information, the younger lawyer let the topic alone and accepted a cup of coffee from Myrna.

When the meal was finished, Mason waited until everyone had placed their dishes in the sink before fetching his briefcase. Taking a sheaf of papers from it, he sat back and waited until the others had returned to their seats.

"Since you're all involved in this, I've brought a copy of Bear's will for each of you."

When Griff started to rise, Willow put a hand on his sleeve.

Seeing the flicker of surprise in Griff's eyes, Mason said, "You, too, Mr. Warren."

Shaking his head in denial, Griff sank back down in his chair.

Mason passed around the documents. "There's no need for me to read all the details of Bear's will. It goes without saying, Maddock, that your land remains yours to dispose of as you please, even though it has now been joined to this ranch, with the same team of wranglers handling both pieces."

He motioned to Willow. "And everything owned by Bear is now part of your trust. The house, the barns, the stock."

He turned to include all of them. "But you should know that once Bear learned of Griff's existence, he insisted that all three sons share equally in his land. Though the ranch will continue to operate as one owner, each of Bear's sons may choose a plot of land on which to build a home, as long as that location is approved by Willow. Furthermore, Bear stipulated that if any of his sons refused to abide by the terms of the will, they could take a cash settlement, in the amount of five hundred thousand dollars, and leave here to make their future elsewhere, with no hard feelings."

Around the room there was complete silence.

"Brady."

The ranch foreman looked up.

"Bear asked if you would stay on as ranch foreman and lend a hand. And he left you a sum of money which has been deposited in this account." He handed over a bank passbook to the startled foreman.

Mason turned to the old woman, who was loading the dishwasher. "Myrna, Bear didn't forget you."

Caught by surprise, she straightened, still holding a plate.

He got to his feet and crossed the room to hand her a bank passbook, as well. "Bear hopes you'll remain here, too. And he wanted you to have a sum of money as a cushion when you decide to retire, though he invited you to spend your retirement years here."

"Retire." She huffed out a derisive breath.

"It happens to everyone at some point in their lives." Mason looked around. "It even happens to lawyers. Which is why I've included Lance in my visits lately. I'm turning over my practice to my son. He assures me that everything will be handled as efficiently as it ever was." He turned to smile at Willow. "That's about it. Everything is spelled out clearly in your documents, but as always, if you have any questions or concerns, you know you can turn to me."

"Just a minute." Willow cleared her throat. "This is all so...thorough. Did Bear mention having some premonition that something was going to happen to him?"

"He never said a word to me. But you should know that Bear was in the habit of updating his will periodically. He often said that he had no respect for men who didn't look out for all the people entrusted to their care."

"But..." She spread her hands. "Bank accounts? Equal splits of the land he loved? That sounds like a man facing certain death."

Mason shrugged. "When Bear met with me over this latest update, he seemed like a man who loved life and was ready to take on even more challenges. But I will admit that when he learned he had another son, it shook him to his core. He told me he felt a deep sense of responsibility for a young man who was forced to grow up without a father, and if he'd known about it sooner, he would have included the young man in his life."

He snapped shut his briefcase and circled the table, shaking hands with the men, pausing to embrace Willow, before walking to the door, trailed by his son. "Our plane leaves in an hour. We'll be in Helena this afternoon, and Lance will be available at any time if you need him."

The two lawyers were gone as quickly as they'd arrived, leaving Griff looking stunned, Myrna weeping over the sum of money in her new bank account, and Brady snapping shut the bankbook with a look of astonishment.

The family of Bear MacKenzie moved about the kitchen aimlessly, trying to process all that had just transpired.

It was Griff who first broke the silence. "Am I correct in reading that Bear wanted me to live here in this house?"

Willow nodded. "As long as you're comfortable with the arrangement, it works for me. This house is certainly big enough that we can all enjoy our privacy without stepping on one another's toes." She paused. "Unless the whole idea is unappealing to you?"

He chose his words carefully. "I guess I could stay. At least for a while, until I sort it all out. But I have to tell you, this isn't the reception I'd expected."

Willow gave him a gentle smile. "It isn't what I'd expected, either. Or maybe I should say, *you're* not what I expected. I thought this would be awkward." She glanced at her younger son across the table, staring at the document in his hand. "Maybe we all thought it would be very different. But I think, for now, we need to pool our resources to see what works and what doesn't."

Griff nodded. "All right. And again, Willow, thanks for your warm hospitality. This can't be easy for you."

He glanced at Brady. "You asked me earlier if I'd like to head to the high country with you. At the time, I thought I'd be leaving today. But now, since I'm going to be staying on, I'll take you up on the invitation. I'd really like to learn all I can about the operation of the ranch. And I'd like to think I can contribute something."

"Good." Brady turned to Whit. "I'd still like your help, too."

"You got it. I'm always up for a visit to the hills." Whit grinned as a sudden thought struck. "I just wish I had that book Brenna offered me." He winked at Mad before casually turning to Ash. "Think you could stop by her place and get it?"

Ash, busy pouring himself another cup of coffee, looked over in surprise. "You want me to pick up a book at Brenna's and haul it to high country?"

"If you're back in time, I'll take it when I'm leaving. If I'm already gone, you can just leave it in my room and I'll take it along next time."

Ash shrugged. "Sure. I don't mind."

Whit shared a conspiratorial grin with his grandfather. "I figured you'd jump at the excuse to call on your old ... friend."

Ash chuckled. "Oh. I get it. You think you're setting me up?"

"I think I'm ..."

Ash didn't hear a word. He was too busy whistling as

he carried his mug of coffee from the kitchen and up the stairs to his room.

Whit turned to those left in the kitchen, "That was too easy. I must be losing my touch."

He exited to a round of laughter.

An hour later, while Brady led a convoy of trucks and all-terrain vehicles along the road leading to the highlands, Ash was in his truck and heading in the opposite direction toward Brenna's ranch.

Though it had been obvious to him that his little brother had set him up, he was too excited about the thought of seeing Brenna again to mind the obvious trick. In fact, he was glad for any excuse to pay a call.

When he turned off the highway and onto the dirt road that led to the Circle C, he felt the old familiar rush of anticipation. His friendship with Brenna went back to their childhood days.

He would never forget their first chance encounter. As usual, he'd had a verbal run-in with his father, and he had taken off on horseback across a pasture. After a hard gallop he'd slowed his mount to a walk when he spotted a figure huddled against the base of a pine tree. The figure heard his approach, a head came up, and he saw blue eyes go wide before watching him with the wariness of a wild creature.

It was a girl. Small, wiry, wearing torn, dirty denims and a shirt with holes in both sleeves.

"Hey." He'd slid easily from the saddle and dropped down into the tall grass beside her. "You lost?"

She shook her head.

"I'm Ash. Ash MacKenzie. This is our land."

She glared at him, and he had the distinct impression she was ready to hiss and spit like a cat to fight him if he ordered her to leave. "You want me off it?"

"No." He tried a smile, hoping she might do the same. "I just wondered how you got here."

She pointed to a spotted pony, nibbling grass in a stand of trees some distance away. It blended so perfectly into the landscape, he hadn't noticed it.

"Where do you live?"

"Over that hill."

"The Crane place? What's your name?"

"Brenna Crane."

Most folks avoided the Crane ranch, though Ash didn't know why. It certainly couldn't be because of this little-bit-of-a-thing.

"You hungry, Brenna?" Without waiting for her answer he reached into his pocket and pulled out a candy bar, breaking it in two.

"Thanks." She accepted half and devoured it in two bites.

Ash broke his half into equal halves and offered her more. She ate that just as quickly, before giving him a timid smile. "You bring any milk, too?"

He shook his head. "Wish I had. It's hot."

"Yeah."

They sat side by side, but when he leaned his back against the trunk of the tree, she remained rigid, refusing to relax. Like she had a rod up her back, and couldn't bend.

"Want to ride to my place and get some lunch?"

She shrugged. "I guess."

She whistled up her pony, and pulled herself up in the saddle before following him back to his ranch.

Once there he led her into the cool interior of the kitchen, filled with the wonderful aromas of bread baking and pot roast in the oven.

Brenna stood in the doorway, looking around like Alice in Wonderland.

"Hey, Myrna. Can I make a sandwich for me and my friend?"

The old woman turned and, seeing the thin little figure behind him, broke into a wide smile. "Well now, who's this?"

"Brenna Crane. I told her she could have lunch with me."

"How nice to meet you, Brenna. Ash, why don't you take your young friend to the mudroom and wash up first?"

As they started out of the kitchen, Myrna followed, intent upon fetching clean towels. Trailing behind them, she could see that the little girl's shirt had several torn spots, and long red lines of something that looked suspiciously like blood trailing down her back.

Myrna swallowed back the gasp that sprang to her lips. Forcing her voice to remain steady, she said, "What's this, honey? You bleeding?" At the same moment she tugged the back of the girl's shirt up, revealing dark purple welts across her pale skin. The sort of welts that could only have come from a whipping.

Ash stared at the welts before looking up at Myrna, who touched a finger to her lips.

The little girl tugged down her shirt and stared hard at a spot on the floor. "Sometimes I fall and...hurt myself."

"Well, you need something on those cuts so they don't

get infected." Myrna hurried away and returned with a vial of ointment. "This might sting a bit, but it'll help those injuries heal, honey."

If she expected the little girl to shrink from the pain, she was surprised. Though the ointment on all that exposed flesh must have burned like the fires of hell, Brenna stood very still, until Myrna lowered the torn shirt. "There. All done."

She caught the girl's hand and led her to a chair in the kitchen. "You sit right here, honey. I've got some turkey left over from last night's supper. I think there's just enough for sandwiches for you and Ash." She turned to the boy, whose eyes revealed too many questions. To keep him from asking, she'd commanded, "And you can fill two glasses with milk, Ash."

"Yes'm." Like a robot he did as he was told.

Though she was barely half Ash's size, Brenna managed to eat two sandwiches, and polished off a tall glass of milk, along with several of Myrna's freshly baked chocolate chip cookies.

When she announced that it was time to get home, Myrna had handed her a bag. "Cookies. For later, honey, when you crave something sweet."

The housekeeper had uncharacteristically hugged the little girl before saying, "Brenna, you're welcome to come back here and visit me whenever you want. Even if you're not with Ash, you hear?"

"Yes, ma'am."

For the rest of the summer, Ash and his new best friend would meet on horseback in the meadow between their two ranches, and they would spend lazy summer afternoons climbing trees and swimming in Copper Creek, which snaked between grassy rangeland and towering buttes.

Brenna often followed him back to his ranch, where she would, at Myrna's invitation, stay on for lunch and even supper before riding home before dark. And always, Myrna would ask the girl if she'd had any cuts that needed tending.

When she did, the old woman applied the ointment without comment.

One day Ash surprised Brenna by riding all the way to her ranch to fetch her.

Though it wasn't even noon, her father, reeking of alcohol and slurring his words, directed Ash to the barn where Brenna was hard at work mucking stalls.

Ash fell into step, working alongside her, until her chores were completed. When they walked into the house an hour later, her father and mother could be heard in the upstairs bedroom, engaged in a war of hateful words, followed by the distinct sound of a loud slap.

Except for Brenna's eyes, wide and fearful, she showed no other reaction. Though Ash had probably always known that the many injuries endured by Brenna weren't the result of falls, there was now no doubt in his mind.

That night, after supper, Ash relayed to his parents what he'd seen and heard at the Crane ranch. Myrna turned from the sink to spare a meaningful look at Bear and Willow.

Bear had cleared his throat and said softly, "I want you to stay away from the Crane ranch, son."

"Brenna's my best—"

Bear held up a hand to silence his protest. "I didn't say

you couldn't see Brenna. I just don't want you going near her folks again. You hear me?"

"Yes, sir."

Later, when he left the kitchen, Ash heard his mother and father talking in low tones, and though he couldn't make out what was being said, he did hear his father say, "...pay a call on Ira Pettigrew."

Later that same summer, Brenna's father had left, never to return. Her mother took a job in town and did her best to work and keep the ranch going, but it soon fell into disrepair.

Brenna was sixteen when her mother died. Folks in Copper Creek made bets on how long a teenaged girl could manage a ranch before being forced to give it up.

But Brenna Crane, Ash thought with a sense of pride in his friend, had learned at an early age how to endure, and how to beat the odds life stacked against her.

CHAPTER TEN

Ash looked around as the ranch house came into view. The barns and outbuildings looked neglected. The back porch of the house was sagging, and the roof had seen better days. The truck parked beside the house was at least ten years old.

Ash parked beside Brenna's old truck and climbed the steps to knock on the back door. From inside he heard only silence.

Assuming Brenna was busy with chores, he descended the steps and made his way toward the barn.

The door of an old house trailer, parked beside the barn, was yanked open, and a white-haired cowboy in faded denims and rough plaid shirt stepped out.

"Vern Wheeler?" Ash stopped in his tracks before starting forward to offer his hand.

The old man peered at him before a wide grin split his

lips. "I'll be darned. Ash MacKenzie. I figured you were long gone."

The two shook hands.

"I've been gone almost ten years, Vern. But I'm back now."

"Well, I figured you'd be home for the funeral before heading out again. I heard about your daddy. I'm as sorry as I can be, Ash. Bear was a good man."

"Thanks, Vern."

"So." The old cowboy looked him up and down. "Looks like you've been doing some heavy lifting. You've kept yourself in good shape."

"I have a ranch in Wyoming."

"Do you now? So, you figure to build it as big as your daddy's?"

Ash chuckled. "That was my plan."

"And you're here to see Brenna?" The old man took a moment before saying softly, "She got herself engaged."

"Yeah."

"To a city slicker. Wears a suit and tie."

Ash managed to keep from laughing. "I met him."

"What'd you think?"

Ash shrugged. "It's Brenna's life. She has the right to fall in love." He couldn't resist adding, "Even with a city slicker."

Vern gave a shake of his head. "You might be saying what you think you ought to, but I'm betting you aren't here to wish her a happy life with some other guy."

"Brenna deserves a happy life."

"Yes she does. Nobody deserves it more. But I'm not sure she's picked the right horse for this race. He doesn't look like a finisher." He nodded toward a second, smaller barn. "If you'd like to pay a call, she's busy over there in her studio."

"Studio?" Ash's lips curved into a smile. "She did it? She actually made some space for herself?"

"Yeah." The old cowboy's grin widened. "Who'd have believed our little Brenna could turn a lump of clay into something people would actually pay good money to own?"

"Is she making a living, Vern?"

"It's tight." The old cowboy shrugged. "I had to let all the wranglers go. A couple of weeks ago I hired a drifter to handle the herd while they're up in the hills. I figure I'll have to take on a couple of extra hands at the end of summer. Other than that, you're looking at the crew. It's just me. You can look around and see that she's not making enough yet to handle more than bare bones. But her sculpting actually pays more of the bills than ranching does." He shook his head. "Ain't she something?"

"Yeah. Something." Ash slapped the old man on the shoulder. "Good seeing you, Vern. I think I'll visit Brenna's studio."

As he walked away he marveled at finding Vern Wheeler still here. Vern was an old-fashioned cowboy who had worked every ranch from Montana to Manitoba until, sensing Brenna's need, stayed on to lend a hand, and he had apparently become a fixture around the place.

It was hard to picture the old man staying in one place longer than a single season, but it would seem that he considered Brenna's needs more important than his own.

Before Ash reached the door to the barn he heard the high-pitched yip of a puppy. He opened the door and a ball of yellow fluff launched itself against his ankles, yipping and wriggling.

"Hey, little guy." He picked up the pup and scratched his ears before turning him loose and staring at Brenna.

She wore an old, stained shirt over faded denims. Her long hair was tied back with a rubber band. Her hands were holding a shapeless lump of clay. She had a smudge of clay on her cheek, another on her chin.

The sight of her took his breath away.

"Ash." She glanced down at her hands, caked with clay, and reached for a rag.

"Hey. Don't clean up for me. I didn't come here to disturb your work."

She shrugged. "I already finished my work for today. This was just something I thought I'd play around with, to see if I could come up with something inspiring."

Ash looked around, at the shelves holding tubes and cans and bottles, and at the sunlight streaming through the oversize windows that had replaced an old barn door. "This is amazing."

She dimpled. "Thanks."

"Did Vern help?"

"I drew the plans, and he did most of the labor. Thank heaven for Vern these past years. I don't know what I'd have done without him. He's been my handyman, my helper, my hand holder through all the hard times."

Hard times.

Ash winced.

When he held his silence Brenna picked up Sammy before asking, "What brings you here, Ash?"

"Whit's heading to high country today, and he wanted me to pick up that book you promised him."

"Okay." She set down the pup and removed the big shirt she used as an apron. Underneath she wore a skinny T-shirt in deep plum.

Leading the way to the house, she climbed the steps and held the door while Ash stepped inside.

Nothing had changed. The same small, cramped kitchen, the same sink and fixtures, the same scarred wooden table and chairs. But it smelled of disinfectant and furniture polish, and the old linoleum floor sparkled in the sunlight, and there were crisp white curtains at the window, tied back with bright red sashes.

"Do you have time for tea?"

"I guess so."

He stood to one side while she set a kettle on the stove.

Sammy hurried over to his bowl and made snuffling noises while he ate dry kibble and slurped water before settling down in a wicker dog bed.

"I'll get that book for Whit."

She hurried away and returned minutes later.

Ash studied the title. "*Nautical Knots*?" He couldn't hold back the laughter. "I guess we'd all have a need to read this one. We have so many boats and yachts floating around Montana."

She joined his laughter before turning away to collect cups and saucers. Over her shoulder she said, "I found it in the barn and thought about Whit. He has an amazing appetite for unusual reading material. You wouldn't believe the things he can talk about. That is, when you get him started."

"I guess you'd know more about my little brother than I do these days."

"I guess so. For starters, he's not your little brother

anymore. In case you haven't noticed, Ash, he's all grown up."

"Oh yeah. I've noticed." Ash was still grinning as he set the book aside. "Maybe I'll engage him in a fascinating discussion of nautical knots."

The two shared an easy laugh.

When the tea was ready Brenna filled two cups and set a plate of biscuits and jam on the table.

Ash sat across from her and bit into a biscuit. "You bake these?"

She shook her head. "Picked them up at Rita's yesterday before leaving town."

"They're good. I'll have to check out Rita's. A new shop?"

"Yeah. She calls it Rita Bakes. And she does. She bakes the best carrot cake ever."

"Better than Myrna's?"

Brenna laughed. "Don't ever tell her I said this, but yeah, better than Myrna's."

"Now I know I'm going to Rita's." He looked around. "It looks good in here, Brenna. Nice and homey. You made it your own."

"Thanks. I try. But sometimes..." She let her voice trail off.

"A working ranch is a lot for one person to handle."

"Two people. Don't forget Vern."

He grinned at her. "Right. I should have said one person and a grizzled old cowboy."

"And Noah," she added, grinning. "I almost forgot, since I hardly ever see him. Noah Perkins. Vern hired him to tend the herd up in the hills. That frees Vern to handle everything else."

Brenna glanced at the clock over the stove. "I'd better get going. I promised to deliver a sculpture to Percy Hanover for his anniversary."

"If you're heading to town, why not go with me? I'm heading there, too."

She considered it. "If you don't mind waiting for Percy and his wife. He asked me to meet them at Reels, after they see *Casablanca*."

"They're still showing that one? How many times did you and I see it?"

She laughed. "Twenty-three times. And that was just in a year."

"You used to know almost every word of the dialogue."

"Still do. Remind me to rattle it off sometime." She touched a hand to her heart. "There's just something so romantic about love lost and then found."

She glanced at Ash and saw the quick frown that came and went, and she realized what she'd just revealed. To cover herself she said quickly, "Anyway, *Casablanca* is Percy and Pearl's favorite movie, and it happens to be today's matinee feature. He said it should let out at three, and then he's taking Pearl to dinner at the Boxcar right after that, where he plans to present her with my sculpture."

"I've got all the time in the world."

"All right." She stood. "I'll be right back. I'm going to leave Sammy with Vern in the barn."

When she returned, she was carrying a large white box.

Minutes later she was seated beside Ash in his truck.

As they started away, Vern stepped to the doorway of

the barn and, in a courtly gesture, tipped his hat. Brenna waved and blew him a kiss.

"Always the gentleman," Ash said with a laugh.

Her tone was almost reverent. "That's Vern."

Her earlier comment played through Ash's mind.

Thank heaven for Vern these past years. I don't know what I'd have done without him. He's been my handyman, my helper, my hand holder through all the hard times.

Through all the hard times.

That thought weighed heavily on Ash's heart. Especially knowing that he had been the cause of at least some of her hard times.

Brenna opened the truck window to enjoy the fresh breeze. She'd removed the rubber band from her ponytail, allowing the wind to play through her hair.

Ash's hand tightened on the steering wheel to keep from reaching out to touch it. He could still remember the way it felt, spilling through his fingers. The way it smelled, especially after a rain, when the scent of her shampoo was stronger. Even after all these years, whenever he smelled lavender, he was reminded of Brenna. Her hair. Her skin. The way she tasted when they kissed.

"...to see your eye is healing."

He pulled himself out of his thoughts. "Yeah. Another day or so and the bruise will be completely gone."

"Chris is still furious with me for jumping into your fight."

"I don't blame him. Luther was in no condition to care who he carved up with that jagged glass."

"Oh, he cared. It was you he wanted, Ash. He's always been jealous of you and your family's success."

"I know. And I'm really grateful for what you did. Without your warning, I'd have been in for the fight of my life."

"What started the fight?"

He glanced at her. "You don't know?"

She shook her head. "Chris hustled me out without giving me time to ask any questions."

"I see." Ash slowed down as they neared the town. Ira Pettigrew was a stickler for driving the speed limit within the town boundaries. "Luther made a couple of comments about Griff Warren, and how much he looked like Pop."

Brenna nodded. "The resemblance is amazing."

"Yeah. But of course, Luther couldn't let it go. He added an insulting insinuation about Pop, and that was all Whit needed to go into pit-bull mode."

"The famous MacKenzie temper. I guess you'd know a thing or two about that."

Ash grimaced. "Yeah. A thing or two. I'm afraid it's imprinted on our DNA."

"How is your mom taking all this major drama at one time?"

"Losing Pop has to be the hardest thing she's ever had to get through. But then to learn that Pop had a son just made it harder. I think Pop's acceptance of the situation, once he learned of it, went a long way toward the rest of us falling into line."

"How did he hear about Griff?"

Ash recounted the information he'd learned since his return home. "Everybody was pretty much caught off guard. And we're still sorting it all out. But Griff makes it easier for all of us, because he's such a nice guy."

Brenna lay a hand over Ash's. "I'm glad. I hope it all works out for you and your family."

"Thanks." He absorbed the heat of her touch as he drove slowly along Main Street.

"Has Luther Culkin apologized?"

"Luther?" Ash gave a huff of annoyance. "Can you recall a single time when Luther apologized for anything?"

She sighed. "You're right. What was I thinking?"

"The man's a loose cannon. Every time there's a problem in Copper Creek, you can count on Luther being a part of it."

Spotting an empty space across from Reels, Ash parked the truck. Moments later he stepped down and hurried around to open the passenger's-side door and take Brenna's hand.

When she stepped out he glanced at the box. "Do I get a peek at the anniversary gift?"

"Sure." She slid open the lid and held up a sculpture of a bride and groom standing side by side, staring into one another's eyes. The female figure wore a long white gown with a lacy skirt, and the man wore a suit and string tie.

"That's old Percy. But younger. Without his glasses and wrinkles. I'd know him anywhere. And look at Pearl. You even captured the lace on her gown."

"Percy gave me an old black-and-white photo of their wedding."

Ash shook his head from side to side. "He's going to be a hero in his wife's eyes when he gives her this." He held the box while she carefully arranged tissue around the sculpture before returning it to the container. "Do you have any idea what an amazing gift you have?"

Her eyes went wide with surprise, while the sweetest smile curved her mouth. "Ash, that's just the nicest thing you could say."

"I mean it. You're amazing, Brenna."

"Thank you." She looked across the street. "The doors are opening. I'd better get over there and watch for Percy."

"I'll go with you."

They crossed the street and stood waiting until the couple walked hand in hand from the movie theater.

"Happy anniversary." Brenna placed the white box in Percy Hanover's hands.

"Oh. What's this?" His wife, Pearl, as plump as her husband was lean, had soft white hair around a heart-shaped face that was still as pretty as when she'd been eighteen. Girlish eyes were dancing with excitement.

"All in good time, Pearl." Percy turned to Ash. "My sympathy on the loss of your pa, son."

"Thank you, Percy."

His wife leaned close to press a kiss to Ash's cheek. "You tell your mama I send my love."

"Thank you, Pearl. I will."

"Now," she said, turning to her husband. "How long are you going to keep me waiting to see what wonderful treasure our Brenna has made for us?"

"Patience, Pearl." He turned to Brenna. "Did you remember to put that photograph in the box?"

"I did. You told me it was the only copy you had. So I made half a dozen copies of it for your children. The copies are all inside an envelope, along with the original."

"Aren't you just a sweetheart?" He brushed a kiss on Brenna's cheek before taking Pearl's hand. "Come on, girl of mine. You'll get to open this after dessert."

As the couple started away, Pearl was muttering a feeble complaint, but it was apparent that she was enjoying the suspense every bit as much as her husband.

Ash caught Brenna's hand. "How about a sundae at I's Cream before we head back?"

Brenna nodded. "I'd love one."

As they started across the street toward the brand new ice cream shop, Brenna couldn't help laughing. "Don't you love the name Ivy gave it? I heard she originally planned on calling it Ivy's Ices, but then somebody suggested using just her initial, and it all fell into place."

"Pretty clever. How's she doing with it?"

Brenna shrugged. "I think it's too soon to know. I'm sure she'll be busy all spring and summer, but once the weather turns cold, she'll have to come up with some other way to lure..."

They both looked up at the sound of a truck careening along the street and heading directly toward them.

The closer it came, the faster it raced, actually picking up speed instead of making any effort to slow down or stop.

Ash reacted instinctively, pulling Brenna toward him into a bear hug and leaping out of the path of the vehicle seconds before it blew past them, missing them by mere inches.

Ash managed to twist in midair, so that as they landed, he cushioned Brenna's fall with his own body. They hit the pavement with a terrible thud.

The truck continued on; the driver made no effort to stop and see whether or not they'd been hurt.

For long moments they were too dazed to move. Finally, when the world stopped spinning, Ash touched a hand to Brenna's face. "You okay?"

"Yes, thanks to you. How's your head?"

"My head?"

She framed his face with her hands and stared down into his eyes. "Oh, Ash, you took a terrible blow."

Slowly, painfully, he sat up and touched a hand to his head, feeling the sticky warmth of blood. "It could have been a whole lot worse."

Several people gathered around, anxious to help both Ash and Brenna to the curb.

Chief Ira Pettigrew pushed through the crowd and knelt beside them. "You two okay?"

"Yeah. No thanks to that damned fool driver," Ash muttered.

"I didn't see it, but I heard the revved engine, and heard what other people told me." He offered a hand to Brenna, and then to Ash, helping them both to their feet.

"This was no accident, Chief." Ash stepped up onto the sidewalk, holding a handkerchief to his head. "That driver actually speeded up."

"Did you see the driver?" Ira demanded.

Ash shook his head. "I was too busy trying to get us both out of the path."

"If Ash hadn't reacted so quickly, we wouldn't be talking to you right now." Brenna's voice lowered with feeling. "I'm certain of that, Chief."

"I'd like you both to come with me." The chief walked

briskly toward his office up the street, with Ash and Brenna trailing along more slowly.

Once they were inside the police station, Ira marched over to his desk and withdrew a formal document.

"Tell me in your own words exactly what happened."

As they spoke, he jotted notes in his distinctive scrawl.

Halfway through their narrative, Ash suddenly stopped.

"What?" Ira asked. "What did you just think of?"

Ash glanced at Brenna. "This happened once before. On the day I arrived in town. Brenna's puppy dashed out in front of my truck, and I stopped and got out to hold the dog until she came for him. While we were kneeling in the street a truck nearly hit us."

"And you didn't think to report it?" The chief looked annoyed.

Ash shook his head. "I figured it was our fault for kneeling in the middle of the street. I didn't really think of it as a deliberate act until now."

"And now you think it was?"

Ash slowly nodded as the scene played out in his mind. "Yeah. The more I think about it, the more convinced I am that it was no accident."

"Was it the same truck?"

Ash glanced toward Brenna for confirmation. "It was dark. Maybe black. Older model, but it happened so quickly, that's about all I know."

Brenna nodded in agreement.

Ira's tone hardened. "You got any enemies, Ash?"

"My first thought is Luther Culkin. He tried to attack me with a broken bottle the other night at Wylie's."

The chief glared at him. "You didn't think to swear out a complaint against him?"

Ash shrugged. "It was a bar brawl, Ira. I came into it a little late, and I was as guilty of fighting as Luther. But he could still be carrying a grudge because he didn't get to carve up my face the way he was hoping to."

"Luther had better have an alibi about where he was and who he was with when this went down." The chief steepled his hands. "Anybody else come to mind?"

Ash shook his head.

Ira turned to Brenna. "How about you? Anybody out to hurt you?"

Ash looked stunned. "You can't believe this was directed at Brenna."

The chief's eyes narrowed slightly. "You claim there was an earlier incident, and you were with Brenna when it happened. Now the two of you are together again, and it happens all over again. Who's to say someone is after you? They could just as easily be out to harm Brenna." He turned to her. "So, can you think of anyone who would want to hurt you?"

She'd gone deathly pale. But when she looked at the police chief, her voice was strong. "No."

He studied her a moment longer before giving a slight nod of his head. "Okay. So for now, our only suspect is Luther. I'll check on him right away. But in case that doesn't pan out, I'd like both of you to think long and hard about anybody in your life, whether past or present, who might want to see you harmed, and quite possibly killed." He leaned back. "Now Ash, I want you to drop over to the clinic and have that head looked at."

"Right." Ash stood, and offered a hand to Brenna.

As they left the police station, they walked stiffly up the street until they came to the Copper Creek Clinic. Once inside they filled out the necessary papers, and were ushered into an examining room.

Minutes later Dr. Dan Mullin walked in.

The doctor still wore his shaggy brown hair in what the folks in Copper Creek called a bowl cut. It fell in wispy bangs over his prominent forehead. He stood no more than five and a half feet tall but was considered a giant by everyone in the town. He stitched up bloody wounds, treated everything from sore throats to tumors, from a ruptured appendix to a ruptured disc, delivered babies, and eased the dying over to the other side, and all with the same droll humor and dry wit that everyone in town admired.

"Banged your head on the pavement, did you, Ash?" He examined the wound before thoroughly cleaning and disinfecting the site. "Good thing you have a hard head. You'll need a couple of stitches, just to help it heal."

"Thanks, Doc."

The doctor winked at Brenna. "He won't be thanking me in a couple of minutes." As he began stitching the wound, Ash swore between gritted teeth.

"Told you so." Doc finished up his work and then handed Ash a pill. "Take this when you get home. Don't take it before you finish driving, though. It'll knock you for a loop."

Ash sat up and felt the room spin for a moment. "No, thanks, Doc. I don't need anything that'll knock me out."

"That's what they all say. Take it with you, and when you get home, swallow it. You'll sleep like a baby."

Ash dropped the pill in his shirt pocket and slid off the table. "I'll think about it."

"Don't take too long to think. That'll only add to your headache."

Before Ash could object, the doctor was gone and off to the next examining room, and they could hear the sounds of a baby protesting loudly.

CHAPTER ELEVEN

When they walked to Ash's truck Brenna held out her hand. "I'll take your keys."

He stopped dead in his tracks. "Why?"

"Because you've just had stitches. You shouldn't drive."

"I didn't take the pill Dr. Mullin gave me."

"I saw the way you swayed when you got off the examining table. You're not steady on your feet." She poked a finger in his chest. "Hand me the keys."

He thought about arguing, but the truth was, he was enjoying the fact that Brenna wanted to take control of the situation. It was rare when anyone argued with him, but in their youth, she'd always had plenty of opinions. It was one of the things he'd always loved about her.

Love.

The very word stopped him in his tracks.

It was too late for that. Too late for a lot of things.

"Okay. Suit yourself." He opened the driver's-side door for her and handed her the keys before circling to the passenger's side. Then he shot her a teasing grin. "Want to fasten my seat belt for me, too, Mama?"

"I would if you were wounded, but you're just light-headed."

"And it's all your fault." He watched as she started the engine and backed out of their parking slot.

"It's my fault that you're dizzy?"

"I always get that way around you, Sunshine."

At his use of the nickname he'd given her all those years ago, her fingers tightened on the steering wheel.

"Or have you forgotten the time I fell flat at your feet?"

She shook her head with a grin. "I haven't forgotten. You cracked your head falling out of a tree, and the next thing I knew you dropped to the ground and I couldn't get you to wake up. I was so scared I rode my horse at a full-out gallop all the way to your ranch and made your father come with me. By the time we got halfway there, you came riding across the meadow like nothing had happened."

"As I recall, Pop was spitting mad at being dragged away from his chores on the whim of a girl named Sunshine."

Brenna and Ash shared a laugh at the memory.

"And that's why I'm driving, and you're sitting. I don't want you passing out again."

"I won't." He lifted his right hand in the air. "Promise."

They laughed together easily as the truck rolled along the highway.

"Want me to turn off at my place, or drive you to your ranch?"

He chuckled. "Then I'd just have to turn around and drive you back to yours."

"You could always ask Whit or Griff to drive me back after I delivered you safely home."

"Not a chance. They're up in the hills."

"Okay." She turned off the highway onto the single dirt lane leading to her ranch. "Don't say I didn't offer."

As they pulled up in front of her house, Vern ambled out of the barn and headed their way, with Sammy racing ahead to yip and yap until Brenna climbed down from the truck to pick him up and cuddle him.

"Perfect timing," Vern called out to Ash. "Got a water valve that's stuck out here in the barn. I've been working on it, but it needs more muscle."

Brenna was already voicing her protest. "You shouldn't be doing anything strenuous. You could pull out those stitches."

"I don't need to use my head for this. You heard Vern. He just needs my muscles."

As he walked away Brenna stared after him. She'd give him that. In the past years, he'd developed some very sexy muscles.

Annoyed at the direction her mind was taking, she climbed the steps and let herself into the house. In the kitchen, while Sammy pounced on his food dish, she set about fixing something for dinner.

Ash knelt in the hay and studied the water valve.

He looked up at Vern, who was standing over him. "Got a pipe wrench?"

"Sure thing." He handed over the wrench and watched while Ash strained to turn the pipe.

It didn't budge.

"How'd it get stuck?"

"I'm thinking it froze. We had a lot of freezing nights, and if there was moisture in the line, it probably froze and then expanded when it thawed."

"You're lucky it didn't burst. You'd have had a mess in here."

"Yeah." The old man watched as Ash leaned into his work, until at last the pipe wrench inched forward.

Another few twists of the wrench and the valve opened, allowing water to spill into the bucket Vern had set beneath it.

"Bless you, Ash." He reached into his toolbox for a towel and handed it over.

"Any time, Vern." He glanced around the cavernous barn while wiping his hands. "Anything else you need some help with?"

Vern shrugged before saying, "If you don't mind. I've got a tractor needing repair, and I need to get it closer to the door so I can use the daylight to see what I'm doing."

Ash looked toward the rafters. "What happened to your lights?"

"Shorted out. I've been meaning to work on the electrical, but first I need to get that tractor up and running."

Ash followed the old cowboy across the barn to the spot where an ancient tractor was parked. After taking it out of gear, the two men leaned their shoulders against it until it started rolling. Both men were sweating by the time it rolled to a stop just inside the barn door.

Vern wiped his forehead with a handkerchief. "I thank you, Ash. This old machine's been worrying my mind for weeks now. If I don't get to the spring planting, those cattle will starve next winter."

Ask sat down on an overturned bucket. "I know you had to let your wranglers go, except for the drifter..."

"Noah Perkins," Vern said.

"Yeah. Do you think Brenna could afford a few more to lend you a hand?"

Vern shrugged. "I was lucky to get even one worker for so little pay. I had to convince him there was nothing much to do up in the hills except watch out for predators around the new calves. Anybody strong enough to do ranch chores signs on with the big ranches these days. Besides, I just can't ask Brenna to dig into her savings, Ash. I see how she watches every dime just to make enough to pay the taxes and keep this place going."

"Does Brenna have any enemies that you know of?"

"Enemies? Brenna?" The old man looked at him as if he'd just sprung two heads. "Why would you ask such a question?"

Very quickly Ash told him about the incident in town. "I don't think it's a coincidence that it happened twice now. Chief Pettigrew asked if I have any enemies. But then he suggested that since both times I was with Brenna, this might have something to do with her instead of with me."

The old man took a great deal of time putting his handkerchief back into his pocket. When he lifted his face, his eyes looked thoughtful. "Your daddy wasn't the only one who made a few enemies when he was alive."

"Brenna's father?" Ash frowned. "He's been gone for years. You think somebody with a grudge with old Raleigh Crane would come after Brenna?"

The old man shrugged.

"What about Raleigh? Is he dead or alive?"

Vern shrugged. "Don't really know. Never heard one way or the other."

Ash's eyes narrowed. "Wouldn't Brenna be notified if her father died?"

Another shrug. "I guess you'd have to ask her. But whether Raleigh Crane's dead or alive, I expect he's left behind a very long enemy list."

"Or maybe, if he's still alive, he's the one with the grudge. Against Brenna." Ash got to his feet.

As he and Vern walked from the barn, Brenna stepped out onto the back porch and called, "Supper's ready."

When Ash started toward his truck Brenna called, "You're invited, too, Ash. It's just meatloaf and mashed potatoes, but I made enough for an army."

His smile was quick. "That's great, because I can probably eat like an army."

He followed Vern up the steps. Inside the two men rolled their sleeves and washed up before stepping into the kitchen.

Ash breathed in the wonderful aroma as Brenna opened the oven and pulled out the covered pan before transferring everything to a platter. A glance at the dog bed in the corner of the room showed little Sammy sound asleep after a day of exploring the barn.

The three of them gathered around the old wooden table.

As Ash reached for the platter, Brenna shook her head and turned to Vern, who caught her hand in his. Seeing them, Ash caught her other hand and fell silent as Vern said, "Bless this food, and these good people."

Ash hoped his jaw hadn't dropped, but the sight of a

weathered old cowboy saying a blessing over their food
had caught him completely by surprise.

As they began passing around hot rolls, fresh from the
oven, along with thick slabs of meatloaf and mounds of
mashed potatoes, a strange feeling of being home washed
over him.

He could still remember the look on Brenna's face
whenever she'd joined his family for supper. It had been
obvious to everyone that she loved being part of that big,
noisy assembly. She'd bonded with his younger brother,
and learned early on how to tease him as unmercifully as
he teased her. As for Myrna, it was no secret that the old
woman had fallen completely in love with the wounded
little girl. Brenna Crane had become the granddaughter
Myrna never had.

And now, this old cowboy had turned Brenna's tired
ranch into a home with his very presence.

Vern cleared his throat. "Ash told me about that incident in town."

Brenna buttered a roll. "I don't know what I'd have
done if Ash hadn't pulled me to safety when he did."

"So the chief thinks one of you has an enemy."

Brenna nodded. "That's what he said."

The old cowboy set aside his fork. "I never asked about
your pa. Figured it was none of my business. But now I'm
asking."

Uncomfortable, Brenna took her time breaking off a
piece of her roll. When she looked up, both Vern and Ash
were staring.

"As a matter of fact, I got a letter from him. He said
he's now in an assisted-living place somewhere here in
Montana."

"Where?" Ash demanded.

She shrugged. "All I got was a post office box number. He said the doctors told him that he's in the final stages of multiple organ failure. Heart, lungs, liver. He didn't know if I was still living on the old ranch, but he wanted me to know he was still alive, in case I wanted to send a letter or...some money to help him out."

Ash and Vern exchanged a look, though neither of them asked the question uppermost in their minds.

Brenna clasped her hands in her lap, her appetite gone. "I sent both. A letter and a check, in case there was anything he needed."

Hearing Vern's quick hiss of annoyance, she glanced over. "I know. I hated dipping into my emergency fund. But I wanted to do the right thing, and at least let my father know I forgive him before he leaves this world."

"Did he ask your forgiveness?" Vern's tone sounded reproachful.

"Yes. He said he was sorry for all the things he'd done while he was drinking. I wanted to do the right thing and let him die in peace."

"So you forgive him?" The words were spoken before Ash could stop himself.

She shrugged. "My mother said he used to be a good man until liquor took over his life. Then he turned into a mean drunk. Before she died, she told me she'd forgiven him in her heart, and she hoped one day I could do the same. I figured this letter, coming right out of the blue, was my last chance to make things right."

"How long ago did you send the letter and check?" Ash asked.

"About three weeks ago."

"And you've heard nothing else?"

She shook her head.

He reached over and caught her hand. "You've got a good heart, Sunshine. But now, with the timing and all, you've got to tell this to Chief Pettigrew."

She shook her head. "I'd feel uncomfortable telling him what I've done. He...knows about the things my father did. He came to talk to us that summer before my father left us."

"Did you tell Ira what your father had done to you?"

"I didn't have to. He knew." She looked away. "The chief made me show him my back. Then he told my father that if he wasn't an officer of the law, he'd whip him with a leather strap until his back was as bloody and scarred as mine. He said he would ask a judge to swear out a warrant against him for child abuse. The next day, my father was gone and we never heard from him again."

At that her cell phone rang, breaking the silence. Brenna pushed away from the table and spoke quickly. Afterward, she returned to the table.

"That was Chris. He's in town, and heard about the incident. He's pretty upset. He said he'll stop by later."

Ash tamped down the quick flash of annoyance, reminding himself that Brenna's fiancé had every right to be concerned for her safety.

He got up and crossed the room, filled three cups with coffee, and passed them around. Next to the coffeemaker was a bakery box, sitting on a fancy plate.

He lifted the lid and glanced over with a grin. "I hope this is Rita's famous carrot cake."

That had the smile returning to Brenna's lips. "It is."

"Want me to slice it or would you rather do the honors?"

"I'll let you do it." The smile slowly returned to her lips. "But see that you don't give yourself the biggest piece."

"Me?" He touched a hand to his heart. "How could you even suggest such a thing?"

When he carried two stingy slices to each of them, and then a huge slice for himself, Brenna rapped his knuckles with her fork. Vern burst out laughing, while Ash, grinning from ear to ear, returned with second pieces for both of them.

Then, measuring his big slice against Brenna's two, he switched plates and began eating her portion.

She turned to Vern with a mock frown. "See? Mr. Brave-and-Noble-of-Heart just can't be trusted when it comes to sweets."

"Or beautiful women," he muttered between bites, wiggling his brows like a mock villain. "So be warned, me fair beauty."

With the mood considerably lighter, they lingered over desserts and coffee, talking easily about ranch chores and filling Ash in on the latest town gossip.

"Oh, and I think you'll enjoy hearing this, Ash." Brenna's eyes danced with unconcealed happiness. "While you and Vern were in the barn, Percy Hanover called to say Pearl was overjoyed when he gave her my sculpture. In fact, he said it was one of the few times in his marriage that he'd ever seen his Pearl cry. He assured me they were happy tears."

Ash sat back, enjoying the moment. "What did I tell you? You have a rare gift, Sunshine. One that made even the stoic Pearl Hanover weep for joy. You can't argue with that success."

Her laughter filled the room. "All right. I concede to your superior knowledge, Mr. MacKenzie."

He turned to Vern. "I want you to remember this moment. It has never happened before, and may never happen again in our lifetime. Please note that Brenna not only agrees with me, but has admitted that I have superior knowledge."

Laughing, Brenna added, "In fact, I'm already regretting my remark. Knowing you, I'm sure you'll hold it over my head forever."

"You got that right." He winked at the old cowboy, who was thoroughly enjoying their teasing banter. "And I happen to have a very reliable witness."

CHAPTER TWELVE

That was a fine supper, girl." Vern circled the table and rested his big hand on Brenna's shoulder. "See you in the morning."

He nodded to Ash. "It's good seeing you again, son. Thanks for all your help in the barn."

"Maybe I'll swing by tomorrow and give you a hand with that tractor."

The old man brightened. "I'd appreciate it. I'll take all the help you can give me. Especially if you happen to have a new starter switch in your bag of tricks."

"I wouldn't be surprised if we have half a dozen in the equipment barn. Brady is prepared for every emergency."

Vern nodded. "Your daddy got a good one when he found Brady Storm. He'd be a fine addition to any ranch."

"Yeah. Brady's been there since before I was born, and I remember Pop saying having Brady around freed him up to enjoy his ranch instead of resenting all the things that could go wrong. He was able to leave all the annoying details to Brady, knowing they'd be done to perfection."

"I hear he's a stickler for 'em. And he works right alongside the wranglers, so they know he doesn't ask them to do the dirty work unless he's willing to do it, too."

Ash grinned. "That's Brady. He gets down and dirty with all of us. It was Brady who taught me to fly, even though Pop and Mad were both licensed pilots. They just didn't have the patience to teach me or Whit the basics." Ash shook his head, remembering. "Come to think of it, I'd have to say Brady taught us every bit as much about ranching and life in general as Pop did. And with a lot less shouting."

At his admission, the old cowboy grew thoughtful before taking his leave of them.

When Vern was gone, Brenna began gathering the dishes. As she filled the sink with soap and hot water, Ash caught the glint of metal at her wrist and stilled her movements to study the delicate filigree bracelet.

"You still have it?"

She glanced down with a smile. "Since the day you bought it for me, it's never been off my wrist."

"You sure it never turned your wrist green?" His voice was warm with laughter. "I think I paid five bucks for it in the notions section of Green's Grocery."

"I don't care what it cost. You bought it for me. And you put it on my wrist yourself."

"Yeah."

As she started to wash the dishes, Ash picked up a towel and began to dry.

She arched a brow. "I know you don't do this at your family's ranch."

"That's because Mad and Myrna don't want anyone else getting in their way. But I've been gone a long time, and while I was in Wyoming, if I didn't take care of things, they didn't get done. There was nobody around to lend a hand."

She washed a plate and set it on the drying rack. "How did you survive when you left here? What did you do for money?"

"What didn't I do?" He gave a dry laugh. "I did every job imaginable on ranches from here to Wyoming. And when I couldn't find ranch work, I took whatever offer I could get. For a while I worked the night shift in a gas station. I even cooked in a diner."

She shot him a look. "You cook?"

"Simple fare. Burgers. Fries. I make a mean grilled cheese sandwich."

"Maybe I'll let you cook for me one day."

"You're on." He shot her a grin. "Hell, I learned to do whatever it took to stay alive. I was nineteen and hungry and scared, and the only thing I knew was ranching. Wherever I worked, whatever I had to do, I knew that one day I'd have my own place."

"And you did it." She turned to study him as he set a plate in the cupboard. "Is it satisfying?"

"Yeah." He reached for another plate and began to dry. "I like being my own boss. But it's lonely being so far from home. That's why I took online college classes at night. It helped fill a lot of sleepless hours."

She finished washing the last of the serving pieces. "Why didn't you ever come back?"

He took his time stacking the dishes. "I think a part of me was afraid of what I'd come back to. I'd grown up, and I knew I couldn't ever be the son Pop wanted. I'd become a man, but there were already two men in my father's house, Pop and Mad. And the two of them butted heads a lot. I knew I'd have to fight for my place in the pecking order. And then there was you..." He picked up the pretty serving platter and began to dry it. He took his time, choosing his words carefully. "I was afraid I'd come back and find you married with a couple of kids. And I wasn't sure I could take it."

She turned, unaware of the water dripping from her hands. "You... stayed away because of me?"

He reached over her head and set the fancy plate on a shelf before looking down at her.

"I figured I'd done enough damage to everybody. My mother. My brother, Whit. Pop and Mad. And you. Especially you. You were... my best friend. And I abandoned you without a word. I don't mind taking the blame for it. But I didn't think my heart could stand seeing you with another man's children."

"Ash..."

"Shhh." He closed his hands around her upper arms and stared down into her eyes. "The hardest thing I've ever done was leave you behind."

"Then why...?"

"We were a couple of kids. You especially."

"I was sixteen, and already on my own."

"You were a kid, Brenna. I didn't know a whole lot, but I knew one thing. I had no right to ask you to leave your ranch, your friends, your life here, to tag along with me, when I had absolutely no plans and no future. All I had were these hands and a willingness to do whatever it took to stay alive."

She reached up to close her hands over his. "That would have been enough for me. I'd have gone if you had asked."

"I knew that. And it would have killed me to see you taking odd jobs all over the West, just to follow me."

"We'd have been together."

"Yeah. In fleabag motels and run-down bunkhouses. No man wants that for his woman."

His woman.

Once the words were spoken, they hung awkwardly between them.

Brenna was staring up at him with wide eyes.

His own darkened. A frown suddenly furrowed his brow.

He stepped back and dropped the damp towel over the back of a chair. "It's time I got home."

"I could make a fresh pot of coffee."

"No." He spoke the word harshly. To soften it, he added, "I...really need to leave."

As he started toward the back door, Brenna followed him.

He plucked his wide-brimmed hat from a hook by the back door. As he started to go, Brenna touched a hand to his arm. Just a touch, but the heat of it danced through his veins.

"Ash..."

He turned to her.

She was looking up into his eyes, her smile wrapping itself around his heart and squeezing. "Thanks for driving me to town. And for helping Vern. Tonight was... special." She shrugged, looking shy and awkward.

He seemed about to say something. Instead he swore and let his hat drop to the floor, while he dragged her into his arms.

"Why do you have to be so sweet and forgiving? Why can't you just hate me for leaving you?"

"Hate..." She blinked. "Ash, I tried that. But I realize now I could never hate you."

His eyes were hot and fierce as he lowered his head. His kiss was so hot, so hungry, it rocked her back on her heels. A kiss that was all fire and flash and sizzle. It drained her even as it filled her. There was nothing tentative or teasing about this. It was bold and possessive. Demanding. And it spoke of a blazing-hot need.

With lungs straining, he lifted his head. For a moment he merely touched a finger to her cheek while he stared into her eyes, as though trying to read her feelings.

Then, muttering an oath, he lowered his head and kissed her again.

This time it was achingly slow and thorough, his mouth whispering over her eyelids, her cheek, the corner of her mouth, until, with a guttural moan, she laced her fingers around his head, clinging to him as her lips found his.

Now it was all heat and frantic need, as each took from the other with a hunger that bordered on desperation, mouths seeking, bodies straining.

His hands were in her hair, though he couldn't remember how they got there. Hers were raking his back, her nails digging through the fabric of his shirt in a frantic effort to get closer.

He turned her, pressing her against the closed door, his body imprinting itself on hers as he took the kiss deeper, then deeper still, his mouth restlessly seeking what he really wanted. He couldn't get enough of her.

The quick, jittery charge to their systems had them practically crawling inside each other's skin. And still it wasn't enough.

When he took a moment to change the angle of the kiss, his name was torn from her lips in a frantic cry. "Ash!"

At the sound of his name on her lips, he suddenly went very still.

Chests heaving, they stepped a little apart, waiting impatiently for their world to settle.

Was the floor tilting? Was the room spinning? Or was it their heads? Their hearts?

When he could finally catch his breath he managed to whisper, "Sorry." He shook his head. "Not for that kiss. I've had a hunger for that since I first saw you again. But I…almost crossed a line. I guess I let myself forget for a moment that you've moved on with your life, Sunshine, and I'm not a part of it anymore."

When she said nothing, he bent and retrieved his hat.

He left without another word.

Brenna stood as still as a statue, watching from the doorway as Ash climbed into his truck and started down the lane.

She remained there, clinging to the door, until her heart rate slowed and her breathing returned to normal. Then she closed the door and returned to the kitchen, staring around as though seeing it through Ash's eyes.

It looked the same as it had for years now. Old. Tired. Worn. But tonight it had been a room filled with warmth and laughter.

She hadn't laughed that hard in ages. Even Vern had enjoyed himself.

Because of Ash.

When he'd left all those years ago, without one word to her, all the sunlight had gone out of her world. Her grief had been so deep, she'd convinced herself that she hated Ash MacKenzie for abandoning her. For breaking her heart. But here he was, back home, back in her life, and she'd not only spent a wonderful evening in his company, she'd allowed him to kiss her.

Allowed? What a lie. It shamed her to admit that she'd been a full participant in that kiss.

In truth, it had been much more than a kiss. They'd practically devoured one another. They had been making love without the physical culmination.

She lifted her left hand. The diamond ring winking in the lamplight mocked her.

What kind of woman was she that she would commit to a future with one man and fall willingly into the arms of another?

Chris was a good and decent man. He certainly didn't deserve to be betrayed like this.

She closed her eyes, allowing the image of Ash holding her, kissing her, to play through her mind.

Even now, just thinking about him, had her so hot she pressed her hands to her cheeks in an effort to cool them.

She began pacing the length of the room and back, her mind awhirl with erotic images and thoughts of what she'd just done.

And then her mind took a turn and she thought of what she'd wanted to do. She'd wanted, more than anything, to make mad, passionate love with Ash. To erase all the years that had slipped away. To forget the man to whom she'd pledged her future. She'd wanted desperately to lose herself in the dark, mindless passion Ash had been offering.

What had she been thinking?

She hadn't been thinking. That was the problem. She'd allowed herself to get caught up in the moment, losing herself in the dark, compelling world of passion.

Chris would be here soon. He would expect her to be the warm, affectionate woman he thought he knew. But now there was a third person in their relationship. A person who had shattered her young heart in the past, and now had come back to test her once again.

It shocked her to think that she would ever trust Ash again. Even more shocking was the thought that she might allow him to come between her and a good man who had just given her a ring to seal their engagement.

What kind of woman would even think twice about a choice between a practical, sensible man who had already pledged his love, and a loose cannon whose temper had once taken him far away from all that he'd known and loved?

Ash had kissed her. Nothing more. And he certainly hadn't declared any feelings for her.

Her throat was suddenly so raw, it felt as though she'd shed a million tears. But her eyes were dry as she peered out the window and watched the approach of Chris's new car gliding slowly up the lane toward her house.

Ash drove the entire distance to his ranch without even being aware of the road. His thoughts were as dark as the night sky spread out like a canopy over all the countryside, leaving the buttes, the hills dotted with cattle, in shadow.

He'd known, from the first moment he'd decided to return to Montana, that he would have to deal with his feelings toward Brenna. He'd half expected to find her married. The thought had struck terror in his soul. But that might have made things easier. It would have demanded a clean break. He knew in his heart that he would never violate a marriage vow. No matter what feelings were resurrected when they met again, he would have been able to keep his distance if Brenna were someone's wife.

She was engaged. Practically married. And though he thought of himself as an honorable man, he'd nearly crossed a line tonight. Hell, he would have, if she hadn't cried out just in time.

But had she called his name to stop him? Or to encourage him to do more?

She hadn't held him at arm's length. If she had, he would have respected her wishes and walked away sooner. But she'd been as much a partner in that kiss as he.

Kiss? He swore under his breath. That was just a kiss the way a Montana blizzard was just snow flurries. They'd practically taken each other right there on the cold, hard floor.

And didn't he wish they had? Didn't he wish they were together, acting on all their desires, right this minute?

She'd felt so good in his arms again. So right.

But it was all wrong. And he needed to face up to the fact that his little Sunshine was now in love with another guy.

He had no future with her, and no right to ever cross that line again.

But, though it would be easier for all involved if he just didn't see her again, that wasn't possible. Even if he took pains to avoid her, the town of Copper Creek was too small for him to avoid running into her.

Besides, there was Raleigh Crane.

He intended to impress on Brenna, first thing in the morning, how important it was for her to talk to Chief Pettigrew about that letter. If her father was pulling a con, she needed to be protected, even if she didn't agree. The man had been a mean drunk, and he wouldn't be above using his own daughter if he had something to gain.

And then there was his promise to lend a hand to Vern. He'd keep that promise, not because he was some noble hero, but because it would give him a chance to see Brenna, if only from a distance.

And there it was. The bare, unvarnished, shameful truth.

Even knowing she loved someone else, he was willing to settle for just seeing her.

How pathetic.

By the time he'd reached his ranch, he was in such a foul mood, he saddled one of the horses and, tucking Brenna's book into his pocket, headed into the hills.

He patted his pocket with a grim smile. *Nautical Knots*. There were other kinds of knots. Some of them pretty tricky to unravel.

A solitary, midnight ride would be just the thing to help him work out some of the knots in his crazy, twisted life.

CHAPTER THIRTEEN

Seeing Chris step out of his car, Brenna opened the door wide before returning to the kitchen.

As he climbed the steps, she called over her shoulder, "I've got carrot cake. I'll start a fresh pot of coffee."

Ordinarily she would greet him with a kiss. Not tonight. Her heart was pumping a little too fast, and she told herself it was best if she didn't let him close until she had her feelings under control.

Was her face a little too flushed? Her eyes a little too bright? Would he know, just by looking at her, that she'd been with Ash?

She didn't need to wonder. He was apparently dealing with issues of his own. He flung his car keys on the kitchen table the minute he stepped into the room. Brenna spun around and saw the look of thunder on his face.

"The buzz going around town is that once again you nearly got run down by a crazed truck driver. And once again, you were with Ash MacKenzie when it happened. Looks to me like bad things started happening the minute the prodigal son came back to Copper Creek."

"You make it sound as though Ash is somehow to blame."

"The way I heard it, the police chief wondered if you have enemies. Is he blind? Or just stupid?"

"Chris..."

He cut off her words with a raised hand. "I heard the reason MacKenzie left town all those years ago was because of a hair-trigger temper. I saw the proof of it at that drunken brawl at Wylie's. If he's anything like his old man, he has as many enemies in this town as he has friends. There are probably a hundred people gunning for MacKenzie, and Ira Pettigrew suspects that these incidents might be about you?"

In his anger he grasped her by the shoulders and started to shake her. "Wake up, woman. You hang with a badass like that long enough, your future won't be any brighter than his. I give MacKenzie another month in this town before he's either dead like his father or back on the road looking for another place to pick a fight."

Her voice was pure ice. "Take your hands off me. Don't you ever touch me in anger."

At her curt command, he released her and backed away. "Sorry. You told me about your father. I know how you feel about...I didn't mean..." He lifted both hands in the air, in a symbol of surrender. "But you can't deny that all of this drama started when MacKenzie came back."

"Drama? Are you suggesting that this has all been orchestrated by Ash to draw attention to himself?"

Chris shrugged. "I wouldn't put it past him. This is a

guy who walked out on his family and never looked back. If that isn't drama, I don't know what is."

"You don't know anything about Ash except what you've heard at Wylie's. When he left, he was young, and he believed that he'd taken enough bullying from his own father. Some folks may have blamed him for leaving, but there were plenty of others who not only understood but approved his courage. As for those dangerous incidents with a runaway truck, I was there. I saw Ash's reaction. He was as shocked as I was. Does that mean I was in on it, too?"

"I'm saying that it seems very convenient that both *incidents*"—he emphasized the word with growing sarcasm—"occurred when MacKenzie was with you, giving him a chance to look like a hero in your eyes."

"Now you're being ridiculous."

"Am I? Listen to yourself, Brenna. You've suddenly become his fierce defender." He moved in closer, his face inches from hers. "Tell me the truth, Brenna. Is MacKenzie's strategy working? Have you started to think that maybe you should forget about past hurts and start to trust him again?"

Seeing her stunned reaction to his words, his eyes narrowed on her. "Uh-huh. I thought as much. And are you wondering what your life might have been like if only you'd waited all this time for your white knight to come riding back to rescue you?"

"Rescue me? From what?"

"From a backwater town like Copper Creek. And from this." He waved a hand. "This miserable, failing piece of land that's draining all your money and energy, just the way it did your mother's."

"Don't talk about my mother—"

"You mark my words, Brenna. You stay in this mess long enough, it'll take you down."

"There's no need to put down my ranch or my town. I'm happy here. I'm happy with the way my life is going."

"Really? Well, if this is all it takes to make you happy, I've got some news that will make you ecstatic."

At his sudden change of direction, she paused. "What news?"

"I've been offered that hot promotion I've been working for."

Caught off guard, she waited, feeling suddenly wary.

"They want to send me to Helena first."

"First?"

"I requested the opportunity to work at the headquarters in Washington, D.C. That's where the real power is within the bureau. My connection in Helena thinks there's every chance I'll get my wish."

"You're leaving?"

"*We're* leaving. You and I. As soon as the transfer documents are completed."

She could feel him watching her reaction. Carefully schooling her features, she said, "And what am I supposed to do about my life here? My ranch? My career as a sculptor?"

"The ranch is a no-brainer. Sell it. Take whatever you can get for it and put it in the bank. With my promotion, we won't need your money. Before I'm through, I intend to be a director of the bureau. As for your hobby, there's no reason why you can't pursue it wherever we settle."

"My . . . hobby?"

"Oh yes. I forgot. Your...career. I noticed you like to call yourself a sculptor."

"Do you have a problem with that?"

He gave a snort of disgust. "Face it, Brenna. If you had to live on what you earn as a sculptor, you'd starve. I don't think you can justify calling it a career."

"You mean, the way you call your job a career?"

"I have a future. And it's not some pie-in-the-sky future. I'm already on my way. I can actually see where I'm heading. And I won't stop until I've reached the top of the heap."

"So I should just walk away from everything I love here in Copper Creek and follow you as you climb your career ladder?"

"That's what a partner does." He narrowed his gaze. "Unless you're having second thoughts."

She lifted her chin like a prizefighter, a sure sign of the temper brewing.

Before she could say a word, he gave a wry laugh. "Oh. I get it. Now that the old boyfriend's back in town, you were hoping to string us both along until you made up your mind."

He fixed her with a look. "Understand this. I won't play second fiddle. It's me or MacKenzie."

"Chris..."

He reached out and caught her hand, staring meaningfully at the diamond that caught and reflected the lamplight. "When I gave you this ring, I knew you were the woman I wanted to spend the rest of my life with. I thought you felt the same way. If you have any doubts at all, I deserve to know. Do you love me enough to sever ties with this place and move on, or am I going to Helena alone?"

She snatched her hand away. "You're not being fair. This is too sudden. You can't expect me to agree to sell my ranch and leave everything I love, without time to think about what I'm doing."

"You knew, from the time we met, that I considered this a temporary assignment. I never lied to you about my intentions to move on."

"But not this soon."

"Now, or a year from now. What's the difference?" He looked into her eyes before taking a step back.

She held her silence.

His tone was resigned. "Don't lie, Brenna. Not to me. Not to yourself. It's MacKenzie. That's the real difference, isn't it?"

When she said nothing in her defense, he held out his hand. "Truth-or-dare time, Brenna. Choose to be with me, and leave this backwoods town behind for the big city, or give me back the ring. And don't tell me you need more time to figure things out. If you really love me, you don't need another minute."

She continued looking at him as she removed the ring from her finger and placed it in his palm. "I'm sorry, Chris. I never meant for this to happen."

He closed his hand over the ring and studied her face, his eyes going from angry to resigned before he turned away.

Snatching up his car keys he yanked open the door. "Maybe you didn't mean to do this, but I'm betting MacKenzie did. He knew exactly how to play you, Brenna."

He paused. "I'll be driving to Helena in the morning for meetings the rest of the week. I'd intended to invite you along so you could do some shopping before the big move."

He gave a long, deep sigh. "I'll be back on the weekend to settle my affairs before moving on. You know where to reach me if you change your mind. I can't say I wish you luck with MacKenzie. I just hope you don't get your heart broken again. But if you do, don't say I didn't warn you. He's bad news, Brenna. You hang with a loser long enough, he'll take you down."

The door slammed behind him.

Brenna stood perfectly still, listening to his footsteps as he descended the porch steps and made his way to the car. She heard the crunch of gravel, and the opening and closing of the car door, and then the purr of his engine and the flash of headlights across the walls and ceiling as he turned his car and drove away.

And then the silence of the night closed in around her as she methodically unplugged the coffeemaker. Sammy lifted his head and crawled from his wicker basket to hurry over and whine.

She carried him to the door and let him out. Within a minute he was back inside and wriggling around, hoping to be picked up.

She lifted him into her arms and switched off the lights before climbing the stairs to her bedroom.

Once there, she deposited the puppy on her bed before walking to the window to stare at the distant hills, layered in darkness.

She wrapped her arms around herself, suddenly chilled to the bone.

Though some of the words Chris had hurled at her had been hurtful, others had hit too close to home.

It was true that she'd carried the image of her youthful hero in her mind for a long time. But he'd been gone for almost a decade. A lot could happen in those years to change a man.

She didn't really know Ash now. He'd been forced to experience a lot of things in order to survive on his own. Things he couldn't share with her. There were rough edges to him now that hadn't been there before.

Had he acquired a list of enemies? Men who would go to extremes to see him hurt or even dead?

Had he brought danger here to their town? To her very doorstep?

So many questions. So many doubts and fears.

As for Chris, she'd hurt him deeply. Hurt a good man who, though angry and frustrated, had declared his love for her.

When he'd asked her to marry him, he'd been forthright about his desire to move on. At the time, she'd convinced herself that it would be good for her to go with him, to see the world, to test her wings and fly as far away as she could from all the old memories. But she never allowed herself to think too deeply about it, because it had all seemed to be something she would do in the distant future. A future filled with so many possibilities.

All that had changed when she'd seen Ash. She'd known, in that very instant, that the last thing she wanted was to leave her ranch, her friends, her studio.

Her old best friend.

Sadly, Chris had known the truth even before she had.

She'd burned a bridge tonight. One that could never be rebuilt.

She crawled into bed and lay in the darkness, her eyes dry, her throat tight with unshed tears.

As if sensing her discomfort, Sammy moved close and snuggled against her

She wouldn't cry over what she'd done. Her future was now as uncertain as it had been when she'd been that scared little girl. But she'd survived her father's drunken episodes, the beatings, the angry, hate-filled words hurled behind closed doors in her parents' room. More, she had survived the terrible knowledge that Ash had left town without a word to her. She had survived all the years that followed, without a single word from him.

She buried her face in the puppy's fur.

She would survive this, as well.

Besides, it was far too late for tears.

Brenna forked wet straw and dung into a wagon before heading toward the next stall. She'd been up before dawn, after a long and restless night. Always, when her mind was troubled, she found solace in hard, demanding work. Today was no different. While she bent to her chores, her mind kept returning to the angry words she'd exchanged with Chris.

Angry was too mild a term

But there was no point in dwelling on something she couldn't undo. All she could do now was keep moving and hope she hadn't made too big a mess of things.

Sammy's barking alerted her that she wasn't alone.

"Hey. You're up early."

At the sound of Ash's voice, her head came up sharply. "What are you doing here?"

"I brought Vern that starter switch."

"He's up in the hills, checking in on Noah Perkins and the herd. He should be back in an hour or so."

"Okay." Ash held out two mugs of coffee. "I hope you don't mind. I checked in the kitchen and helped myself. Want a break?"

"I don't mind." She leaned on the handle of the pitchfork and removed one battered work glove before accepting the mug.

He tipped over a bucket and indicated the seat.

When she settled herself on it, he perched on the edge of a bale of straw and took a long drink.

Sammy jumped up beside him, and he idly scratched behind the pup's ears as he studied her over the rim of his cup. "Did you have breakfast?"

She shook her head. "Not yet. Vern and I usually have something in midmorning, after first chores."

"If you'd like, I'll finish mucking in here. Or if you'd rather, I'll make breakfast. Your call."

She eyed him. "Honestly? I'd rather muck stalls any time than have to cook."

He laughed. "Okay then. I'll do the cooking." He gave her a long, slow look. "I'd feel guilty about taking the easy job if I couldn't see how good all this hard work is for your body."

"Yeah. Right, MacKenzie."

"You don't believe me?" He shook his head. "You ought to see what I see."

She'd removed her parka and tossed it over the rail of the stall, rolling the sleeves of her plaid shirt, which she wore with torn, faded denims tucked into tall rubber boots. Even with her blonde hair pulled away from a face devoid of any makeup, she took his breath away.

"You could be one of those fashion models in an ad for healthy living."

"I see all those years away have taught you how to sweet-talk the ladies." She sipped her coffee. "I bet you've learned all kinds of other things, too."

He merely smiled and raised a brow. "Maybe I'll show you a few of them sometime."

"Maybe I'll let you." Her remark, spoken before she had time to filter it, had her blushing furiously before she tossed aside the last of her coffee and got to her feet to hide her embarrassment. "Thanks for the break. Now I've got to get back to work."

She pulled on the work glove before picking up the pitchfork.

"Come in the house whenever Vern gets back. I'll have breakfast ready."

Brenna watched him walk away. He didn't so much walk as saunter, those long legs eating up the distance to the house with ease. He hadn't bothered to shave, and the dark growth of stubble only added to his rugged appeal.

He could have been in an ad, too, she thought. An ad inviting travelers to rough-and-tumble Montana, home of the authentic, rugged American cowboy.

The image fit him perfectly.

Sammy stood in the doorway, alternately staring at Brenna, then at the man walking away.

Finally he made a mad dash to catch up with Ash, happily trailing him up the steps of the porch.

"Traitor," Brenna muttered as she returned to her chores.

* * *

"Now this was worth dealing with a cranky cowboy, and having to mend a section of fence with nothing but a pair of rusty pliers." Vern tucked into the plate of scrambled eggs, thick slices of ham and fried potatoes and didn't stop until his plate was empty.

"Why was Noah feeling cranky?" Brenna asked.

The old cowboy shrugged. "I found him asleep, and told him to get his sorry...hide over to the herd. I'm not paying him to sleep on the job."

"If I found a wrangler of mine asleep on the job, he wouldn't have the job anymore." Ash set a steaming skillet on a hot pad in the center of the table and handed the old cowboy a long-handled serving spoon. "There's seconds. Help yourself."

"Don't mind if I do." Vern filled his plate again and ate more slowly, pausing now and then to sip his coffee. "As for Noah Perkins, I can't fire him. He's all we've got."

"If he knows that, then he knows he's got you over a barrel, and he figures he can do whatever he pleases on the job. I'd do double duty before I'd let one of my hires run roughshod over my rules." Across the table, Ash watched the old cowboy with a grin. "You act like you haven't seen food for a year."

"Not food like this." Vern winked at Brenna. "Not that I'm faulting you, girl. You got your hands full being an artist and hardworking rancher."

Brenna laughed. "That's a polite way of saying that when it comes to cooking, I won't win any awards."

"You got that right." Vern glanced at Ash. "How'd you learn to cook like this?"

"Necessity." Ash buttered a slice of wheat toast.

"When you're alone, you cook or starve. Plus, it gave me a source of income when I was broke."

"You cooked for a living?"

Ash shrugged. "When I had to." He deftly changed the subject, turning to Brenna. "When I finish helping Vern with the tractor, I thought I'd drive you to town."

She looked up sharply. "Why?"

"So you can tell Chief Pettigrew about that letter from your father."

"I have no intention of telling Ira about it."

"Why?"

She shrugged. "I've given it some thought, Ash, and I don't see any possible connection between that letter and those incidents in town."

"Maybe you don't see the connection, but I think that should be up to the chief. It's a simple matter of showing him the letter and letting him decide whether to investigate it further or choose to let it alone."

Her eyes flashed fire, a sure sign that she was becoming agitated. "I wish I'd never mentioned that letter."

"Too late, Sunshine. Now that I know, I'm not going to rest until you agree to show it to the police chief."

She turned to Vern. "Why don't you take him out to the barn and let him work off some of this energy on that tractor?"

Vern drained his coffee in one long swallow. "Come on, Ash. You heard the lady."

Ash glanced around at the mess he'd left in the sink. "I'll help Brenna with the dishes and then join you in the barn."

Brenna shook her head. "If you think I'm going to give you any more time to press me about talking to Ira Pettigrew, think again. Just go with Vern and do whatever you need to do in the barn."

As the two men headed out the door, trailed by her puppy, Brenna poured herself another cup of coffee and watched through the window as Ash and Vern crossed the distance from the house to the barn.

Though she watched both men, her mind was only on one.

He had the loose, easy stride of a cowboy. His muscles, toned from years of ranching, rippled beneath the sleeves of his plaid shirt. His dark hair, in need of a trim, was wind-tossed. His laughter, rich and warm, was carried on the breeze.

Ever since Ash had returned to Copper Creek, her carefully laid plans had come crashing and burning to the ground. Her life had become one long, crazy freefall.

She could only hope that somewhere in her future lay a smooth, easy landing.

CHAPTER FOURTEEN

Hold that light a little higher, Vern."

Ash leaned in as far as he could, using daylight and the extra illumination from Vern's handheld flashlight to remove the faulty starter switch.

The older man peered over his shoulder. "Why are you so determined to force Brenna to tell the police chief about her pa's letter?"

Ash's words were muffled as he leaned deeper into the tractor's engine block. "I still think those two near accidents in town were targeting me. But since the chief suggested that Brenna could be the target, we have to take precautions. One thing we all know is that her old man was no good. He may be older now, and his health failing, but I figure a tiger doesn't change his stripes. As long as he's alive, we should consider him a threat."

Vern nodded his agreement. "You make a good case. I'm with you on this, son."

"Good." Ash grunted as he replaced the old starter switch with the new one.

He tightened everything before lifting his head and turning to Vern. "Then be sure to let Brenna know how you feel. She respects your opinion, Vern. I want her to go to town with me before the day is over and let Ira Pettigrew decide how to proceed." He nodded toward the tractor. "Okay. Give it a try."

The old cowboy climbed up to the tractor seat and turned the ignition key. The chugging of the engine had his face creasing into a wide smile. "That'll do it, son. You do good work."

"Good. Glad it was a simple fix."

Wiping his hands on a rag, Ash looked around at the lack of lights in the barn, the door hanging by a single hinge, the ladder leading to the hayloft missing several rungs. "I can't believe how many things are falling apart around here."

"It's getting old. Like me."

"You're in a lot better shape than this place. You have to be a miracle worker to keep this old ranch and its ancient equipment running. How do you do it?"

"Rubber bands and duct tape, boy."

The two shared an easy laugh.

Vern sobered. "But sometimes it's frustrating, especially after a long day of having to fight a lazy drifter, a leaking roof, a flat tire, and always old Mother Nature."

"Yeah. It has to be tough to take. You need help around here, Vern. And so does Brenna." Ash squinted up at the exposed rafters of the barn. "Now tell me about those lights. Where's the source of the problem?"

Vern shrugged. "They all went out at the same time, so it has to be the wiring."

"I'm no electrician, but Brady's a whiz at such things. And if he can't fix it, he knows someone in town who can. I'll see if he can spare some time to take a look at it."

"I'd be grateful for his help." Vern crossed to the far side of the barn and hung the flashlight on a hook on the wall. He took his time wiping his hands on a rag. "You notice anything about our girl this morning?"

"Other than the fact that she was grumpy?" Ash grinned at his own joke.

"Maybe she has a right to be."

"What's that supposed to mean?"

The old man folded the rag once, twice, three times before tucking it into his back pocket. Only then did he look directly at Ash. "I noticed she kept her left hand in her lap over breakfast. But I caught a glimpse of it before she pulled on her work gloves around dawn this morning. She didn't think I noticed, but I did. That fancy diamond ring was missing."

He saw the stunned surprise in Ash's eyes before it was blinked it away.

Ash cleared his throat. "Maybe she doesn't like to wear it while she's working."

"That ring hasn't left her finger since the city slicker put it on." The old man continued studying Ash while he added, "Speaking of which...he paid a call last night, shortly after you left. I was sitting outside my trailer, enjoying a beer in the dark. He stormed up the porch steps like a wounded bear. Wasn't inside the house very long. When he left, there were tires spitting gravel, like somebody being chased by the devil. Afterward, the kitchen lights went out. The only light I saw was in Brenna's room upstairs. That one was on and off most of the night until I fell asleep after midnight. I suspect that our girl may be feeling a mite conflicted right now. Even though, from Revel's reaction, I'd say the final decision came from her, not him."

Vern paused a beat. "Not that it matters who said what. The fact is, Brenna's no longer wearing Revel's ring."

Ash dropped down on the edge of a bale of hay and stared in silence at the ground.

Seeing the thoughtful look on his face, Vern climbed up to the seat of the tractor. Though Ash hadn't said much, the look on his face spoke volumes.

The old man was whistling as he drove out of the barn and steered the tractor along the lane heading toward a distant meadow.

"All I'm asking is that you show Ira the letter." Ash pulled on his sunglasses as the truck ate up the miles from Brenna's ranch to town.

Brenna shot him a dark look while her fingers continued worrying the edges of the envelope.

"I'm trying to do as my mother asked, and be a forgiving daughter. And now you're suggesting that I name my father as a suspect in something that could be criminal."

"I'm not suggesting that you make any accusations or point any fingers. Let the chief come to his own conclusions."

She held up the letter. "He says he's near death. His organs are failing. How could he possibly be strong enough to drive a truck across Montana just to target me?"

"I'm not saying he did or didn't do anything wrong.

But if he'd been holding a grudge all these years, it's a possibility." Seeing her stricken look, he added gently, "Listen, Brenna. I'm not pointing a finger at your father. I'm just doing as the chief said, and offering any name that could be a suspect. It would be wrong to withhold something that could turn out to be important information during an investigation." To keep things light he winked. "Can you tell I spent a lot of nights watching cop shows on TV?"

That brought a smile to her lips. "All right. I get it." She set the letter back in her lap. "And I'll show him the letter. But I want Chief Pettigrew to know that I don't believe my father is capable of this."

"Fair enough." Ash glanced at her hand, then away. He'd gone over and over in his mind how to approach the subject of the missing engagement ring, but he couldn't come up with a way to keep it light. So he continued avoiding the obvious.

Finally, when she reached into her purse for her sunglasses, he caught her hand in his. "Hey."

Her eyes went wide before they narrowed on him. "What?

He shrugged. "Nothing. I just noticed this hand is looking...a tad naked."

She snatched it away and folded it under her right hand in her lap.

"Chris and I are...taking some time off."

"Time off. Is that like a vacation?"

"Yeah." She looked over to see his lips curling into a smile. "Are you smirking?"

"Just smiling. Is smiling allowed?"

"Not if it means you're laughing at me."

"Me? Laugh at you? Now why would I do a thing like that, Sunshine?" He waited a beat before asking, "Are you happy or sad about this...vacation time?"

She didn't answer for so long, he started to regret his question. Maybe he'd struck a nerve. The last thing he wanted to do was add to any pain she might be suffering.

Finally she started speaking in halting sentences. "I'm not sure just what I'm feeling. Maybe a little...relieved. Chris is being reassigned to Helena, and then, if he gets his wish, to Washington, D.C. It's where he's always wanted to be. We both knew his assignment out here was temporary. He never tried to hide that fact from me."

"So, he didn't invite you along for the ride?"

"As a matter of fact, he did. To Helena, and then to Washington. When he first talked about it, I went along with the plan. It seemed like...a fantasy, I guess. But now that it's real, and not just some far-in-the-distant-future goal, I have a lot of doubts. My home is here. My family ranch. My studio." She swallowed. "My friends." She glanced at him. "When he pressed for an answer, I felt a real moment of panic."

"And now?"

She shrugged. "Maybe there's still a little panic. But not as much. And honestly, I just can't see myself ever living in a big city. Look at me." She glanced down at her faded jeans and T-shirt, and the scuffed sneakers that she'd bought in a resale shop a year ago. "I'd never fit in."

"Sunshine, you'd fit in anywhere you wanted to be. But I know what you mean about leaving all this." He felt his heart soar as the truck came up over a ridge and the little town of Copper Creek came into view. "Most people would see only the dingy buildings and struggling ranchers. Not to mention miles of wilderness. But after years away, I see old friends who share my grief at the loss of my father, and who ask about my mother and grandfather and brother." He turned to her. "It has to be the same for you. When your mother passed, there was old Vern, offering to stay awhile and help out with ranch chores, and ended up staying for all these years."

She nodded. "And Nonie Claxton over at Wylie's, who used to send home bowls of soup with me after school. And Reverend Hamilton's wife, Francis, who made my dress for graduation after my mother passed away. And your father, who paid my taxes without telling a soul. I only learned of it when I went to plead my case, and learned it had been settled." Her smile bloomed as she remembered. "So many good friends who got me through some really hard times."

Ash shot her a look of absolute astonishment. "I didn't know about Pop doing that, but I guess I shouldn't be surprised. He could be the toughest, meanest slave driver around. But he had a soft spot for good people in need."

"If it hadn't been for your father, Ash, I know I'd have lost my land years ago. He not only paid my back taxes, but paid them forward, too, so I wouldn't have to worry. When I found out, I rode old Thunder over to his place to thank him. He was working out in one of the barns, and his face got all red and his eyes were watering. He said he had a cold, but I think he was remembering you."

Ash's voice was rougher than he'd intended. "What makes you think that?"

"Because when I was leaving he hugged me, and said he hoped some day my best friend would come back."

She looked out the side window, avoiding Ash's eyes. "And we both knew who he was talking about."

"Yeah?" There was a softness in Ash's voice that hadn't been there moments earlier.

She turned to study his profile. "Yeah."

They drove through the town in complete silence.

By the time they parked the truck and walked into the police chief's office, they were both smiling and feeling as though a heavy weight had been lifted from their shoulders.

Ira Pettigrew read the letter several times before setting it aside. He steepled his hands on the desktop and peered at Brenna, who was seated across from him and beside Ash.

"The handwriting's pretty shaky. You recognize it as your father's?"

She glanced helplessly at Ash. Of all the questions she'd been anticipating, this hadn't been one of them. "I wouldn't know. I never got a letter from him before."

"Do the bank records show whether your check has been cashed?"

"It's only been a couple of weeks. But I can ask Sarah over at the bank."

"You do that. And let me know." Ira leaned forward. "I'll give you back this letter as soon as I make a copy for my files. Until I figure out what's causing these incidents, I need to question anything that seems unusual."

"And you think my father could be involved?"

He kept his tone impersonal. "Not at all. It sounds to me as though he's hoping to make peace before facing his Maker. But I can't discount any theory, no matter how thin. It's my job to be suspicious."

He studied both of them. "Anything else I should know

about? Ash, you remember any new enemies I ought to be checking up on?"

Ash shook his head. "How about Luther?"

"He was up in North Pond, hauling a load of grain at the very time that rogue truck was bearing down on you two. I checked out his story, and half a dozen witnesses were able to verify it."

Ash swore. "I was wishing it was Luther. Then we could all catch a breath and relax."

"I expect the two of you to be vigilant about your safety. As a lawman, I view one runaway truck as an accident. But I consider two a conspiracy."

He got to his feet, signaling an end to their meeting. "I've got to get over to the courthouse. I'm grateful that you brought this letter in, Brenna. It may mean nothing, but I'd rather follow a dozen false leads, even if they don't lead to a solution, than overlook something and have it turn out to be important."

Brenna flushed. "I didn't want to bring it here. I just don't see any connection between the letter from my father, and these accidents. The only reason I'm here is because Ash insisted."

The chief offered a handshake to Ash. "Then I thank you for doing the right thing."

He crossed to the opposite wall and set the letter in a copier. When a page was printed out, he handed back the original to Brenna.

Before the chief left, Ash put a hand on his sleeve. "What about your investigation into Pop's death, Ira? Any leads?"

The chief met his look of concern with one of his own. "I've asked the state police to assign a couple of their best detectives to the case, Ash. They have the bullet taken from your father's body, and, after interviewing you and your family, they've been checking out every item your family listed as possibilities. Rustlers. Poachers. Anyone who owed your father money. Even old friends from his past who may be down and out, and jealous enough of his success to hold a grudge. So far, they've come up empty. But I gave your mother my word that this investigation won't end until we have the guilty party."

"Thanks, Ira."

When the chief walked away, Brenna laid a hand on Ash's arm. "I'm so sorry that you and your family have to go through so much pain. My little problems are insignificant compared to what you're dealing with."

He looked down at her hand and absorbed the warmth of her touch. Just hearing her words of comfort lifted his spirits. "Thanks, Sunshine." He nodded toward Wylie's. "Ready for some lunch?"

At Brenna's murmur of approval, he caught her hand and led her across the street.

It was a simple gesture, and something he'd done since they were kids. But now, with her hand tucked firmly in his big palm, he felt a sudden rush of heat that had nothing to do with the spring sunshine.

He knew he would be considered shameless for what he was thinking. He ought to be at least a little sorry that Brenna was going through these doubts and concerns, not only about her father, but about her broken engagement to Chris. But the fact was, now that she'd shed that sparkler from her left hand, even a runaway truck, or the fact that the state police had no leads in his father's death, couldn't put a damper on this day.

CHAPTER FIFTEEN

W ell, look who's here." As Ash and Brenna stepped inside the smoky saloon, Nonie Claxton dashed past them with three plates balanced on one arm, and a tray of beers in her other hand. "Grab a table and I'll be right with you."

Ash kept hold of Brenna's hand as he led her through the crowded tables of raucous cowboys toward a booth in the rear of the room, both of them pausing often to greet old friends and neighbors.

Minutes later Nonie sidled up beside them. She was grinning from ear to ear. "Brenna Crane, what're you do-ing here with this bad boy?"

Brenna flushed. "Just catching up on old times."

Nonie winked. "That's what they all say."

She turned to Ash. "Mind your manners today. Wylie just replaced half a dozen chairs and he'd like to keep them around for a few months."

Ash and Brenna joined in Nonie's teasing laughter. She was still laughing as she set down two glasses of ice water. "I remember when the two of you would come in and sit at the bar, drinking sodas and eating burgers. You were both too young to be here alone, but Wylie knew your daddy, Ash, and so he'd let the two of you eat, as long as you never tried to sneak a beer. And you never did. At least not while I was looking. Now, what'll you two have to drink?"

"Now that I'm older and wiser, I'll have a beer." Ash turned to Brenna. "How about you?"

She shrugged. "I'm well past legal age and still don't drink. I'll have a lemonade, Nonie."

"Sure thing." The older woman paused. "Today's special is Wylie's famous ranch chili and fries. Guaranteed to make your eyes water and your tongue cry uncle."

"Sold." Ash winked at Nonie. "I've got years of missed Wylie's chili to catch up on."

"I'll have the same." Brenna shared a smile with Ash as Nonie flounced away.

A short time later she was back, serving up two bowls of steaming chili topped with onions and shredded cheese, and ringed by an assortment of crackers.

After his first bite Ash sighed. "For years I've tried to duplicate Wylie's recipe. But mine has never captured the fire like this."

Brenna ate hers, pausing to soothe her throat every few minutes with sips of cold lemonade. "You're right. There's definitely fire in this bowl."

Ash polished off his first and signaled for Nonie to bring him a second.

"Try not to eat that white thing. It's the bowl." Brenna

laughed as, just minutes later, she stared at his empty dish. "You going for thirds?"

He shook his head and sat back, drinking his beer slowly and looking around before taking her hand in his. "I really missed this. Not just Wylie's, but being here with you."

"I missed it, too." She looked away, avoiding his eyes.

"Wylie's? Or me?"

She turned to him. "You fishing for compliments, MacKenzie?"

His sexy grin was quick and dangerous. "Hell, yes."

"Okay. Honestly? I even managed to miss you a couple of times."

"A couple? I guess that means I'm better'n I thought. I figured the minute I was out of sight, every guy from here to Helena would be plying you with their charms."

"Oh, they did." She laughed at the look that came into his eyes. "And I decided to let them charm me. After all, a girl's got to do what a girl's got to do."

He glanced at their linked hands and closed his other hand over them. "I hope you'll do that girl-thing on this guy some day."

She tossed her head. "I don't know what you're talking about."

Laughing, they drew apart as Nonie paused beside their table. "You ready for another, Ash?"

He shook his head. "One more and I'd explode. But tell Wylie that was the best lunch I've had in almost ten years."

"I'll do that. But if word gets out to your granddaddy, Mad'll have your hide. He's always bragging on his cooking."

"Swear you'll keep our secret, Nonie." He caught her hand and kissed it.

The old woman visibly melted.

With a sigh she turned to Brenna. "A word of warning. Guard your heart, girl, 'cause this cowboy oozes pure sex."

When she walked away, Brenna deadpanned, "Another conquest."

"It's a curse. All the MacKenzies have to bear it." He caught her hand. "Come on. It's time we breathed fresh air."

Ash veered off the highway and cut across a stretch of meadowland blanketed with soft spring-green vegetation. He continued driving until he came to the banks of a stream. Turning off the engine, he stepped from the truck and circled around to hold open the passenger's-side door.

Brenna didn't need to ask why he'd come here. She was smiling, her eyes looking soft and misty. "Our spot."

"Yeah." He took her hand and led her to a large, flat rock overlooking the stream.

They sat side by side, watching as the swollen waters from melting snow in the highlands tumbled over hidden rocks. The stream was at its highest point this time of year, nearly spilling over the banks as it raced past them.

"Did you come here a lot of times without me?" He kept his face averted, watching the play of sunlight on the water.

"I haven't been here at all." She drew her knees up before wrapping her arms around them.

He turned to her. "Why?"

She shrugged and said simply, "It was our place."

His heart took a couple of hard bounces before settling back to its natural rhythm.

They sat in companionable silence, listening to the soothing sound of rushing water.

Ash leaned back on his hands. "I'm glad you told me about Pop paying your taxes."

"He was a good man, Ash. Oh, I know he was a tyrant. Especially with you. But he really loved you. And after you left, he seemed even more driven to look out for all the people that mattered to you."

"Like you."

She nodded. "Your father had never been to my ranch until you left. Then he started stopping by on his way to town just to see if I needed anything." She chuckled. "The first time he did that, I got so scared. Seeing his stern face, I thought he was coming by with some bad news about you, and before he could say a word I burst into tears." She flushed as she realized what she'd just admitted. "He was so sweet, insisting that he hadn't heard a word. But then, when he offered to pick up grain or groceries, or anything I needed, I couldn't think of a thing to say. After a while, it got easier for me. And before long, we became friends."

"You and Pop?"

"Yeah." She laughed. "Isn't that a hoot?"

"Yeah." He fell silent, digesting what she'd just told him. He felt a sudden warm glow just thinking about his father befriending Brenna and looking out for her in his absence. And then, he felt a sharp pang of regret for all the years he'd missed.

Her voice grew dreamy. "At first, after you left, I

stayed away from your ranch, afraid that I wouldn't be welcome, with you gone. But one day your dad insisted that I come over for lunch, and once I got there, it was just like before. I was treated like one of the family. And when I was leaving, Myrna made me promise that I'd come by at least once a month."

"Did you?"

"I tried. But it was hard, with all the ranch chores, and life and things. Lately, I'd been putting off my visits, because..." She shrugged. "There was just a lot going on."

He caught her hand. "You don't have to talk about it."

She withdrew her hand from his. "I want to. I haven't been entirely honest about my reason for giving Chris back his ring." She decided to say nothing about the kiss she and Ash had shared. A kiss that had caused her a good deal of worry. That was still a little too confusing to talk about. She needed more time to sort it all out in her mind.

She waited a moment before saying, "Chris doesn't respect me for struggling to keep my ranch going, and for spending time on what he calls my 'hobby.'"

"Sculpting?" Ash's eyes narrowed. "Did he actually call it a hobby?"

"He did. He thinks I'm wasting my time. As for my ranch, he wanted me to sell it."

At Ash's hiss of annoyance she was quick to add, "You need to understand. His parents spent their lives trying to stay out of debt on a small ranch, and Chris decided early on in life that he would never be like them. I can respect him for whatever he chooses to do with his life, but the fact that he can't respect me for my choices is something

I won't accept. I tried, but lately, a few things have made
me realize that I can't go on allowing him to disrespect
me like that."

"What changed your mind?"

She lifted a shoulder. "Several things. The first was
the day I gave your mother my sculpture of your father.
Seeing how touched she was made me so grateful that
I'd followed my heart and didn't wait, as Chris had suggested. And then when Percy Hanover phoned to tell me
that my sculpture had made Pearl cry, it did something to
my heart and soul. I'm beginning to realize that my art
can bring real pleasure to others."

He put his hands on her shoulders and simply stared at
her. "You honestly didn't know?"

She shook her head. "I wasn't sure. But when Chris
called it my hobby and hinted that it didn't matter to him,
it really hurt. How can I share my life with someone who
doesn't share my values?"

"He's a damned fool."

At his outburst, she couldn't help laughing. "And
you're not saying that because you're jealous?"

"Jealous as hell." His snarl turned to a grin. "But that
doesn't change the fact that he's a fool."

They were both laughing then. Laughing so hard, they
fell into each other's arms.

"Oh, Ash, I've missed this. It feels so good to be laughing again with my best friend."

"I know what you mean. I've missed this, too. Missed
you, Sunshine." He lowered his face and brushed his lips
over hers.

His mere kiss started a flame deep in her soul.

Her first instinct was to lean into him and enjoy the

moment. But instead of returning his kiss she stiffened and pushed a little away.

"What's wrong?" He looked hurt and genuinely puzzled.

"Me. You. Chris. I need time. This is all too much, too soon. I feel all jittery inside. Like I have a fever and any minute now I'm going to be sick."

"Okay." He drew away, giving her the space she needed.

They sat in silence for a while.

Finally he slid from the rock and offered his hand until she was standing beside him.

Keeping her hand in his, he led the way to his truck and held her door before circling to the driver's side.

"Let's see how Vern is doing now that he has a working tractor."

As they turned onto the long, winding gravel driveway, Sammy came rushing toward the truck, yipping and yapping.

Ash stopped the truck and waited while Brenna scooped him up into her arms.

She climbed back inside, gently scolding the puppy. "You silly little thing. Did you sneak out the barn door when Vern wasn't looking? Don't you know that's how little guys like you get hurt?"

She pressed a kiss to his wet nose as they moved along the lane.

Ash pointed to deep grooves in the gravel. "What's this? Have you been doing wheelies lately?"

Brenna stared out the windshield. "I can't imagine Vern ever driving that hard and fast. I wonder who's been here."

They came to a stop outside the barn. The door had caved inward and lay in a heap of splintered wood. Beyond that, the tractor lay tipped on its side, gasoline spilling from a ruptured gas tank.

Vern stood to one side, staring at the mess.

"Are you okay?" Ash leaped from his truck.

Before he could open Brenna's door, she was out and rushing to stand beside the old cowboy, her hand on his arm.

"I'm not hurt. It was a close call, but I'd just stepped down when I heard a crash, and looked up to see the barn door falling in on me."

Both Ash and Brenna breathed a sigh of relief, just knowing that Vern wasn't harmed.

Vern looked from one to the other. "I jumped back just as a truck came barreling through the door and slammed right into the tractor. If I'd been sitting on it, I'm sure I wouldn't be talking to you now."

Brenna wrapped her arms around the old cowboy's neck and buried her face against his chest.

He patted her arms and drew her a little away. "I'm okay now, girl. Don't you go getting all weepy on me."

She sniffed. "You know I never cry."

"That's right. So don't start now." He gave her a gentle smile. "Poor little Sammy was running around and around in circles in the dust."

"Did you see who did this?" Ash demanded.

The old man shook his head. "Between the splintered door and the tipped-over tractor, all I saw was a blur of a truck barreling out of here in a cloud of dust so thick, I couldn't even tell much about it, except that it was a dark color. Black. Maybe dark blue." He scratched his head.

"Why would someone crash into the barn, hit a tractor, and then drive away without stopping?"

Tight-lipped, Ash glanced at Brenna, whose face had gone ashen. "How long ago did this happen?"

"No more'n a few minutes before you got here." He shook his head. "Well, maybe more like half an hour. I'm not sure. I waited until my head stopped spinning and my ears ringing. Then I tried mopping up the gas with some rags. All that gas is a fire hazard with this straw and old barn wood."

Ash was already dialing his cell phone. Turning away from the others he spoke into the phone. "Ira? Ash MacKenzie. There's been an incident out at the Crane ranch. A truck plowed into the barn and upended a tractor. Nobody hurt. Vern was the only one here at the time, and he didn't get a very clear look at the truck or driver before it took off in a cloud of dust." He paused before saying, "Yeah. We'll be here."

He tucked his phone in his pocket. "Chief Pettigrew is on his way. He'll want a statement, Vern."

The old cowboy nodded. "That'll give me time to clean up the gas."

Ash touched a hand to his arm. "Leave it. The chief will want to see everything just the way it is before we start cleaning anything up. Besides, you need to sit down."

Seeing the stunned look in Vern's eyes, he put an arm around the old man's shoulders and another around Brenna, who looked equally alarmed. "Let's go inside and have a cup of coffee while we wait for Chief Pettigrew."

* * *

The police chief's SUV sported oversized tires, a heavy-duty caged backseat section for unruly passengers, and a rifle rack holding an assortment of weapons.

Hearing his arrival, Brenna followed Vern and Ash out the door, leaving her puppy safely in the house. Though Sammy yammered his objections, she firmly closed the door and descended the steps.

By the time she stepped into the barn, Ira Pettigrew was walking around the upended tractor.

"Was the barn door open when this happened?"

Vern shook his head. "Closed. I'd just driven it in from the field and parked it, then closed the door, figuring I'd go out the side door over there." He pointed to the small side entrance.

"So, if someone was watching you drive in and closing the door, they might think you were still standing in front of it?"

The old man shrugged. "Why would anyone be watching me drive in?"

"I don't know. I'll ask you what I asked Brenna and Ash in my office. Do you have any enemies, Vern?"

The old man grinned. "When you've lived as long as me, you probably have more than you can count. But none come to mind."

The chief turned to Brenna. "Have there been any visitors here lately?"

She shook her head. "No one."

"Any deliveries?"

She thought about it before turning to Vern. They both shook their heads at the same time.

The chief addressed both Brenna and Ash. "This could very well be connected to those near misses that happened in town. But right now, I feel like I'm missing something. Something important. None of this makes sense. So for now, until I figure out what's going on, I'd like the two of you to be extra cautious."

"Are you thinking whoever did this will come back?"

Ira turned to Ash. "Those first incidents happened in town. Because the two of you were together both times, I couldn't figure out which of you was being targeted. Now, the fact that you're both here clouds the issue somewhat, because of what happened to Bear. But since this is Brenna's ranch and Brenna's property that was damaged, I'm going to assume, for now, that she's the primary target. It isn't much, but it's a start. Now I just have to figure out why, and that may lead me to who the culprit is."

Ash speared a glance at Brenna before asking, "Have you checked on her father?"

The chief nodded. "Honey, that was the news I'd been planning on bringing you. It was there in a fax in my office when I returned."

Ira cleared his throat. His tone softened. "The assisted-living place informed me that your daddy checked himself out."

Ash's eyes grew stormy. "And that letter to Brenna, about being near death, was all a lie?"

"Maybe. Maybe he was testing the waters, to see if Brenna was still living here." The chief turned to Brenna. "Or maybe it was just a way of getting enough money to move on. Sarah at the bank confirmed that your check was cashed."

Brenna looked stunned as the chief handed her a slip of paper. "Here's the name and number of the director of the nursing home." His voice lowered. "The director said your daddy left in the night, with only the clothes on his back. Nobody saw him go. The belongings he left behind don't amount to much, but if you're agreeable, the director would like to donate them to a charity. He'll need your permission."

Seeing her pain and confusion, he touched a hand to her arm. "You think on it, Brenna honey. There's time to make a decision before you talk to the director."

"I will. Thank you, Chief."

He nodded before turning toward his vehicle. He motioned for Ash to follow.

Leaning on the door of his SUV, he kept his tone low. "At least now I have a suspect. Though I can't for the life of me figure out why old Raleigh Crane would come back here and try to hurt his daughter and Vern."

"Maybe in his twisted mind he blames Brenna, because it was his treatment of her that caused you to order him to leave all those years ago."

"Maybe. All I know is, I can't be here day and night, and I'll tell you, Ash, I don't like knowing Brenna and old Vern are out here, so far from town and at the mercy of a someone out to hurt them."

Ash's tone was pure ice. "They won't be alone, Ira. I give you my word on that."

CHAPTER SIXTEEN

Thanks, Mad." Ash slipped his cell phone into his shirt pocket and approached the barn, where Vern and Brenna were cleaning up the gasoline spill. Snatching up a handful of rags, he dropped to his knees and helped.

Afterward, Brenna carried the bucket of rags outside and wrinkled her nose. "I smell like gas."

Ash took the bucket from her hands. "A nice long shower ought to take care of that." His tone lowered. "I'd be happy to scrub your back."

"I just bet you would." She turned back to look at the pile of splintered barn wood littering the floor. "And what will take care of my barn door?"

"I'll get a crew over here tomorrow."

She shook her head in protest. "I can't afford to pay a crew of workmen."

"I'm talking about some of our wranglers. Those that aren't needed with the herd can lend a hand."

Vern dropped down onto a bale of hay. "That was our only tractor."

At his words, Brenna glanced at the upended vehicle, and then at the old man, looking with such sadness at the destruction.

She walked over to lay a hand on his arm. "Think how much worse it might have been. Seconds earlier and you could have been—"

He stood and touched a finger to her lips. "Don't start looking for trouble now, girl. I'm fine."

"I know. But—"

"We could all use a change of scenery." Ash ambled over to clap a hand on Vern's arm before turning Brenna toward the sunshine outside. "First, you both need to take a long, hot shower. Then we're driving to my family's ranch for supper. Mad just told me he's grilling steaks and his special potatoes, and Myrna's baking lemon meringue pies."

Vern touched a hand to his heart. "Lemon meringue? Now that's worth a shower in the middle of the day."

His words had them all smiling as Vern made his way toward his house trailer and Brenna headed toward her back door.

Ash trailed slowly behind her, uttering a thank-you to his grandfather for insisting that he bring both Brenna and Vern back with him. It wasn't a solution, but at least they'd deal with their problems on a full stomach.

"Now this is what our family's been missing." Mad looked up from the grill when Brenna stepped into the kitchen. "Where've you been keeping yourself, lass?"

"I'm sorry, Mad." She crossed the room and leaned

down to give him a hug. "I should have been by to see you."

"That you should've, lass." He returned the hug before glancing at Vern, who stood hesitantly in the doorway.

"And look who you've brought. Vern Wheeler. It's been too many years."

"That it has, Mad. That it has." The old cowboy offered a firm handshake before turning to Myrna, who had both arms around Brenna and was hugging her fiercely.

He gave a courtly bow. "Myrna."

"Vern." Her face was wreathed with smiles as she kept her arms around Brenna. "How good to see you." She pressed a kiss on Brenna's cheek before releasing her.

The back door opened and the rest of the family began streaming in, fresh from their chores, pausing to hang their hats and wash at the big sink before stepping into the kitchen.

There were hugs and handshakes as Willow, followed by Brady and Whit, greeted both Brenna and Vern. Willow handled the introductions to Griff, who had stood back watching and listening.

Vern gave the young man a long, slow appraisal before saying, "It's nice to meet you, Griff. You've got your daddy's face, son."

Griff surprised all of them by saying, "Thank you. The more I learn about Bear MacKenzie, the more I like what I hear."

Ash glanced at Willow in time to see the slow, haunted smile that touched her lips.

"Go ahead and sit." Mad turned toward the oven. "Dinner's ready."

The family took their usual places, and Willow directed their guests toward the empty chairs. Ash held a chair for Brenna before settling himself next to her.

Mad and Myrna passed around platters of sizzling steaks, a salad of early spring greens from Myrna's garden, and Mad's special potato dish. A basket of rolls warm from the oven was placed in the center of the big table, where everyone could reach them.

Vern cut a bite of steak and closed his eyes in pleasure.

Seeing it, Brenna laughed. "Enjoy yourself. Tomorrow is soon enough to get back to reality."

"Which one of you does the cooking at your ranch?" Myrna asked.

"I do. If you want to call it cooking. It usually ends up being burned toast, or slimy eggs along with whatever cold meat hasn't turned moldy," Brenna said.

"Now that sounds really appetizing." Whit grinned around a mouthful of Mad's potatoes. "Maybe you could take a few lessons from Mad and Myrna. The one thing we've always been able to count on here is good cooking. It's what keeps our crew of wranglers coming back year after year."

Brenna tasted the potatoes before turning to Mad. "I'd love this recipe."

He winked. "Not sure I'd like to share it, lass. It's an old family secret."

Myrna deadpanned, "Which he stole out of my cookbook. If you'd like to know how to make this, just ask me."

Mad shot her a look. "Careful, or you'll be banished from my kitchen."

"*Your* kitchen?" she huffed. "I ran this kitchen before you and your . . . inventions moved in, and I expect I'll be running it long after you and all your clutter are gone."

"And just where am I going?"

She looked down her nose at him. "I don't think you want me to answer that, Maddock MacKenzie. Heaven knows you're no angel, so that only leaves that other place, which will be a lot hotter than this kitchen."

Around the table, the entire family roared with laughter.

As they continued eating, the talk turned easily from crops, to the size of their herds and the number of new calves, to the whims of nature, which they and their neighbors faced every day.

"So hot yesterday, we were shedding our coats, then our shirts. Today we were shivering inside our parkas," Griff muttered.

"Welcome to springtime in Montana." Vern looked over at him. "Where'd you grow up, son?"

"Billings."

"Then you already know how fickle Mother Nature is in Montana."

"I do. But it seems even crazier here on the ranch, when you're dealing with newborn calves getting buried in snow, and trees budding one day and freezing the next."

"Sounds like you're having a real baptism of fire, son."

Brady sat back, sipping strong, hot coffee. "Griff here is a natural. Today he helped birth a newborn calf without flinching."

When everyone turned to Griff, he managed a quick grin. "Well, I may have been wincing inside, but I knew I had to get that calf out quick, or its poor mother was in trouble."

"Messy, isn't it?" Ash said in an aside.

Griff nodded. "Bloody messy. But when you look beyond the blood and gore, it's beautiful. And amazing, too. Within minutes that old cow was licking her new baby clean, and the little guy was up and nursing. And I was standing there thinking I'd just assisted in the miracle of birth."

Whit winked at his grandfather before turning to Griff. "Well, since you're feeling all soft and mushy right now, how'd you like to go up in the hills tomorrow with the crew? There are probably a couple hundred cows ready to provide you with all the miracles you can stomach."

When he'd finished laughing, Griff sobered enough to say, "Actually, I've already offered to go. I told Brady that I want to learn all I can about the operation of a ranch."

Vern, who'd been listening in silence, turned to Griff. "You didn't grow up on a ranch in Billings?"

Griff shook his head. "My mother taught school. I lived in town, and when I was old enough, I got a job in a woodworking shop after school."

Ash looked over with interest. "So you'd know how to fashion a bunch of broken timbers into something useful, like a barn door?"

Brenna shot a quick glance at Ash, but he silenced her with a wink.

"Sure. That's what I did. I can cut wood, shave it, saw it, fashion it into whatever you'd like." Griff paused. "Why?"

Ash shrugged. "Some crazy guy drove his truck through Brenna's barn door, smashing it to bits."

Willow's fork clattered against her plate. She turned to Brenna with a look of concern. "What's this about?"

As briefly as possible Ash explained what had happened.

Willow's concern grew. "I don't like the sound of this. Brenna, why don't you and Vern spend the night here? We have plenty of room for both of you."

Brenna was already shaking her head. "I can't just leave. The chores would pile up without the two of us there to stay ahead of them. Besides, what if this guy decides to come back and do even more damage?"

"You think he'll be back?"

Brenna looked down at the tabletop. "I don't know what to think."

"All the more reason why you and Vern ought to stay here where you're safe."

That had Brenna looking around at the others. "I'm not about to abandon my ranch to some nutcase who wants to destroy it."

"I'm with you." Ash turned to Griff. "This is why Brenna needs a new barn door as soon as possible. Think you can turn her mess into something useful?"

Griff nodded. "I don't see why not. I may have to buy a few pieces of lumber, if the remnants she has left are too small. But I'm sure I can put together something that will keep out the elements."

"But will it keep out crazy drivers?" Mad muttered.

"We'll leave that up to Chief Pettigrew." Ash patted Brenna's hand and she shot him a quick smile.

Willow's brows knit into a frown. "I still think the two of you ought to stay the night." She turned to her foreman. "Brady? How do you feel about this?"

He glanced across the table at Mad before turning to her. "I think Ash is right. For now, let's wait for the chief to do his job." He turned to include Brenna and Vern. "But if Ira decides he needs help, you know we're here."

Vern nodded thoughtfully. "It's a comfort to know you folks have our backs."

As Myrna began cutting slices of pie and passing them around, the old cowboy's smile returned.

At his first taste, he was murmuring words of appreciation. "Now, for this I'd sell my ranch, if I had one to sell."

That had the others smiling and nodding along with him.

Griff sat back, letting the conversation and laughter flow around him. This was all so new and different from anything he'd experienced before.

He'd grown up an only child in a house where silence and secrecy was the rule. Because his mother spent her days teaching school and her evenings grading students' papers, he'd learned early in life to avoid bringing friends home. Instead, he'd often spent long hours at their houses until hunger would drive him to return home. Dinner was a quiet affair, just him and his mother. The few times he'd broached the subject of his father, the pain in his mother's eyes always caused him to retreat. After a while, he'd learned to keep his questions to himself. He'd loved his mother. She was a good woman, if a bit stern. And so he'd held his silence, in order to spare her any further pain.

Now here he was, in his father's home, with his father's family and friends, and the love, the laughter, were as enjoyable as they were unexpected. Nothing was as he'd expected. Not Willow, his father's wife, or her sons, or his grandfather.

Grandfather. The very word took his breath away.

As a boy he'd yearned for family. There hadn't been

so much as a cousin, or an aunt or uncle. His mother had allowed few friends to get close. Maybe that was why the military life had been so appealing. There was a brotherhood, a camaraderie that had filled a void in his life.

Suddenly, there were so many people around him, and all of them family.

Because of Bear MacKenzie. A man he'd wanted to meet. And in truth, expected to hate. Instead, he was learning a great deal about the mysterious Bear and the people who had been closest to him. And with each new fact he learned, he liked and admired the man more, despite his famous temper.

"What do you say, Griff?"

At Ash's question, his head came up sharply. "Sorry. What?"

"I said, are you willing to give up a day in the hills, experiencing...miracles..., to lend a hand at Brenna's place first?"

"Yeah. Sure thing." He saw the winks and smiles being exchanged, and decided to simply enjoy being the butt of their latest joke. "I guess I can give up the mud and the blood and the gore for a little while longer. It'll give me a chance to try my hand at woodworking again."

"Great." Ash caught Brenna's hand. "See? I told you we'd get that door fixed. Now..." He winked. "How about staying the night? You know Myrna will pamper you. Right, Myrna?"

The old woman was nodding. "No burned toast or slimy eggs here. The only leftovers will be a thick steak, hot off the grill. I'll fix you and Vern a breakfast fit for royalty."

Brenna ducked her head. "How I wish I could take you

up on that. And I know Vern wishes he could. But we really need to get back. I left Sammy home alone."

"Sammy?" Whit's attention was immediately caught. "Did you add a brother you never knew you had, too?"

Everyone chuckled.

"He's better than a brother. Sammy's my new puppy."

"And the great love of her life," Ash added.

"I have to admit, he's stolen my heart." She spent the next five minutes describing him in great detail, right down to his habit of licking the side of her face every morning if she didn't wake up when he was ready to start the day.

After second cups of coffee, and more easy conversation, Brenna and Vern made ready to leave.

Myrna hurried over to envelop the young woman in a warm hug. "One of these days we'll get you to stay longer."

Brenna returned the embrace. "You've always made me feel so welcome here."

"This is your other home. And has been since you were just a kid. Don't you ever forget it."

"Thanks, Myrna." Brenna kissed her cheek before turning to say her good-byes to the others.

Myrna handed Vern a brown paper bag. He shot her a questioning look.

"A big slice of my lemon meringue pie. Enjoy it later tonight with a glass of milk. Of course, it would even taste good with a cold beer."

His face creased into a smile. "You do know my weakness."

"Now that Brenna has come back to the fold, there will be lots more where this came from."

With a wide smile, Vern followed Ash and Brenna out the back door before settling into Ash's truck.

As they drove away, the entire family gathered on the porch to wave good-bye.

Seeing them, Brenna turned to Ash. "Do you know how lucky you are to have so many people who love you?"

He nodded. "I can't believe I allowed nearly ten years to slip away before coming to my senses."

"At least you finally figured it out, son." Vern lowered the passenger's-side window and breathed in the cool night air. "Some folks go a lifetime and never appreciate all the good people in their life."

As the truck moved along the driveway to Brenna's house, the three of them were laughing as they discussed the running feud between Myrna and Mad.

"She had the run of the house until my grandfather moved in. He was like a dictator, ordering her about and expecting her to do his bidding, just because he was in that wheelchair. Now I understand, to make things worse, he'd started inventing things that he swears will make their lives easier. All Myrna sees is that it uses up her good utensils for inventions that never work. As always, she's let him know that she doesn't take orders from anybody."

"That has to be a shock to old Maddock MacKenzie." Vern chuckled. "A man like that wouldn't take kindly to having a woman stand toe-to-toe with him."

"He has no choice but to accept the fact that he's met his match. Now they seem to have figured out some kind of truce."

"Truce?" Vern shook his head. "One wrong word and that so-called truce will erupt into all out fireworks..."

His words trailed off as the headlights flashed across the gravel path, illuminating Sammy, trembling and whining.

Ash braked, and Vern stepped out, scooping up the shivering pup before handing it over to Brenna.

She hugged the little guy and buried her face in his ruff. "How did you get outside? I know I locked the door when I left. Oh, Sammy, I wish you could tell me what's wrong."

Just then the truck's headlights swung across the back porch, showing the back door.

It was hanging open at a crazy angle by one hinge, swinging back and forth on the breeze.

CHAPTER SEVENTEEN

Ash came to an abrupt halt and swung out of the truck with a terse command to Brenna and Vern. "Call Ira Pettigrew and stay here with the doors locked."

He reached for a rifle from behind the seat and was up the steps and inside the kitchen when he heard footsteps behind him. He swung around, prepared to do battle, only to see both Brenna and the old cowboy just stepping inside.

He snarled a warning. "I told you to stay outside."

"This is my house, Ash. I'm not hiding in your truck while you face danger alone."

He looked beyond Brenna to the old cowboy. "What's your excuse for this foolishness?"

"I take my orders from her," Vern said with a grin.

Ash took a breath. "And Ira?"

"I called him." Brenna's voice was tight with worry. "He's on his way."

"All right. But it'll take him an hour to get here from town, and whoever did this could still be hiding inside."

"He won't get past all three of us." Brenna opened a drawer and pulled out a long knife.

In Vern's hands was a tree limb he'd picked up outside. It looked sturdy enough to break a man's legs. Or a head, if he aimed high enough.

"Where's Sammy?" Ash demanded.

"I left him safe in your truck."

Just then they heard the sound of breaking glass.

"Someone's here," Brenna shouted.

With Ash leading the way, they raced through the house to the old-fashioned parlor, only to find a window smashed and a figure darting across the backyard into the darkness.

"I'm going after him." Ash called over his shoulder, "And this time, stay here."

He didn't dare attempt to go through the broken window. The shards of glass were as forbidding as daggers.

Though it cost him precious time, he raced through the house and into the night. But as he made his way across a meadow behind the barn, he knew, with a sinking heart, that he'd lost any chance of catching up. Whoever had broken in was long gone, having been swallowed up by darkness.

After a cursory check of the barns and outbuildings, Ash turned to make his way back, only to find Brenna and Vern coming up behind him.

"Can't the two of you understand anything? This isn't just a break-in. This guy could have a gun."

"And haven't you heard there's safety in numbers?" Brenna's voice was breathless, either from running or from pure terror.

Hearing the catch in her voice, Ash caught her hand and guided her through the darkness back to the porch. Inside, they began turning on lights as they moved through the house checking rooms. When they stepped into the living room and switched on the lamps on side tables at either end of the sofa, they were startled to see a pile of plaster and debris littering a corner. They looked up to discover a hole in the ceiling.

"I'll get a flashlight." Brenna hurried away and returned minutes later.

Ash dragged a chair across the room. Using the flashlight, he climbed as high as he could before shining the light into the gaping hole.

"See anything?" Vern asked.

"Nothing but dust. Tomorrow, in better light, I'll check it out and see if there's anything more." He climbed down and handed the flashlight to Brenna. "You have any idea what an intruder could be looking for?"

She shook her head. "I don't have a clue. And why in here? I haven't used this room for ages." She pointed to the fireplace, with logs on the grate and kindling in a basket beside it, gathering dust. "Mom and I used to watch TV in here. But after she passed, I put the TV in my bedroom."

"I'm going to check upstairs." Ash turned away, and once again Brenna and Vern trailed behind.

Though they looked carefully in every room, there was no further sign that the intruder had been there.

In the kitchen, Ash nodded toward the stove. "You may as well put on a pot of coffee. By the time Ira gets here, he'll welcome something hot."

"I'll fetch Sammy," Vern called as he headed outside to the truck.

* * *

"Okay. Now let's see what you found." After hearing their story, and bemoaning the fact that the intruder got away, Ira studied the debris on the floor of the living room.

Vern set up a stepladder he'd retrieved from the shed.

The chief climbed up to peer into the gaping hole. Using a flashlight, he studied the old timbers clouded by years of dust and cobwebs before climbing down and wiping his hands on his handkerchief.

He turned to Brenna. "Looks to me like whoever broke in here knew exactly where he was going and what he was looking for. Why here? Why not tear up the kitchen ceiling? Or one of the bedrooms?" He thought a minute. "Did your ma ever mention hiding anything in the ceiling?"

Brenna shook her head. "She never said a word to me. And I'm sure if it was something important, she would have told me. When she was sick and knew she didn't have much time left, she was careful to get her life in order. She put my name on her bank account so I could give her a proper burial. She showed me where she'd filed all her documents. Her birth certificate, her marriage license. They were all in a metal box in her bedroom. Ma didn't have much, but she used to say I was her only real treasure, and she was determined to leave me armed with as much information as possible."

Ira Pettigrew patted her shoulder. "Your ma was right, Brenna. You're her treasure. And you've done just fine with your ma's legacy."

Brenna glowed from the chief's praise as they made their way to the kitchen, where she filled four cups with steaming coffee and passed them around.

They sat at the table, sipping coffee and mulling all

that had happened. Across the room, the puppy had settled into his bed, but not before whining and shivering uncontrollably for half an hour. Though Ash held his silence, he felt certain that the poor little thing had been traumatized by the intruder.

Ira broke the silence. "The fact that you scared off this guy makes me think he didn't have time to get whatever he came for. And that's a problem."

He glanced at Brenna, then Ash, and then at Vern, hoping to impress upon them the importance of what he was about to say. "This pretty much cements what we'd already been thinking. These acts against you weren't random. The runaway trucks that nearly ran you over. The smashed barn door. And now this. We have to assume that this guy means business. He's after something. Something important enough to have him targeting anybody who happens to be in his way. You may be his target, Brenna, but he was willing to do real harm to both Ash and Vern. That tells me he's a desperate man."

"Look around you, Chief." Brenna swept her hands to indicate her simple surroundings. "There's nothing of value here. Why target a ranch like mine?"

"If I knew that, Brenna, I'd be known as some kind of police guru. Right now, all I have are questions."

"If he'd come to me and tell me what he wanted, I'd be happy to give it to him, just so he'd leave me alone." She lowered her hands to her lap where she nervously twisted them. "How do we deal with the fear that he won't quit until he gets whatever it is he's looking for? How do we know that next time he won't just settle for smashing a door or a tractor, but one of us?" She looked across the table at Ash before reaching over to catch Vern's hand

in hers. "I can't bear the thought that he nearly killed
Ash just to get to me, or that he nearly hit Vern when he
slammed into my barn door. Next time, maybe we won't
be so lucky."

Ira and Ash exchanged a knowing look, then Ash
turned to Brenna and Vern. "I'm going to take both of
you to my place. I'd like to see our intruder try something
there."

Brenna shook her head. "I want to take you up on your
offer, Ash. Believe me, I'm terrified. I'd feel much safer
with your family. But I can't just walk away and let this
intruder win."

"This isn't about winning or losing. It's about staying
alive." He reached across the table and closed a hand over
hers. "Think about it, Sunshine. You said yourself next
time it could be you or Vern."

A tear trickled from the corner of her eye. "I couldn't
stand to see anyone hurt because of me." She turned to
Vern. "I want you to go to the MacKenzie Ranch with
Ash."

"And you?" The old cowboy was staring at her with
the tender look of a doting grandfather.

"I can't leave. I'm not running away."

"Bren—"

At Ash's protest she lifted a hand. "I have a rifle in the
bedroom and I know how to handle it. I'm not going to
allow this stranger to enter my house at will, and trash it
and maybe burn it to the ground along with the barns, just
because I'm afraid."

Vern drained his cup. "That's it, then. If Brenna's staying, so am I."

Ira looked to Ash, hoping he could change their minds.

Ash shot him a look of resignation before taking Brenna's hand in his. "I guess I should have brought along my toothbrush. If you and Vern are staying, so am I. Looks like I'll be spending the night."

Brenna pulled her hand free. "You can't—"

"I can." He shot her a wicked grin. "It won't be the first time I slept in your barn."

Ira finished his coffee and got to his feet. "I wish I could spare a deputy to park himself here until we catch this guy, but I can't. I want you to know, though, that my deputies and I will swing by whenever we can, at different hours of the day and night so this guy won't ever know when it's safe to try something like this again. But I can't say this strongly enough. At the first sign of trouble, you call. See that you have my number on speed dial."

Brenna offered her hand. "I will. Thanks, Chief."

He nodded. "I wish I could do more. But at least I know I'm leaving you in capable hands."

He motioned for Ash to follow him out the door.

At his car he paused. "This guy is familiar with the house. He knew right where he was going. I've got the state police searching for Brenna's pa. Right now, everything points to him."

Ash nodded. "That's my thought, too."

"Raleigh Crane was a mean drunk, Ash. If he's still in the bottle, there's no telling what he's capable of doing. And now that he got money from Brenna, he'll want more. Maybe that letter was just his way of getting traveling money. In the meantime, until the state police locate him, I hope you can get some backup from your wranglers. I'm thinking you won't be getting any sleep tonight."

"Don't worry, Ira. I've had a lifetime of going without sleep when the chips are down."

Ira patted his arm. "I know that. You're a MacKenzie. My money's on you."

As he drove away, Ash pulled his phone from his pocket and called home to let them know he wouldn't be there, before climbing the steps to Brenna's house.

In the dark of night Vern and Ash stood on ladders on either side of the living room window and hammered nails into place, boarding up the gaping hole.

"You do good work, son." Vern climbed down and stepped back to examine their handiwork.

"Now if I could only nail down the rest of Brenna's troubles as easily." Ash tucked the hammer into his pocket before lifting the ladder to his shoulder.

The two men hauled their ladders and tools to the barn and returned them to their proper storage before looking around.

Ash kept his tone low. "Ira thinks Brenna's father is behind all this."

"Yep." The old cowboy nodded. "My thinking, too. But where's he hiding? He had to know when the house was empty so he would have time to do his dirty work. And when I drove that tractor into the barn, he had to be watching."

"I've been thinking the same thing. He has to be somewhere close enough to keep an eye on the place."

The two men paused outside Vern's trailer. "But what did he leave behind in the ceiling? Cash? If so, why wouldn't he have taken it with him when he left all those years ago?"

Vern shrugged. "Maybe there wasn't time. As I recall, he left in a hurry, one step ahead of the police chief." The old man offered his hand. "Thanks for staying, son." He gave Ash a long, steady look. "I'm thinking the barn is too far from the house to hear an intruder."

Ash nodded. "You're right. I'll sleep in the house so I can be close enough to hear anything out of the ordinary. 'Night, Vern." Ash shook his hand before walking toward the house.

"'Night, Ash. I'll sleep a whole lot better knowing you're here."

Ash frowned, deep in thought. He was glad one of them would sleep better. As for him, he knew there wouldn't be much time to sleep tonight. He intended to stay awake and alert.

Maybe, if they were lucky, Raleigh Crane would decide to push his luck and try one more time tonight to retrieve whatever it was he hoped to find in the ceiling. And when he did, Ash would be waiting.

CHAPTER EIGHTEEN

As Ash climbed the steps, he could see Brenna through the window. She was standing in the kitchen, hands gripped tightly at her waist, watching the door. The look of fear on her face twisted a knife in his heart.

The minute he stepped inside, she hurried toward him with a smile. That only made the pain worse. He knew at once she was putting on an act to hide her true feelings.

Her voice was a little too cheerful. "You decided not to sleep in the barn?"

"Too far from the house. I need to be here."

"There are two unused bedrooms upstairs. The one in the front has a softer bed. The one in back is warmer."

He shook his head. "I won't need either. I'll be sleeping on the sofa in the living room."

"But..."

He held up his rifle. His eyes had a steely look about them. "This will be beside me. Just in case."

She swallowed. "Okay. Are you hungry?"

"After that meal we had?" He touched a hand to his stomach. "I wouldn't need to eat again for a week, and I'd be fine."

"If you'd like more coffee..."

"Nothing..." He touched a finger to her lips to silence her, and was forced to absorb the quick thrill that shot through his system.

At the same moment he looked down, she looked up at him. Their lips were a whisper apart, sending a cascade of tremors down his spine.

Still holding his rifle, his other hand closed around her shoulder and he drew her up hard against him, until he could feel every part of her inside himself. Her breasts, flattened against his chest. Her thighs brushing his. Her quick intake of breath, and then the way she released it slowly, feathering his cheek.

The image of their kiss flashed through his mind. Just as quickly he struggled to banish any thought of it.

Very deliberately he lowered his hand to his side and took a step back. "You've had a long, exhausting day, Brenna. You need to go up to bed."

"I don't like thinking about you all alone down here. There's an overstuffed chair in a corner of the parlor. I could—"

"No. You can't do another thing." He shook his head firmly. "Go on. Get out of here. Before I do something we'll both regret."

Her eyes widened as his meaning dawned. She turned away, picked up Sammy, and exited the room.

He stood perfectly still, watching as she climbed the stairs. Then he turned out the kitchen light and made his way toward the parlor in the back of the house.

Just knowing he was alone with her changed everything. There was a tension in him that had nothing to do with the danger they were facing. The air around him was charged with it.

He could hear the floorboards creak as she moved around her bedroom, just above him. He closed his eyes, imagining her taking off her boots, her jeans, her shirt. His hand clenched at his side. He wanted, more than anything, to be there with her, undressing her.

He moved woodenly around the room, trying vainly to blot out the thought of her so close. Just a few steps away, and he could have everything he'd ever wanted.

Even the debris still littering the floor and the boarded-up window couldn't serve as distractions. Despite the danger that threatened, despite the threats that had already been made, all he could think about was making love with Brenna.

She was finally alone here with him. After so many years apart. The thought taunted and tempted him.

Hoping to clear his mind, he set aside the rifle and pulled off his shirt, tossing it over the back of a chair. Sitting on the arm of the sofa, he pried off his boots and kicked them angrily against the wall before unsnapping his jeans, all the while calling himself every kind of fool. If he didn't have this damnable code of honor, he could have everything he'd ever wanted. After that kiss they'd shared, he knew it wouldn't take much to persuade her. But though he wanted her, he knew she needed time to sort out all her feelings. And right now, with all that was going on in her life, the last thing she needed was any kind of complication.

He heard a sound, and caught sight of a shadow in the doorway. In one smooth motion he snatched up his rifle and took aim, only to find Brenna standing in the doorway holding an armload of bed linens.

She backed up a step. "Sorry. I thought you'd need a pillow and…"

"Yeah. Thanks." Exhaling a long, slow breath he set aside the rifle before taking the items from her arms and tossing them on the sofa.

He turned back to her. Now that her arms were free he realized she was wearing nothing more than a skimpy pair of boxer shorts and a skintight camisole that revealed more than it covered.

In the moonlight her eyes seemed too wide. Too unblinking. Fear? Nerves? Was it possible that she was as achingly aware of him as he was of her? Or was he just so hungry for her that his mind was playing tricks on him?

"I ought to…"

"I figured I'd…"

Each stopped in midsentence and stared at the other.

He held out his hand, palm up. "You first."

"Well, I see"—she started to turn away—"you were undressing. You need your sleep…I'd better…"

"Brenna." He lay a hand on her arm, then just as quickly withdrew it. "We both know this isn't going to work."

"I don't…" She shook her head. "Are you saying you're not staying?"

"Wild horses couldn't drag me away." His voice lowered. "What isn't going to work is me sleeping down here and having you in my space, unless you don't want me sleeping…alone."

The silence stretched between them for so long, he could feel each anxious stirring of his uneven heartbeat. He knew he'd overstepped his reach. Hadn't she made it perfectly plain that she needed time? After all, she'd just given back an engagement ring. A woman didn't go from loving one man to sleeping with another.

"Sorry…" He turned away. "My mouth got ahead of my brain. Go upstairs now, Brenna. And don't come back down here again tonight. You don't want to be around me when I'm in this mood."

His words were met with stunned silence.

He fisted his hands at his sides, mentally cursing himself.

With no warning he absorbed a shock to his system at the press of a hand on his bare back.

Her voice was hushed. "You're right, Ash. This really won't work."

He stood perfectly still, afraid if he'd move, if he'd even breathe, he'd frighten her away. He would let her say what she'd come here to say, and then he'd let her walk away with her dignity intact.

"I can't allow you to sleep down here…" he heard her take a long, deep breath "…alone."

He froze. He hadn't really heard that. He'd only imagined it because he wanted it so desperately.

"Say something, Ash."

When he held his silence he felt her shift, until her arms slid around his waist. She pressed her face to the naked flesh of his back and whispered against his skin, "Please don't send me away. I couldn't bear it."

A ripple of blazing heat snaked along his spine.

He turned and grasped her by the upper arms, holding her a little away. "Do you know what you're saying?"

She lifted her head, her chin jutted in that way he'd come to recognize, whenever she was ready to dig in her heels. "I've been trying for so long to deny the truth."

"The truth?" His eyes fastened on her, so hot, so furious, she actually flinched.

"The truth I didn't want to face. I wanted to hate you for leaving me without a word all those years ago. I tried. I really tried. But I couldn't then. I still can't. It's you, Ash." Her voice lowered to a whisper. "It's always been you."

He went absolutely still for the space of a heartbeat, digesting what she'd said. And then there were no words as he dragged her into his arms and kissed her until they were both gasping for air.

"Dear God, Brenna." He lingered over her lips. He'd never known a mouth so perfectly formed. A mouth so clever, it was driving him mad. It was a mouth made for kissing. And he did, over and over again. He wasn't so much kissing as devouring.

He'd have gladly gone on feasting on that generous mouth forever, except for the wild rush of need that had him pressing her firmly against the wall while his hands fisted in her hair. He drew her head back and resumed kissing her, pressing moist, hot kisses down her throat to the sensitive hollow between her neck and shoulder.

"Ash."

Just as he worried that he was being too rough, and started to pull back, she whispered his name again.

"Ash. Ash."

Then she wrapped herself around him and began to drive him slowly mad, running hot, wet kisses over his face, while her clever hands moved over him as though she couldn't get enough of him.

Those strong fingers, which could steer a tractor or mold a lump of clay into a thing of beauty, had him sweating. And when she sighed and laid both palms flat against his hair-roughened chest, he had to take a moment to breathe. But when her greedy mouth began nibbling a trail of fire across his chest, he wondered that his heart didn't explode.

"Wait." He nearly shredded her camisole in his haste to strip it aside. For a moment his heart forgot to beat as he studied the sight of her, so perfect.

"Brenna." He bent to her, nibbling one breast, then the other, until he heard her whimper.

"Sorry. I'm trying to go slow." He pressed his forehead to hers, struggling vainly to calm the passion raging inside him. "I'm so damned hungry for you, but I don't want to hurt you."

His quiet whisper had her going still.

And then she smiled. A woman's knowing smile. "You won't hurt me, Ash."

At her words, spoken so simply, he framed her face with his big hands and stared into those incredible blue eyes. "I just want you to be sure."

"I'm not sure of anything but this. I want you, Ash. Only you. Only this. Right now."

A smile curved his lips. Warmed his voice. "And I want you. It's always been you, Sunshine."

She stared into his eyes before wrapping her arms around his neck. "I love it when you call me Sun—"

He stole her words with a kiss that spoke of all the long, lonely days and nights they'd been apart. A kiss so desperate, he could feel himself going up in flames. Burning to ash. And still he kissed her, devoured her, and wanted more. He wanted all she had to give.

His hands moved over her at will now, touching her in all the ways he'd always wanted to, all the ways he'd dreamed of on those long, lonely nights, driving her and himself half mad with need.

She slid his unsnapped jeans over his hips and closed her hand around him, touching him as he was touching her.

He moaned with pure pleasure and pressed her against the wall, while his big, work-worn hands moved over her, making her writhe with need.

Against his mouth she whispered, "The sofa…"

"Too far." He bent his head and began nibbling, suckling until the air between them grew so hot, it filled their lungs and blurred their vision while it pearled their flesh with a sheen of moisture.

In one smooth motion he tore away her boxer shorts and found her hot and wet.

"Wait…" It was all she could manage as he stole her words with a savage kiss and took her on a wild ride to a peak of pleasure that left her dazed.

He loved watching her. He loved the way those trusting eyes widened, before they glazed over as she lost herself in the pure pleasure he offered. When she reached the very edge, her hands gripped him fiercely before going limp.

He gave her no time to recover as he began leading her to the next peak, then the next.

With a frantic burst of energy she ran her hands across his chest, down the flat planes of his stomach, then lower, and was rewarded by his low, guttural moan as she found him and began to pleasure him.

"Now. I can't wait." He'd wanted to move slowly. To touch and taste and savor until he'd had his fill. But now he could feel the need taking over, clawing to be free. It was a tidal wave sweeping over him, bearing down on him, and he was helpless to stop it.

Frantic for release, he lifted her and she wrapped her legs around him. The need, the momentum, had him driving himself inside her with all the force of a raging storm.

On a low moan of pleasure she closed around him, taking him deep.

And then they were moving together. Climbing together.

Outside the boarded-up window, the wind sighed. Night birds called. Cattle lowed.

The two people locked in each other's arms heard nothing except their two hearts beating wildly, and their breathing. Fast. Labored. And their sighs. Low. Frantic.

The world could have come to an end, and neither of them would have noticed. Their world had narrowed to this room, this moment, this intense, driving pleasure.

"Ash."

His name on her lips was the sweetest sound. It was the only thing he heard as he took her with him to the very edge of a high, steep cliff. For a moment they hung suspended. Then, on a shattering climax, they soared through space.

For the longest time they remained locked in a fierce embrace, their bodies fused, their hearts beating wildly.

Brenna was grateful for the cool wall at her back, and those strong arms holding her up. Without Ash's support, she would surely fall, fluid and boneless, to the floor.

"You okay?" He nuzzled her neck.

"Umm."

"Is that a yes?"

She lifted a hand to his cheek and smiled.

"Okay. I'll take that for a yes." Still high on adrenaline, he lifted her in his arms and carried her across the room before depositing her on the sofa.

As he settled in beside her, she snuggled close enough to feel his heartbeat inside her own chest. "Oh, this is nice."

He shot her an incredulous look. "Nice?"

"You don't think it's nice?"

"Sunshine, 'nice' is hot chocolate on a cold night. 'Nice' is flannel sheets after a bone-chilling ride through waist-high snow. But you naked against me...?" He grinned. "It may be a lot of things, but I'd never call it nice."

Her fingers trailed the thick mat of hair on his chest. "Naughty, then."

His warm chuckle rumbled through her system. "Right now, I'm feeling a whole lot naughty. In fact, when you start touching me like this, I'm feeling downright illegal." He caught her wandering hands. "And if you don't stop that, we'll have to go for seconds."

"Oh yeah. Right. This soon?" She studied him through lowered lashes. "Are you joking? Or just bragging?"

His sexy grin widened. He looked like a sleek mountain lion studying its prey. "You know me better than that, woman." He rolled her on top of him until she was straddling him. Then he framed her face with his big hands and tugged her head down until their lips were brushing.

Against her mouth he whispered, "Sunshine, all I have to do is think about you and I'm ready."

"Umm. It's the same for me." She returned his kisses, losing herself in the pleasure.

As their kisses grew more heated, her heart rate speeded up. Her body, already highly sensitized from their lovemaking, moved over him, lighting fires wherever she touched.

She gave a little cat smile. "Okay. Now I know you're as good as your word. But we need to take it slower, Ash. This is all happening so fast."

"Your fault." He shifted positions until she was pinned beneath him. Against her throat he murmured, "You unleashed a very hungry monster. Now you have to feed him."

She was laughing as he entered her.

Suddenly her laughter turned to a sigh of pleasure.

And then there was no need for words. They showed each other, in the way of lovers from the beginning of the world, all the feelings they'd stored up for a lifetime.

CHAPTER NINETEEN

Ash stirred.

Some time in the night he'd added kindling to the logs on the grate and started a fire. Sammy had padded down the stairs and lay curled up on a rug in front of the fireplace.

The fire had burned to embers, casting a warm red glow over the room.

Ash studied Brenna's face as she slept. He loved looking at her. She was so lovely, she took his breath away.

He lifted a hand to trace her lips and heard her sigh in her sleep.

He drew her close and felt her breathing go all soft and easy, as she drifted back to a deeper sleep.

He loved the feel of her body against his. A body he now knew as intimately as his own.

All night they'd loved, then dozed, then loved again. Each time it was new. Sometimes more passionate and powerful than a sudden summer storm. At other times slow and easy, like lovers who'd known each other all their lives. And each time more satisfying than the last.

He experienced a moment of guilt. She worked so hard, and he'd stolen precious hours of much-needed sleep by indulging himself. Not that she'd complained. She'd been an eager partner. What pleasure she brought him. What great joy.

And now, after a night of lovemaking, he knew her in a way he never had before. Had any other woman's body ever fit itself to his so perfectly? Had any other woman ever filled his heart with so much quiet happiness? At the moment, he couldn't recall a single one. There was only Brenna. She was like the missing part to the puzzle of his life. His other half.

He'd foolishly thought that if he fed this hunger for her, he could then resume picking up the pieces of his life and settling into his old routine. But everything had changed. The more of Brenna he experienced, the more he wanted. Not just her body, though he knew now that he'd never have enough. He wanted it all. Her heart. Her soul. He wanted to be the first thing she thought of each morning. The last each night.

"Greedy," he muttered as he slid from the sofa and made his way to the kitchen.

Sammy lifted his head and watched, before falling back into a troubled sleep.

A short time later Ash was back, carrying a tray of coffee mugs and a muffin he'd found in the fridge.

Light from the hallway spilled through the open doorway, bathing the sleeping figure on the sofa.

Brenna sat up and, aware of her nakedness, slipped into his shirt. "Do I smell coffee?"

"You do."

"Oh." She took the mug he offered and sipped before giving a long, deep sigh. "This is wonderful. Thank you."

"No. Thank you." At her arched brow he grinned. "For looking so damned fine in that shirt. Of course, I like the way you look without it, too."

She laughed as she glanced at the tray. "Is that food?"

"A muffin. It's all I could find that looked tempting."

"It's banana walnut. From Rita's."

He broke it in half and settled himself beside her on the sofa.

"Bless Rita." He devoured his half in two bites while she broke off a piece of hers for Sammy, who showed his thanks by licking her hand.

They sat companionably side by side, sipping their coffee.

Brenna was the first to break the silence. "Ira suspects my father, doesn't he?"

Ash nodded.

"And you agree?"

He shrugged. "This isn't your typical break-in. The intruder didn't rifle through your dresser drawers, or any of the other places where folks usually hide valuables. This guy went straight for the ceiling in the corner of the room. That points to someone who knows this house. And that makes your father the obvious suspect."

"I wish there could be some other explanation."

"Why are you reluctant to admit the obvious?"

She sighed. "Because I wanted to believe that he'd turned his life around. Because I promised my mother that

I'd try to forgive him for the things he did to me in the past. I even sent him money. And now, I feel…betrayed. And I feel so foolish for believing that he could actually change."

Ash wrapped an arm around her shoulders and felt her shivering. That only reinforced his feelings of resentment for the man who had made her childhood a living hell and had now returned to add to her pain. "It isn't foolish to want to believe the best about people, even when they fail you. You should be proud of yourself for being able to put the past aside. As for the money you sent him, you can't beat yourself up over it. It's gone, and probably spent on a bottle of whiskey."

"Or a good meal."

"There you go. The eternal optimist." He took the cup from her hand and set it aside along with his own. Then, gathering her close, he dipped his head and brushed his mouth over hers.

Against her lips he whispered, "Did you ever wonder why I've always called you Sunshine?"

"Because I'm so bright?"

He chuckled. "There's that, too. But I called you that because despite all that you've had to go through, you've always been so optimistic. You always see the good of things, instead of the dark side. You're the most honest, decent, genuinely good woman I know."

She flushed and pushed a little away. "I'm not a saint, Ash. Now you've made me feel really guilty."

"Of what?"

She ducked her head. "I have an admission to make."

Ash held his breath, hoping she wasn't about to tell him that she was having second thoughts about what they'd shared.

He tried to prepare himself for the worst, and wondered how his poor heart would ever recover if she pushed him away yet again.

"It's about my... boxer shorts and camisole."

He nodded, trying to follow her line of reasoning. "Very sexy."

She took a deep breath and started speaking as quickly as possible, so she wouldn't lose her nerve. "I... usually sleep in an old ratty dorm shirt. I put on those shorts and that cami because I—" she took in a deep breath "—wanted to seduce you."

He was staring at her with a bemused look. "*You* seduced *me*?"

She looked away. "I'm sorry, Ash. That was sneaky..."

He swallowed back the laughter that threatened before framing her face with his hands. "Why, Ms. Crane. That was *very* sneaky. Who'd have believed this of sweet little Brenna?"

"I know it wasn't fair. It's just that you'd pushed me away. And I just wanted to... to tempt you."

"Oh, you did. Believe me, you tempted me. You had me so hot, I was close to a meltdown." He brushed his mouth over hers before drawing her down against the sofa cushions. Against her throat he muttered, "That was a damned fine seduction. Now it's my turn. Let's see. If I just touch you like that... and then if I... and follow it up by..."

Her laughter turned into a series of soft sighs and low moans as he proceeded to show her his version of a perfect seduction.

* * *

"What's this?" Brenna sat up, tossing back her hair, to see Ash standing in the doorway holding a tray. "More food?"

"We've been burning a lot of calories. It's time to gear up for the next round."

"Wishful thinking, cowboy." Laughing, she nudged a coffee table closer to the sofa.

Ash deposited a tray bearing a plate of eggs and toast and orange marmalade, along with two mugs of steaming coffee.

She touched a hand to her heart. "Now this was worth burning off all those calories. But wouldn't it be easier if we ate in the kitchen?"

"Probably. But this is cozier." He sat beside her and offered her a bite of toast spread with orange marmalade.

"Umm. I've never been fed before. I think I like it."

"You've spent a lifetime taking care of everything and everybody. Now it's time you were taken care of."

"And you've assigned yourself the task?"

He brushed a kiss over her mouth and tasted the sweet orange flavor that clung to her lips. "A tough job. But somebody's got to do it."

They shared bites of egg and toast until they'd had enough. Then they sat back, sipping strong, hot coffee, and watching Sammy nibble a treat.

As dawn began to paint the horizon with ribbons of pink and mauve and purple, they shared all the things that had happened to them in the years they'd been apart.

"Why didn't you contact your family and let them know where you were?"

Ash frowned. "In the beginning, I was just angry and hurt. Sick and tired of being my father's whipping boy.

And suffering a lot of growing pains, I guess. I figured I'd show my father I could be just as tough as he was." He huffed a breath. "Then reality set in, and I found out how little I knew about the real world. I took every odd job I could find, and still there were nights I didn't know where I'd sleep, or whether I'd earn enough to eat the next day. I shoveled manure on ranches, pumped gas, cooked in a diner. It took me longer to grow up than some, but gradually I began to figure out what I wanted to do with the rest of my life. And it turned out to be exactly what I'd been doing since I was born. Wonder of wonders, I wanted to be a rancher."

"After all these years." She closed a hand over his. "Are you sorry it took you so long?"

He mulled her question before shaking his head. "I think if I'd stayed here and toughed it out, it wouldn't mean as much to me today. Now that I know how much blood, sweat, and tears went into taming this land and making it a success, I won't ever take my inheritance for granted."

His voice lowered with passion. "Don't get me wrong. There are regrets. Plenty of them. I never got to say good-bye to my father. And I know how much my absence hurt my mother." He turned to her, his eyes reflecting his sadness. "And I wasn't here for you when you needed me."

"Ash..."

He touched a finger to her lips. "Don't worry. I'm not going to dwell on the 'could've, should've, would've' litany. I'll learn to live with my regrets and move on with my life. As for you, it can't have been easy managing this ranch alone all these years."

Ash linked his fingers with Brenna's. They sat with an afghan across their laps, Sammy dozing at their feet, as they finished the last of the coffee.

Brenna smiled. "My mom used to say that nothing worth doing is easy. And I haven't been alone. I couldn't have done this without Vern."

"Yeah. That old cowboy is worth his weight in gold. He could really use some help."

"I'm glad he was able to find Noah Perkins."

"Where'd he find him?"

Brenna shrugged. "Noah knocked on the door of his trailer and asked if he knew of anyone looking for an extra ranch hand. Vern brought him to the house and I hired him on the spot. From the sounds of things, Noah's not very reliable. Vern found him asleep up in the hills when he was supposed to be tending the herd. But like Vern said, if Noah gets us through the calving season, that's good enough. Then maybe we'll earn enough when we sell off some of the herd to hire a real crew."

"I'm hoping Brady can spare a couple of our wranglers. That ought to ease Vern's burden..."

The ringing of his cell phone had Ash snatching it from the end table. "Yeah, Vern. What's up?"

He listened, then swore. He was on his feet and reaching for his clothes before the old man was even finished speaking.

Brenna shot him a look of alarm. "What's happened?"

"Range fire. Looks like it started up in the hills and is headed right for your herd." He tossed her his phone. "Call Brady. Tell him what's happened, and warn him to keep an eye out in case the fire jumps the creek and heads for our land."

She did as he asked. By the time she'd hung up, Ash was heading for the door.

She grabbed up her clothes before rushing across the room to hand him his phone. "I'll join you as soon as I'm dressed."

"Suit yourself. You might want to stay here and keep an eye on the fire from the hayloft. If it looks like it's heading this way, get out the hoses and start soaking the house and barns."

Her eyes widened. "You think it could get this far?"

"There are a lot of ifs with a range fire. If there's enough dry brush to feed it. If the wind shifts. If we don't catch a break, we could be in for a tough battle."

"I'll dress and join you before deciding. Stay safe, Ash."

"You do the same. And be sure you lock up Sammy in the house." He drew her close for a hard, hurried kiss.

He strode out the door and raced toward his truck without a backward glance.

CHAPTER TWENTY

Ash's four-wheel-drive truck moved slowly along a rutted trail that cut across the high meadow. Already a pall of thick black smoke was forming above the nearest hill. As he drew closer to the center of the smoke he caught up with Vern on horseback. When he glanced in his rearview mirror, he caught sight of Brenna and her horse galloping up behind him.

He came to a halt and lowered his window. "You made good time."

"It's easy when your range is burning." She turned to Vern. "Any sign of the herd?"

He shook his head. "I figure they're still safe if they're in high country."

Ash pointed. "You two lead the way and I'll follow."

"Our range shack is up there." Brenna pointed to a cluster of trees at the top of the hill.

As she and Vern urged their mounts into a run, Ash put the truck in gear before trailing behind.

When they came up over the ridge they paused to take in the sight of a smoldering heap of ash where the shack had once stood. The clearing around it was devoid of vegetation. It was now a charred ruin.

Ash stepped out of his truck and walked around the smoking rubble. "Not much left. Did you have anything valuable?"

Brenna nodded. "Just the supplies necessary to survive up here. A couple of bunks and sleeping bags. A generator to run a heater, stove, refrigerator, coffeemaker. Enough nonperishables to last through winter. Extra parkas, boots, and gloves in case of sudden snowstorms."

Ash turned to peer into the distance, where he could see the herd milling about, far ahead of the flames that were burning through the brush.

"Okay. There's the herd. Do you see a horse and rider? Where's Noah Perkins?"

Vern looked around in frustration. "If that lazy drifter's run off, I'll have his hide."

Ash looked equally furious. "You won't need to. If I find him first, I'll do it for you."

Just then they saw a figure emerge from the stand of trees.

The man, hair shaggy, face bearded from his days spent alone in the hills, was moving slowly, using a sturdy tree limb as a cane.

Vern's tone was stern. "What's happened to you? I thought you'd be with the herd."

"Can't. I'm hurting too much." As Noah drew closer, they became aware of his injuries.

There were cuts on his face, leaving his beard matted with blood. His sleeves and the legs of his denims were streaked with more blood.

"Looks like you tangled with a wildcat," Vern muttered.

"The cabin." Noah dropped into the grass, looking exhausted. "I woke and found it in flames. Had to jump out a window."

"What was wrong with the door?" Vern looked skeptical.

"It was a wall of flames."

Vern looked around at the smoldering embers. "How'd the fire get started?"

Noah shot him a look of irritation. "How should I know? I told you I was sleeping."

Vern moved in for a closer inspection. "Looks like you're cut bad."

"Yeah." The bloodied man turned to Brenna. "Sorry, boss lady." He nodded toward Ash. "Who's this?"

"Ash MacKenzie. His ranch is over there." Brenna pointed to the lush fields to their south.

Now that she'd had time to note the extent of Noah's injuries up close, Brenna made a decision. "You need more medical care than I can give from a medical kit. You need to see a doctor."

"I agree." Ash nodded. "Take him to town in my truck and leave your horse here."

"But the fire—"

"—will eventually burn itself out. It's not looking nearly as bad as I'd feared. If it started here, it's being fed by wind and dry brush. But now that the wind has shifted, it's heading toward Copper Creek, which will act as a natural fire break."

"And my herd?"

"Looks like they're already at the creek. Vern and I can take them across, if it looks as though the fire might not be contained."

She took a breath. "All right. As long as you don't need me."

"Noah needs you more."

Ash turned to the man half-sitting, half-lying on the ground. "Need some help getting to the truck?"

Noah shook his head and pushed himself up with the aid of his makeshift cane, limping slowly behind Brenna. Once in the passenger's side of the truck, his head dropped back and his eyes closed.

Brenna started the truck and turned it around before heading down the trail.

Ash watched their descent before taking the reins of Brenna's horse and pulling himself into the saddle.

He turned to Vern. "Let's get moving. We've got a lot of ground to cover."

Brenna maneuvered Ash's truck along the rutted trail. With each bump and dip she glanced over toward the man who remained perfectly still, eyes closed, saying not a word. She was grateful that he wasn't moaning in agony, but his stoic silence weighed heavily on her. He was in this situation, after all, because he'd been working on her behalf.

Her tender heart went out to him.

As she rounded the barns and drove closer to the house she slowed her speed. "Can I get you anything to ease your pain before we head into town to the clinic?"

"Some water would be great."

"All right." She parked beside the porch and stepped out. "I'll just be a minute."

She returned a short time later carrying a tall plastic glass of ice water in one hand, and cuddling Sammy to her chest. She handed Noah the water through the open passenger's-side window before walking around to the driver's side.

Before she could step inside Sammy was yapping wildly and wriggling about so frantically, she nearly dropped him.

"Sammy. Stop that." She opened the truck door and set the yapping pup on the seat, but he jumped out and began circling the truck while continuing to bark.

She glanced apologetically at Noah, who watched without emotion. "Sorry. I was hoping to take him with us. He usually loves riding in my truck. Maybe it's the fact that Ash's truck isn't familiar. I guess I'll have to leave him here."

She picked up the puppy and returned him to the kitchen before firmly closing the door.

When she returned to the truck, Noah sat slumped in the seat, head back, eyes closed.

Worried about the extent of his injuries, and suffering a wave of guilt, she drove the entire distance to town without a word.

Once there she parked outside the medical clinic. "Do you need help going inside?" He nodded, and she hurried around to help him exit the truck.

In the clinic, they were greeted by Dr. Mullin's assistant, Kate. After hearing a brief explanation of their visit, Kate said to Brenna, "If you'll wait here, I'll take Noah to an examining room." She held out a handful of documents to Noah and said to him, "I'll need you to fill these out before the doctor sees you."

A short time later Dr. Dan Mullin stepped into the waiting room to speak with Brenna. "Your wrangler's got a lot of cuts. A couple of them are deep. I removed whatever glass I could find embedded in his cuts, and I stitched him up where he needed it. I applied disinfectant and he's currently getting an IV antibiotic. I think he ought to stay for at least twenty-four hours so I can observe those wounds that are problematic, just to make certain he doesn't get an infection. I'll call you when I'm ready to release him."

"Thanks, Doc."

He lowered his voice. "Noah said there was a fire up in the hills."

"My range shack. I'm just glad he was able to get out in time."

"Yeah. That's what he told me. I wanted to test his lungs, to be certain he hadn't inhaled too much smoke. But he said no."

"Did he give a reason?"

The doctor shrugged. "He says he has no insurance, and since he's working for you, you'd just have to pay for another test he doesn't feel he needs."

She sighed. "That's very thoughtful of him, but if you think he needs anything, see that he gets it, Doc. I'll wait for your call."

Under his shaggy bangs, the doctor's eyes were hawk sharp. "I see by Noah's forms that you don't carry any insurance on your ranch hands, Brenna."

She flushed. "Don't worry, Doc. I'll pay you tomorrow."

"I'm not worried about getting paid. I'm concerned for you."

"There's no need. I keep enough money for emergencies." She offered her hand. "Thanks for everything, Doc."

"Yeah." He seemed about to say more, but Kate was already beckoning him toward a second examining room where a mother and her infant were waiting.

He turned away, leaving Brenna alone in the waiting room.

On the drive home, she thought about the debts that kept piling up. A barn door. A range shack. And now Noah's medical bill.

She hadn't been exactly honest with the doctor. Though she kept an emergency fund, it wasn't nearly enough to cover all the emergencies that had cropped up this year.

That had her thinking about Chris, and his scornful attitude about ranching in general and her ranch in particular. He'd made a passionate case for walking away from a lifestyle choice that demanded so much and promised so little. He'd called it a crapshoot that seduced ranchers into thinking they were living a life of freedom when they were really putting everything on the line against thievery, the tax man, and the whims of nature.

Annoyed at the direction of her thoughts, she switched on the radio in time to hear Willie warning mamas about letting their babies grow up to be cowboys. But while she tapped a hand on the wheel in time to the music, the nagging little fear remained. With every day that passed, she seemed one step closer to losing everything she'd spent a lifetime struggling to hold on to.

* * *

The sight that greeted Brenna back at her ranch lifted her spirits considerably.

Several trucks bearing the logo of the MacKenzie Ranch were parked in her yard. Down at the barn, a handful of wranglers were picking through the remains of her shattered barn door, setting aside any boards that could be reused, while tossing the badly damaged pieces into the back of a truck.

Her once-upended tractor was now sitting in the yard, looking no worse for having been hit by a truck and toppled. As she stepped out of her truck she could hear the tractor engine chugging smoothly. The sound of it brought a smile to her face.

What brought an even bigger smile was seeing Ash and Vern standing to one side, talking with Griff and Whit. At their feet was Sammy, happily chewing on a stick. When the pup spotted her, it ran up and was scooped into her arms. The men looked over as she drew near.

"My herd?" She waited, hoping for good news, but bracing for something else.

Ash touched a hand to her arm. "I had my wranglers take them across the creek. I thought with only you and Vern able to work, we ought to keep them on MacKenzie land for now, where my crew can keep an eye on them. If that's all right with you."

She felt herself breathing easier. "It's the perfect solution, until we know when Noah will be able to work again. Thanks, Ash."

"How is Noah?" Vern asked.

"Doc said he stitched some of the deeper cuts, and

has him on an intravenous antibiotic as a precaution. He wants to observe him for twenty-four hours or so. The clinic will call when they're ready to discharge him."

"That's good news, girl." Vern nodded toward the tractor. "More good news. Look at that. Good as new."

"Yeah." Just seeing the old cowboy's smile had her spirits lifting considerably.

Ash turned to Griff. "Now that we've got our woodworking expert here, let's get to work. We have a barn door to build."

With Griff directing them, they began putting the boards together into some semblance of order. Whit drove a truck loaded with new lumber to a spot beside the barn, where the wranglers began hauling more boards until they had enough laid out to construct a huge barn door.

"Okay, boss man," Ash called to Griff. "We know how to do the grunt work, but the finishing touches will be all yours."

Griff strapped on his tool belt and began calling orders as he and the men bent to their task.

"What can I do?" Brenna asked.

"How about a pot of coffee for openers?" Ash called.

"I can handle that." She set Sammy on the ground and hurried off toward the house.

As the coffee perked, she filled a tray with mugs, cream, and sugar, and rummaged through her refrigerator, wishing she'd stopped at the store in town. What she wouldn't give for some man-sized food for all these workers.

When the coffee was ready she nudged the door open and carried the tray to the barn. The minute she set it down, the men gathered around, filling mugs and sighing with pleasure.

"Caffeine." Whit closed his eyes. "Now this is all the fuel I need to keep going."

"Yeah," Ash said in an aside. "That and a half-dozen roast beef sandwiches."

"The more I see of him, the more I realize that would be just an appetizer," Griff muttered.

Whit joined in their laughter. "I do like to eat. So as long as we're talking about food, I figure I could eat a couple of bowls of Wylie's extra-hot chili, followed by some juicy burgers smothered in grilled onions, and washed down by a few ice-cold beers."

"Why settle for a few?" Griff winked at Brenna. "Why not go for a whole case?"

"And a couple of hot barmaids to serve you," one of the wranglers called, causing everyone to nod in agreement and add their own comments.

"Sorry, guys," he said with a laugh. "You know it's my curse. I've had to learn to live with the fact that women just can't resist me."

As the men returned to their work, they were still moaning and teasing Whit about his famous, numerous appetites.

CHAPTER TWENTY-ONE

Though it was early spring, the sun burned so brightly, the men were soon removing their shirts and tossing them over low-hanging bushes beside the barn.

Brenna watched Ash as he and Whit followed Griff's directions, fitting each board into place before nailing it securely.

The muscles of Ash's back rippled with each movement, and she felt her throat going dry at the sight of him.

She knew that body. Knew how strong he had become. Strong, yet tender. He'd been such an attentive lover. The thought had her smiling as she turned away to see Vern watching her.

"Can I get you some water, Vern?"

He merely grinned. "You might want some for yourself, girl. You're looking a mite warm."

She flushed and turned away, aware that there were no secrets between them. Somehow he knew, just by looking at her, that she and Ash had progressed from friends and neighbors to something more.

Something more.

But just what were they now? She wasn't yet ready to probe the topic too deeply. She was in over her head, and willing to drown, just to be with him for however long he chose to be with her. And wasn't that a road leading straight to heartache?

A short time later, while Brenna busied herself mucking stalls, Whit hooked up a hose and turned it on himself to cool off. Once he'd cooled down he couldn't resist turning the hose on his brother.

"Hey." Ash gave a yelp of surprise when the first frigid spray hit him.

He turned and, seeing that Whit was cranking up the faucet to a full stream, made a mad dash across the distance that separated them, hoping to snatch the hose away.

Whit saw him coming and turned the spray nozzle until it was streaming water like a fire hose. Despite the fact that he was walking headlong into freezing water, Ash kept on coming until the two brothers were wrestling for control of the hose.

The rest of the wranglers forgot about their work as they circled around, cheering on the two brothers and howling with laughter.

Water sprayed everywhere as Ash took Whit down and struggled to get the hose. Whit fought back, and the two rolled around and around in the grass, all the while sending water over everyone nearby.

"Children. Children." Griff cupped his hands to his mouth in a valiant effort to end this before it turned into an all-out MacKenzie brawl. "Recess is over. Time to get back to work."

Ash and Whit didn't hear a word he was saying. They were too busy fighting for control. By now fists were flying, and the air was turning blue from their muttered oaths as they matched blow for blow.

Whit threw a punch and the hose slipped from his hand. He barely noticed as Ash's fist connected with his jaw.

While the two continued pummeling one another, Brenna saw her chance to intervene. Putting aside her pitchfork, she sneaked up behind them and grabbed hold of the hose. When she turned it on the two of them, the stinging cold spray had them forgetting all about the fight.

Now they saw only one thing. A common foe. A meddling female.

Ash turned to Whit. "Does she really think she can get away with that?"

Whit was grinning like a conspirator. "I'm with you, bro. The traitor must pay."

The two of them started advancing toward her.

"Oh, no you don't." At first, she managed to hold them at bay with a steady stream of water.

Wise to her strategy, they separated, each one coming at her from a different side.

Now, while she was busy spraying Ash, Whit moved in. When she turned to spray Whit, Ash crept in behind her, wrapping his arms around her before lifting her off her feet.

"You're not playing fair," she cried. "There are two of you and only one of me."

"You should have thought of that before you jumped in

the game, Sunshine." Ash yanked the hose from her hands and tossed it to Whit, who turned to the two of them with a grin.

"Thanks, bro. Now I'll take you both down."

"Hey."

That was all Ash managed before Whit turned the full spray of the hose on both him and Brenna until they were thoroughly drenched.

Ash pushed her behind him before turning to Whit. "Now you pay, little bro."

The two wrestled again until the wet grass had them slipping and sliding.

Brenna tried to step in and ended up falling, with Ash and Whit landing on their backsides next to her.

By the time Griff managed to turn off the spigot, the entire yard was a puddle, and the three lay in a heap of arms and legs, laughing so hard they were wiping tears from their eyes.

Whit leaned up on one elbow. "Pretty sneaky of you, Bren. I guess since you couldn't take your shirt off like the rest of us, this was the only way for you to cool down."

She was laughing so hard she could barely get the words out. "Gee, Whit. Thanks for taking care of that for me. I'm cool enough now."

"Anytime. That's what friends are for."

Ash got to his feet and offered a hand up to Brenna, then helped Whit to his feet.

"I guess we're all cooled off enough to get back to work," Whit muttered as he strolled away.

Brenna turned. "And I guess it's time for me to go inside and change."

"Don't change on my account." Ash studied the way her shirt clung to every curve of her body. "I like you just the way you are. But if you'd like my help getting out of those wet things…"

"In your dreams, MacKenzie." As she walked away, he stood where he was, watching the way her soaked denims molded to her backside like a second skin.

"Yep. That's some dream." He turned away with a smile of pure male appreciation, only to see everyone watching and grinning like conspirators.

"Get back to work," he said gruffly.

"Yeah. Right." Whit winked at Griff, and the two of them shared a moment of secret laughter before turning back to the job at hand.

Brenna looked up at the sound of trucks arriving. Willow was at the wheel of the first, with Mad seated beside her. Ash and Whit set aside their hammers and hurried over to assist their grandfather from the truck and into his wheelchair, which was stowed in the back.

Myrna drove up in a second truck. Stored in the back were more than a dozen covered aluminum steam trays.

Both Myrna and Mad were issuing orders like drill sergeants as they directed that a plank be set up on sawhorses beneath the shade of a huge aspen. This would serve as a perfect buffet table.

Brenna hurried over to lend a hand as they began setting out a feast that would put a church potluck to shame.

There were trays of baked ham and fried chicken, as well as thick slices of rare roast beef swimming in gravy. There were baskets of dinner rolls warm from the oven. There were steaming casserole dishes filled with scal-

THE MAVERICK OF COPPER CREEK   261

loped potatoes, others with garden peas and green beans. There were cold dishes of potato salad, tossed salad, and a layered salad of red beans, salsa, chips, and sour cream.

A tub of ice was filled with soda, beer, and bottled water.

And then there were the home-baked desserts. A chocolate layer cake. A giant carrot cake. Brownies. And a banana cream pie topped with real whipped cream.

Whit looked at the makeshift table groaning under all that food and turned to Myrna with a wink. "Okay. I see what you made. But where's the stuff Mad was supposed to cook?"

That had everyone howling with laughter. All except Mad, who felt the need to defend himself.

"As a matter of fact, most of this is my handiwork, lad. I only allowed Myrna to slice the ham."

She shot him a look. "I'll have you know the potato dishes are all mine. And the brownies and chocolate cake."

Ash nudged his brother, hoping to get a rise out of their housekeeper. "You're lucky Mad even allowed you in his kitchen."

"*His* kitchen?" Myrna's hands were at her ample hips, her eyes flashing fire. "It was my kitchen long before it became Mad MacKenzie's, I'll have you know."

"What I know is—" Ash put his arm around her shoulders and kissed her cheek "—we're all grateful for the two of you. And speaking for Vern, I'd say he's the happiest of all, since he gets a day off from having to eat Brenna's cooking."

That brought another round of laughter before Vern felt compelled to defend Brenna. "Now, Ash, she may not be the best cook in the world, but she's managed to keep me here for a number of years, and I haven't died from starvation yet."

"Yet." To soften his teasing, Ash wrapped an arm around Brenna's waist and drew her close to press a kiss to the top of her head.

Seeing it, Willow and Mad exchanged looks before the old man called, "These men have put in a long morning. Let's stop all the chatter and eat."

The others didn't need to be coaxed. They began circling the table and heaping their plates before finding shady spots in the grass to sit.

Their voices grew muted while they enjoyed the feast.

Most of them went back to load their plates a second and third time, until they'd eaten their fill.

While they were eating, Brady Storm and a group of wranglers rode up on horseback to report that there was no trace of fire in the meadow, and all of Brenna's cattle had been accounted for and were now grazing contentedly on MacKenzie land.

"Thanks, Brady." Brenna shook his hand. "I'm so grateful for everybody's help."

"That's what neighbors are for," Willow said as she came up beside them.

"But this is above and beyond." Brenna waved a hand to include the food, and the happy wranglers. "I know your crew is neglecting work at your ranch while they help out here."

"They'll make it up tomorrow." Brady smiled at her, showing white, even teeth in his deeply tanned face. "And believe me, I'll see to it."

"I'm sure you will." She returned his smile. "Now,

please eat. And you don't have to worry, I didn't cook any of it."

Everyone shared a laugh at her self-deprecating humor.

"Thanks." Brady removed his wide-brimmed hat and shook it against his leg, sending up a cloud of trail dust. He glanced at his wranglers, who were already lining up to eat. "Don't mind if I do."

As he strolled away and began filling a plate, Brenna turned to Willow. "You're lucky to have a foreman like Brady."

Willow nodded before adding, "And you're equally lucky to have Vern Wheeler with you all these years. Bear used to say Vern was the kind of man he'd like to have watching his back."

"I agree. He's the best."

When Willow walked away to speak with Mad, Brenna dropped down in the grass between Ash, Griff, and Whit, and leaned back, sipping from a bottle of water. "Your family's a lifesaver in so many ways. Not only taking in my herd, and lending me the use of their wranglers, but all this." She spread her hands to indicate the food. "I was thinking about driving all the way to town to buy enough chili at Wylie's to feed everyone, and then they did this." She shook her head from side to side. "I don't know how I could ever repay them."

Whit shared a smile with Ash and Griff. "If you try, they'll be insulted. You heard Ma. That's what neighbors do for neighbors in need. Next time, it may be one of us, and we know you'll be there, doing what you can." He got to his feet. "Time to get back to that door. Griff says we'll have it finished and installed before dark." He glanced at Griff. "You still think we'll make that deadline, Griff?"

"You bet. Come on. I'll join you."

As the two strolled away, Brenna turned to Ash. "Your family's amazing."

"Yeah." He looked around with a satisfied smile. "They are." He leaned close to press a kiss to her cheek before getting to his feet. "And I've got you to thank for reminding me."

When he joined the others, Brenna remained seated, looking around at the beehive of activity.

An hour later, Mad and Myrna, along with Willow and Brenna, began packing up the leftovers and storing them in containers. Brenna carried an armload toward one of the trucks.

Willow stopped her. "That's going in your fridge."

Brenna shook her head. "Willow, there's enough here to feed an army."

Mad winked at his daughter-in-law before saying to Brenna, "I'm thinking there's just enough there to feed Vern and Ash for another day or so. The way those two eat, you'll soon have to think about cooking again."

With a laugh Myrna led the way to the house, where they stowed the food in Brenna's nearly empty refrigerator

When they were done, Brenna shook her head. "That's the most food this place has ever seen at one time!"

She trailed them outside, where Mad patiently waited at the foot of the steps.

Without a word she began pushing his wheelchair toward the truck, where Ash and Whit were waiting to lift him up to the passenger's side.

"Thanks again for all you did." Brenna leaned in the open window to press a kiss to Willow's cheek.

"You're more than welcome." Willow squeezed her hand. "I'm so glad we could help."

Ash and Whit ambled away to join the workers.

Brenna stepped back and waved as the trucks began rolling out, with Willow and Mad in the first, and Myrna following in the second truck.

She recalled that when she was a girl, the MacKenzies had always been the family she'd wished she had. Whenever her father got drunk and mean, she would close her eyes and pretend that she was in a room somewhere in the MacKenzie house, warm, fed, and feeling safe.

Wasn't that exactly what they'd done for her today? They'd taken charge of the fire, her herd, and her ranch. And they'd done it all with such good humor, they'd made it feel like just another day on the range.

And that was exactly what she'd always most loved about them. From the first time she'd met them, they'd welcomed her into their home and hearts, and made her feel that it was the most natural thing in the world to make her a part of their wonderful family.

It was why she loved them so.

It was why, the minute Ash returned to Copper Creek, she'd begun to think she'd made a terrible mistake in accepting Chris's proposal of marriage. How could she give her heart to one man, when she'd already lost it completely to the entire MacKenzie family all those years ago?

CHAPTER TWENTY-TWO

With a satisfying meal under their belts, the crew returned to their task with renewed energy.

Once the planks were joined, Griff handled the intricacies of mounting the hardware to both the barn and the doors so that the two sides would open smoothly on a well-oiled track.

While he worked on the finishing touches, he sent the crew scrambling over the interior and exterior of the barn and outbuildings, looking for needed repairs. The missing rungs of the ladder leading to the hayloft were repaired, as were the chinks in the walls that needed to be filled. The tools hanging along the wall were examined and repaired, and harnesses were mended.

The tractor, which had been tested and found to be in good working order, was now parked in one corner of the barn.

By the time Brenna had finished mucking the last stall,

the doors were ready to be hung. She stood back, watching as the crew strained under the task of lifting each enormous door onto the track. She held her breath while Griff tested them, not once, but twice, before giving his nod of approval.

Now her barn boasted a pair of doors that slid open on tracks, and could be pulled closed by the simple tug of a handle.

Griff pointed to the large brace hanging from a leather strap. "Throw this brace whenever you see a storm brewing. It's just a good backup to use to secure the doors in rough weather. And then, there's this." He handed her a padlock and key.

Brenna was beaming. "This is just beautiful. Thank you, Griff." She gave him a warm hug before turning to the crew. "My thanks to all of you." She caught Vern's hand and pointed to the interior of the barn. "And just look at all the other things they managed to do today. New rungs on the ladder. Handles on some of the tools. The tractor up and running like new."

The old man was grinning from ear to ear before shaking Griff's hand. "We're beholden to you, son." He turned to include everyone. "We're beholden to all of you. This has been one fine day."

The men were smiling and slapping each other on the back as they picked up their tools and loaded them into the back of MacKenzie trucks.

Whit tousled Ash's hair. "How about you, bro? You coming home with us, or are you still watching out for the big bad wolf?" Though his words were spoken with a grin, both men understood the seriousness of Brenna's situation.

Ash smacked his shoulder. "I think I'll just hang here and watch for villains."

"My money's on you, bro." Whit punched his arm before climbing into a truck.

Ash turned to Griff. "That's some fine workmanship."

"Thanks." Griff cast a final glance at the barn door before turning toward the truck.

"And Griff?"

At Ash's words he paused. "Yeah?"

"Thanks, bro."

For a moment Griff was speechless. Just as quickly he recovered and managed a grin. "You're welcome, bro."

As he settled into the truck beside Whit, he opened the window and leaned an arm out.

They started along the gravel drive, and Whit cast a sideways glance at the man in the passenger seat.

Maybe he was making more of this than he should, but he figured they'd built more than a barn door today.

This wasn't just about being related by blood. That had been an accident of birth. Today they'd built something much better. They'd built a bond. A tenuous one, but a bond all the same. And maybe, just maybe, he didn't resent this man as much as he'd expected to.

In fact, right now he really liked Griff Warren. If not as a brother, at least as a friend. And it would appear that the same could be said for Ash. There'd been genuine warmth in his tone when he'd called Griff Warren "bro."

Brenna stripped off her grubby work clothes and stepped into the shower. As she worked shampoo into her hair, she felt strong hands grip her shoulders.

"Ash." She barely managed to speak his name before

he stepped under the spray and his mouth began trailing delicious kisses across the back of her neck.

Against her ear he whispered, "I've been thinking about this for most of the day. Just this. It's what kept me working in the hot sun."

She turned and wrapped her arms around his neck, feeling the warm spray play over her upturned face. "And here I thought you were just a workaholic."

"I think I'm turning into a loveaholic." He ran nibbling kisses over her face while his hands moved slowly up from her hips to cup her breasts. "And right now, I'm hoping to satisfy this terrible craving."

She arched her neck to give him easier access. "How terrible is that craving?"

He shot her a sexy grin. "So powerful, I think I tore my shirt to shreds while I took the stairs two at a time."

"In a hurry, cowboy?"

"I was." He dipped his head to take what she offered. "But now, I think I'll just take my sweet time."

He kissed her long and slow and deep before dropping to his knees and driving her slowly mad.

Ash knocked on the door of Vern's trailer.

The old man's clothes were freshly laundered, and his hair was still damp from his shower when he opened the door. "Hey, Ash. Come on in."

Ash stepped inside. Though the trailer was old, it was as neat as a pin. The bed in one corner, which also served as a sofa, was covered in a plaid quilt, with pillows at the head of the bed, and a reading light attached to the wall overhead. On a bedside table was a stack of books. On top was a dog-eared copy of the Bible.

The tiny galley kitchen boasted a small table and a chair covered in bright red, yellow, and lime-green stripes. At the window was a crisp white curtain with a valance of colorful fruit: cherries, bananas, lemons, and limes.

Ash couldn't help smiling. "This place has a good feeling about it."

Vern nodded. "That good feeling is home, son." As he looked around, a softness touched all his features. "I've spent a lifetime wandering. I guess I've worked every ranch from Casper to Calgary. I never had any desire to put down roots. But since being here with Brenna, I've come to appreciate having a place to call my own. There's something to be said for home."

"Yeah." Ash cleared the lump from his throat. "Brenna wants you to come over for supper now."

"Are you kidding? After that lunch we had today?"

Ash chuckled. "That was hours ago. Besides, Ma and Myrna put all the leftovers in Brenna's fridge. So we're having another feast." He held the door. "Come on, Vern. You know you've worked up an appetite for more."

The old cowboy winked. "I may be old, but I'm not addled. I've never been known to turn down some of Myrna Hill's fine cooking, son."

They crossed the distance from the trailer to the house, where Brenna turned from the sink.

The table was as festive as any party, with the leftovers arranged on pretty platters and trays.

Vern's face creased into a wide smile. "Looks like somebody's celebrating."

Brenna blushed. "It didn't seem right to set all this out

in those aluminum pans. Mad and Myrna went to so much trouble cooking and baking, I wanted to do them justice."

"And you did." Ash held her chair. "Now Vern and I will just have to do our part."

The two men exchanged grins as they helped themselves to heaping portions of everything.

While they ate a leisurely meal, they replayed the events of the day.

"How about Griff?" Ash tucked into the steaming scalloped potatoes. "That was some of the finest woodworking I've seen around here."

Vern nodded in agreement. "He knows what he's doing, that's for sure."

Brenna was beaming. "It's a much better door than I had before."

"And why not?" Ash winked at her. "That barn was probably new when your father bought this place thirty or more years ago."

Brenna shook her head. "My dad never bought the ranch. I think it belonged to his father or grandfather."

"So, the barn could be a hundred years old?"

She shrugged. "I guess it could be." She turned to Vern. "Do you know anything about the history of this place?"

He paused to butter a roll. "Can't say as I do. But I guess you could find out from the county offices. They keep track of such things. Speaking of the county offices... Chief Pettigrew called me. He heard about the range fire from Doc Mullin, and wanted to know why we never told him about hiring a drifter. I told him I just never thought about it, but he wanted details, so I gave him Noah's name and vitals, like his Social Security number and his sketchy work record. Sounded to me like the chief intends to check him out."

"Good." Brenna passed around another platter.

The talk moved on to the repairs of the ladder, the tools, the tractor. By the time they'd run through the litany of good things that had happened over the course of a single day, they'd managed to make a huge dent in the leftovers.

Ash turned to Vern with a smile. "And you didn't think you could eat again, after that feast at lunch."

The old man patted his stomach. "Like I said, it's hard to resist Myrna's cooking."

Brenna pointed to the array of desserts on a sideboard. "Did you leave room for a slice of her banana cream pie?"

The old cowboy shook his head. "Not right now. But I wouldn't mind taking some back to my trailer for a snack later tonight."

Brenna cut a generous slice and set it on a plate before covering it with plastic wrap. "How about some coffee to go with it?"

He shook his head. "I might have a beer first. And then, when I'm finished reading for the night, I'll have this with a glass of milk."

He turned to include Ash. "This has been one fine day. And this just guarantees it'll be one fine night."

As Vern let himself out, Ash poured coffee into a carafe. "Let's take this in the parlor."

"All right. How about dessert to go with it? Pie or brownies?"

"Save the pie for Vern. I'll always choose chocolate over anything."

"Brownies then." She placed several squares on a plate

and followed him to the other room, with Sammy trailing behind.

As soon as Ash got a fire started on the hearth, the puppy curled up in front of it on his favorite rag rug and was soon dozing contentedly.

Ash settled himself beside Brenna and drew her close to nuzzle her lips. "Vern was right. I'd say this guarantees it'll be one fine night."

"You mean with coffee, brownies, and a cozy fire?"

"Sunshine, none of those things matter. This is what matters to me." He drew her into the circle of his arms and poured himself into the kiss.

His tenderness was her undoing. It was so easy to lose herself in exquisite pleasure as he showered her with long, deep kisses that had fireworks exploding behind her closed lids. His touches sent slivers of fire and ice coursing along her spine.

When she tried to touch him as he was touching her, he pressed her down among the cushions. Against her mouth he whispered, "Not tonight. Right now I want to go slow and easy, and take the time to taste and touch and savor. I want to just be with you. Now."

She was helpless to do more than sigh and cling to him as he moved over her, tasting to his heart's content. Touching her at will, and watching as her eyes glazed over with passion, and her world narrowed to him. Only him.

She felt like the most pampered woman alive.

So alive. With each touch, each kiss, her heartbeat quickened, and her blood warmed and flowed through her veins like molten lava, while her breath hitched in her throat. A throat clogged with wants and needs. And all of them focused on him.

Instead of rushing, as she'd anticipated, he treated her to a long, slow journey of love.

The work of the day was forgotten, as were her troubles. All that mattered was this man, this moment, and the pleasure they shared.

CHAPTER TWENTY-THREE

The fire had burned to embers, and still Brenna and Ash remained on the sofa, alternately dozing and talking quietly. The only jarring note to the tranquil scene was Ash's rifle in the corner of the room, beside Brenna's, which she'd brought down from her bedroom.

Brenna sat sipping coffee, while Ash lay with his head on her lap. "I had the feeling that you were pretty impressed with Griff's talents." She ran her fingernails lightly along his arm and shoulder as she talked.

"Yeah. He was as good as his word. If it hadn't been for him, all we'd have had to show for our efforts would have been a bunch of planks and a bucket of screws. But he showed us how to put it all together into a cohesive barn door."

"It's more than a door." She bent down to brush a kiss on his forehead. "It's security."

"Yeah. I like the fact that it's solid enough that any truck foolish enough to ram it might drive away with more damage than it could inflict."

"I was thinking the same thing." She sighed. "And I like the padlock. Not that I have anything valuable to worry about, but it's a comfort to know I can keep vandals out." Her tone lowered. Softened. "I got the impression that your feelings toward Griff were deeper than mere pride in his workmanship."

Ash fell silent for a moment before saying, "Yeah. It's weird, knowing his father was my father. But when I look at him, or listen to his voice, I see and hear Pop. I ought to really resent him for that. But how can I, when he's such a good guy?"

"It's not as though he had any choice in deciding who his father was. In fact, he never had the opportunity to know his father the way you did."

Ash grinned up at her. "Maybe that's a good thing."

She playfully smacked his arm. "Be serious. I know from experience what it's like to grow up with a father who failed me on so many levels. All your father had was the famous MacKenzie temper. Which, I might add, has been inherited by his sons."

"Guilty," he said with a grin.

"But think about the burden Griff has carried. To never know your father? To spend a lifetime wondering who he was, and what he looked like, and what your life might have been like if only you'd had the chance to be with him...?"

"Yeah." Ash shifted so she could run her fingernails over his back. "I know what you're saying. At least, now that he's living with us, and spending time with Pop's friends, he's getting a better picture of the man he never knew."

"It's so generous of your mother to open her home to him. But I'm not surprised. Look how she opened her home to me." Her voice grew dreamy. "You know, Ash, this has been the perfect ending to a perfect day. It almost makes me believe that whoever broke in here has given up and gone away for good. If so, we can just get on with our lives." She sighed. "Wouldn't that be just the best?"

When he didn't respond, she looked down at him. His eyes were closed. His breathing slow and even. On his lips was a smile of pure pleasure.

Asleep.

And why not? He'd worked from sunup until sundown. And all on her behalf. He deserved whatever comfort she could offer. Even, she thought with a grin, getting his arm, shoulder, and back tickled and scratched until he'd drifted off.

He looked so peaceful in sleep.

While awake, he was all energy and motion. From riding into hill country, to nailing boards, to a water fight with his brother. But now, work and play behind him, he was as calm and still as an innocent.

And she loved him. The thought stole slowly over her, filling her heart with quiet peace, and filling her soul with instant awareness.

She loved Ash MacKenzie. She'd loved him as a little girl loves a hero, and she loved him now as a woman loves a man.

She bent forward and pressed a soft kiss to his lips.

Then she shifted a pillow beneath her head and joined him in sleep.

* * *

Ash was the first to wake.

Somehow, during the night, he and Brenna had come together amid the blankets and cushions, their arms and legs entwined, bodies so close, their two hearts beat as one.

A heartbeat so strong and steady. Like Brenna, he thought with a smile. No one who knew her, and knew of her family history, would ever think her weak or fragile. She knew what needed to be done to survive, and she did it without question. Without drama.

Drama. It seemed so much a part of the fabric of his family. Hair-trigger tempers. Fast and furious fights. Raucous laughter. Outrageous teasing.

Murder.

The very word sent shock waves through his system. His father had been murdered. Shot in the back by a coward who'd hidden from view and used a long-range rifle. And the filthy coward was still walking around, free to do more damage, while Bear MacKenzie lay in a grave, ripped from his family too soon.

The coward's identity would be uncovered. No matter how much time it took, or how much effort, he would be caught. All his secrets would be revealed. And he would pay, Ash thought. He would pay the same way Bear had paid. With his life.

He felt the change in Brenna's breathing and knew that she was on the verge of waking.

He watched as her lids fluttered, then opened. It was the sweetest thing to see the sudden awareness, and then the softening in her eyes as she reached up to brush a lock of hair from his forehead.

"'Morning, sleepyhead." He dipped his face toward hers.

"Good morn...ummm." Her greeting ended in a sigh as his lips met hers.

Seeing them stir, Sammy came wriggling over, anxious to be included in their lovefest.

"Hey, little guy." Brenna sat up, shoving hair from her eyes. "I guess we all slept through the night without a single disturbance." She turned a hopeful smile on Ash. "Do you think our intruder has given up?"

It was on the tip of his tongue to say something that would keep that smile on her lips. But he couldn't lie. "I figure, if he's been able to keep an eye on this place, he knows we're here and he's just biding his time until he can get the house to himself. Unless, of course, he already found what he was looking for."

Brenna glanced toward the gaping hole in the ceiling. "What now? Do we tear down the entire ceiling, or patch it?"

"My gut feeling is that we tear it down. I know it will create a huge mess for you, but Vern and I can help clean it up after we've torn out every bit of old plaster to see if something's been hidden in the interior."

"And if we find nothing?"

He shrugged. "Then we'll have to figure that he got what he wanted. Or that he was here on a wild goose chase."

She gave a reluctant nod of her head. "Okay. We tear down the ceiling."

When Sammy trotted toward the door, Brenna scrambled to her feet. "Come on, sweet Sammy. You need to go outside. It's been a long night, and you've been such a good boy."

She padded to the kitchen and opened the back door. The puppy raced down the steps and returned minutes later, happy to find his food dish ready.

Brenna called out to Ash, "I'm going to grab a shower."

He followed her up the stairs. "May as well join you."

At her quick glance he merely grinned. "Hey, I'm just doing my part to save water."

"My hero." She touched a hand to her heart in a mock salute as she stepped into the bathroom, with Ash in hot pursuit.

"Something smells good." Vern ambled into the kitchen in that loose-limbed gait.

"Ash is cooking." Brenna sat at the table sipping coffee. She held up her cup. "Want some?"

"Yeah. About a gallon, if you don't mind." The old man had shed his hat at the back door. Now he pulled out a chair and straddled it, as he accepted a mug of coffee and watched Ash flip eggs and ham in two skillets, while buttering toast like a short-order cook. "You got that down real good, son."

"Practice. Practice."

At his words, the two men grinned.

"No activity last night," the old man said.

"So we noticed," Brenna said. "Think he's gone for good?"

Vern glanced over her head to where Ash had turned to shoot a warning glance at him. Though he caught Ash's message to keep things low-key, he knew better than to sugar-coat what he believed.

"No sense fooling ourselves, girl. One night isn't some kind of milestone."

"I know. But I can hope, can't I?"

He grinned as he blew on his coffee before taking a drink. "You can hope all you want. But that fire seems like the work of a desperate man. Any fool knows a range fire could wipe out an entire herd if those cows can't stay ahead of it."

She met his eyes. "So you agree with Ash. Unless he's already found what he came for, he'll be back."

"Girl, if he'd found what he came for, he'd have never started that fire that cost Noah a night in the hospital." He paused. "Speaking of Noah... Heard anything from Doc Mullin yet?"

She shook her head. "Not a word. But it's early. Dr. Mullin will probably make an assessment sometime this morning. If Noah's ready to be released, I can drive into town and pick him up."

"Let us know. If he's up to working, we can bring the herd back to the hills. No sense leaving the herd on MacKenzie land any longer than necessary. We've already made more work for their wranglers than we wanted to."

"You know we don't mind." Ash winked at Brenna. "We're a full-service neighbor."

Brenna had an idea that he wasn't just talking about his wranglers now. She felt herself blushing as she had a quick vision of their passionate scene in the shower.

She turned to Vern. "Ash thinks we should tear down the ceiling."

Vern nodded. "I'm with Ash on this. Either we'll find what our intruder was looking for, or we find nothing, in which case we're right back where we started. But at least it will be one more thing crossed off our list of possibilities."

As Ash began setting out plates of scrambled eggs and
ham and toast, Vern added, "Maybe we should plan on
dealing with the herd first thing this morning, and then
later today I can give you a hand tearing out the ceiling."

Ash pulled out a chair and sat down. "Good idea. We'll
leave after breakfast."

"Speaking of which…" Vern spread thick strawberry
jam on a slice of toast and took a bite, closing his eyes in
pleasure as he did. "I'm starting to look forward to morn-
ings a whole lot more these days."

Ash and Brenna shared a smile at the look in the old
man's eyes. It was very clear that he was enjoying the re-
wards of having a new cook.

In fact, Ash's presence at her ranch had changed so
many things, it was hard to remember what it had been
like before.

How was it possible for one man to make such a difference?

It wasn't just the physical improvements. A barn door.
A herd safely under the care of watchful wranglers. All
the little things, old and broken and failing, that were now
mended and working like new. But there was also a feeling of hope now, where before there had been a quiet
despair that too many things were beyond fixing. He'd
brought laughter back into their lives.

That was Ash's true gift to them.

Hope. Passion for life. And so much laughter.

Her heart felt lighter than it had in years.

And that could only be attributed to Ash's presence in
her life.

CHAPTER TWENTY-FOUR

Kate's cheerful voice over the phone assured Brenna that Noah was strong enough to be released from the clinic. While Brenna made plans to drive to town, Ash and Vern left on horseback to return the herd to her highland range.

"See that Noah brings an insulated sleeping bag, now that he has no range shack for protection," Vern called. "The nights are still pretty cold, especially in the hills."

Brenna nodded and waved them off before tossing one of the spare sleeping bags into the back of her truck. She let Sammy out for a quick run before closing him up in the kitchen.

On the drive to town she was distracted by thoughts of Ash. Despite the fact that he was a different man from the one who'd left in a temper all those years ago, his basic goodness hadn't changed. He was still fun to be with, silly and teasing, but with a fundamental integrity that couldn't be shaken even while he'd struggled to survive.

Maybe that was another reason they were so good together. He understood her struggles, because he'd been forced to live his own. Despite his family's wealth and success, he'd had to make it on his own.

He'd said nothing about remaining on his family ranch. Maybe he wasn't ready to make that decision yet. Maybe he was just testing the waters, to see where he fit in.

She hoped he would stay. She wished it with all her heart.

But if he decided to go, she wouldn't hold him. It might break her heart, but she would never ask him to do something he didn't have his heart set on doing. And that included staying because of her.

She'd almost settled for something less than perfect with Chris. She'd tried to convince herself that even a taste of happiness, at the expense of all she wanted, was better than none at all. Never again, she thought, clenching a fist on the steering wheel. She would never settle for less than unselfish love. And if that meant giving up the one person who mattered most in her life, so be it.

She parked in front of the clinic and hurried inside.

Kate looked up from her desk with a wide smile. "I've been waiting for you." She rounded the desk and lowered her voice. "I have a favor to ask."

"Of course." Brenna followed her example, lowering her own voice, as well. "What can I do for you?"

"I don't know if you're aware of it, but Dr. Mullin and the clinic will be celebrating twenty-five years here in Copper Creek this June. I was hoping you could make a sculpture in time for the anniversary. And I'd like it to be a surprise."

Brenna couldn't hide her pleasure. "What a fine idea. Do you have anything in mind?"

Kate rummaged through her desk drawer and produced a picture cut from a magazine. It showed a man in a white lab coat, with a stethoscope around his neck. "I'd like something like this, but with Dr. Mullin's face and body type. Think you could do it?"

"I don't see why not. I can certainly try." Hearing the doctor approach, Brenna stuffed the picture into the pocket of her jeans and looked up with a smile.

"Brenna. Your wrangler is all set." Dan Mullin paused to scratch his name on a document before handing it to her. "He has no sign of infection, and he claims to have no pain, so there's no need for any prescriptions to be filled."

"It's safe for him to resume working?"

"You bet." He nodded toward Kate. "I already told him to get dressed. You can tell him Brenna is here to drive him back."

Minutes later Noah Perkins walked down the hall beside the doctor's assistant. In his hand he carried the crudely fashioned cane he'd made from a tree limb while up in the hills.

Dan Mullin turned. "I told Brenna that you're able to resume your chores. Do you need that cane?"

Noah shook his head. "I just thought I'd keep it for a souvenir. I'm good to go. Thanks for stitching me up."

"A couple of those cuts were deep. Next time you have to escape out a burning building, try the door, okay?" The two shook hands before Noah followed Brenna out the door and into her waiting truck.

Brenna glanced at the man in the passenger seat. From the shaggy beard and hair, to the long-sleeved flannel shirt and worn denims, still smeared with his blood, he looked much the same as when she'd brought him to the clinic.

"I wish I'd thought to ask Kate for your clothes when you were admitted. I don't know if all that blood would have come out in the wash, but at least they'd be clean."

He shrugged. "Cows don't mind dirty clothes."

She smiled. "That's true." She nodded toward the rear of the pickup. "Before Vern and Ash left to fetch the herd, Vern reminded me to bring along an insulated sleeping bag. With no shelter, you'll be glad to have it on these cold nights in the hills."

"So Vern and Ash are already with the herd?"

She nodded. "Vern didn't want to impose on the generosity of the MacKenzies any longer than necessary."

Noah leaned his head back, a sure indication that he was through talking. Not that Brenna minded. She was already thinking about the sculpture Kate had commissioned. She would have no problem sculpting Dan Mullin's face, or the lab coat or stethoscope, but she'd already moved beyond that. She wanted to show his love, his compassion for the people of Copper Creek. Maybe she would add a baby in one arm and have his other arm around the shoulder of a cowboy in denims, wearing a Stetson.

Her mind was working overtime, mulling all the possibilities.

By the time she arrived at her ranch, she was itching to get started.

As she passed the porch and headed toward the trail

that led around the barns and into the hills, Noah lifted his head.

"Think you could spare a couple of bottles of water?"

"Oh, of course. Not a problem. I'll get them."

She parked the truck and left it idling as she climbed the steps of the porch. When she opened the back door, she realized that Noah was right behind her.

"You startled me. There's no need to exert yourself. I can bring it out to you."

"I can help."

When she hesitated, he shoved her inside with such force she stumbled across the mudroom.

In the kitchen she caught hold of the edge of the table and steadied herself before turning to him with a flash of anger. "What do you think you're doing? I nearly fell."

Sammy was halfway across the room, yapping hysterically, when he suddenly halted in midstride and cringed when Noah lifted the cane menacingly.

"Smart mutt. He remembers what the toe of my boot feels like." No longer hunched over in pain, Noah was standing straight and tall.

"What are you saying?" Brenna was too stunned to do more than stare at him in open-mouthed surprise. But as his meaning dawned, her eyes went wide. "It was you? You broke in? You frightened my dog?"

"You're lucky I didn't kill him. All that yapping. Then he tried to bite my leg. That's when I kicked him and tossed him out the door."

She thought of her poor, frightened puppy, hurt and wandering around in the darkness until Ash's truck's headlights had found him alongside the road. He'd probably been shamed by the fact that he hadn't been able to guard his territory.

"Why? What do you want?"

"Shut up. I'm sick and tired of you yapping just like your dog." He pointed with his cane. "Now pick up the mutt or I swear this time I will kill him."

She scooped Sammy into her arms and did her best to soothe his trembling response to this stranger. She could feel his poor heart thundering. It matched her own heart rate, which had gone sky-high.

She was terrified of this man. And confused. Had his injuries all been part of some elaborate scheme? That wasn't possible. Dr. Mullin would never have tolerated a hoax.

"Get in there where I can keep an eye on you." Noah shoved her roughly ahead of him into the parlor. When he spotted her rifle leaning against the wall, he tossed aside his makeshift cane and grabbed the weapon.

Seeing the boarded-up window, he muttered a curse. "If it hadn't been for that..."

His words had her stopping in midstride. "That's where you cut yourself. Not up at the range shack."

She could still hear the shattering of glass, and see in her mind's eye the figure fleeing across the darkened yard, leaving a trail of blood.

And then it all became perfectly clear.

"That fire up in the hills was no accident. You set it, didn't you? It was all an elaborate cover-up to get help for your wounds without anyone getting suspicious about how you got them."

"You're too damned smart for your own good. But I'm a whole lot smarter."

"But why...?"

"I told you to shut up." He brought the rifle down hard on her head.

The blow had her seeing stars as she dropped to her knees. Though Sammy yelped and wriggled, she managed to hold fast to him, afraid if he broke free this man would follow up on his threat to kill him.

"Give me your cell phone," Noah demanded.

"Wha...?" When she didn't move quickly enough he snatched it from her pocket.

"Now. Don't move," he ordered. "Stay on the floor and face that wall."

When she didn't turn away quickly enough he brought the rifle down again, this time across her back, sending her sprawling.

With a moan of pain she lay on the floor, desperately cuddling Sammy against her chest. As she struggled to remain conscious, she could hear the sound of something heavy being shoved across the floor. Minutes later she heard a chair creaking under Noah's weight.

If only she could see. But the pain of the blow had rendered her dizzy and half blind, with blood from the open cut in her head slowly trickling down her face.

She could hear Noah grunting and swearing as he began tearing down huge sections of the ceiling and allowing it to fall to the floor. Dust and debris fell on Brenna, coating her hair, clogging her throat.

Her eyes burned from the effort to open them in the cloud of powdery dust that rose up from the old plaster. Sammy gagged and coughed, and still she clung to him with a kind of desperation.

"Yes! It's true. That old son of a bitch didn't lie."

She heard his muttered exclamation, and felt her heart stop.

It was obvious that this drifter had found whatever it was he'd been searching for.

Now he would no longer have any use for her.

She heard him grunt as he leaped from the chair and landed with a thud on his feet. In quick strides he was across the room and standing over her. She could hear him breathing. She could smell him, a foul, sour smell of sweat and filth and unwashed clothes.

Instead of the gunshot she'd been anticipating, he reached down and yanked her painfully to her feet.

The figure of him swam in front of her eyes and she blinked furiously, trying to clear her vision.

"You're going with me." He shoved her ahead of him.

When she realized what he was doing, she thought about Ash and Vern, in the hills with the herd, and completely unaware of the drama being played out here. Even when they returned and found her gone, they wouldn't have a clue what had happened here, or if she'd been taken against her will.

It was tricky, keeping hold of a wriggling pup while sliding the slim bracelet from her wrist, but she managed it, and let it drop silently to the rug.

Muttering every rich, ripe oath he could think of, Noah shoved her ahead of him toward the kitchen and out the back door.

"Now we'll take that ride."

"I can't see enough to drive."

"No need. From now I'll be driving, cuz I'm in charge. See. You didn't know it, but from the beginning, I've been in charge." He opened the passenger door and shoved her so hard she fell across the seat.

In that instant Sammy wriggled free and began running around and around the man's feet, yapping frantically.

"No, Sam..."

Her words were cut off at the sudden, loud report of a rifle shot as Noah fired at close range. The puppy's yelp died in its throat, as the little dog dropped to the ground in a heap.

"Sammy. Oh, Sammy..." She sat up, but before she could rush to him, the rifle slashed out, knocking her backward.

"That's better." Enraged, Noah stepped over the puppy's lifeless body and slammed the passenger door before circling around and climbing into the driver's side.

He withdrew some rope from his pocket and tied Brenna's hands and ankles so tightly she cried out in pain.

"Aw. Did I hurt you?" He gave a strange, high-pitched laugh at his little joke before his voice turned into a snarl of rage. "If you say a word, I'll tape your mouth. You hear?"

She nodded, while tears ran silently down her cheeks.

He put the truck in gear, and took off with the tires spewing gravel.

Brenna stared out the side window, cursing the tears that blurred her vision. But what she could see of Sammy was nothing more than a tiny bundle of yellow fluff lying still and lifeless on the ground.

And then the truck was racing toward the highway, leaving behind a cloud of dust.

As her ranch receded from view, she thought of Ash,

herding her cattle to the highlands, expecting to find Noah there to tend them.

By the time he returned, she could be hundreds of miles from here. Even if he found her bracelet, there was no way of letting him know what had happened, or where this madman was taking her.

Though she struggled through a mist of pain and sorrow, her mind, her body betrayed her. The blow to the head had left her brain fuzzy and her vision blurred.

The young woman who had always prided herself on being able to take care of herself and resolve any situation, no matter how impossible it may have seemed, was now reduced to an odd, numbing silence.

CHAPTER TWENTY-FIVE

Ash and Vern, working together in companionable silence, moved slowly behind the herd. Occasionally one of them would veer off to force an errant calf back to its mother's side, or lasso an ornery cow that wandered too far from the rest.

It was a perfect spring day. Sunny but cool enough that they were comfortable in the saddle.

Once they began the climb toward the hills above Brenna's ranch, the cattle moved along the familiar territory at a faster pace. They were soon milling about their spring range, feasting on the abundant grass that grew there.

Vern looked annoyed. "Now what's keeping that lazy drifter?"

"I'm sure he's on his way." Ash pulled out his cell phone and punched in Brenna's number. The phone rang and rang before her message played.

"Hey, Sunshine. Vern and I are here with the herd. What's the holdup with Noah? I hope he didn't develop any complications before the clinic could release him. Call me when you get this message."

He dropped the phone into his shirt pocket. "I'm sure we'll hear from her in a few minutes."

Noah played Ash's message and shot a triumphant grin at Brenna. "Sounds like your boyfriend's not happy being stuck babysitting your cows. But that's all good news for me. It means he and the old geezer haven't been to the house yet, and don't know you've gone missing. We've just bought ourselves a whole lot of time."

At his words, Brenna's heart fell to her toes. How long, she wondered, would Ash and Vern wait in the highlands before giving up and heading toward her place?

By the time they realized she was missing, she could be hundreds of miles away.

Or dead.

Noah had shown no mercy toward Sammy. Why should she expect him to treat her any differently?

"Where are you taking me?"

"You'll see when we get there."

"But why? Why take me, when you got what you came for?"

"Maybe what I really came for is you."

She visibly paled.

Seeing how his words affcctcd her, he became animated, clearly enjoying the role of tormentor. "So, your old man was a drunk. A mean one. I know a thing or two about that."

She went very still. "How do you know about my father?"

"Maybe I heard people talking."

"Up in the hills with the cattle?"

He shot her a narrowed look. "You're too smart for your own good. If you're not careful, I'll tape that mouth. Or maybe I'll just silence you the way I did your dog."

She refused to be cowed. "Tell me how you know about my father."

He swore. "You're just like him. There was no shutting him up, either."

"So you did know him. You talked with him?"

"Oh yeah. Mostly, he talked and I listened. You might say I took notes." He chuckled at his little joke.

"Where? Where was he? How did you meet him?"

His head swiveled to study her. "I see I got your attention now." He took his time, measuring words, parceling them out like a miser. "I met your daddy in an assisted-living place where I was working. You might say I was his...personal aide."

"How did he look?" Her tone was nearly pleading. "Was he clean and sober?"

Noah gave a dry laugh. "I don't know about clean, but he was sober. He also got religion, which turned him into a real bore. There's nothing worse than a recovered drunk who's ashamed of his past and wants to spend the rest of his life converting the whole world."

Brenna sat back, trying to imagine her father sober and religious. It was almost more than she could take in. "Did he ever...mention me?" Her voice trembled slightly.

"When didn't he? You're all he talked about. How you looked just like your mother. How she'd forgiven him before she died, and how he hoped and prayed his beautiful daughter would do the same."

His beautiful daughter.

Brenna fell silent, trying to reconcile the image of the angry, abusive father she'd known with the man he'd apparently become in his old age.

He'd never called her beautiful. Or pretty. Or even sweet. All he'd ever hurled at her were angry, hurtful names.

Feeling full of himself, Noah managed a sly smile. "You're about to join him, you know."

Despite her pain, her terror about the very real danger she was facing at this man's hands, she latched onto the only thing that he was willing to talk about. "You're taking me to my father? Why didn't you tell me that sooner?"

"Would it have made any difference?"

"Of course it would. I want to see him. And if you'd been honest from the beginning, you wouldn't have had to go through any of this. I'd have been happy to give you whatever you wanted, and I'd have come willingly, without being tied or forced."

She saw an odd look come over him. Smug at first, as though he'd won the lottery. But then his eyes went hard as flint, and he looked at her in a way that had her blood turning to ice.

"The only thing I hate more than a reformed drunk is a woman who pretends she can forgive the drunk who abused her."

"I do forgive him." She said it simply, from the heart.

His hand shot out so quickly she didn't see it coming and slapped her hard. Her head snapped to one side, and the prints of his fingers left red welts on her cheek.

While tears welled up in her eyes and spilled over, he

merely laughed. "We'll see just how forgiving you really are. Before I'm through with you, you'll be cursing my name. And just for fun, I'll let you call me Daddy."

"Okay. I've waited long enough." Ash plucked his phone from his pocket and dialed the clinic in Copper Creek. After several rings he said, "Hey, Kate. Ash MacKenzie here. Was there a holdup on Brenna's wrangler, Noah Perkins?"

He listened, then said, "Thanks, Kate. I'll check her place."

He turned to Vern with a frown. "Brenna and Noah left the clinic two hours ago. You stay with the herd. I'm heading to Brenna's house."

He dug in his heels, urging his mount into a gallop. Along the way he tried her phone several times, but always got her message. By the time he came around the barn and saw no trace of Brenna's truck, he'd gone over a dozen different scenarios in his mind, and all of them too frightening to accept. Now, as he struggled to dismiss yet another vision of Brenna in harm's way, he came closer to the back porch and caught sight of Sammy lying still and small in the yard.

He vaulted out of the saddle and raced toward the puppy. The earth around his tiny body was wet with blood.

Cradling the bloodied pup in his arms, Ash sprinted up the steps, shouting Brenna's name.

The silence of the rooms mocked him.

He gently settled the still form of the pup on its bed and felt the feeble, thready pulse. Alive, but barely. He covered him with a sun-warmed afghan before walking to the parlor. He took one look at the ruined ceiling, and the piles of dust and debris, before turning away. Then he realized that Brenna's rifle was missing. As he started out of the room he caught sight of something glittering on the rug near the door.

He bent and picked it up, at the same moment punching in the police chief's number.

"Ira. Ash here." His voice was tight as he fought to control the absolute terror rising within him. "I'm at Brenna's place. Her puppy's been shot and left for dead. Her parlor ceiling has been trashed. No sign of Brenna, her truck, her rifle, or the drifter she'd picked up at the clinic this morning. I'm certain she didn't go with him willingly."

"Did she leave you any message?"

Ash opened his hand to stare at the delicate gold filigree. "She left me a sign. It's unmistakable."

"All right. That's good enough for me." The two exchanged terse words as the police chief asked the make and model of her old truck before saying, "I'll get the state police on it right away. They can have aerial observation going within the hour."

"My family can have a plane up even sooner than that." Ash rang off and called his brother.

In quick, staccato phrases he explained what was happening and what he needed.

Whit didn't waste time with unnecessary questions. There would be time enough later for answers. For now he said simply, "Brady and I will have the plane ready when you get here."

"Thanks. I'm on my way." Ash called Vern and told him what he'd found, including the near-lifeless body of

Sammy. "Leave the herd and get here as fast as you can. If Noah got what he wanted from that ceiling, there was no reason to take Brenna along, unless he plans to hurt her. He shot Sammy, probably with Brenna's own rifle. I have no doubt he's capable of much more violence."

The old cowboy heard the pain and fury in Ash's voice and said simply, "I'm heading there now. You go after her. And Ash?"

"Yeah."

"You bring her home, son."

"You know I will, Vern. Or die trying."

CHAPTER TWENTY-SIX

By the time Ash reached his family's ranch, Brady and Whit had the Cessna Skyhawk fueled and had completed their preflight check.

The entire family, including Mad in his wheelchair, were gathered outside the barn that housed the aircraft. Beyond was an airstrip for easy takeoffs and landings, which they'd built years earlier.

Though they were bursting with questions, one look at Ash's face warned them to hold their silence and let him speak. He filled them in as quickly as possible.

"Brady, I'd like you to handle the controls so I can take the copilot's seat and watch for Brenna's truck."

The foreman nodded and climbed aboard.

Ash turned to his mother and brothers. "I'd like you to take our ranch trucks and fan out to cruise some of the roads and trails. You'll be looking for Brenna's tan pickup, but check out any vehicle with a man and woman.

This guy may have already tried to ditch Brenna's truck for something less conspicuous."

"Where do you think they're headed?" Mad asked.

"That's the million-dollar question. I don't have a clue. But since everyone in Copper Creek knows Brenna, I'm sure he'll avoid the town."

Mad slammed a hand down on the arm of his wheelchair. "I'm going up with you and Brady."

"Mad…"

The old man shook off Ash's protest. "I know this land better'n anyone. There's nothing wrong with my eyes or my brain. Now lift me up to the seat of that plane, and let's get moving."

Ash did as he was told, stowing his grandfather and the wheelchair in the two rear seats.

He turned to close a hand over Willow's shoulder. "We have to find her, Mom. She's in the hands of a madman."

Willow touched a hand to his cheek. "If there's a heaven, Ash, and I truly believe there is, your father is already keeping Brenna safe until you can get to her."

"I'll hold on to that thought." He gave her a fierce hug before turning away to climb into the Cessna. With a roar of engines, it taxied along a strip of asphalt before lifting into the air.

Willow, Griff, and Whit checked their cell phones and chose to search in different areas in order to cover as much ground as possible.

"Check in with me at least every half hour," Willow called before climbing into one of the ranch trucks and driving away in a cloud of dust.

Whit and Griff followed and veered off in separate directions when they reached the highway.

* * *

Brady guided the plane over lush rangeland and followed the meandering course of Copper Creek past green highland meadows and cool mountain peaks.

While he easily handled the instruments, he encouraged Ash to go into detail about what had happened, knowing it would help if he could be encouraged to talk it out.

Ash was filled with remorse. "I should have never left her alone. I should have been with her when she went to town to pick up that drifter from the clinic."

From the rear seat Mad's voice was low with passion. "You didn't know she was in any danger, lad."

"I didn't like him. From the moment I met him, I sensed something about the guy." Ash shook his head. "Vern felt it, too. He kept calling him lazy. He only hired him because he was desperate for some help. But the guy was more trouble than he was worth. Always asleep instead of tending the herd. Never around when Vern needed him. The old cowboy isn't to blame. He has too much on his shoulders. But I should have caught on to this drifter sooner..."

At the ring of his cell phone, he said gruffly, "Ash MacKenzie."

Recognizing the police chief, he turned his phone on speaker, so the others could hear as Ira's voice boomed.

"The state guys got a report on the drifter Vern hired. Noah Perkins, alias Nolan Parker, was fired from a nursing home when his background check showed a record as long as his arm. They alerted the authorities, but by then he was long gone. Now we suspect he's the same guy that's wanted, under various aliases, in four

Western states for everything from armed robbery to murder."

Murder. It was the only word Ash heard. "Then this isn't larceny any longer."

"That's right. This guy is a real psycho."

"Could he be responsible for Pop's murder?"

"You know we'll be checking every move he's made to see if we can connect the dots." The chief's tone lowered. "There's one more thing. Raleigh Crane checked himself out of that nursing home the same day that this guy was fired. Nobody has seen either one since."

Ash's heart contracted with fear. "You think they've concocted some kind of scheme? Or is Raleigh a victim? I don't like the sound of this, Ira."

"I know what you mean. I don't like it, either. My thinking is that Brenna Crane is in serious danger." The chief cleared his throat. "The state police are on watch on the ground, and they'll be getting their aircraft up any minute now."

"Thanks, Ira. We're airborne, and the rest of the family is searching the roads and trails. Do you have any idea where this guy could be heading?"

"I wish I had my crystal ball, Ash. But there was one thing. On his employment records he listed a ranch about a hundred miles east of Copper Creek as the place where he grew up. It's probably a needle in a haystack, but it might be worth checking out."

While the chief gave directions, Brady brought it up on the GPS and pointed. "There. Really desolate land."

Ash nodded. "Thanks, Ira. We're heading that way now."

"I'm going up in a helicopter with the state boys. Stay

on our frequency. If you spot any life there, let us know. We'll be right behind you."

The plane made a sharp turn and the three men fell silent as they charted their course toward what they hoped and prayed was the destination of the man who held Brenna's life in his hands.

The thought twisted inside Ash's brain.

She was in the hands of a man already wanted for murder.

If a man killed once, did it matter to him how many more he added to his list of victims?

Brenna's head ached from the blow she'd absorbed from her rifle. The throbbing at her temple had her wanting to close her eyes against the constant glare of sunlight reflecting off the truck's cab. Between the motion of their vehicle, bumping along like a covered wagon, and the piercing light burning her eyes, she was forced to fight back nausea. But she continued watching every turn, in the hope that she could somehow make her way back home when this was over.

When this is over. It played like a litany in her mind.

Right now, all of this seemed like a bad dream. But it was all too real. And she'd already seen the price poor little Sammy had paid for trying to defend her.

She watched as the scenery slowly changed from ranches and herds grazing on rangeland to uninhabited stretches of land that could have come right out of the old West. An occasional shack, timbers rotted, roof caving in on itself, was the only sign that anyone had ever inhabited this land. This isolated area looked as though it had been defeated by plagues of grasshoppers, drought, and windstorms, until nothing was left but rocks and barren soil.

Noah had long ago left the highway and was now following a dirt track, sending up a plume of dust. They followed the trail for what seemed miles until they came up over a rise and spotted, in the distance, a decaying shack.

"Very soon now you'll get to join your daddy," Noah announced with a laugh. "The old bag of bones was obsessed with asking your forgiveness, but he was too ashamed to do it."

Brenna blinked back tears. "That's what he told me in his letter."

Noah threw back his head and laughed.

Brenna looked over. "Why do you find that funny?"

Instead of answering her, he began in a whiny voice, " 'Dear Brenna. My dear, sweet darling child. I'm so sorry it's taken me all these years to contact you. But even though you never heard from me, you were always on my mind...' "

Brenna's smile turned to a look of stunned horror as the truth dawned. "That letter wasn't from my father. *You* wrote it."

"Pretty good, wasn't it? All gooey and heartbreaking. I actually stole some lines from a Willie Nelson song."

"But why?" Brenna could feel tears welling up in her eyes and hated the fact that she was allowing him to see how deeply he'd hurt her.

"Why? That's easy. I needed some traveling money to get here."

"You cashed the check I wrote to my father?"

"He'll never miss it." He paused a beat before adding, "See. The joke's on you. You financed my trip here so I could steal from you."

"Steal what? What did you take out of my ceiling?"

"Nothing you need to worry your head about. Once we get where we're going, you'll know everything you need to. And then you can join crazy old Raleigh Crane."

"Why would my father choose such a dismal place as this to meet?"

"One place is as good as another. Especially when you're..."

She turned to him, tense, expectant. "When you're what?"

"When you're full of religion. Yeah. That's it. When you're full of sobriety and religion." His laughter grew, high and shrill, reminding her of nails on a blackboard.

There was, she knew, a madness to his laughter. And madmen were too dangerous to trust.

She quickly dismissed that thought and concentrated instead on the fact that she was joining her father. Whatever pain he'd inflicted in the past, he was now remorseful and eager to see her. She would be able to tell him in person that her heart was filled with only love and forgiveness. And Raleigh Crane, in turn, would deliver her from this crazed drifter.

"I hope there's someone tending my dad. I can't imagine how he left a nursing home for this."

Noah's laughter stopped abruptly. His eyes narrowed on her. "You don't think this is good enough for him? Or are you worried that it isn't good enough for you? There was a time when folks thought it was the only thing good enough for me."

Hearing the simmering fury in his tone, she was quick to placate him. His moods changed so abruptly, she needed to keep things as calm as possible. "I wasn't implying anything. I'm just worried about my father's health."

"Don't you worry about that." He smiled, showing yellowed teeth. "You're like him, you know. Always asking questions. Talking. All he wanted to talk about was you. How brave you were. How good. How perfect." He made a gagging sound and swore again. "After awhile I just wanted to stuff a rag in his mouth, or better, slit his throat and shut him up permanently."

He turned off the ignition and opened the door, circling around to yank the passenger's-side door open. In his hand was something dull, until he touched a button releasing a long, sharp blade that glinted in the sunlight.

Even as Brenna was recoiling, he grabbed her feet and the blade sliced through the rope binding her ankles as neatly as though it were butter.

His eyes gleamed. Cold. Feral. "Thought I was going to stick you, didn't you?"

When she said nothing he smiled. "You see how sharp this is? I could cut out your heart before you had time to blink. And don't you forget it."

He pulled her by the arm, knocking her off balance. She fell to her knees in the dirt, and he hauled her roughly to her feet. "Must have hit you harder than I thought. Or else you're just a prissy lightweight."

Though her limbs were numb from having been bound so tightly for so long, she staggered forward and stepped into the shack. In the gloom she stared around hopefully.

"Where is he? Noah, where's my father?"

His smile was wide. It was plain that he was enjoying his little joke.

"Oh. Did I forget to tell you?" He waited a beat, drawing out the moment, clearly savoring his private little joke. "Your daddy's out back. Six feet under."

Ash studied the land below. "I grew up here in Montana, and I don't recognize any of this. All rocks and sand and not a single sign of civilization. It looks like some kind of moonscape."

Brady nodded. His eyes were hidden behind the mirrored sunglasses, but his tone revealed his somber mood. "I know a little about this part of Montana."

Ash glanced at him.

"I grew up not far from here."

"I don't think you ever mentioned that before."

Brady shrugged. "Not something I like to talk about."

Ash waited, but when the foreman offered nothing more, he didn't press.

From the rear seat Mad's voice was triumphant. "See that dust cloud?"

They turned to study the dust billowing upward from a vehicle moving along a rise. It was impossible to see the vehicle through the dust, but, since it was the only sign of life they'd detected, Brady kept the plane on course, while slowing their speed.

Ash pointed to a shack that was little more than a dark spot in the distance. "That could be where they're headed."

Brady nodded and slowed the plane even more so that it didn't get ahead of the vehicle on the ground.

When at last the movement came to a halt outside the shack, the dust began to settle, and they could clearly see the tan truck.

"It's Brenna's." Ash's voice trembled with feeling.

With binoculars trained on it, he watched as Noah circled the truck and hauled Brenna from the passenger's side.

"She's alive," he whispered.

Those two words had all three men breathing again.

Ash continued watching through the binoculars, hungry to store up every image of Brenna that he could.

What he saw had his eyes narrowing in anger, as she was dragged from the truck so hard she dropped to her knees before being yanked to her feet and shoved roughly inside the shack. Noah followed her inside.

Ash dialed his cell phone to alert his family members at the same time that Brady spoke into the plane's headset, to give the information to Ira and the state police.

After feeding all the information they had, Ash added, "We've found her. She's alive. We're going down."

CHAPTER TWENTY-SEVEN

Brenna looked around as if in a daze. She'd come here expecting to be reunited with her father. And now Noah was telling her he was dead? How could this be? It was simply too much to take in. And yet hadn't she known that something was very wrong? All those hateful words he'd hurled. He'd been telling her, over and over, how he'd hated her father. Hated her.

Her legs wobbled, and though she knew she shouldn't let this evil man see any weakness in her, it couldn't be helped. She dropped to her knees on the dirt floor of the crumbling shack and felt tears sting her eyes.

He stood over her, his tone pure sarcasm. "Oh. Poor baby. You crying?"

The sound of that nasal whine had her head coming up sharply. Though her wrists were still bound, she lifted them to wipe her eyes with the backs of her hands. There would be no tears. She would not meet the same fate as her father without a fight.

"When did you kill my father?"

"A couple of weeks ago."

Weeks. Her heart plummeted. "Why? You said he was in a nursing home. He was old and sick. Why did you have to kill him?"

"Because he was a necessary part of my plan."

"Your plan for what?" She stared at the switchblade in his hand, her rifle in the other, and knew what her fate would be. The finality of it made her more determined than ever to let him see no weakness.

"For having my own place. While your dear old daddy was yakking on endlessly about the family ranch he'd left all those years ago, I realized that he was offering me a chance to have what I've always wanted without having to work for it."

"I don't understan—"

He lifted a hand. "See this dump? This place that you consider unfit for your father? This was home when I was a kid. If that isn't dismal enough, consider this. Like your old man, mine was a drunk. A mean, let's-slap-Junior-around-until-I-break-some-bones drunk. And when he was through having fun with me, he'd turn all that charm on my mother. Only she was big enough to get out, leaving me alone to face my own private hell. I didn't get out until I was twelve, and big enough and smart enough to stash a knife under my pillow." He caressed the blade of the knife as though it were a lover, sending chills along Brenna's spine. "The next time my old man attacked me, I fought back. And won. I buried him out behind the barn, packed up as much as I could tie behind my saddle, and left. Nobody even knew he was missing. Nobody cared. And that meant I was free." He gave a chilling laugh. "I've bounced around the country, getting by. And then this old drunk tells me how he wants to make it up to his little girl. How he's got a deed hidden up in the ceiling of his ranch house that dates back to the eighteen hundreds. His family ranch is some kind of historical treasure. He wants the deed framed, so his little girl will have something of his that can make her proud. Once I heard that, I figured if I hold that deed, and I'm the last living heir, it can all be mine, and I'll be more than proud. I'll be a respected land owner."

"The last living heir?"

He laughed again. "It has a nice ring to it, doesn't it? But if you and your old man are dead, who's to deny my claim?"

"Everyone who knows me in Copper Creek. And there's Vern. He's been with me for years. He'll never believe you're an heir to my family's ranch."

"They will if you and the old guy go missing. Out here, the only ones who'll ever uncover your grave are the wild things. Meanwhile, back in Copper Creek, I'll see that old Vern gets what he should've got when I drove through that barn door."

"It was you."

He frowned. "You and that old geezer have more lives than a cat. I got sick and tired of stealing rancher's trucks trying to run you down. But I knew sooner or later I'd win. I always do. And once the two of you are out of the picture, I'll get all cleaned up and show up at the county with proof of my claim." He opened his shirt and removed the yellowed document. "This is the deed to your land.

All nice and tidy and legal. And it says that all that land belongs to the one who holds it. Did you hear me? It belongs to the one who holds it. And then there's this." He held up a letter. "This is signed by Raleigh Crane, naming me beneficiary of his estate. Estate." He cackled. "Has a nice ring to it, doesn't it?"

"My father would never sign such a thing."

"Oh he would if there was a knife to his throat." He gave her a long, icy look. "Sorry, girly. But if it's any comfort, your old man thought he was arranging your future when he told me about this historic deed. He may have been sober, but by telling me all his secrets, he was nothing but a sober fool. And now he's a dead one."

He set aside the rifle and advanced toward her with the switchblade glinting in his hand. "A bullet's cleaner. But I've come to enjoy the feel of my knife cutting deep into flesh. And your pretty flesh ought to be as soft as butter."

His voice was drowned out by the roar of a plane's engines, so loud they sounded near enough to tear off the roof of the shack.

Startled, he raced to the doorway to peer skyward.

The Cessna skimmed low over the ground before touching down a hundred yards distant.

"I can land right there." Brady pointed to a flat stretch of dry creek bed. "But there's no way to pull a surprise when you're landing a plane practically in his shack." He turned to Ash. "Got a plan?"

"No time for one. Just land."

As the plane bumped along the rocky stretch of soil, Ash checked his rifle.

When they came to a halting stop he turned to Mad. "You'll have to stay here."

The old man snatched up his rifle. "Like hell I will."

"Listen, Mad." Ash's eyes blazed. "I don't have time for anything right now except Brenna."

"You said this nutcase has her rifle. What makes you think he's going to let you get within a foot of her?"

"I don't know." Ash pulled open the plane's door and stepped down. "But he'll have to kill me to stop me."

Brady stepped down from the other side of the plane. "I'm going with you."

"You're staying here. Somebody has to be able to fly our bodies out of this godforsaken wilderness." Ash didn't give him time to argue. Without a backward glance, he circled the plane and started toward the shack.

Behind him, Mad growled, "Brady, get over here and help me get this damnable wheelchair out of this heap of metal."

Brady lifted out the chair, and then the old man, who was cradling his rifle to his chest. "What about Ash's orders?"

Mad shot him a sly grin and cupped a hand to his ear. "Huh? Sorry, I'm too old to hear you."

"I'm going with you," Brady shouted.

As he lay the rifle across his lap and hit the wheels, propelling himself forward, Mad called, "You heard Ash. Stay here and tend the plane. Somebody has to be sensible."

As he rolled away Brady muttered under his breath, "Yeah. That's what I'm going to be. Sensible."

He rummaged around the plane for a weapon and located a flare gun. He figured it was better than nothing as he raced to catch up with crazy old Mad MacKenzie.

* * *

When the door to the plane opened, Noah stared open-mouthed at the sight of Ash MacKenzie coming boldly toward him with a rifle in his hands.

"Oh, this should be fun." Noah yanked Brenna to her feet and dragged her outside before wrapping an arm around her neck.

Pressing the switchblade against the tender flesh of her throat, he called out, "Toss aside that rifle, hero, or I slit this pretty little thing from ear to ear."

Before Ash could comply, Mad rolled into view. "What're you going to do after you kill her?" he shouted. "Think that knife will go up against two guns?"

"Big talk, old man. You can shoot me, but the woman will still be dead." To prove a point Noah pressed the blade firmly enough against Brenna's throat to draw blood.

Hearing her cry out, and seeing the blood spilling down the front of her shirt, Ash let out a roar before tossing his rifle aside. "Let her go. We'll do what you want." He turned to his grandfather. "Drop your weapon, Mad."

The old man swore as he released his hold on his rifle.

"That's more like it." Throwing Brenna to the ground, Noah shoved the switchblade into his back pocket and took aim with the rifle. "Looks like I'm going to be real busy digging graves."

He took his first shot, and as the bullet ripped into Ash's shoulder, he had the satisfaction of watching the fountain of blood spurt from the wound before Ash dropped to his knees in the dirt.

Noah swore. "My second shot won't miss your heart, hero."

"Hold it right there." Brady stepped out from behind the plane and aimed his weapon at Noah.

The drifter's eyes narrowed on him. "You think I'm stupid enough to believe that useless flare gun can kill me? Drop it."

When Brady hesitated, Noah took aim. "Another hero."

Just as his finger touched the trigger, he caught the slight movement behind him and turned. Despite her bound wrists, Brenna managed to ram her body against his, sending him stumbling forward. His rifle shot went wild, the bullet flying harmlessly into the dirt.

Noah regained his footing and spun around, hitting her on the side of her head with the rifle. With a cry she fell to the ground.

By the time he'd turned back, Ash was advancing on him with a snarl of rage.

With no time to aim, Noah fired, and had the satisfaction of watching Ash take a second bullet to the arm.

Instead of falling, or even slowing down, Ash kept coming.

Mad tugged on the wheels of his chair, propelling himself forward.

From behind him, Brady started running toward them.

"You're all fools," Noah shouted. "Dead fools."

This time he took careful aim, but before he could fire again, Ash dropped down and the bullet rang over his head. That was all the time Ash needed to reach out and wrench the rifle from Noah's hand.

It fell to the ground between them as Ash's fist met Noah's face, sending blood cascading down his chin and staining his already filthy shirt.

"Now you'll have to fight me like a man, you coward."

The words were no sooner out of Ash's mouth than Noah reached into his pocket and withdrew the switchblade. With the touch of a button the deadly blade was exposed, and aimed directly at Ash's heart.

"I'd rather fight you the way I fought my miserable excuse of a father," Noah said with a chilling laugh. "And your pretty girlfriend can tell you how that ended."

Before he could take a step forward, he was stunned by something hitting the side of his head. Brady's flare gun left a bruise on his temple as it fell to the ground.

Before Noah could react, something else hit him hard enough to have him swearing a blue streak. He turned in time to see Mad taking aim with another rock.

"You just sealed your fate. All of you. But first, I'll take care of this hero." Noah swung out his hand holding the blade, slicing the front of Ash's shirt. With a savage oath he lifted the knife for a deadly thrust and lunged forward.

Ash gripped Noah's wrist and managed to halt his momentum, but barely. With a grunt of rage Noah slammed Ash to the ground, and the two men fought for control of the knife, rolling around and around in the dirt.

Ash managed to wrench the knife free, and it slipped from Noah's grasp. He slammed a fish into Noah's face, and threw a second punch to his chest, sending Noah into a fit of wheezing.

As the two men rolled around, trading punches, Noah's fingers dug in the dirt, searching for his knife.

Brenna, kneeling in the dirt, closed her bound hands around the open switchblade and used it to slice through her bonds.

The loss of so much blood had Ash staggering to his feet, barely able to stand. Seeing his ashen features, Noah gave a triumphant laugh. Like a fighter in the ring who sensed his opponent's weakness, he raised his fists, ready to end it with a quick knockout punch.

"No!"

Hearing Brenna's cry from behind him, Noah turned to see her holding the knife.

Seeing what she intended, his lips split into a cruel grin. "Nice try, girly. But we both know you haven't got the guts."

Staggering, Ash fell facedown into the dirt.

As Noah reached down to take the knife from her hands, she brought the blade upward with all her strength, sinking it deeply into his chest.

For several seconds he merely stared at her blankly, as though unable to accept what she'd done. Then he dropped to the ground, his hands clutching at the knife protruding from his chest.

When she realized what she'd done, Brenna burst into tears.

"There now, lass." Mad leaned down from his wheel-chair to touch a hand to her hair.

"I was too late, Mad. Look. He's killed Ash."

"No, lass. Ash isn't dead. You have to know a MacKenzie's too tough to die from a couple of bullet wounds."

She crawled closer to roll Ash over and touch a hand to his throat. "I can feel a pulse. It's weak." *Dear heaven, so weak*, she thought. "But he's still alive."

"And where there's life, there's hope. You see, lass? You saved his life."

"And he saved mine." She was crying now, big, gulping sobs, as she wrapped her arms around the still figure of Ash and rocked him like a baby. "Oh, Ash. Please don't die. You have to live."

Those were her last words as pandemonium broke loose. State police helicopters, directed to the spot by Brady, landed nearby, sending up little sandstorms that were nearly blinding.

Ranch trucks roared up in a convoy as Willow, Whit, and Griff arrived on the scene. They were out of their vehicles and gathering around both Ash and Mad, asking a million questions and watching helplessly as Brenna continued holding onto Ash.

While state police detectives examined Noah's lifeless body and began bagging and tagging evidence, the police medics pried Brenna away from the half-conscious Ash. After a cursory exam they injected him with painkillers and loaded him onto a gurney. When they'd finished, Brenna once again caught hold of Ash's hand and refused to let go.

When they rolled him into a police helicopter for the ride back to Copper Creek, Brenna was at his side, still weeping, still whispering words of comfort, though he had long since lapsed into blessed unconsciousness.

The rest of the family piled into the Cessna to follow the police copter to town, leaving a small band of officers to tend to the brutal business of crime and death.

CHAPTER TWENTY-EIGHT

The little town of Copper Creek had never seen anything quite like the scene it was witnessing on a tranquil spring afternoon.

A state police helicopter landed in the Copper Creek High School parking lot, and an emergency vehicle whisked Ash MacKenzie and Brenna Crane down Main Street to the clinic, starting tongues wagging.

A Cessna Skyhawk landed on the interstate highway. It looked like a clown act at a rodeo when the doors opened and the pilot, Brady, Whit, Griff, Willow, and Mad, as well as his wheelchair, exited and hitched a ride to the clinic in Chief Ira Pettigrew's squad car.

A convoy of ranch trucks pulled up with Vern, Myrna, and half a dozen wranglers, who rushed inside the clinic to visit the wounded.

"Oh, Ash." Willow fell on her son, hugging him as he

lay on an examining table, while Brenna, on the gurney beside him, was still clinging to his hand.

"You did it, lad." In his excitement, Mad slapped a hand on his grandson's shoulder, causing Ash to wince in pain.

The old man looked up at the others, gathered around the beds. "You should have seen him. Like Superman, taking bullets and moving forward toward that bas—" he stopped and corrected himself "—that miserable excuse of a drifter, who tried to slit Brenna's throat."

"Oh, how horrible." Seeing the fresh dressing Brenna was wearing like a scarf, Myrna ran across the room threw her arms around the young woman, and hugged her fiercely.

Vern, who'd been standing back watching and listening, moved closer to solemnly touch a hand to the young woman's shoulder. "You okay, girl?"

"Fine. It's just a flesh wound." Brenna patted his hand and gave him a weak smile before turning her attention back to Ash.

Once Dr. Dan Mullin and his assistant, Kate, returned to the examining room, they soon turned the chaos into calm.

"My primary concern has to be for my injured patients. The rest of you need to leave."

Mad crossed his arms over his chest. "I'm not leaving my grandson alone."

"He's hardly alone." Dr. Mullin glared at the crowd. "This is a medical clinic. There are sick and injured people here. You can throw a party at your place later. Right now, you all need to leave."

Kate, more diplomatic than her boss, opened the door

and indicated the outer waiting room. "At least until the doctor has had a chance to talk to his patients."

One after another they moved past the beds, touching a hand to Ash or patting Brenna's shoulder before moving to the other room.

When they were alone Dr. Mullin checked Ash's vitals and then Brenna's, before pulling up a chair between their two cots.

"All right, you two. First the facts. Ash, the bullets have been removed, and you're on antibiotics to prevent infection. Brenna, the cut is clean and stitched, and I'm betting my reputation that it will heal without a scar. Thankfully, you're both young and strong and healthy. You've had some physical trauma, not to mention a frightening emotional ordeal. As your friend and your doctor, I'm going to recommend a couple of things. First, while you're here, let everything go and rest. I can give you a prescription for something to help you, if your sleep is disturbed. Then, when I release you both tomorrow, you have that crowd out there dying to pamper you. Let them have their way. Let them feed you and smother you with love. But only for a while. And then, if you're wise, get away from everything for a few days or, instead of feeling smothered with love, you'll feel simply smothered." He looked first at Ash, and then Brenna. "Any questions?"

Brenna looked confused. "You're keeping us overnight?"

The doctor nodded. "I've given you both something for pain. You're exhausted. You'll sleep. And Kate and I will keep an eye on you to see that when we do send you home, there will be no setbacks. Now, if you're smart, heed my advice and catch some rest."

Brenna couldn't help laughing. "That's it? Rest, food, love?"

He winked at them. "Best medicine in the world." He turned toward the door. "Okay. Now I've got to deal with that mob in the outer room. That will definitely be a bigger challenge than the two of you."

When the door closed behind him, Brenna caught Ash's hand. "Are you in any pain?"

"Doc's got me so numb, I can't even feel my toes." He wiggled them, just to be sure they were still working. "Other than that, I'm fine." He squeezed her hand. "And so are you. You're the most amazing woman I've ever known."

She shuddered. "What's amazing about being abducted by a crazy killer?"

"You survived." His tone was rough with emotion. "We both did. Because of your courage."

"What about yours?"

"Sunshine, that wasn't courage. That was desperation. The minute I saw him holding that knife to your throat, my brain shut down and I knew I'd die if I had to. But he wasn't going to go on hurting you as long as I had breath in me."

She felt fresh tears burn her eyes. "It was the same for me. I couldn't stand to watch what he was doing to you. I knew I'd die before I'd see him hurt you anymore."

When her words were met with silence she looked over to see his eyes closed, his breathing soft and even.

She lay very still, watching him breathe. And then, as her sedative kicked in, she joined him in a deep, dreamless sleep.

* * *

It was midafternoon before Dr. Mullin agreed to allow his patients to return home. He was gratified by the fact that both Ash and Brenna had logged in more than ten hours of sleep each.

"You're healing nicely. No infection. And best of all, you got through the night without any complications. I'm comfortable letting the two of you go home."

He looked up as the door opened and the MacKenzie family burst in on them, making further conversation impossible.

"Doc says you can come home," Whit announced. "Mad and Myrna have been cooking and baking all morning. They're planning a celebration. When they refused to leave the kitchen long enough to come to town, we figure this is going to be one heck of a feast." He grinned at his own joke. "Griff's bringing the truck up to the door. And Brenna, Mad phoned Vern and told him to come for supper."

Kate walked in pushing a wheelchair.

Seeing it, Ash started to protest, until she stopped him. "Sorry, Ash. I'm sure this insults your manhood, but it's procedure. Once you leave the clinic, you can walk. But from here to the door, you're my prisoner, and you have to ride."

With Brenna and Ash in side-by-side wheelchairs, they were rolled down the hall.

At the front door their truck was idling, with Griff at the wheel.

After giving calls of thanks, Ash and Brenna were whisked away.

Despite Brenna's protests that she ought to go home, she was outvoted, and she found herself in the midst of a huge celebration at the MacKenzie Ranch.

Myrna and Mad had outdone themselves, with several whole, roasted chickens, stuffing, mounds of mashed potatoes, sweet potatoes, and an enormous salad of tomatoes and cucumbers and red onions in a homemade vinaigrette dressing. There were rolls hot from the oven, and a seven-layer chocolate torte with hot fudge and whipped cream topping.

Vern, who was in on the celebration plans, walked into the kitchen carrying a blanket-wrapped bundle.

Brenna looked over with a smile, which quickly turned to shock when she realized what he was holding.

"Sammy?" She raced to the old man's side. "Oh, Vern. I was so afraid he'd..." She couldn't bring herself to say the word.

"He's doing just fine." Vern unwrapped the blanket and the puppy lifted his head to lick her hand.

"Oh, you little darling." Tears filled her eyes. "How did he survive?"

"The bullet went clear through and didn't hit any of his organs. He lost a whole lot of blood, but he's a tough little guy." Vern looked at her with moisture shining in his watery eyes. "Just like the lady who loves him."

"Oh, Vern." She wrapped her arms around his neck and hugged him fiercely. "I was so afraid..."

"Here." Worried that he might embarrass himself, the old cowboy shoved the bundle into her arms. "He needs you to hold him."

She cradled the little pup like a newborn baby, cooing to him and lifting him to her face just to breathe him in.

Around the kitchen, the others watched with matching smiles.

Hearing the arrival of yet another vehicle, everyone

turned to the door. Chief Pettigrew stepped inside and hung his hat on a hook by the back door before stepping into the kitchen.

"Good." He inhaled all the wonderful aromas. "I was afraid I'd miss the party."

"Not a chance," Mad called from the stove. "Tonight's a celebration, and we want everyone here to join us."

"Anytime I can have a hand in a satisfying resolution, I'm happy to celebrate. This could have ended very differently." He accepted a lemonade from Myrna and sipped. "The state police have been busy checking all their sources, and what they've learned is that the drifter who called himself Noah Perkins and Nolan Parker is really Norman Posey. He's a suspect in a string of crimes that include armed robbery and murder. I'm sure before they're finished with their investigation, there will be plenty of unsolved crimes that can finally be closed."

He turned to Ash. "But the most important fact is this—because of you and your family, he wasn't able to add one more crime to his string."

Ash shook his head. "We can't take the credit, Ira. Brenna not only saved my life but her own, as well. If it hadn't been for her quick thinking, leaving her bracelet behind, I might have missed what was really happening. And then, when he was inches from killing me, she found the courage to stop him, even though he'd cut her throat."

"And what about your courage?" Brenna was staring at Ash with a look of adoration. "At the clinic, Mad called you Superman. That's what you were. Even when that madman shot you, you kept on coming." She turned to the police chief. "Seeing how brave he was, how could I do less?"

The chief winked at Mad. "Looks like I've walked into a mutual admiration society love fest."

While the two men chuckled, Willow startled everyone by bursting into tears.

"Hey, now." Ash hurried over to put a protective arm around his mother. "What's this?"

"Nothing. I'm just... always close to tears these days. But all the time I was out searching for that madman, I was thinking about Bear, and how he would have dealt with this. He would have been so proud of all of you. But I couldn't help thinking that after just burying your father, I couldn't bear to lose another member of my family."

"You didn't lose me, Mom." To ease the tension, Ash added, "Didn't you hear? You can't kill Superman."

While everyone else laughed at Ash's joke, Willow sniffed and fumbled around for a handkerchief.

"Here." From behind her, Brady offered her his.

"Thanks." She blew her nose, obviously embarrassed at having made a scene.

He closed a hand over her shoulder before turning to the chief. "Is there any way this drifter could be responsible for Bear's murder?"

Ira shook his head. "The state boys traced his movements. He wasn't anywhere near Copper Creek on the day Bear was shot." He added, "I know we'd all like to have the filthy coward who shot Bear caught once and for all. But it won't be today. I'm sorry."

The chief's declaration had Willow softly weeping again.

To distract attention from her, Brady called to Myrna, "I thought this was supposed to be a celebration. How about opening that champagne?"

While the others were busy passing around tulip glasses, Willow shot him a grateful smile. "Thank you."

He leaned close. "You okay now?"

"Yes. I'm fine."

He handed her a glass of champagne before holding a chair and waiting for her to take a seat. Then he engaged in a quiet conversation with Vern. But while they talked, he kept an eye on the pale woman who sat sipping her drink, her eyes still red and swollen from the tears she'd been holding back until her son was safely home.

"Maybe this is the perfect time to give you this, Brenna." The chief held out a yellowed document. "This is what our killer was after."

She nodded and accepted it from his hands. "He told me it was a historic deed to my ranch that dates from the eighteen hundreds. My father wanted me to have something that would make me proud of him. But then, with a knife to his throat, he was forced to sign a letter naming Noah his next of kin." She looked at the chief. "My dad never got the chance to make amends for what he'd done in my childhood."

Ash put a hand on her shoulder, before glancing at his mother, pale and quiet. "When I was heading out to find you, Mom told me something that kept me going." His voice lowered with feeling. "She said she believed in her heart that Pop would keep you safe until we could get to you. She's made a believer out of me. And I believe in something else. Redemption. Since your father expressed regret for his behavior, it makes perfect sense that he and Pop were probably working together to see that you came through this alive." He took her hand. "Why not just enjoy the gift your father left you, without any regrets about the past?"

In the silence that followed, Mad cleared the lump that was threatening to choke him and managed to say, "All right. Enough of this. Didn't we promise you a celebration?" He turned to Myrna. "A celebration needs food. Let's get to it."

As they took their places around the table, Mad lifted his glass. "What will we drink to first?"

It was old Vern who came up with the perfect toast. "Here's to putting the past behind us and looking to the future."

With smiles and tears all around, they drank before tucking into their feast. But while everyone around him ate, Ash had grown strangely quiet. Quiet and thoughtful.

It had grown dark outside before the party broke up. The rush of adrenaline was slowly replaced with a feeling of lethargy.

Chief Pettigrew offered handshakes as he took his leave. "This was a good day."

"Yes, it was." Ash accepted the chief's hand. "You do good work."

"We all do." Ira donned his hat as he walked out the back door.

Brady shoved back his chair. "I've got a crew to see to in the morning." He touched a hand to Willow's arm. "You all right?"

"Fine." She glanced around the table. "This was a perfect celebration. Thank you, Mad. Myrna. We couldn't have done it without the two of you."

Vern turned to Brenna, seated beside Ash, still cradling

Sammy in her arms. The pup had long ago given up and drifted to sleep. "I need to get you home, girl."

She nodded. "I think after a long, hot bath, I'll probably sleep for hours."

She kissed Mad's cheek, then Willow's, and finally was embraced by Myrna, who held her for long, silent moments before releasing her.

Ash got to his feet. "I'm going with you."

She paused. "You don't need to keep watch anymore, Ash. Vern and I are safe now."

"I know." He saw the way the others were watching and listening. "There are things...I need to say."

She looked at his eyes, narrowed on her with an intensity that had her heart dropping. Whatever he had to say, it wasn't going to be easy for him, and that meant that it wouldn't be easy for her to hear. She turned toward the back door, feeling all the joy of this celebration melting away.

Ash kissed his mother and grandfather, before solemnly shaking hands with Whit and Griff. With his arm around Myrna he spoke to all of them. "Without you, I wouldn't be here tonight. I want you to know how much I love all of you." He followed Brenna and Vern toward the truck.

In the kitchen, it was Mad who broke the silence. "If I didn't know better, I'd say that sounded a whole lot like good-bye."

The drive to Brenna's ranch was made in complete silence. At the wheel, Vern cast sidelong glances at the woman next to him and the man beside her, looking everywhere but at each other.

The only time they touched was when Sammy stirred.

Both of them drew back the blanket to peer at his little face. The pup yawned, stretched, and fell back to sleep.

Vern deposited them at the back porch before calling good night and crossing to his trailer.

He was too wired to go to bed. Instead he pulled a beer from his fridge and kicked off his boots before dropping into his easy chair.

He leaned back, puzzling over these past days. He prided himself on being able to read people. It was plain to see that Brenna was still head-over-heels for Ash MacKenzie. Ash was another story. Maybe it was the fact that he hadn't been able to spare her the horror of what she'd been through. Maybe he was suffering from some kind of posttraumatic stress. Whatever was going on in Ash's mind, he'd looked fierce enough to slay dragons.

In the kitchen Brenna gently set Sammy, still wrapped in the blanket, in his bed. He was so sound asleep, he never even moved.

She straightened to find Ash still standing at the door. "Will I make coffee?"

He shook his head. "I'll make it."

She sank down on one of the kitchen chairs and braced herself.

Minutes later Ash set a steaming cup of coffee in front of her and poured a second for himself. Crossing to the table, he took the seat opposite hers.

"You said you'd like to talk."

He nodded. His voice was quiet and careful. Too careful. "After Pop's funeral, I promised my mother that I'd give myself time to think about staying."

She felt her hand shake, sending coffee sloshing over

the rim. She set aside the cup. "I know you have a ranch in Wyoming."

"Yeah. My ranch. For nine years I struggled to prove something to myself. Maybe I wanted to prove that I was as tough, as independent, as shrewd as my father. But those nine years taught me so much. I realize now that I'm my own man. I don't have to measure up to Pop. What I do going forward isn't about Bear MacKenzie. It's about what I want. And I realize now that I'm not at all content at home. Maybe I've been away too long. I can't go back to being the boy I was when I left."

Brenna wondered that she could speak. How was it possible, when her heart was shattering? "So you're going back to your ranch in Wyoming."

His head came up. He looked directly into her eyes. "I'm not doing this very well. But I'm trying to tell you that I want to live here, on your ranch."

"Until you're strong enough to return to Wyoming?"

"I've been in contact with my neighbor. He's been tending my herd. He loaned me the money for the repairs to my irrigation system. He's been wanting my spread ever since I bought it. And now I've decided to sell it to him."

"So you can buy a bigger one?"

"Maybe that was my dream once upon a time. But now..." He reached across the table and caught her hands. They were cold as ice. "Sunshine, let me try again. We're getting off track. What I'm trying to say is that I love you. And all I really want to do is settle in here with you on your 'historic'..." His smile came now, curving the corners of his mouth. "...Yeah. Your historic ranch, so that the two of us can make it all that it ought to be. That is, if you'll have me."

Brenna held up a hand. "Wait. I'm confused. Is this a merger or a marriage proposal?"

"I'll make this easier." He stood and rounded the table, before dropping down on his knees before her. "Brenna Crane, the day I stumbled upon you sitting under that tree, I knew I'd found my best friend. Since then, I've spent my days and, to be honest, a lot of my nights dreaming of you. It didn't take me long to figure out that what I felt for you was love. But when I left, I figured I'd killed any chance of ever getting that love back. Seeing you with Chris…" He shook his head. "It was almost as shattering as seeing you with a knife to your throat. And through it all, through all those days and nights and years, through the hard work and the tears, I knew one thing. I love you. I've always loved you. I thought I'd really messed up and lost everything that mattered to me. But now that I have a second chance, I want, more than anything in the world, to marry you and live with you, and ranch with you, and raise Sammy with you, and…"

She stopped him with a long, slow kiss. Against his mouth she whispered, "You had me at 'best friend.' Because, friend, I love you, too. So yes. And yes. And yes…"

And then there was no need for words.

Out in the trailer, Vern saw the kitchen light go out. He waited to see if a bedroom light went on. The ranch house was dark. And silent.

He smiled and tipped up his beer.

Whatever those two were up to, he'd put his money on Ash MacKenzie. Now there was a dragon slayer if ever there was one.

EPILOGUE

Summer had come to Montana. Meadows were lush and green. Hawks soared on warm currents of air, making lazy circles over cattle growing sleek and fat. Copper Creek lured many a cowboy to strip off his clothes, just as in childhood, and take advantage of a cool, refreshing dip before returning to his chores.

Brenna's house glowed in the summer sun under a fresh coat of white paint. Her porch had been widened, and new steps added.

Ash had enlisted the aid of Griff, whose skill as a woodworker had turned the interior of the old house into a showplace. Walls had been removed, opening the kitchen and parlor into one big sunny space. Upstairs, two bedrooms had been turned into a master suite, with a walk-in closet and master bathroom, complete with a deep soaker tub and shower big enough for an army.

Out back, the sagging, ancient barn had been shored up

and sported a spiffy coat of red paint. Everyone for miles around referred to it as Big Red.

In the kitchen, Myrna and Mad were bumping into each other as they put the finishing touches on a wedding supper fit for a MacKenzie. The wranglers had been put to work setting up planks on sawhorses that graced the yard beneath the big old aspens. The planks looked glorious with their white linen tablecloths and centerpieces of white roses and ivy.

Soon they were groaning beneath trays and platters of rare, fork-tender beef tenderloin, fried chicken, and honey-glazed ham. There were steam trays swimming with mushroom gravy and Myrna's famous garlic mashed potatoes. There were too many salads to count. A garden salad with Mad's own dressing of creamy gorgonzola cheese. Potato salad, pasta salad. There was a kettle of chili hot enough to make a cowboy weep.

There was a sweet table, filled with enough cakes and pies and cookies to satisfy the sweet tooths of everyone in the town of Copper Creek, all of whom had been invited to share the joy of this day.

Mad studied the figures atop the four-layer wedding cake that he and Myrna had fashioned. The bottom layer was carrot cake, to satisfy Ash and Brenna. The second layer was chocolate, the third yellow, and the top layer white, with bits of fresh strawberries from Myrna's garden.

On top of the creamy white frosting stood a cowboy with dark hair and, just beneath his plaid shirt, a tiny strip of bright red Superman S. Mad and Myrna shared a conspiratorial grin. The female figure was blonde, wearing denims and boots, and holding a yellow fluffy pup in her arms.

"Ye've outdone yerself, lass." As always, when he was feeling emotional, Mad's Scottish burr became more pronounced.

"So have you." Myrna looked around with satisfaction. "I believe our work is finished."

"Then let's enjoy ourselves. We've earned it." Mad turned his wheelchair toward the porch and waited for Brady to take him to the yard, where the others had gathered.

Out in the yard, Willow stood back, admiring the flowers she'd ordered from the tiny shop Flowers by Flo, in Copper Creek. It had been the largest order the owner—Florence Hanover, daughter of Percy and Pearl—had ever filled.

Tall urns filled with long-stemmed white roses and spilling over with ivy dressed the makeshift buffet tables, as well as each side of the porch.

More white roses and ivy adorned the steps, and small, round bowls of them sat on every table beneath a white tent.

A hundred chairs with big white bows tied to their backs were set in a semicircle around a raised platform, which was ringed with roses.

Seeing that Mad and Myrna had finished with the food, Willow caught Myrna's hand and whispered, "Brenna asked if we'd join her upstairs when we're ready."

Myrna nodded, and the two women disappeared up the stairs together.

Ash stood in the cool interior of the barn, where a plank set over two sawhorses formed a bar of sorts. Several ice buckets held chilling bottles of alcohol and soda.

He looked up as Brady pushed Mad toward him, trailed by Whit and Griff. Vern, wearing his best Western suit, his boots polished to a high shine, stepped out of his trailer and strolled over to join them.

Whit poured fine Irish whiskey into tumblers and passed them around. "Here's to you, bro." He lifted his glass. "And to your bride. I don't know what took you so long to figure out what the rest of us knew years ago. You and Brenna were meant to be together."

With a laugh, they drank.

Griff lifted his glass. "Here's to the family I wish I'd had growing up. I'm proud to know all of you."

"Right back at you, bro." With a grin, Ash drank again and they joined him.

Mad's burr thickened. "Here's to my son, who gave me this fine big family. I know he's smiling today."

"To Pop," Ash said.

"To Bear MacKenzie," Griff added.

As they drank, Vern cleared his throat before saying softly, "I'd like to toast Brenna. A finer woman you'll never find."

They all nodded before drinking.

Willow paused outside the bedroom door and knocked.

"Come in," Brenna called.

Willow and Myrna stepped inside and paused to stare at the vision before them.

"Oh, Brenna. Look at you." Willow felt tears spring to her eyes and cursed the fact that she'd shed more tears in the past weeks than she had in a lifetime.

"Do you like it?" Brenna twirled. "It was my mother's. I found it in the attic."

She wore a long, slender column of ivory silk fashioned with a high, dog-collar neckline of lace that ringed her throat, and short, cap sleeves that fluttered at the tops of her arms with each movement.

Her blonde hair worn long and loose, her only jewelry was the band of filigree at her wrist, and the effect was simple and stunning.

"It's perfect," Myrna sighed. "It suits you."

"Thank you." Brenna hugged Willow and then Myrna before removing two boxes from the dresser. "I made each of you something."

She handed the first to Willow, who opened it and gave a gasp of pleasure.

It was a sculpture of her surrounded by Ash, Whit, and Griff, with Mad seated in front of them—and behind, with his arms spread as though gathering them all close, stood Bear.

Willow couldn't stop the tears, and was forced to reach for a handkerchief before embracing Brenna. "I will cherish this. I love it so much."

"I'm glad."

Brenna handed the second box to Myrna. When the older woman opened the box, she simply stared, too stunned to speak.

It was Myrna with her arms around a very young Brenna, who was looking up at her with eyes wide and smiling. On the base of the sculpture were the words, *The grandmother heaven sent me*.

"I never knew you felt that way." Myrna fought her own tears.

"I let my sculpture say it for me." She pressed a kiss to the old woman's cheek.

At a knock on the door they looked up to see Vern standing in the doorway.

For several moments he merely stared at Brenna, unable to say a word. Finally, clearing his throat, he managed to say, "Reverend Hamilton and his wife are here. It's time to go, girl."

Seeing the look in the old cowboy's eyes, Willow caught Myrna's hand and stepped away. "We'll be downstairs."

When Willow and Myrna left, Brenna turned to Vern. "Are you ready to give away the bride?"

"I don't know if I am."

At his words she moved closer to touch a hand to his arm. "What does that mean?"

He merely shook his head. "I've watched you grow up. Watched you struggle against all that life threw at you, and look at you, girl. Still standing, and looking like some kind of angel." He touched a leathery finger to her cheek. "I'm so proud of you. And I know your mama and daddy are, too."

"Thank you." She smiled then, because she didn't want her tears to mar this day. She wrapped her arms around his neck. "I couldn't have done it without you, Vern. You were always here for me. And I'm so grateful that you've agreed to stay on."

"You're my family, girl. And I'll say this now. You've picked the right man to spend the rest of your life with. Ash MacKenzie is a finisher. That man will never let you down."

She linked her arm with his and leaned close to kiss his cheek. "Come on. Let's make it legal before he gets away."

With a laugh, the two of them stepped out of her room and descended the stairs.

When they reached the porch, they paused.

Half the town of Copper Creek milled about the yard. Ira Pettigrew, and Percy and Pearl Hanover. Nonie Claxton and Wylie. Thurman Biddle and Alf Green, the grocer. Mason McMillan and his son, Lance, looking out of place in their fancy suits. Beside them stood Dr. Dan Mullin—in a lab coat, since he would be returning to the clinic immediately after the wedding—and his assistant, Kate, chatting up all her neighbors.

There were boys and girls playing hide-and-seek, and teenage boys and girls flirting, while their parents kept a close eye on them.

The minister, in his best vestments, stood near the raised platform, which was banked with roses. To one side Willow stood beside Brady. Mad's wheelchair was parked next to Myrna, who already held a handkerchief to her eyes. On the other side of the minister stood Whit and Griff in their best denims and shiny boots. Whit winked at Brenna, and she shot him a grin. Griff gave her a thumbs-up, and she gave it back to him.

And then she caught sight of Ash, looking so fierce and handsome as he walked toward her.

She was vaguely aware of Vern taking her hand from his arm and placing it in Ash's hand. Could hear Rascal Flatts in the background singing about the broken road they'd traveled, from her favorite CD. But all she was really aware of was Ash. Smiling down at her, his eyes on hers, his hand so big and rough and callused, holding hers with such strength.

"Oh, Ash, I love you," she whispered.

"I love you more, Sunshine." He leaned close. "Last chance. Want to skip all this fuss and go swimming in Copper Creek?"

"Not on your life, cowboy. I let you get away once. This time, you're not going anywhere until you make me your wife."

"Okay. But tomorrow you and I are going skinny-dipping." He winked, then turned away. "Almost forgot." He handed her a nosegay of white roses. As she buried her face in them, he leaned down and straightened, holding Sammy, who was wriggling happily and wearing a white bow on his collar.

At her raised brow, Ash shrugged. "If we're going to make it legal, we have to include the entire family."

Family.

While the onlookers smiled and laughed, Brenna looked around at the wonderful family she was acquiring.

For a girl who'd been alone for most of her life, it was heady indeed to know she now had a grandmother, a grandfather, and tall, sturdy brothers who would always be there for her.

Above all, she was finally free to spend the rest of her life with the boy who had won her heart all those years ago.

Her very own Superman.

Real life didn't get any better than this.

MAD MACKENZIE'S GARLIC MASHED POTATOES

(Adjust the quantity if some family members are absent)

When the entire MacKenzie family is present:

- 5 to 10 lbs. potatoes, peeled, quartered, and brought to a boil in a huge pot of water, along with 4 cloves of garlic

Simmer until cooked to a soft consistency (approx. 20 to 25 minutes), depending on amount of potatoes.

Drain and pour into large mixing bowl.

Add ½ a cup of milk and ½ a stick of butter, depending on amount of potatoes.

(For a creamier potato, add a package of cream cheese as well.)

Mix all ingredients well and serve with Mad's tender pot roast.

After his mother passes away, Griff Warren ventures to Copper Creek to meet the family he never knew. But the handsome cowboy still feels like he doesn't fully belong there—until he meets a beautiful woman with a heart of gold...

Please see the next page
for a preview of

THE REBEL OF
COPPER CREEK.

CHAPTER ONE

Get 'im in that chute, Griff."

The cowboy's shrill voice had Griff Warren singling out the next calf from the portable corral and urging it into the narrow passageway toward a branding cradle. At least that was what the wranglers called it. Griff thought of it as a torture chamber.

Once in there, the headgate slammed shut, the walls of the chute closed in, and the entire cage tipped to hold the calf on its side while Ash or Whit MacKenzie pressed a sizzling branding iron to the calf's right hip area.

The entire operation took only a few seconds, and the bawling calf was righted, released, and sent racing toward its mother in a second holding pen, while Griff, amid shouts and catcalls, was forced to prod the next calf toward the same fate.

The process was repeated over and over, for five hot, sweaty, endless days, until every calf born this spring on the MacKenzie Ranch had been branded with the unique MK on its left shoulder. Then they were herded by a team of wranglers, or in some cases trucked to the highlands in cattle haulers for a summer eating frenzy on the lush grasses that grew in the hills around Copper Creek.

When the last of the calves had met its fate, Whit, Griff's brother, dropped an arm around Griff's shoulders. "Great job, cowboy. You just had your baptism of fire. And look at you. Still standing."

"Barely." Griff, his shirt so wet it stuck to his skin, eyes red from the dust of frantic cattle, managed a weak grin.

Brady Storm, foreman of the MacKenzie Ranch, offered a handshake. "Welcome to Ranching 101, son. It's hard, dirty work. And not one of us would trade this job for a suit and tie in the city."

Griff shook his head. "Don't tempt me, Brady. At the moment, that almost sounds like heaven."

"Another fine supper, Mad." Griff sat back, sipping coffee.

Fresh from the longest shower of his life, he was feeling almost human again.

He'd been living with the MacKenzie family on their ranch since mustering out of the Marine Corps. He'd arrived in time to bury the stranger who had been his father. But though he'd been acknowledged as the son of Bear MacKenzie, he resisted accepting the MacKenzie name, choosing instead to continue using his single mother's last name as it had been recorded on his birth certificate.

"From what Brady told me, son, you deserve a good meal." Seventy-year-old Maddock MacKenzie, Bear's father, and therefore Griff's biological grandfather, was called Mad by all who knew him. It was a well-deserved name, since his temper was legend in this part of Montana.

The cantankerous old man winked at ranch foreman Brady Storm. "Brady tells me you've been jumping into ranch chores with both feet. But branding's another thing altogether. For a novice, branding can be pretty grueling, even for those of us who cut our teeth on ranch chores."

"Tell me about it." Whit, at twenty-five, the youngest of Bear MacKenzie's three sons, shot a grin at his brother, Ash, seated across the table. "The first time Pa took me with him to help with the branding, I was five or six. The wranglers were still branding the old-fashioned way. Wrestling calves to the dirt, holding them down, and driving that hot iron into their rump. I've never forgotten the smell of burning flesh and the bawling of those calves. I was sick for a week."

"I guess, to a kid, it's pretty barbaric." Mad polished off the last of his garlic mashed potatoes, one of his favorite side dishes, which he prepared at least once a week.

"Not just to a kid." Willow MacKenzie, mother to Ash and Whit, turned to her father-in-law. "I may have grown up on a ranch, but I'm still troubled every spring during branding."

"Can't be helped." Mad shared a knowing look with the foreman. "We can tag a cow's ear or implant a chip, but the process our ancestors came up with is still the most efficient. The state of Montana is open range. We've got thousands of acres of rangeland. Those critters can hide in canyons, wander into forests. But the state demands that we register our brand with the state brand office. Not only the brand, but the exact location on each calf. That's why we've got that MK on the right hip of every one of our cattle. It's pretty hard for a thief to explain what he's doing with your property."

Griff shook his head. "All I know is, I'm glad that particular chore is finished for the year. Now I can get back to learning the easy stuff."

"You think tending herds in the high country in blizzards or summer storms is easy? You like mending fences and mucking stalls?" Ash shared a look with the others. "I guess that's what happens when you survive three tours with the Marines in Afghanistan. Everything after that is gravy."

The others around the table joined in the laughter.

Myrna Hill, plump housekeeper for the MacKenzie family, set a tray of brownies on the table before passing around hot fudge sundaes. "You have Brenna to thank for the dessert. She drove all the way into Copper Creek, to that cute little shop I's Cream, for Ivy's special chocolate marshmallow walnut ice cream."

Ash nudged his bride, Brenna, seated beside him. "Is this a special occasion?" He put a hand to his heart. "Don't tell me I've forgotten an anniversary or something already."

"Now you've done it, lad." Mad's Scottish burr thickened along with his laughter. "Don't you know that the first rule of a new husband is to never admit that you've forgotten a special day? You're supposed to just smile and remain silent, and your bride will think you've known about it all along."

"Now you tell me." Ash put his arm around Brenna's shoulders and nuzzled her cheek. "Whatever the occasion, you know I'm happy to be celebrating it with you."

"Uh-huh." With an impish grin Brenna smiled at Myrna, whose cap of white curls bounced with every step she took. "I suppose, if you're feeling guilty enough, I could get a new washer out of this. Or maybe something really big, like a new truck at Orin Tamer's dealership. But the truth is, babe, you haven't forgotten a thing. I just thought you'd want some comfort food after dealing with all that branding for the past week."

"Whew." Across the table, Whit made a big production of wiping imaginary sweat from his brow. "You really ducked a trap this time, bro."

"Yeah." Ash lifted Brenna's hand to his mouth and planted a wet kiss in her palm. "See how she pampers me?"

"Don't be fooled, bro." Whit dug into his sundae. "Our Brenna's smart. That means she'll figure a way to get what she wants even without playing on your guilt."

Brenna dimpled. "Better eat that dessert as fast as you can, or you may find it dumped over your very adorable head, my sweet brother-in-law."

"That's 'bro-in-law' to you, Bren." He held up his now-empty bowl. "And you're too late."

Around the table, the others enjoyed the banter while they polished off their desserts.

Afterward, they lounged comfortably, drinking coffee and discussing the week's activities on the thousand plus acres that made up the mighty MacKenzie ranch.

With the sudden, shocking murder of Bear MacKenzie, the operation of the ranch had fallen to his three sons and his widow, Willow. Bear's father, Maddock, was confined to a wheelchair since a ranch accident nearly fifteen years previous. Since then he'd merged his ranch with that of his son, and had commandeered the kitchen chores, much to housekeeper Myrna's dismay. Though the two shared some cooking skills, Mad's overbearing personality often drove Myrna to hide out in other parts of the house. But when she did work in the kitchen, she was more than ready to stand up to the old curmudgeon. And though they enjoyed spirited arguments, there was an underlying affection that was obvious to everyone.

Ash turned to his mother. "Any news from Chief Pettigrew?"

Willow shook her head. "As a matter of fact, Ira called this morning, just to touch base and let me know he was doing all he could. The state police crime lab has concluded the estimated distance the bullets traveled. That's an important step in the investigation. Once they determine the exact location where the shooter was concealed, they can begin going over the area with a fine-tooth comb. Ira assured me that if even a single thread of evidence exists, they'll find and identify it."

Mad patted his daughter-in-law's hand. "Keep the faith, lass. They'll get the coward who shot Bear."

She nodded. "I know, Mad. But every time I go into town, I can't help thinking that someone smiling at me, talking to me, could be Bear's killer." She shuddered. "I can't bear the thought that such a monster is still walking around, enjoying his life, while Bear is..." She couldn't bring herself to say the word.

Brady Storm, always sensitive to Willow's emotions, quickly changed the subject. "I saw Lance McMillan fly in that sleek new plane. What did he want?"

At the mention of their long-time lawyer's son, who had recently taken over his father's practice, Willow sighed. "I told him his father knew better than to interrupt a rancher at branding time. And without even the courtesy of a phone call. But he said he was on his way up to join his father on a fishing trip in Canada, and it was Mason who'd wanted me to sign some papers."

Mad looked over. "What kind of papers?"

Willow shrugged. "Lance said they were just routine documents needed after the death of a spouse. I told him to leave them and I'd read them later, when I have my wits about me."

"Good." Mad nodded his approval. "Mason would have never brought documents for a signature without taking the time to explain them thoroughly."

Willow gave a short laugh. "That's what I said, though in truth I didn't want to give him any more of my time. The irony is, after I took my shower I went to Bear's office to read them, and they weren't there. When I phoned Lance on his cell phone, he said he'd mistakenly dropped them back into his briefcase. He has them with him in Canada. Now he'll have to mail them to me when he gets back to Billings after his fishing trip with Mason."

"So his visit was a waste of time."

"I don't know about Lance's time, but it was certainly a waste of mine."

Willow looked up as Whit clapped a hand on the foreman's back. "How about a beer at Wylie's?"

Brady nodded. "I'm in." He turned to Griff. "You joining us?"

Griff smiled. "Good idea. Willow? Mad? Ready for a night in town?"

Both Willow and Mad shook their heads.

Whit turned to the newlyweds. "Ash and Brenna?"

The two turned to each other, smiled, and shook their heads in unison.

Ash spoke for both of them. "Thanks, but we'll pass tonight."

Whit waved a hand toward the others. "What did I tell you? The way those two are looking, I'm betting that before the night's over my big brother will be promising his lady love that new truck she's been mooning over."

"Nobody deserves it more," Ash said, stonefaced.

"Oh, man." Whit turned away with a mock shudder. "Now I really need a beer at Wylie's, to wash away the taste of all that sugar."

At that, everyone burst into gales of laughter. Even Myrna joined in as the men made ready to leave for town.

Copper Creek, more than an hour's drive from the ranch, was little more than a main street, with rows of shops and stores, a church, a school, a medical center, a town hall connected with a jail and a courthouse, and Wylie's Saloon, the official watering hole for the surrounding ranchers. "Hey, Whit. Griff." Nonie Claxton, a waitress at Wylie's since it first opened, paused while juggling a tray holding half a dozen longnecks. She wiped stringy orange bangs from her eyes as she gave Brady Storm a long, admiring look. "How lucky can a girl get? Three sexy cowboys. Park somewhere, boys, and I'll take your order in a minute."

Seeing no seats left at the bar, they grabbed a table in the middle of the smoky room. Within minutes Nonie was there as promised to set three frosty longnecks in front of them.

Griff nodded toward a noisy table in the corner. "Who're the guys in uniform?"

Nonie glanced toward the assortment of men in wheelchairs, others balancing crutches or canes across their laps. Several wore faded military fatigues. "They call themselves Romeos."

At Griff's arched brow she laughed. "They're all part of the band of veterans who spend time at the Grayson Ranch. It's a take on the owner's name. The widow Grayson. Her name's Juliet. Get it? Romeos? Juliet?" She nodded toward Whit. "Your brother here could probably tell you about the place."

Whit shrugged. "I'm afraid I don't know that much about it, except that when Buddy Grayson's widow came back to Montana to take over the ranch, she offered to turn it into some kind of therapy place for wounded vets."

"How can a ranch be a therapy place?" Brady asked.

Again that shrug as Whit said, "I don't have a clue. I'm thinking it's like a dude ranch. All phony, and not a working wrangler in sight." He turned. "Maybe we ought to ask the Romeos about their Juliet."

Just saying those names had him grinning, and Griff and Brady chuckled at the joke.

A short time later Griff felt a hand on his shoulder and looked up to see a bearded man in a faded denim shirt and torn jeans, seated in a wheelchair and grinning from ear to ear.

"I thought that was you, Captain. What in hell are you doing in Copper Creek?"

It took Griff a moment to place the face, but the gravelly voice was unmistakable. "Jimmy? Jimmy Gable?"

He was up and leaning over to grab the bearded man in a bear hug.

When the two had stopping punching one another's shoulders, Griff stood back. "I thought your home was somewhere out East. What are you doing way out here in Montana?"

"Wanted to see how the other half lived." The man chuckled at the look on his old Marine buddy's face. "Okay. Truth. After my little...accident..." He looked down at his empty pant legs before smiling. "...a guy I met at the VA hospital invited me to join a group called the Romeos. They spend a lot of time at some ranch."

"Playing cowboy?" Griff asked dryly.

Jimmy shrugged. "Something like that, I guess. And since that was just about the best excuse I could think of to get away from my doting family, I jumped at the chance."

With a grin, Griff turned to introduce Jimmy to Whit and Brady. After a round of handshakes, Griff took a seat beside the younger man's wheelchair. "I thought you were leaving the Corps when I did."

"I planned on it. I had only another month when my luck ran out."

"How bad is it?"

Jimmy's voice lowered. "I won't be running any marathons." He brightened. "But then, I was never much of a runner anyway. The doctors think I'm a good candidate for a prostheses."

"That's great. How long will you have to wait?"

The younger man shrugged. "I'm working with a doctor who is hooking me up with a guy he calls a genius at these things. But it all takes time. And while I'm waiting,

I thought I'd take a break from my family. Ever since I got home, they've been all over me. Won't let me do a thing. Running ahead to open doors, picking up anything I drop before I even know I dropped it."

Griff chuckled. "Don't fault them, Jimmy. You know they love you."

"Yeah. And they're smothering me with all that love."

He studied Griff, whose already muscled body was now honed to perfection, his skin tanned from weeks in the hills with the herd, his wide-brimmed hat hanging on the back of his chair. "Something tells me you've turned into the real deal. A cowboy."

Griff couldn't stop the grin that spread across his features. "Guilty."

Jimmy nodded toward Whit, seated across the table. "Did I hear you call him your brother?"

Griff chuckled. "You did. And yeah, before you ask, I'm as new at this family thing as I am at being a rancher."

Jimmy looked at Brady, whose handsome, tanned face and white hair, along with a perfectly toned body made him look like a poster for the State of Montana. "And is this your long-lost father?"

That had all of them chuckling.

"Brady is the foreman of my father's ranch."

"Okay." Jimmy rubbed his hands together. "Now tell me about your mysterious father."

With a glance at Whit, Griff was quick to say, "Maybe some other time. Right now, tell me about those Romeos."

"Better than telling you, why don't I have you join us?"

Griff shrugged. "Join you for what?"

"A military reunion. We're heading over to the Grayson Ranch tomorrow. Want to join us?"

Griff was already shaking his head. "Maybe, after chores—"

Brady interrupted. "After the week you put in, I think you deserve a day off. Grab it while you have the chance."

Griff looked pleased. "You're sure?"

When Brady gave a quick nod of his head, Griff didn't need time to consider. "Why not? If it's got something to do with veterans, I'm intrigued. Just tell me where and when."

"We'll be heading over around noon. I'm told it's somewhere out in that vast expanse of wilderness folks around here call a hop, skip, and a jump from town."

Whit was smiling as he added dryly, "I know where it's at. I'll give you directions before you head out tomorrow, bro."

Jimmy drained his beer. "I'd better get back to my buddies. I'll see you tomorrow, Captain. We'll reminisce about the good times we had in the hills of Afghanistan."

With a twinkle in his eye he turned his wheelchair and returned to the table in the corner, where the voices grew louder with each round of longnecks.

Whit narrowed his gaze on Griff. "Captain?"

Griff tipped up his longneck. "Not anymore. Now I'm just a ranch hand learning how to shovel manure."

"And doing a damned fine job," Whit said with a laugh as he caught Nonie's eye and lifted his empty bottle.

Within minutes she'd brought them another round of drinks, and the talk turned, as always, to the daily grind of running a ranch the size of Rhode Island.

CHAPTER TWO

Summer had settled in to Montana, bringing with it hot, sunny days and warm nights perfumed with bitterroot. The pale pink blossoms covered the hills around the MacKenzie ranch.

Griff leaned a hip against the sill and stared at the scene outside his window. Everything on this vast ranch seemed more. More space to roam. More cattle than any one man could count.

An eagle soared high above the herds that darkened the landscape. For as far as he could see, this land belonged to the MacKenzie family. His family now. The thought had him frowning. It didn't seem possible. After growing up dreaming about the father he never knew, he'd now acquired a grandfather, two half brothers, and a stepmother who still looked more like the model she'd once been than the rancher's widow she was now.

What was even more impossible to process was the

fact that before his death, Bear MacKenzie had not only accepted the truth that Griff was his son but had included him in his will, leaving a portion of all of this to him, if he decided to stay and become a rancher. If he chose instead to walk away, he would relinquish his share but would find himself a very rich man.

He shook his head at the absurdity of it all. How could anyone starved for family turn his back on all this for mere money? What Bear had offered, and what Willow MacKenzie had agreed to when she'd learned of her husband's will, was worth so much more than wealth. She and her family had accepted him as one of them.

He'd arrived here an angry, bitter man, war-weary from three tours of duty, expecting to resent the sons who had been privileged to grow up alongside their powerful rancher father. Instead, he'd been made welcome, and was learning, by trial and error, to become worthy to be called Bear MacKenzie's other son.

"Hey, bro."

Outside in the hallway, Whit pounded a fist on the closed door as he headed for the stairs. "If you're late for breakfast, I get your steak."

Griff was still buttoning his shirt and tucking it into his jeans as he made a wild dash to the kitchen. "If Mad's making steak and eggs, you'll lose your hand if you even think about touching mine."

The old man looked up from his wheelchair positioned in front of the stove, where he was flipping steaks onto a platter. "Any fighting at the table, the two of you will be shoveling manure for the rest of the day."

"Yes, sir. Thank you, sir." Whit grinned at Griff as the two shared a laugh behind Mad's back.

The old man turned to give them a hairy eyeball. "Don't think I don't know what you're doing. Even grown men can misbehave, given the opportunity. But I do like the way Griff's military attitude is rubbing off on you, lad."

Whit shot his grandfather one of his famous grins. "Now if only my charm with the ladies would rub off on Griff."

At Willow's raised brow, Whit chuckled. "There were half a dozen hot chicks at Wylie's last night, all giving big bro here that 'let's hook up' look, and he spent all his time ignoring them and talking to a bunch of military guys over in the corner."

"Military guys here in Copper Creek?" Intrigued, Willow set down her coffee cup and turned to Griff. "There's no military base for hundreds of miles. What were they doing here?"

He shrugged. "They call themselves Romeos, because they're involved in some kind of therapy at the Grayson Ranch."

"Ah." Willow nodded. "I heard rumors that Buddy's widow was living there, but I hadn't heard any details. What kind of therapy are they involved in?"

Griff shook his head. "I don't have a clue."

Whit chuckled. "Since you're going over there later today, Mom will expect you to have some gossip ready when you get home."

"You're going to the Grayson Ranch?" Willow flushed, knowing she sounded a bit too eager. "It's not gossip. But like everyone around town, I'm curious to know what's going on there."

"We all are." Mad wheeled closer to the table and began filling his plate as Myrna Hill passed around platters of steak and eggs, cinnamon toast, and little pots of jam.

"What's that supposed to mean?" Griff turned to Willow. "Isn't it a working ranch like all the others around here?"

"It was." She tasted her steak and smiled at her father-in-law. "Perfect, Mad. How do you always manage to get my steak exactly the way I like it?"

"Because I'm a genius in the kitchen." He winked at his youngest grandson. "And don't you ever forget it, laddie."

"As if you'd let me," Whit deadpanned.

Willow turned to Griff and picked up the thread of their conversation. "The Grayson Ranch is fairly small by Montana standards, but it used to be one of the finest around. Buddy Grayson was the last remaining member of his family. When he died, we expected the place to go up for auction. Instead we heard rumors that his widow had shown up to take over the operation."

"Good for her." Griff took his time, savoring every bite of his breakfast. There'd been a time when he had only dreamed of meals like this. Now that it was a reality, he was determined to enjoy the moment. "So Buddy Grayson married a rancher. Did she grow up around here?"

Willow shook her head. "I'm not sure, but I heard she comes from the Midwest."

Griff arched a brow at Whit. "Not exactly ranching country. But then, I grew up right here in Montana, and the closest I ever came to a working ranch was on a field trip in third grade. We all got to feed some hogs and milk a cow."

"What?" Mad grinned at him over the rim of his cup. "Those teachers didn't have you shoveling manure?"

"They knew better. With a bunch of city kids like us, we'd have been holding our noses and climbing back onto the school bus, ready to hit the road at the first smell."

That had everyone around the table laughing.

Griff returned his attention to the Grayson Ranch. "So, if this guy's widow doesn't know a thing about ranching, how does she expect to keep it going?"

"That's the million-dollar question around these parts." Willow shrugged and turned to Brady Storm. "Have you heard how she's doing?"

He shook his head. "Word is, Jackie Turner, ranch foreman since old Frank Grayson was running things, retired right after he heard about Buddy's death. His heart was broken, and so was his spirit. Without somebody to ride herd on the few wranglers that are still there, the place is looking pretty shabby these days."

Willow pinned Griff with a look. "As long as you're going there today, I expect a full report."

"Yes, ma'am." He shot her a grin. "Maybe you'd like pictures?"

"Words will be enough. At least for now," she added with a smile. "Your father was a good friend to Frank Grayson. I think he'd be appalled at the thought of all that rich grazing land going to seed."

Mad nodded. "While some outsider turns the place into a spa."

Griff was quick to defend, even though he knew it was useless. "I don't think it's a spa. It's a place for some kind of therapy."

"Massages. Therapy." Mad scowled. "Same thing in

my book. It's probably some fancy dude ranch and spa."

Brady pushed away from the table. "I'm heading up to the highlands today. Whit, you coming with me?"

"Yeah." Whit turned to Griff. "I wrote directions to the Grayson Ranch. The far end of their ranch butts up to our north ridge. Take the interstate highway and you'll be there in an hour. If you take the back roads, it'll take closer to an hour and a half. But if you'd like to take up the Cessna, you could be there in no time. I don't know if their airstrip is still in good repair, but I know that Buddy used to keep a single-engine plane in one of the barns."

Mad's head came up sharply. "You licensed to fly in Montana, lad?"

Griff nodded. "After flying with Brady for the past month, I went to the county offices a couple of weeks ago and took the test. The formal documents came in the mail the other day."

The old man gave him a long look. "You're just full of surprises, aren't you?"

Before Griff could respond, Mad's mouth curved into a wide smile. "I see you play your cards close to the vest. Just like your pa."

Griff had no words.

It was, he realized, the highest compliment Maddock MacKenzie could have paid him.

It was a perfect day for flying. The sky was a clear, cloudless blue. A gentle breeze was blowing in from the west.

Griff had thoroughly enjoyed being tutored by Brady, who had regaled him with hair-raising stories of the early years working with Bear MacKenzie. During those long airborne hours, Griff and Brady had formed a bond, discovering that they both preferred reading biographies to fiction, watching suspense movies over outrageous comedies, and both had grown up without a male role model in their lives.

Griff could see, through Brady's eyes, the sort of man his father had been. Blunt, hardworking, driven to succeed. A tough, demanding taskmaster who saved his harshest criticism for his own sons, believing it was the only way to assure that they would be able to survive in this unforgiving land.

Maybe, Griff thought, he was lucky to have been spared that part of his education. Military school had been bad enough. He'd been forced to fight his way through the first couple of years. Growing up under the thumb of Bear MacKenzie would have been a lot tougher. Which explained why Bear's son, Ash, had left in a rage after a particularly unjustly earned tirade, returning only after his father was dead.

Griff adjusted his sunglasses before peering at the land below. Just as Whit had promised, it was easy to discern where MacKenzie land ended and Grayson land began. The undulating hills of MacKenzie land were black with cattle, with dozens of capable wranglers to tend the herds. The sparsely populated hills to the north were nearly barren, with only the occasional small herd grazing. Griff saw no sign of horsemen below.

As the plane drew near the Grayson house and barns, the distinction was even clearer. There were gaps in large portions of fences. The roofs of the buildings appeared worn and shabby, the barns were in need of paint, the sprawling house sported a sagging porch, and shingles were missing from the peaked roof.

A couple of trucks and a shiny new bus were parked near one of the barns.

After circling the barn and concluding that the asphalt strip looked safe enough, Griff brought the little Cessna in for a smooth landing.

He was smiling as he opened the door and stepped down.

"I hope you have a good explanation for making me wait a whole week."

The feminine voice was low, the words spoken in a tone that left no doubt that the one speaking was furious.

Griff turned to see a slender girl in torn denims and a skinny T-shirt standing just inside the doorway of the barn, hands on her hips, dark eyes barely visible beneath a faded baseball cap, spitting daggers at him.

His own eyes, hidden behind the mirrored sunglasses, widened in surprise.

He stepped closer, his tone lowering to a growl to reveal his annoyance at this unexpected greeting. "I beg your pardon."

"You'd better beg my pardon. You were supposed to be here last Monday. You know how critical your equipment is to my operation. I can't believe I haven't heard a single word from you. And after you promised to repair that lift as soon as possible."

"Look." Griff reached out a hand. "I don't know who you think I am, but—"

She was too busy chastising him to hear a word he said. "Just take a look at the mess I've been dealing with."

She turned away and stalked into the barn, expecting him to follow.

He did, reluctantly, and was forced to remove his

glasses in order to let his eyes adjust to the gloomy interior. As he did, he became aware of a cluster of men in wheelchairs, all watching him in sullen silence.

A movement to one side of the barn had him looking over at two little boys, cowering in the corner, staring wide-eyed at him.

Sensing their alarm, he immediately tamped down on the angry words he'd been about to unleash. At least now, having met his new family, he understood why he'd spent a lifetime fighting that hair-trigger temper. It was a legacy from his father and grandfather, and he was determined to curb it before it took control of him.

The girl snapped on a series of lights before pointing to the ceiling. "I hope you've brought all the right parts. I don't want to hear that after keeping me waiting all this time, you can't get this lift up and running properly without another holdup."

Using these moments to cool off, Griff studied the track that had been mounted to the ceiling, forming a circle around the midsection of the barn.

Though his tone was still gruff, the words were muted. "I'm sorry about the missing parts, but you've made a mistake. I'm not the person you were expecting."

She spun around to face him. "Don't tell me..." Her look went from fury to bewilderment. "You're not here from Endicott Medical Supply?"

"I'm here because a Marine buddy of mine invited me to stop by and see the Romeos in action today."

For just an instant Griff thought she might break into tears. Then she composed herself. "Sorry. It's just that I've been waiting..." She turned away and stuck her hands in the pockets of her torn jeans before shaking her head and kicking at a clump of dirt. "It doesn't matter..."

"Captain?" A voice from the group of men had him looking over.

"Jimmy." He watched as one wheelchair separated itself from the others and Jimmy Gable rolled forward, his face wreathed in smiles.

"Hey. You came to see us. I was engaged in a serious poker hand with my pal Hank when you came in. Since I figured it was the medical supply guy, I wasn't paying attention. Sorry."

"I said I'd come, so here I am." Griff reached down to clap a hand on his friend's back.

Jimmy turned to the young woman. "This is Griff Warren. He and I served in Afghanistan together. He left shortly before me. Who'd have believed we'd run into each other here in the middle of nowhere?"

Griff smiled at the young woman. "I'm from the MacKenzie Ranch just over those hills. I guess I'm looking for your mother."

"My mother?" Her head came up sharply.

"Jimmy said this place belongs to Juliet Grayson."

"I'm Juliet."

At her words he couldn't hide his surprise. "But I thought..." He swallowed and decided to try again. "Sorry. I was expecting someone..."

"Older?" She nodded. Though she was trying for sarcasm, her voice betrayed a deep pain. "I guess 'the widow Grayson' confuses some people." She turned away. "You've come all this way for nothing. I was just telling the Romeos that today's therapy session is cancelled. In fact, it remains cancelled until I get this lift repaired."

Now that Griff had time to study the lift, he understood. "So this device is used to lift the men from their wheelchairs—"

"—into the saddle. Exactly. Until this machine is repaired, everything grinds to a halt."

"And the repairs aren't handled locally?"

She shook her head. "The company is supposed to be flying the parts in from Helena. At least that's what they've been telling me for the past week. But every day, they come up with another excuse to put me off. When we spotted your plane, we thought we'd finally had some good luck."

"I'm sorry to get your hopes up and then have them dashed. How about your wranglers? Any of them know a little about electronics?"

She gave an expressive lift of her shoulders. "I didn't think to ask. The few wranglers left are so overworked, they can barely keep up with the day's chores as it is." She turned to him hopefully. "I don't suppose you...?"

"Sorry. I'm pretty good with my hands. But my specialty is woodworking." He glanced at the ceiling, considering. "Besides, this isn't something that can be done on a ladder. In order to take a look at that track, the company will need to send along a bucket lift for the repairs."

She nodded. "I suppose you're right."

He turned to the two little boys, who hadn't moved. "Yours?"

She beckoned them closer, and when they hurried over to stand on either side of her, she gathered them close and hugged them.

Getting down on her knees, she said, "This is Ethan and this is Casey."

Griff followed her lead and knelt down so that his eyes were level with theirs.

He turned to the older one. "Hey Ethan. How old are you?"

The boy buried his face in his mother's arm.

Jimmy Gable said in an aside, "The kid doesn't speak."

"Efan's six." The younger one held up six fingers. Then he held up three fingers. "And I'm free."

Griff's smile grew at the little boy's attempt to speak clearly. "Three? And your brother is six? I bet you two are a big help to your mom."

The younger one nodded. "Efan can pour the milk on our cereal. Mom won't let me 'cause I spill it." He looked down for a moment while he considered his own skills. "Sometimes I feed the chickens, don't I, Mama?"

"Yes, you do. And you both do a fine job of helping."

When she got to her feet, Griff noticed that Ethan clung tightly to her leg and refused to look up. Little Casey, on the other hand, was content to stand beside her while he studied Griff with a look of open curiosity.

He tipped his head back to peer up at him. "Are you a giant?"

That had Griff laughing. "No. Sorry. I'm just a man."

The little boy pointed to the Cessna. "Is that yours?"

"It belongs to my . . . family." The word still caused him such a jolt, he had to give himself a mental shake.

"My daddy flied planes," Casey said proudly.

"Flew," Juliet corrected.

The little boy nodded. "My daddy flew planes."

"Did you ever get to fly with him?"

The little boy's eyes grew round with surprise. "I

wasn't borned yet. But Efan got to watch, didn't you, Efan?"

The older boy buried his face in his mother's frayed denims.

Juliet turned to the group of men, who'd been watching and listening in silence. "I guess you all know what this means. No lift, no riding. I'm sorry. Whenever Endicott gets this up and running, I'll contact Heywood Sperry, and he'll let the rest of you know. But at least we got in a little talk about exercise and nutrition."

As the men began moving toward the bus parked outside, they paused beside Jimmy for an introduction to Griff.

"Hank Wheeler." The heavily tattooed man gave a smart salute. "Any friend of Jimmy's is welcome here."

"Stan Novak." Rail-thin, head shaved, the man maneuvered his wheelchair close. "Did four tours of Afghanistan. One too many," he added as he passed with a wave of his hand.

"Billy Joe Harris" came a Southern twang. The young, bearded man had a face so round it resembled a basketball. His stomach protruded over the waist of his tattered shorts. "I saw you with Jimmy last night at Wylie's."

"Yeah. Hey, Billy Joe." Griff shook the man's hand.

A big man in a muscle shirt in red, white, and blue stripes started past Griff in his electric scooter until Jimmy Gable stopped him with a hand to his arm. "Hey, Sperry. Take a minute to say hi to my friend, Griff Warren."

The man, who from the waist up looked like a bodybuilder, with bulging muscles in his arms, and a lean, chiseled face that might have been handsome if it weren't for his dark, glaring frown, looked Griff up and down before dismissing him completely. "What's he doing here, Gable? He doesn't look to me like he needs therapy."

"The captain and I served together in Afghanistan. I invited him to come here and meet my . . ."

The scooter rolled on before Jimmy had finished talking.

The young veteran shot an embarrassed look at Griff. "Sorry. As you can imagine, there are a lot of angry hotheads in the group."

"No need to explain that to me. I served with guys like that. Remember?"

Jimmy chuckled. "Yeah. I'm just glad you were the one who had to deal with them and not me." Hearing the sound of an engine roaring to life, he turned his wheelchair away and headed out of the barn. "Gotta go. It's Sperry's bus, so he gets to call the shots."

"That's some vehicle. Had to cost a few bucks to install that hydraulic lift."

"Not to mention the custom interior. It's like a rock star's." Jimmy chuckled. "Rumor is that Heywood Sperry's family has millions."

"Nothing like flaunting his wealth."

"Hank Wheeler says Sperry should have painted some rust on the outside as a joke, so folks would feel sorry for us poor old vets." Hearing the engine, Jimmy started rolling toward the bus. "No time to chat, Captain. Sperry's made it clear that when he says he's leaving, we'd better be aboard or we're left behind."

Griff frowned. "That's not the way of a Marine."

"Yeah. But it's Sperry's way. I hope you'll come back another time and watch us in action, Captain."

"I'll try, Jimmy."

Griff stood in the barn watching as Jimmy's wheelchair was boarded onto the bus by the hydraulic lift. When all their wheelchairs were secured, the vehicle left in a cloud of dust.

"Can he stay for lunch, Mama?" Casey asked.

Griff turned in time to see the annoyed look on Juliet's face. "I'm sure Griff isn't interested in peanut butter and jelly."

"Is that what we're having?" The little boy brightened. "I like peanut butter and jelly, don't you, Griff?"

Griff thought about the wonderful ranch meals he'd been enjoying since arriving at his father's home. He hadn't once had anything so simple.

If he hurried, he could join Whit and Brady Storm up in the hills for a close-up lesson on wrangling thousands of cattle on the range in the highlands.

Still, the pull of this angry young woman and her two sons was surprisingly strong. And there was something in his nature that had him enjoying the fact that he could annoy her even more.

"That's one of my favorites, Casey." He looked at Juliet. "I'd be happy to stay and have lunch with you."

"Well then. I guess, since you're not my repairman, I have no reason to stay here. We may as well head on up to the house."

Looking about as happy as a fox caught in a trap, she turned away and steered her sons from the barn.

Fall in Love with Forever Romance

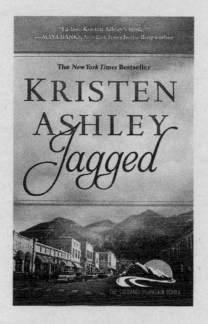

JAGGED

Zara is struggling to make ends meet when her old friend Ham comes back into her life. He wants to help, but a job and a place to live aren't the only things he's offering this time around...Fans of Julie Ann Walker, Lauren Dane, and Julie James will love the fifth book in Kristen Ashley's *New York Times* bestselling Colorado Mountain series, now in print for the first time!

ALL FIRED UP

It's a recipe for temptation: Mix a cool-as-a-cucumber event planner with a devastatingly handsome Irish pastry chef. Add sexual chemistry hot enough to start a fire. Let the sparks fly. Fans of Jill Shalvis will flip for the second book in Kate Meader's Hot in the Kitchen series.

Fall in Love with Forever Romance

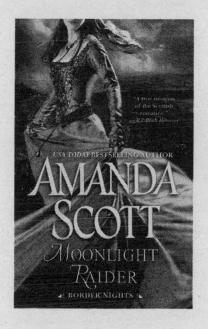

MOONLIGHT RAIDER

USA Today bestselling author Amanda Scott brings to life the history, turmoil, and passion of the Scottish Border as only she can in the first book in her new Border Nights series. Fans of Diana Gabaldon's *Outlander* will be swept away by Scott's tale!

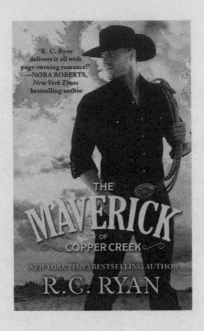

Fall in Love with Forever Romance

IT HAPPENED AT CHRISTMAS

Ethan and Skye may want a lot of things this holiday season, but what they get is something they didn't expect. Fans of feel-good romances by *New York Times* bestselling authors Brenda Novak, Robyn Carr, and Jill Shalvis will love the third book in Debbie Mason's series set in Christmas, Colorado—where love is the greatest gift of all.

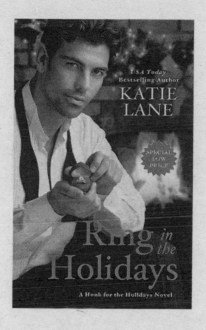

Find out more about Forever Romance!

Visit us at
www.hachettebookgroup.com/publishing_forever.aspx

Find us on Facebook
http://www.facebook.com/ForeverRomance

Follow us on Twitter
http://twitter.com/ForeverRomance

NEW AND UPCOMING TITLES

Each month we feature our new titles
and reader favorites.

CONTESTS AND GIVEAWAYS

We give away galleys, autographed copies,
and all kinds of exclusive items.

AUTHOR INFO

You'll find bios, articles, and links to personal websites
for all your favorite authors—and so much more.

GET SOCIAL

Connect with your favorite authors, editors, and
other Forever fans, and share what's important to you.

THE BUZZ

Sign up for our monthly romance newsletter,
and be the first to read all about it.

VISIT US ONLINE AT

WWW.HACHETTEBOOKGROUP.COM

FEATURES:

**OPENBOOK BROWSE AND
SEARCH EXCERPTS**

•

AUDIOBOOK EXCERPTS AND PODCASTS

•

AUTHOR ARTICLES AND INTERVIEWS

•

**BESTSELLER AND PUBLISHING
GROUP NEWS**

•

SIGN UP FOR E-NEWSLETTERS

•

**AUTHOR APPEARANCES AND TOUR
INFORMATION**

•

SOCIAL MEDIA FEEDS AND WIDGETS

•

DOWNLOAD FREE APPS

BOOKMARK HACHETTE BOOK GROUP
@ WWW.HACHETTEBOOKGROUP.COM